FIRST FLIGHT

THE
HYBRID
ARCHIVE

Book One

FIRST FLIGHT

S.F. WIDLACKI

For more information, visit sfwidlacki.com

First paperback edition: April 2021

Summary: Upon learning about a chemical that dangerously alters plants and animals, drastic measures are taken. Rory finds herself at the mercy of such measures, waking up ten months later with wings, among other adaptations.

ISBN 978-0-578-88382-3 (paperback)
ASIN B091RSFL3X (KDP ebook)
LCCN: 2021906919

Going down in flames;
That empty space eating you.
But ashes rise,
ashes fly.
So I ask you —
how do you fall in flames?
If you're going down,
go down in flames.
Yes,
RISE.
Because falling is the only way, after all...

— from your own lovely author

PROLOGUE

"What you're saying is — it's *preposterous.*"

"What I'm saying," the doctor said, "is *true.* We need to prepare, and that can only happen with your authority, Mr. Secretary."

The Secretary laced his worn fingers, leaning back agitatedly in his black leather chair with a heavy sigh. Instead of dismissing the idea rashly, he paused to listen, albeit with a slight discomfort.

The doctor saw this as his opportunity to continue persuading the Council and his heart beat faster, knowing his ability to sway them could mean the difference between life and death. "This natural event is unlike anything we've seen before, nowhere in records kept for hundreds or *thousands* of years, and we *cannot* stop it — we can only hope to prepare for it." Without looking behind him, he raised his hand and tapped on the massive projector board, a certain hysteria in his urgent fingers.

This board displayed a diagram of a mid-ocean ridge, playing through what they predicted to happen in the following months. "Once this event happens, it will release a chemical that would normally stay dormant under the usually slow process of oceanic plate divergence. It's released in a gaseous form, and once it escapes the ocean — which it will — it will spread through the very air we breathe. There will be no escaping it."

"Do you have anything *good* for us, Doctor?" the Chairman entreated in an exasperated manner.

The doctor wagged an eager finger in the air at him. "Yes, I do. Upon testing, we found that this chemical doesn't affect humans due to genetics we all possess," he mentioned. His expression darkened as he continued. "However, it affects everything else, with drastic side effects. The animals exposed to the chemical showed heightened brain activity in areas responsible for aggression, and higher cerebrum functioning, especially in mammals, but also in avian and even aquatic species. In fact, we predict those aquatic animals to be affected first. Even plants were affected, with abnormal growth rates."

The Council remained silent, sitting around the massive oak table, absorbing this heavy information.

"Also, and even more terrifying, the animals exposed to the chemical show a change in makeup on a physical level, basically evolving at a rapid rate," the doctor informed solemnly. His hairs visibly raised as goosebumps encroached his arms. "We can't keep up, Sirs. The human species will no longer be the apex predator once this event happens, and *no one* will be safe."

"Earlier, you said all we can do is prepare for it. I'm assuming you do have a preparation in mind," the Director drawled, inclining his unruly eyebrows in question.

The doctor nodded and flipped the projector to the next screen with a small remote, its smooth black surface like a bar of soap in his clammy hands. Diagrams of alleles, complicated genetic material, and various species popped up, consuming the board and the deplorable gazes of the half dozen Council members. Not every possible attendee was there. No, they couldn't risk bringing everyone in, not on this.

He had to be careful how he went about presenting his precarious intentions. "Now, the Council was not made previously aware of our studies," the doctor tried cautiously. "We've been tracking things for a while now, but it hadn't been a real threat until seismic activity was detected to be stirring up." He cleared his throat, his hands shaking slightly from the seriousness of the situation he was presenting. "I've said no one will be safe. No one *fully human…*"

"And what is that supposed to mean?" the Chairman reproached.

The doctor opened his mouth to explain but faltered hesitantly, trying to figure out how to go about his next words in a manner the Council would understand. He licked his chapped lips and testingly asked, "Have you heard of, eh, hybridization, Chairman?"

"Can't say I have, Doctor," the Chairman responded coolly. "Please explain."

"Just as sexual reproduction can bring different sets of alleles together in a common genetic background, hybridization between species allows alleles from one genetic background to integrate into another. Now, fusing the genomes from different species to generate a new hybrid species lineage was mostly studied in plants... Until recently," he stated with pride. He paused, and placed a hand on the screen behind him. His fingers practically caressed the images, lingering in the fruits of his studies. "Our scientists have found a way to hybridize *human* genetics with that of other species."

The Director leaned forward with great interest. "Wouldn't that only be possible to accomplish in the developmental stage, then? We don't have the years to do this." He was better versed in some of the scientific areas than, say, the Chairman.

"No, indeed we don't have that kind of time. This is why we've found a way to put the subjects *back* into a state where their makeup is willing to be altered."

The Secretary had been silent all this time, but now he finally called attention to himself. "What does *hybridization* have to do with this chemical lying dormant in the sea? What are you saying, Doctor?" he asked, a dangerous edge in his words.

"I'm saying…that we've done it," the doctor said. "We have a way to stay alive. That's the goal of all of this, Mr. Secretary."

Unease and tension were palpable among the Council. They looked around at each other in shock and dismay, but a certain hopeful excitement also glinted in their eyes.

"The only way is to evolve with the rest of the world, or get left behind and die," the doctor pushed, his voice rising a notch.

The members nodded to the doctor in passing then bent their heads to collaborate, talking amongst themselves. The doctor let out a long, silent breath. He could only pray now as they made a decision.

After what felt like a lifetime of anxiety, the talking subsided, and the Council looked toward the doctor. He could tell nothing from their gazes, some even avoiding his searching eyes as if ashamed.

"We will begin the next phase," the Secretary said solemnly.

The doctor felt his heart skip a beat after hearing that and had to discreetly catch himself on the edge of the table. He gave a terse nod. "Right away," he agreed.

"We are at your disposal," the Chairman said gruffly.

With this consensus, the Secretary got up and left the room, and others filed out uncomfortably behind him. The doctor began putting his papers back in order, but his hands kept shaking.

The Director stood off to the side for a lingering moment, watching the doctor with growing unease. Finally, he eased forward around the table. "Doctor," he began quietly. "How many will have to be tested on? How many will be...*altered?*"

The doctor laid his papers in a neat stack, his finger pressing against the top. "As many as we can get, Sir. The gene responsible for allowing this human hybridization is most malleable in ages sixteen to mid-twenties."

"How do you know it will *work*?" he insisted, his body shaking as his quiet voice strained.

The doctor turned his head toward the Director, whose face was lined with hard decisions. The doctor's eyes were dark, hiding the wealth of fear threatening to swallow him. "It has to."

With those simple words, he swept up his papers and exited the room. The double doors flapped shut behind him, leaving the Director alone in the massive room.

CHAPTER 1

Nothing's better than feeling like you can fly. Tearing down an empty stretch of road on my dual sport motorcycle, blaring the song "You Get What You Give" by New Radicals, that's exactly how I felt. Thick fields of corn stalks on both sides of the road whipped by like two walls of gold, my olive utility jacket billowing in the wind.

I had to braid up my curly, breast-length, hickory-colored hair, the ends bleached a strawberry-blonde from the daily sun exposure, to keep it from lashing my face, but little strands still managed to get loose.

"*Pleh.*" I spat out a rogue curl from my mouth. Not even my helmet kept them away.

The air seemed to rumble, past the usual exhilaration of my bike. I glanced up through the tinted shield of my helmet to see a dark chopper whirling through the air.

Strange. I didn't usually see choppers coming through this stretch of farmland.

Two more came by, so close I could practically feel the air their blades kicked up. "Woah," I murmured, tensing as the quick *whop whop whop* of the choppers tossed around the dried stalks of corn.

I turned the music volume lower as I slowed down and stopped off to the side of the road, flipping up my visor to look after them. I made a thoughtful sound as I watched the trio head east, toward the town.

After studying them for a while, using my left leather open-finger driving glove, I flipped my visor back down. I upped the volume and rode back into motion, the growl of the engine battling with the music.

Ten minutes later, I turned down a narrow road and pulled into a small gravel parking lot. I drove over to the far end and parked my bike, rumbling to a stop. The engine still crackled after being silenced, and I could imagine watching an ice cube melt on it. Taking my helmet off, I looked out over a gratifying scene: late afternoon sun shining down on a wide, grassy field, an old red barn, horses nipping leisurely at the grass.

I swung my leg over the end of the bike and walked up to a two-story house with my helmet tucked under my arm, one of the few sparse buildings on this large acreage. It was a pretty basic house, with its white siding which had begun to peel away and sun bleached gray shingles.

My black boots clomped satisfyingly against the wooden stairs leading up to the front door. With a loud *creak*, I swung the old door open. I took my boots off and set my helmet down at the doorway, tossed my jacket aside, then swiped an apple off the kitchen table before jogging upstairs.

The upstairs room was pretty simple, with wooden walls and flooring, a slanted ceiling without much insulation... A metal framed bed sat off to one corner, where I'd drift off into nightmares. There was also a wooden dresser, a desk and chair, and a boat load of artwork and plants. The art was all me, mostly of sketches or paintings of animals and fantasy scenes. There were wide windows at intervals that let in plenty of light as well, giving me a nice view of the whole farm. Oh, and a Wing Chun wooden dummy sat in another corner. That dummy was probably the best gift I ever got, given more as a consolation prize by my adoptive mother.

Speaking of Louise (the name I gave the dummy, even though it looked nothing like a person, more like a sad, wanna-be tree), I felt like training, and since I finished my chores before riding out, there was no reason I couldn't. When *wasn't* there a good time to train? It was a lifestyle, really. I'd picked up fighting when I was fourteen, after my parents had died. They'd been attacked and murdered while I was waiting in the car outside an old gas station, and since then, I started training mostly in Jeet Kune Do, brought to life by the skillful Bruce Lee, and Armed martial arts. At first the reason was a mix of self-defense and releasing anger, but now it brought me peace. It had become a way to live; to move on.

My parents died six years ago, as I was now twenty years old, meaning I'd been training almost every day for the good part of half a dozen years. This little area in central Virginia I lived in now with my (adoptive) mom was pretty low-key, the worst thing happening maybe being a car break-in. Therefore, I hadn't run into an instance where my skills were needed, but at least I was prepared. Never knew what could be right around the corner.

I practiced moves on Louise, dealing a series of damaging strikes. *Duck, weave, strike, dodge, strike.*

Some twenty minutes later, I heard the front door open. I had tried to sneak out through that door once, way too early in the morning, like four or five years ago. Let me tell you, if that old door is your only way out, you are *screwed,* my friend.

"Rory, last rides just ended," a familiar voice called up the stairs. "Go deal with it."

That was Jody, my sort-of-mom. You know how I indulged in that little piece of information about my parents being murdered? Yeah. Fourteen-year-olds apparently couldn't live on their own, so I was taken up by Jody seven months later. It had been a relief to get out of the Sinkhole of Sucks (that's what we kids had called it), but Jody wasn't always a peach herself.

Kick, kick, dodge, punch, dodge. I let out a sound of exertion as I dealt a firm kick, sending Louise sliding back a meter. Straightening, I stepped forward and placed a hand on Louise to get him to stop teetering.

Panting slightly, I smoothed the curls back from my face and snatched up a jug of water from a desk, chugging a third of it. "*Ah*," I breathed, setting it back down with a slosh.

I jogged down the stairs and threw my boots and jacket on at the door. The old wooden frame clanked as the door fell back into place behind me. I headed across the field, down a gravel path that needed some TLC. Horses neighed in the distance, and I heard an engine rumble to life as a car pulled away.

See you, I thought, watching what could only have been the last customer of the day, leaving. I slipped into the barn with its paint chipping off and walked down the dirt aisle, the air smelling of sweat and hay. We had ten horses here, all used in a trail riding business run by Jody.

There were horses still tacked, waiting in the stalls for my attention. I unlatched the furthest door and closed it behind me, then started untacking the horse. I finished up all five and started turning them out in the field.

As I unhaltered the last horse, setting him free, the familiar sound of gravel crunching beneath car tires sounded from the lot. I walked back into the barn and, through the open barn door, saw a car pulling in. It clunked and clanked across the small gravel parking lot and came to a painfully slow stop at one of the concrete bumper blocks.

I knew that car! A grin tugged at my mouth.

I grabbed a pitchfork and set it against one of the stables, then went around to the back of the barn to haul a big black muck cart over. When I came back into the barn, a girl wearing an oversized T-shirt sporting the characteristic words NATIONAL SARCASTIC SOCI-ETY — LIKE WE NEED YOUR SUPPORT in big white letters beside a yellow outline box, comfy jeans, and worn forest green sneakers was saying hello to a horse I couldn't let out to pasture yet.

"Hey, Scout, how ya been?" the girl asked, giving the brown and white gelding a pat on the nose.

"Wanna help me clean stalls?" I asked, picking up and dumping a pitchfork-full of dirty bedding into the muck cart. I liked to pull the cart down the aisle and just hook it up to the gator instead of dragging individual buckets to the cart. Less work that way.

The girl sighed and came up to the other side of the door to the stall I was cleaning out. She rested her arms atop the wooden door, watching me work. "Yeah, I don't know about that one," she said.

I glanced up at her to see her grinning at me, her marbled blue eyes crinkling faintly at the edges with humor under gently rounded eyelids. A grin found its way onto my own mouth at her teasing, and I shook my head.

She got up and went down the aisle. I heard her rummaging in the tack room, and a moment later, she came back with a pitchfork that was almost taller than her stance of 5'2". "You use me, I tell you," she joked, setting the pitchfork against the stall to pull her long hair up. She had the longest hair I'd ever seen. It was straight, light brown but tinted red, and nearly reached her butt.

She was my best friend, and she had been there for me through everything.

"How'd that interview go?" I asked.

Her voice sounded echoey across the aisle as she worked in the opposite stall. "Good, I think."

My gaze slanted over to her. Her mouth was set in a thin line. "Vixen," I chided.

She rolled her eyes. "Okay, so I think I screwed up! She kept asking me questions like 'what are your weaknesses,' and 'why should we hire you.' Like, I *have* no weaknesses, and — I need money!" She waved her hands exasperatedly. "My dad is trying to kick me out. He hasn't outright *said it*, but he keeps dropping all these hints."

I was still laughing at her interview answers. "Yeah? That sucks."

"Hey, maybe I can just room with you!" she thought up hesitantly. "You think Jody would go for that?"

"Sure, if you're ready to do manual labor every day," I said with an easy shrug.

Vixen was quiet, so I glanced up. She had her eyes narrowed at me. "Yeahhh, maybe not."

I chuckled. I finished cleaning the stall and moved on to the next one.

"My brother's friend won't stop talking about you, by the way," she said randomly. "Maybe you should call him or something. At least *one* of us might get a boyfriend."

I pressed my boot onto the flat edge of the pitchfork, scooping up a heaping pile of horse crap. Yeah, all the boys just couldn't resist my *parfum de manure*. "Ha, nah, I'm good."

"'Oo, her hazel eyes are so dreamy. That hair? *Soooo* curly.'" She mimicked the boy, pretending to swoon.

"Don't make me miss the cart," I warned, holding up the full pitchfork threateningly. "It would be a shame to miss with you right on the other side…"

"Aye! Fine," she laughed.

A bit of silence passed. "My eyes are dreamy?" I asked. When I looked up, I met Vixen's joking glare, and we both laughed.

My friend and I finished cleaning out the stalls and hooked the cart onto the back of the topless gator. She climbed into the passenger seat beside me as I started the engine, rumbling to life. I shifted gear and eased my foot down on the gas pedal, driving us through the gravel lot, then looked both ways before stomping on the gas, shooting left out onto the paved road.

We had to drive the manure to a neighbor's yard and dump it under this big tree. He liked to use it for his crops. She got out and helped me lift the heavy cart up, and we hooked it back up.

Vixen waved a hand in front of her nose, her face scrunched up in disgust. "Oh, that's just horrible. How do you deal with this every day?" she asked, mortified.

"Just come on," I laughed.

"You really need a break from all this." She pointed at me with a serious expression as she climbed back into the passenger seat.

"This *is* my break." Call me crazy, but hard work and taking care of animals actually made me happy. Why would I want to get away from that?

"I know," she sighed. "Still. Maybe we can go get some lunch together tomorrow. I'm off from classes from noon to two?"

"Tomorrow? Yeah, alright," I agreed.

We drove back out onto the road and to the barn. I parked the gator and climbed out, and a voice called out across the yard from the house.

"Dinner's ready!" Jody called from the porch, her hands cupped around her mouth.

She didn't strike me as a country mom, standing outside with freshly washed, wavy black hair dampening the floral robe wrapped snugly around her. While her voice carried loudly across the distance, the crinkles around her brown eyes gave her a gentle appearance. I raised my hand and gave her a thumbs-up.

"You, too, Vixen!" Jody added.

A smile spread across Vixen's face, giving her the appearance of innocence. "Well alright."

We trudged up the path to the house, joking around with each other. Altogether, a solid day. Mark that one down in the books.

♦ ♦ ♦

"Scooch your butt," Jody said, poised over the couch.

I elbowed Vixen, who was texting distractedly on her phone, and we moved over a bit, Vixen doing so absently. Jody fell back beside me with a sigh, a loaded plate in one hand. She grabbed the remote off the short coffee table in front of us and clicked the TV on.

Okay, so don't get any wrong ideas; we could enjoy a nice family dinner with the whole fancy getup if we wanted to. Us three girls simply didn't have any qualms against enjoying our buttery mashed potatoes, juicy pork chops, and good old fashioned green beans whilst lazing on the couch and watching TV.

"Wait, turn it back," Vixen urged unusually. "My dad just told me to click it to the local news."

"Why? Was there an accident or something?" I asked through a mouthful of green beans.

Jody changed the channel to Vixen's liking. An uptight newscaster appeared on the old TV screen, his urgent voice blaring out at us.

"— *what we can only assume to be extremely dangerous. This virus seems to most seriously affect those between ages sixteen and twenty-six. Any and all persons within this age group should immediately report to Hawking Meadows High School for testing. This is a —"*

"Oh my god, is this for real?" Vixen murmured. "I thought my dad might be joking."

"The government has issued mass testing on every-one within this age group. Further information will be gathered as soon as possible. Please report to —"

"A virus? Did this just happen?" Jody asked no one in particular. The great universe, I suppose.

I waved a dismissive hand at the screen as the news-caster continued to blab on. "They don't even have a name for the virus. What good is testing supposed to do if they don't even know what they're testing for?" I argued.

"What're you talking about?" Jody asked accusingly. "You're getting tested! Both of you!"

I tried to explain it. "Viruses get named based on their genetic structure. If they don't know that, no way could they go through with mass testing."

Jody pinched my arm.

"Aye! What was that for?" I frowned.

She stared at me critically. "I'm not letting you take any chances. You'd better go to that high school tomor-row." She leaned around me to get a look at Vixen. "Make sure she goes."

I squinted my eyes at Jody indignantly. No way would I willingly go to that school.

Vixen merely gave a halfhearted smile, knowing she couldn't make me go anywhere. I shoved a forkful of mashed potatoes in my mouth to prevent myself from saying anything else.

CHAPTER 2

BEEP. BEEEEEP.

Cars honked angrily around me. No, not because of me. Jump to conclusions much?

I was not one to weave around and between people unless necessary. I don't know anyone who doesn't hate when motorcycles just trickle on by while the rest of them are stuck at a stand-still, not to mention it's dangerous.

Luckily, it wasn't a complete stand-still, just really, *really* slow. Seriously though, what was the hold-up? Surely there weren't *that* many twenty-year-olds rushing to the high school.

I took the first turn-off road I came to and drove along a different route. The sun was shining brightly, barely a cloud in sight. Fresh cut grass left a sweet scent in the air while "Crazy" by Gnarls Barkley played. Overall, a nice spring day.

Even though it was the tail end of spring, I was still wearing my usual attire including blue stone-washed jeggings, black boots, white and gray U-neck, and my favorite (and only) olive cargo/utility jacket.

I was supposed to meet Vixen at this sandwich place five minutes ago, and I could imagine her sitting uncomfortably at a small table, trying to avoid people. She was pretty open with me, but around others she was super introverted and shy.

Turning smoothly onto another road, I started passing walls of small shops. It was a cozy little town with two-lane roads and mostly one-story brick buildings. People walked by on clean sidewalks with friends and family, others loners.

Crap. The road I had planned to go down was blocked with orange cones.

"Ah, whatever." I would just walk. The sandwich place was only a short six-minute walk away anyhow. I turned into a small gravel lot outside a manicured garden place and parked my bike. I distractedly unclipped my helmet and pulled it off as I hurriedly headed around the other side of the block. I pushed past people, already feeling bad for being late. "Excuse me, excuse me," I muttered, edging past person after person.

"What's taking so long?" someone I edged past asked in a hushed tone.

"This is some government bull crap is what it is," I picked up from someone else's conversation.

The school was nearby, though still a solid two-minute walk away. The line couldn't actually be that long, could it? I didn't really care though. I just wanted to get by. I made it out to the other side of the jumble of people and continued purposefully on, only glancing over at the commotion with a small frown out of curiosity.

"Woah," I breathed quietly, nearly bumping into someone. My head had spun back around, and standing in front of me was a man in a black uniform, bulletproof vest and all, his light hair clipped almost nonexistent. "Sorry," I muttered, about to go around him.

He shot a muscled arm out, blocking me. I halted. My head turned slowly toward him, my eyes narrowing. I tried to pass him again. He blocked me, *again*.

"Hey, buddy," I snarled.

His eyes wandered over me speculatively, and he pointed to the mass of people. "Everyone in your age range has to go through a quick test. Mandatory by the Department of National Security. It'll only take fifteen minutes, ma'am."

Quick test? Mandatory? Nah. "Can't, I'm supposed to be meeting with someone —" I held my wrist up and pulled the sleeve of my jacket up a couple inches, looking at a watch I didn't have. "— quarter 'till freckle ago."

The muscled man looked over his shoulder, and I followed his eyes. A gruff-looking man off behind him gave a nod, and the one in front of me turned to me again with newfound conviction. "Ma'am, you'll have to come with me," he stated.

I slid my jaw, grinding my teeth. "DNS, huh?" I nodded at him. "Got any proof?"

"That's enough," he said, and reached out to grab my shoulder.

Instincts and years of training sprang into action under a tense situation. I leaned back, dodging his hand. His eyes widened, and he went for me again. I dodged, simultaneously bringing my left arm up to block, hitting his arm away, my right arm still holding my helmet. "Pretty sure what you're doing is illegal!" I said.

"Stop!" he ordered.

How about...*no.* He glanced over at the other guy again, and I saw my opportunity. Tensing, I jumped around him and slipped past his guard. I started running, my boots whisking by across the cement, hoping to disappear in the stream of people. There weren't as many on this sidewalk, though, making it hard to effectively hide.

Suddenly, a guy jumped out from the other side of the road some twenty feet in front of me. My eyes skipped around astutely. A solid wall of storefronts to my right, street to my left. A few more guys in black uniforms were coming up from the street side, all with guns. Whatever they were doing, it was serious.

They stayed a healthy distance from me, two of which actually pointed their guns at me. People that had been walking on the sidewalk freaked out and hurried off.

"Come with me. *Now*," that annoying, familiar voice commanded.

I turned my head, my nose scrunching agitatedly. He moved toward me, and I didn't run this time. The muscled man grabbed my wrists and banded them together, taking my helmet from me. I let out a gasp as the hard plastic bit into my skin. "It's only for precaution," he explained tersely.

I could probably still take him out and slip away with my wrists bound, I thought defensively, but I didn't tell him that.

He led me down the sidewalk, back the way I'd come. We walked past the thick line of people with an armed man taking up position behind us. A white canvas tent outside the low, brick high school came into view as we rounded the line, and he took me to it.

With extra bragging force, he sat me down on a metal folding chair inside the tent. My eyes followed him dangerously. "Stay here."

He waved some other guy over, also in uniform. Only two people at the back of the tent weren't in uniform, instead wearing white lab coats that reached midway down their thighs. I couldn't help but feel that these people were all taking very few health precautions for a supposedly 'extremely dangerous virus.'

This new man in uniform came over to us, holding some sort of hand-held machine in his right hand. It looked like one of those temperature probes doctors might slide against your forehead, but not.

"Her?" he asked, nodding in my direction.

"Just do it," the man who'd brought me over said.

Probe-guy sighed and leaned down to me. "Left or right?" he asked.

"What?"

He swiftly bent around me and twisted my left hand uncomfortably, bringing the probe thing to my finger. I felt a prick in my skin, but the calluses caused from daily labor negated the effects.

I stared after him angrily as he straightened. He was lucky my gloves had open fingers. He tapped on the probe, and I realized there was a small, flat screen over the handle. Feeling agitated and maybe a little panicked, I discreetly tugged against the tight binds on my wrists.

"We got another one," the guy muttered. I barely heard him. He stared at the screen, then raised his eyes to me, something in his expression making me tense, giving me the sudden urge to *get out now*.

A different man next to him, wearing an unfortunate handlebar mustache, grabbed his arm, pulling the device over to take a look. "Well I'll be d*mned, seems we did." He let go of the man with the instrument and took a step toward me, about to lift me from the chair. "Come with me. Further examination is required," he said, all cold-cut and serious.

I avoided his hand and stood up myself. "For what?" I asked defiantly. "What is all this?"

"You've tested positive. All will be explained, but you have to come with me."

Tested positive? "I —"

"*Now*, ma'am." His deep voice had risen, his burly muscles tightening against the black fabric formed to his chest and biceps. He didn't look like someone you wanted to mess around with, more so than the first short-haired man I'd run into on the sidewalk. That first man actually handed my helmet to Mr. Mustache. I didn't want to, but I did as I was told. That didn't stop me from glaring angrily at him though.

"This way," he ordered. He kept an eye on me as he led me away from the lines, away from the school, into a building half a block down a perpendicular street. I may have been imagining it, but there was a certain glint to his eyes that was unnatural.

I was very tense, my senses picking up everything they could. I hesitated at the doorway, but then he grabbed my arm and pulled me harshly in.

"Hey!" I argued. I was *this close* to going into self-defense mode, but he let me go a moment later.

Inside, my eyes quickly flicked around the room. Four men in uniform stood at the side like statues, and the whole space was rather clean and empty.

I glanced back at Mr. Mustache, but he wasn't look-ing at me — his eyes were trained on something in front of us. "We got another one, sir," he said.

I followed his steady gaze. A middle-aged man in a

blue dress shirt rose up from behind a desk, the tabletop illuminated by a harsh fluorescent lamp. His dark hair was somewhat disheveled, and his blue eyes took me in, looking me up and down with a strange energy. He came around the desk and pushed his thin metal glasses higher up the bridge of his pointed nose.

This man stood very close to me, only a meter away as he leaned in a bit. He looked at me like one might examine a specimen.

"Mm. No need to worry, we just need to run some more tests," he said, giving me a lame smile of reassurance. He sounded tired and stressed. "A safety concern for the country. It's very important."

"Tests? Seriously? Who are you people?" I asked, anger slithering into my voice. The presence of four other guys in uniform standing against the side of the room suddenly felt pressuring.

The man in front of me straightened. "You can call me Dr. Fabel." His expression twitched. "Though, that doesn't really matter."

"You're a doctor?" I asked. I eyed the guy who'd brought me here. "And you're not what you're posing to be, are you?"

The uniformed man didn't respond to me. Dr. Fabel laughed, though his amused smile didn't reach his eyes. "Clever one, aren't you?" He shook his head a little. "No, no... We are much bigger than that. All that," he said, waving a hand at the wall, presumably gesturing to the lines outside, "is all so we can treat the people like you."

"Me? Why?" I was feeling uneasy, even though the doctor sounded genuine. Maybe his genuinity is why I felt that way.

He looked as if about to say something, but he stopped himself. With a stifled sigh, he said, "Follow me, and I will tell you everything."

Before I could respond, the burly guy behind me pressed me forward. I really wanted to punch him in the face.

"Easy, Luther," the doctor said over his shoulder. The man behind me huffed.

Wanting to stay away from Luther, I picked up the pace and followed the doctor. We went down a narrow, dimly lit hallway, passing random doorways. Peering through the cracks, I glimpsed mostly empty rooms. There were a couple lit up, people in white lab coats testing dark red vials and peering through microscopes.

I gotta say, that was not very reassuring.

At the end of the hallway, Dr. Fabel stopped and gestured to Luther. The burly man begrudgingly turned me around and undid the bindings.

I brought my hands up, rubbing my wrists with a frown as Dr. Fabel held open a door for me. I didn't move at first. Peering inside, I saw another person. He looked a little under twenty, with neat jeans, a plain jacket that exposed his scrawny frame, and short honey-brown hair tossed over his forehead in a French crop. He seemed anxious, and paused to watch me through the doorway. Nothing about him screamed abnormal or dangerous.

"It's alright, dear," Dr. Fabel said. "Take a seat anywhere. We'll begin once everyone has arrived."

I glanced at my helmet still in Luther's left hand. The doctor seemed to notice this. "It's fine, we'll keep it at the front for you," he smiled.

This was all feeling very sketchy from the get-go. Sure, the building was clean and looked legit, but it felt like a mask, same as the uniforms those 'military' men wore.

Alas, I stepped into the room and surveyed my surroundings. It was clean, with white walls, tiled floor, and square lights spaced at intervals in the ceiling. A dozen metal chairs sat in a row in the middle of the room, and a projection board took up a third of the wall at the front. A plastic, marbled fold-up table at the side held water bottles and some snacks you'd find at a gas station.

I heard the door behind me shut and spun around. It was a solid door, so I couldn't see the two men on the other side. Even so, I went back up to it. I hesitated a moment before pressing my ear to the cold paint. Nothing. Wondering, I brought my hand up to the smooth metal handle and testingly tried to turn it. Locked.

Okay, so that was weird, right? Forcing myself to remain calm, I turned back to face the room. That other kid was watching me, his foot bouncing.

"Locked?" he asked.

I nodded. Walking warily over to the chairs, I sat down two chairs away from him on his right.

"This is crazy," he continued. His foot bounced rapidly, just like his nervous voice. "Apparently I tested 'positive,' whatever that means. I guess you did too?"

He turned to me expectantly, searching for answers. "Apparently," I said, my brows creased with uncertain thoughts.

"What does the military want with us, anyway? Run tests?" He seemed to be racking his mind. "Maybe this really is the beginning of a pandemic or something, and they're trying to quell it before it starts."

Okay, theorist, I exasperated mentally.

I looked around the room again. Still no windows. I felt like someone looking through a fridge the second time and expecting to see that the food fairies paid a visit. I did, however, notice a shiny black orb in the corner of the ceiling. It had to be a camera.

"What's your name?" he asked.

"Hm?" I glanced at him distractedly. "Rory. Yours?"

"Rory," he repeated, the name sounding foreign on his tongue. "Never heard that one before." For the first time, I saw the corner of his mouth flick in an attempt at a smile. "My name is Will."

My phone vibrated against my side, making me jump slightly. I pulled it out of one of my jacket's cargo pockets and looked at the bright little screen. To be honest, I forgot I had a phone.

From Vix: *WHERE ARE YOU? IT'S HALF PAST ONE!*

Ah, oops. I unlocked my phone and typed back: *SORRY, KINDA RAN INTO SOMETHING NEAR THE SCHOOL. NOT SURE WHEN I'LL GET OUT.*

A typing word bubble appeared, the three little dots dancing in a wave pattern.

I waited and waited, but then they just disappeared. My brows creased and I leaned forward in the chair.

What happened?

I exited the chat and checked my signal, but there was nothing wrong with it. Then I thought of Jody, who was under the impression I was having lunch right now. Surprise!

I was about to message her, but my fingers hesitated over the keypad for a good while. Finally, I typed: *GOT TESTED AT THE SCHOOL. THEY SAY I'M 'POSITIVE,' WHATEVER THAT'S SUPPOSED TO MEAN.*

Of course, I conveniently left out the middle part on how *I didn't purposely get tested.* Feeling tense, I clicked my phone off and dumped it back into my pocket.

I looked around the room for a third time. "What the heck is going on?" I murmured to myself.

CHAPTER 3

Over an hour passed and we were still sitting in that darned room. I was more than antsy at this point.

I got up and strode to the door. My fist pounded on it, producing hollow banging sounds. "Hey! How long are you trying to keep us here?" I shouted.

When there wasn't a response (I don't know, maybe there had been a guard outside the door or something?), I started pacing. I checked my phone. Still no response from Vixen. Jody had sent me a relieved text about how it was good they found out about my 'condition' so soon, which only irked me. But hey, at least she wasn't panicking inside like me, right?

Crunch. Crunch.

My gaze slanted over to Will, who was eating from a bag of Cheetos. "Really?"

"What?" he asked, holding a Cheeto mid-way to his mouth.

"You sure you want to be eating that? It's supplied by the same people holding us *captive*," I dissuaded.

His chewing paused. Swallowing whatever he had in his mouth, he said, "That seems extreme. You really think it's like that?"

"Well how would *you* look at it?" I posed.

"Mm." He looked at the Cheeto in his hand, then placed it back in the bag and set it aside, looking like he'd lost his appetite.

I heard something clank on the other side of the door and tensed. It opened, and Dr. Fabel stood in the doorway, the sight of him resparking my anger.

"Hello, my dears," he said. "Sorry for the long wait. We'll go ahead with the next phase of testing now, and then you'll both be on your way."

Will sighed loudly behind me, and I heard metal scratch across the tiled floor as he inevitably got up. "'Bout time," he said, coming to stand next to me. He was at least four or five inches taller than me, and I was 5'8".

Dr. Fabel led Will out and held the door open for me, but I stayed where I was, only looking the doctor up and down skeptically.

"Didn't you want this to be over?" Dr. Fabel asked innocently.

"Uh-huh," I muttered as I walked around him, eyeing him as I went.

The doctor smiled tersely and let the door close

behind us. "Right in there, Will," he said, gesturing to an open door.

I could've sworn that room was unlit before. Will glanced back at me nervously before disappearing into the room. I heard a pleasant voice greet him from within.

Dr. Fabel walked me to the next door and stopped outside of it. "And this is you," he said to me.

I pulled my eyes from their wandering position on the heavily guarded front doors, leading to freedom, to the small room. This room was lit up nice and bright as well, giving it a false sense of comfort. Inside, it reminded me of a lab, with an examination table, scale, microscope, little metal instruments; the whole shebang. A lady in a white lab coat, with dark hair pulled back tightly against her scalp, greeted me.

"Hello, my name is Dr. Jones. I'll be taking a quick look at you," she said. Her voice wasn't commanding like the men in uniforms, but it still made me feel cold. "What's your name?"

"Rory," I said, feeling uneasy.

Dr. Jones gestured to the cushioned exam table, and I begrudgingly sat down, wanting this to be over.

"Treat her well, Dr. Jones. She's special, this one," Dr. Fabel said, waving over his shoulder as the door closed.

Dr. Jones had her back to me, getting set up. "Do you have any eye prescription?" she asked.

I took my eyes from the door. "No."

"Any medications? Allergies?"

"Nah."

"Alright then." She flicked a light switch, turning the room dim, and turned around with a cylindrical instrument in her left hand. "Look at my finger, please."

I followed her gloved finger as she shined a light in each of my eyes. She dropped her hands and went to turn the light back on, and I blinked the lingering blindness from my eyes. "What next?"

This time she turned around with a needle. My eyes widened a sliver. I hated needles.

"Just a quick blood draw. That way it can be tested while we complete everything else," she said easily.

"Ah," I replied weakly.

She walked up to me, and before I knew it, a needle was in the crook of my arm. I cringed internally, pretending it was just a snake biting me. Getting bitten by a snake was so much better, as it'd happened plenty of times on the farm.

"All done with that," she said, retracting the needle, now full of a dark red substance, and walking to some table out of my range of vision.

She did more tests, taking my weight, height, checking my hearing, reflexes, heartbeat, lungs, and more. She even checked my teeth and took full body X-rays! This was feeling more like a prep than an exam, and I was getting pretty tired of it.

A machine beeped softly, and Dr. Jones instantly

turned her attention toward it, striding over to the back table. I shuffled uncomfortably on the exam table.

"Mmm, mixes, mixes." The doctor muttered quietly to herself. I craned my neck to see what she was doing. Little *dings* of glass vials came from the table as the doctor's arms shifted about, her dark ponytail jerking as she looked this way and that.

"Everything alright?" I asked.

She didn't seem to hear me, continuing to mutter to herself.

Suddenly she straightened and turned around to me with a nonchalant countenance. "Okay, just need one more sample and then you'll be on your way," she said smoothly.

"Another one?" I questioned, frowning.

"Mhm." With her back turned to me, she got another needle together. "Lie down for me?"

"For a blood draw?"

"Yes, ma'am," she said lightly.

It didn't make any sense to me, but it was just this last needle and then apparently I was done. I obliged tensely, lying back on the table. "Okay."

She came up to my arm, and I could see her preparing to inject the needle out of the side of my vision. "Just relax," she drawled softly.

I felt the prick of the needle entering my skin and tried not to move. This time felt different, however. It felt like...

"Hey," I argued, lifting my head to take a look. "What're you —? *Ah.*" I seethed, clenching my teeth. My head suddenly felt heavy, too heavy to hold up. It fell back onto the table, rolling about. My eyelids fluttered as I struggled to keep them open, but it was useless. I couldn't feel my body anymore, just a tidal wave of cotton coursing through me.

My thoughts became numb, just like my body, and I sunk into darkness.

Time wasn't relevant, my person was insensible.

Blurry flashes of light came in and out.

Very, very distant rumbling passed through me, clogging my torpid ears.

Then, there was just…

Nothing.

CHAPTER 4

A chill spread over my exposed body. Instinctively, I started shivering, but it hurt to do so. My eyelids felt heavy, but the sudden bright light behind them forced me to crack them open.

Oh geez. It was really too bright, to the point it felt my eyes might melt. I was relieved when something blocked it out, a shadow appearing above me. I blinked hard, and my vision sharpened up a bit, revealing a man standing over me, dressed in white, an intolerable grin on his face.

"Goodmorning, love," he said, his voice hitting me like a freight train. "Welcome to your new hell."

Come again?

"What is this?" I asked, my voice muddled. The man in the white lab coat tried to flash a small light across my eyes, and I brought my right arm up to push him away.

"Hey, now," he warned. "Just let me do what I need

to do, yeah?"

I'm glad he didn't try it again, because honestly, just lifting my arm was a struggle. I realized that my whole body ached immensely. "What did you do to me?" I slurred.

"What did we do? We saved you is what we did. So *maybe*," he said, "a little less resistance would be preferable."

I stared at him under heavy eyelids. I was too out of it to really be annoyed, but it was coming back to me. "They lied," I said.

"Who? Oh, yeah. Didn't know what you were talking about there for a moment." He laughed briskly. "Time passed differently for us I suppose."

My brows creased, but a small headache started up from the effort. "What're you talking about? And where *am* I?"

The indistinct thought that I had to go meet Vixen floated up in my mind. "I have to go," I said, rolling laboriously out of whatever bed I was laying on. I winced from the pain but didn't stop.

"Hey, no no no," the man said, pressing me back down onto the table. "You shouldn't be trying to get up yet. You just got out of stasis."

"I have to get to my friend," I slurred, not understanding what was going on. What had that doctor injected me with?

The man beside me stiffened, and I looked over at

him. He couldn't have been more than thirty, maybe mid-twenties. Dark brown hair a bit too long swirled around his ears and metal glasses, like a kinder version of Dr. Fabel.

"You should forget about that," he said matter-of-factly. "Forget about everything, actually."

What? Why would I do that? I shook my head slowly against the back of the table, squeezing my eyes shut. Man, I had the *worst* headache right now.

"Things aren't how they used to be," he said, a solemn note to his voice. There was a pause, so long it made me anxious enough to open my sore eyes and look at him. "It's been ten months. Ten months since all of you Hybrids were brought here."

"Ten months? You don't understand," I said. "I was *just with the doctor.*"

"Maybe to you, but ten months have passed since they knocked you out and brought you here. You, my friend, are now in post-apocalyptic Iceland."

I stared at him and blinked hard. Did he say…Iceland? *Apocalyptic?* "You sound crazy, you know that, right?" I asked seriously.

He shrugged, looking insulted. "You don't believe me? Look in a mirror." He disappeared for a moment and came back with a hand mirror a foot in diameter. "Here."

Disconcerted, I took the mirror from him and angled it down at myself. He must be crazy.

But then, I jolted, my eyes widening. This mirror

was playing a trick on me, right? My free hand came up to touch my face, around my hairline. Feathers, ranging from the size of my thumbnail to as long as my pinkie finger, formed around my scalp and into my curly hair, the same color as my hair (which for some reason glinted gold under the bright lights), only dappled with lighter tans and whites. And my eyes — they startled even me! Unfamiliar hazel eyes glowed back at me, way too bright and unsettling to be mine.

Then, *oh gosh*, there were little mottled feathers on my shoulders, running down my chest, blending smoothly into my skin and disappearing under the gown the lab coat guy had tossed over me. And behind me on the table, I saw much larger feathers of a creamy color, the edges a darker golden color and splotched with black and white marks.

I sat up, not caring if that guy didn't want me to. Something tugged behind me, against the table, and I could feel it, but it wasn't part of me. I was too stunned to alleve the uncomfortable sensation just then though. My fingers continued to travel over myself, then again, and again. I could see it, and I could feel it.

My hand went numb and the mirror fell from my grasp. It shattered on the floor, and I jumped from the excruciating sound. The noise felt magnified tenfold.

The guy cursed under his breath. "Not like we have an endless supply of those around here." He went to sweep it away, then looked me dead in the eyes. "Promise you won't respond like this when you see your back next."

I gulped, unsure whether I wanted to see more, terrified that there *was* more. "Show me," I said, trying to sound stern.

He begrudgingly helped me down from the table and walked me over toward the far wall. The whole room was maybe half the size of someone's ranch-style house, sporting white, white, white. Laboratory equipment and charts hung up on shelves and desks.

"I can stand," I said a bit harsher than I meant.

He seemed reluctant, and only after a lingering moment did he let me go, unsurely. I wobbled a bit but quickly righted myself. My body felt...*weird.* It still ached, sure, but it also felt stronger, and lighter somehow.

I was led down the rest of the long room, and then he stopped me, telling me to turn to the right. He didn't need to tell me to do this, however; I glimpsed my reflection from the side of my vision already. I was just scared to look.

But I had to.

Taking a deep breath, which felt unusually easy to do, I stiffly forced myself to face the mirror.

Okay, so here's the best way I can explain how I felt. Imagine you go to a party (I don't party, but I think this makes sense), and you're just your normal, expected self when you go. Then you get hammered — total blackout, can't remember anything.

...And when you wake up the next morning, feeling like total crap — your eyes hurt, your body hurts from falling off that porch railing — you go numbly to the bathroom. You look up at yourself in the mirror but nearly jump, thinking someone else is in the bathroom with you, because no way is that *you*. Not even 'messy hair, shaved an eyebrow off' different. I'm talking painting your face purple and adding horns, and *you can't even remember it*, can't *undo* it. It's you now, somehow, and you're staring this new you in the eyes.

Yep, that's sort of what it was like looking in that mirror for me.

I didn't even care that lab coat guy was standing just meters away — I removed the gown covering my body to my knees and tossed it away onto the floor. My figure looked the same, still lean and somewhat hourglass-shaped. My skin was the same color, maybe a little paler from lack of sunlight, but feathers covered parts of my well-toned body. They flowed across my shoulders, over my clavicles, and down and over my curvy B-cup breasts. Not sure a bra was even an option anymore. Some delicate feathers also covered my lower private region, replacing my hair. Curious, I lifted my arm. No armpit hair, or feathers. Weird.

I stared at myself, looking my body up and down, somewhere between horrified and amazed. Something else also pricked my attention: long feathers trailing down behind me. I could see them around my arms and behind my legs. Swallowing my saliva, I forced myself to turn around, my heart in my throat, and looked over my shoulder nervously. In the mirror, I wasn't sure I was seeing things correctly. A blanket of feathers hanging from my back? But I could *feel* them, like I could feel my arms or legs. My breathing quickened and my eyes widened in realization.

It was a new sensation, but somehow I could control it. For the first time ever, I worked muscles and tendons I'm not sure I previously had and stretched out my — wait for it — *WINGS*. I had *wings*.

I was acutely aware of my heart pounding in my chest, for it was abnormally loud and angry. *What did they do to me???*

Lab coat guy let out an amazed laugh, staring at my wings. I had forgotten he was there. "Oh, wow. *Wow*. You really are, just, *amazing*," he marveled with wide eyes. "Hey, hold it like that, will you? I can go ahead and take this measurement."

I wasn't really listening to him. Staring at the back of my wings in the mirror, my vision started acting up. I'd be staring at it normally, then suddenly I'd super-focus and could see tiny, impossible details of my feathers. I blinked hard multiple times.

The backsides of my wings were a sort of caramel gold washed over a tan-blonde. They were mottled with white and black, looking like organized flecks I'd find in a piece of artwork. Dark gold stripes lined those longer feathers reaching toward the ground. Honestly, other than the terror, they were kind of mesmerizing to look at. As the scientist ran off to some desk, I folded them in slightly, the feeling new and somewhat pleasant. I turned back to face the mirror and extended them out again. The undersides were more of a creamy buttermilk color, the ends of my long, sharp primaries and overlapping secondaries sporting pale gold stripes that mirrored the darker gold stripes on the backsides of my wings.

I wasn't sure what kind of bird I looked like. I'd always been interested in animals and knew plenty of birds, but mine didn't look like any definite type. The gold sheen on almost every feather on my body and wings, and even my skin a little bit I realized, was rather peculiar and threw my guess off the most.

Lab coat guy returned. "Hold them out as far as you can," he told me. I did as told, personally wanting to see how far I could go. Plus, despite their wide size, holding them up was easy, not feeling heavy at all. Holding some sort of fancy instrument to the farthest tip of my right wing, a beep sounded and he walked slowly behind me to the tip of my other wing. The width of my wings hid all but the lower half of his shins and the top of his shoulders up. It beeped again and he brought it down to look at it. He let out a long, low whistle. "Twenty feet. Impressive."

I looked over my shoulder at him. "Really?" I asked, feeling a note of dulcet pride amidst the shock.

"Here, come and sit," he said, walking swiftly back to a desk.

Looking over my wings one last time, I still couldn't believe it. I felt numb, convinced this was a dream, as I folded them up. I flicked them into a comfortable position behind my back, the feeling of them folded on either side of my spine unusual but warm. I picked up the gown I'd dismissed to the floor and wrapped it loosely around me, too stunned to be overly self-conscious. He pushed a rolling chair out to me, and I walked over to take a seat. It was probably for the best. Didn't want to faint or anything, ya know?

My wings hung over the back, scraping the tiled floor.

"Get used to those, eh?" he joked, pointing at the chair beneath me. I stared at him. He raised his hands with palms facing out, dropping his grin. "Okay," he murmured.

He spun around to the desk in a chair *with* a back. How convenient. Did this mean I couldn't sleep on my back anymore either? No, I had been lying face up when I'd woken. It must be okay. Comfortable or not, however, I'd have to find out.

"Personally, you're my favorite combination. Siberian Eagle Owl and Golden Eagle?" He huffed in a gratified laugh. "Amazing! Perfect power soaring and night glider combination. Can't wait to get you up in the air and test your speed." He wagged a finger at me without looking over. "Jensen thinks his Swainson's Hawk Hybrid takes all the cake, but I'm betting on you."

I stared at him out of the side of my vision. "Is this funny to you?" I asked.

He looked up and leaned forward with a raise of his eyebrows. "If you can't enjoy what you do here, may as well join the Last dying outside." He straightened and slapped the table next to him, making me flinch. It was too loud, my ears too sensitive.

I tried to ignore the noises and asked, "The Last?" My head was hurting really bad again, so I subtly tried to press down on the pressure points in my hands that were supposed to help with headaches.

"What," he asked impatiently, "you don't know who *the Last* are? Hellooo, survivors? You'd have to be living under a rock to not know what's been going on."

"Or *in stasis*," I growled.

He flicked his hand, waving me off uninterestedly. "Yeah, yeah, excuses. People in your state are still supposed to be able to hear things, even if you can't *react* to it."

"What're you saying? You've been talking to an unconscious person this whole time as if they could hear you?"

He seemed to ponder for a moment, his pen hovering over the paper as he looked up at the wall in front of him. "So? It gets lonely." He shrugged, turning his spinny chair back around to a screen. He jotted something down on the keyboard.

I stared at him incredulously. So not only had he seen my naked body, but he'd been having conversations with me while unconscious? Who even was this dude!?

"What's your name?" I asked. Couldn't exactly keep calling him *lab coat guy* in my mind.

He startled pleasurably at my question and lifted his eyes over to me for a long moment. "Carson," he said simply, turning back to his work. "And your name is Rory."

"Yeah." I couldn't help but feel it was creepy he knew without me telling him. Everything he'd said earlier, about ten months passing and being in Iceland, hadn't left me, but my mind was still reeling from my new body. I wanted to ask him questions but didn't even know where to start.

CHAPTER 5

Carson ran through all the same tests that lady doctor had, plus more. Somehow I was still around one-hundred-thirty pounds, even with wings. When he saw my confusion, he explained that my bones were denser and sturdier but also much lighter.

Seeing the X-rays was a serious shocker. My heart and lungs were bigger, more efficient. It explained why it felt way too easy to breathe. Additionally, I had new bone structure on my back, new muscles and tendons to help power my wings, and I could feel the sensation of them tightening when I flexed.

My bones, muscles, tendons, ligaments — they were all stronger. Those in my feet and legs especially so, and they would apparently allow me to jump into the air like an actual bird would do. I had yet to actually test it though.

My senses...they were sharp — too sharp, giving me

a splitting headache. I could hear things in *three rooms over, see* things in great detail. My eyes kept focusing on random spots, drawn to the twitch of Carson's pen, the joints in his metal chair as it creaked, the small particles of dust kicked up from his white shoes — my vision sharpening like a raptor. It was too much.

I frowned as Carson leaned over and plucked one of my arm hairs. He placed it under a microscope to take a look. I rubbed my arm, and to my pleasant surprise it was soft. My hairs felt *incredibly* soft, like bird down. My vision started acting up again as my focus intensified, somehow zooming in on my arm. Each hair had rows of even thinner hairs on both sides, looking like a microscopic version of a simplistic bird feather. Feathers... Oh god, they'd altered my *arm hair*, too?

My vision clicked back to normal. I instantly reached up into my curly hair, wondering what they'd done to *that*. It was also super soft. My fingers ran right through it like silk, something I'd never been able to do before.

"You grew perfectly," he said, his left eye pressed to the eyepiece of the microscope.

"Are you talking to me or the feather?" I asked, feeling wary.

He opened his mouth, then closed it, puckering his lips to one side in thought. "Hmm. You figured that out yourself, huh?" He spun around toward me and brought his chair closer. "How'd you do that?" His eyes wandered my person behind rimmed glasses as if he'd find an answer that way.

I almost didn't want to tell him, scared he'd try to dissect my eye or something. "I can see it," I said, watching him guardedly.

His brows drew in and his brown eyes lifted to mine. A moment later, his expression turned into clarity, maybe a hint of wonder. "Ah. Your eyesight is really that good? I didn't expect such excellent results. We did see a tapetum layer in your eyes early on, however. You should be able to see quite well in the dark."

I blinked blankly at him, feeling shocked, and right when I felt I couldn't get any more shocked. *Night vision?* Well, that explained my response to bright light.

"We saw this develop in anyone mixed with a nocturnal species," he carried on. He paused and rolled his eyes at himself. "Obviously."

His words replayed in my head. "How many people did you do this to?" I asked, practically whispered. My voice sounded dead.

"You say it like it's a bad thing." He frowned at me. "Would you rather be the only one like this?"

I don't know, would I?

"How many are like me?" I asked after some thought.

He flicked his thick eyebrows, seeming pleased. "With your specific hybrid combination? None. Now, if you're asking how many avian Hybrids there are, then that would be a lot more. In this unit, twelve total, including you. But, in total *everywhere*, one-hundred-forty-seven."

So that many people had been experimented on against their will as well? That was…it was…

"How could you do that to all those people?" I asked, appalled.

"Easy," he said. "We had to."

I stared at him, waiting for a better answer.

"Look, I get how it's bad from your point of view, but we really didn't have any other choice," he bargained impatiently. "When you got put down ten months ago, the civilian world didn't know about the disaster about to take place. Major organizations got together to act fast. They wanted to help preserve the human race in one way or another and built bases in remote locations around the world. You don't know what the rest of the world is like anymore. It's not good, okay?"

"Like…how not good?" I asked reluctantly.

"'Total apocalypse' not good," he said. He looked at me very seriously. "Only about five percent of the human population remains, and they're dying every day. Believe it or not, you're one of the lucky ones."

CHAPTER 6

His words hit me hard. Like, dive-bomb off a cliff and faceplant a hundred meters down hard. I'd seen my body modified, *transformed*, but the reality of the situation only really hit me now.

Only five percent remains.

Oh god — Jody. Vixen.

"I need to contact my mom and friend," I said hastily, my brain trying to piece the severity of my new reality together. Even if I didn't totally believe what this scientist guy was telling me, I had to know if they were okay.

Carson frowned sadly at me, making no attempt to help.

"How do I contact them?" I pressed, beginning to look around for something. A phone, carrier pigeon, I don't know. *Something.*

"You can't," he said.

I rounded on him. "Why not?" I argued, feeling panicky.

"Long distance communications stopped working five and a half months ago."

I was momentarily stunned but pulled myself out of it. "Okay? Just let me go and I'll find them myself." All I needed was a map, and I could get back to Jody's house.

He sighed. "What part of 'you're in Iceland' don't you get? Forget it."

"Sure I am," I scoffed. "Just let me go."

He seemed agitated now. "You still don't believe me?" he asked testily. "Fine."

He stood up suddenly and strode over to a tall cabinet. He grabbed something from it and shoved it in my face. "Change so I can prove it to you and we can move on," he ordered.

The clothes were forced into my hands. He sat back down, tapping his foot with his arms crossed. Apparently I was already taking too long, for he spun around to the screen on his desk and continued typing and clicking tensely.

I took my eyes from him, instead examining the clothes I was holding. They were soft and stretchy, and didn't look like any getup I'd ever seen before. Curious, I took my thin gown off and tried to slip into these new clothes.

"Ah. How the hell —?" There were too many components. It had been hard enough just making sure my arms went through the right holes when I'd wear *normal* clothes, but now this? I'd managed to get the pants on easy enough, but this second piece of clothing had half a dozen different holes in it.

Carson sighed exasperatedly. "Let me help you," he grumbled, taking the piece from me and slipping one part over my head. I tensed when I felt his fingers on my bare skin, and eyed him warily. Without much other choice, however, I tried not to be so tense and let him help me. "We had to design it to accommodate your wings," he explained, pulling a strap around under my breasts. Some sort of non-scratchy Velcro. *Cool.*

Once he finished, I walked in front of the big wall-mirror to look myself over. The dark gray mesh material hugged my body comfortably, not too tight and not too loose. It was soft and both warm and breezy at the same time.

The pants stopped just above my ankles and went up to my hips (so, like, normal pants), but the top was an elite fitness bra. The fabric went around my neck like a low collar, and three pieces of the same width fell down to the portion over my breasts, one on either side and one right down the middle. Small feathers fell overtop of the edge of the material where they met. My feathers were still very visible, and the ones that were covered didn't feel uncomfortable under the breezy material. The only part that went around to my back was that wide Velcro strap around my rib cage, laying a comfortable distance under the base of my wings.

After a quick check over, I was ready to head out. "Alright, can we go now?" I asked zealously.

"Uh-huh." Carson led the way through a door flush with the wall.

I padded after him. I noticed the tiled floor beneath my feet didn't feel cold — that it hadn't once felt cold.

"Uh, hey," I inquired quietly as we walked down a wide, never ending hallway. Speaking loudly felt like a crime walking through this echoey hallway, like flushing the toilet in the middle of the night. "Did your genetics treatment do something to change my temperature reception?"

"Temperature reception?" he repeated, more so murmured to himself. "Ah, yeah. Your body is more resistant to temperature changes now, especially to cold. Helps with flying. You know, wind and all." He waved a hand around in the air.

I remained silent. I guess that made sense?

We passed other doors identical to the one we'd walked out of, lining both sides of the hallway. I counted twelve in total. Wait — twelve?

"Are the other people down here?" I asked quietly, feeling my hairs rise in alarm.

"The others in your unit, yes. *They're* still in their rooms, like *you* should be," he scolded.

I shot Carson a stern look. I'd heard voices through the walls earlier thanks to my keen ears, but it didn't occur to me that those voices could belong to others like me.

He took us to the end of a hallway and up three sets of well-lit stairs. There was commotion behind secure-looking, wide double doors at each level, stirring my curiosity.

We reached the top, no more stairs, just an empty section of rubber floor. Set into the wall in front of us was a set of serious-looking double doors. No way was anyone busting through those. I watched as Carson stepped forward and pressed his hand against a foot-long panel beside the right door. The panel beeped, lighting blue, and Carson let his hand fall back to his side.

I stood there in anticipation, but the doors didn't open, making me frown. Then, my astute hearing picked up what sounded like little mechanisms in the walls, flowing through the doors. They cracked outward with a hiss, and cool air rushed in, teasing my feathers. My hands came up to guard my eyes as I was assaulted with brilliant light. Regardless, I took a couple small steps forward, blinking hard. My eyes slowly adjusted to the bright light as whistling wind and the rustling of small plants met my ears.

I stifled a gasp.

Behind a massive grassy court the size of three football fields smashed together, lined in the distance with a tall metal fence rimmed in barbed wire, was a breathtaking and impossible scene.

My right hand involuntarily came to my chest, smashing the tiny feathers there, as if that could possibly slow my pounding heart. Not that it needed to — my heart may as well have stopped and rolled over dead.

There were no trees in sight, only a curvy grassy plain dotted with little flowers ending suddenly, disappearing into a clear blue sky. Waves clashed hungrily in the distance, by the faint sound of it an easy thousand feet down. We were surrounded by endless water on three sides, the other an immeasurable stretch of land connecting to a hazy landmass.

Oh, crap.

This was definitely not Virginia, I'll tell you that much.

CHAPTER 7

Carson was shivering slightly beside me in his white lab coat. "Seen enough yet?" he asked impatiently.

"I..." I had no words. My wide eyes took in my surroundings. Numbly, I walked forward. Soft grass met my feet and the breeze surrounded me.

This was Iceland?

Well what the hell was I supposed to do now??

"Rory," Carson insisted.

Seeing as how Carson was determined on bringing me back inside, I took the opportunity to really scan what was around me.

Besides the empty land and ten-foot-tall fences, a room-sized cement square squatted behind me under a small hill, its two-foot-thick doors hanging open. I spotted another small structure similar to that one hiding under a mound of grass some hundred meters away to my right, facing the courtyard. I didn't doubt there were more elsewhere out of view.

The outside of the structure behind me had cameras built into its walls, which was anxiety inducing but not unexpected.

There really wasn't much else I noticed. It was pretty empty out here. Not another living thing in sight, much less a human.

I followed Carson back inside, and he closed the heavy doors behind us. The natural sounds ceased to exist, and the breeze no longer tossed around my feathers. I looked back over my shoulder at the exit as we started down the stairs.

◆ ◆ ◆

"You'll get used to it," Carson promised once we were back in the lab room.

I seriously doubted that, but I didn't voice my rejection.

"So, why Iceland?" I asked. "Why not Hawaii or something?"

Carson laughed, actual humor in his voice. I glanced at him with a frown. "There are over *twenty-thousand* animal species in Hawaii. Iceland has around *one-thousand-six-hundred*. Compared to Hawaii, Iceland is a walk in the park."

Personally, one-thousand-six-hundred still sounded like a lot to me, but apparently not. "Okay?" I inquired.

He sighed, as if tired of my lack of knowledge. "The chemical — DODG — alters animals. Screws with their brains to make them ultra-aggressive and extra intelligent, and advances their physical forms to make up for it. Trust me, you want an island with as few animals as possible."

Carson had told me before that the world had turned apocalyptic, but I didn't fully understand why. I guess if animals really evolved the way he said they did, humans would be in serious trouble. My wings itched behind me, my thoughts clicking into place.

"All of them?" I asked. "The animals, I mean. Were they *all* affected?"

"Yep," he said with a smack of his lips. "No more Rufus the puppy or Snowball the bunny. Only Fangs the man eater and Bob the Builder tunnel edition."

Oh geez. "What about humans?"

"No humans were affected, unless you count being hunted and killed as an effect," he said a little stiffly.

Pros and cons, I suppose?

"Hey, does DODG stand for anything?" I asked after a while.

"DODG? Deep Ocean Death Gas, of course. What else?" he joked.

I gave him a look. "No, really."

"Yeah, really."

Ah, okay then.

He finished with his tests, finally announcing only a solid twenty minutes later that he was done.

"Great. Now let me just log this in, and we can

continue on as scheduled," he said cheerfully.

While he had been busy running tests, I had been silently figuring out how to get out of here and go find my mom and best friend. If there really were such evolved animals as he said there were, I'd have to find them as soon as possible.

The first major idea to get back was taking a boat. I had wings now (as I kept having to remind myself), but that didn't mean I knew how to use them, or even if I did that I could fly across the ocean. I put this idea on hold. I hadn't seen any sign of civilization when outside the — what was this place? Facility? Bunker? Eh — the *place*, so I wasn't sure how far I'd get with the boat idea.

The second major idea was that I could fly back. Like previously stated, I did not actually know how to yet, but that didn't mean I couldn't learn. But that required...*ugh,* staying put.

Fine, I'd go along with whatever they had planned for now, until I was sure I could get out of here without drowning in the frigid ocean.

Something on Carson's screen caught my eye: pictures of complex DNA structures with information under each of them. Curious as always, not to mention paranoid now, I squinted my eyes a bit at it. Focusing on the image, my vision zoomed in and I could see every little pixel. *Ah, too much.* I blinked and forced my vision to zoom out a bit. It was a super weird ability, but I think I was starting to get the hang of it.

He scrolled through them, and I caught the first pieces of information directly under each DNA structure. I recognized the first one as me.

IM3771NV_Siberian Eagle Owl_Golden Eagle - Rory: (20, Female, 5'8", 20Ft wingspan)

IS6822_Peregrine Falcon - Michael: (23, male, 5'10", 17.5Ft wingspan)

IS5641_Swainson's Hawk - Clara: (18, Female, 5'8", 18Ft wingspan)

IM8772NV_Snowy Owl_Osprey - Iver: (20, male, 5'11", 21.5Ft wingspan)

IS5542_Steppe Eagle - Adler: (20, male, 5'11", 21Ft wingspan)

IS9421_Blue-Faced Honeyeater - Aubrey: (22, Female, 5'6", 14Ft wingspan)

IS4462_Cooper's Hawk - Ronin: (22, male, 5'9", 16Ft wingspan)

IS2561_Mourning Dove - Anna: (18, Female, 5'3", 14Ft wingspan)

IM8731_Tree Swallow_American Kestrel - June: (22, Female, 5'7", 15.5Ft wingspan)

IM5182_Great Cormorant_Violet-backed Starling - Samuel: (25, male, 5'9", 19.5Ft wingspan)

IM3992_Magnificent Frigatebird_Iceland Gull - Will: (19, male, 6'0", 22Ft wingspan)

IS6841NV_Elf Owl - Elena: (17, Female, 5'6", 15Ft wingspan)

Wait, Will? Could the Will on this log of human experiments be the same Will from Virginia?

Carson clicked out of the screen and hopped out of his spinny chair. "Alright, love," he said. "Come with me."

"Don't call me that," I muttered, getting up to follow him.

We walked back down the hallway and up the stairs like before, only Carson stopped us on the second level, a metal plaque above the double doors sporting the label G2. I tensed, picking up on conversations on the other side of the doors. We were gonna go through there? I was going to see people who weren't Carson?

My heart was beating fast in my chest as Carson pushed the left door open, leading the way in. He held it open and looked back at me expectantly.

I forced my feet to move but only made it as far as the other side of the door, where I then halted abruptly.

At a table twenty feet from the door, a group of kids around my age looked up, half having to look over their shoulder, all wearing the same dark gray mesh material I was. Their eyes were trained on me, their expressions and body language ranging from wary, shocked, scared, and sad. That wasn't the shocking part that had caused me to halt in my steps though. You see, they all had *wings*.

"Good luck," Carson whispered. He gave me a quick thumbs-up before closing the door behind him. My keen ears could hear him walking back down the glossy stairs.

I looked around the room, tearing my eyes from the birdkids for a moment. A third of the floor was filled with long metal tables, similar to the ones you'd find pushed together in a cafeteria. Men and women in lab coats and others in dark uniforms sat around tables further back, apparently eating. I could hear them chattering about me and the other kids sitting in front of me, frequently turning to stare.

Despite the numerous seats, the room was very spacious. Four rows of concrete columns three times the width of my body rose in thirty-foot intervals down the room. The floor and ceiling were also a light-colored concrete, though very smooth and level. Bright fluorescent lights hung twenty feet above from the ceiling, effectively lighting the whole space.

More doors sprung off from around the sides of the room, though most of them were single doors. A set of double doors at the opposite end looked just like the ones I'd come out of, and a sudden thought struck me. I bet those led to another staircase that would bring me to the outside doors across the field I'd seen earlier. I quickly estimated the distance and found it to be about a hundred meters, same as the distance from one door to the other outside.

Amidst my quick mental notes, my head whipped over as someone walked over to me from the side.

A man wearing a decorated, dark uniform walked toward me without hesitation, giving me the impression he was a person of power around here. His graying hair was clipped an inch from his skull, standing on-end in a permanent state of surprise. He was on the older side, but he was not lacking in muscle, his uniform tight against his chest.

"Welcome to the living, Rory," he said. He swept a well-toned arm out toward the long table seating seven other kids with wings, consisting of three guys and four girls. "Have a seat and lunch will be provided. I'm sure you've got a nice appetite after sleeping for ten months."

I eyed the man for a hesitant moment, but his stony face, with a Roman nose and squarish features, did not betray him. Was it that *everyone* knew my name here?

"Sure," I replied briskly, feeling uneasy inside.

He gave a curt nod and walked me past a few tables to the one with the birdkids. "Anywhere is fine," he told me from the side.

I glanced around and easily slid onto the metal bench closest to me, keeping a good meter between myself and any others. I sat on the side already holding more people, but I could watch the double doors easier from here.

A moment later, someone came out of one of the single doors at the side, carrying a metal plate. Her white coat looked more like a cook's coat than a lab coat, her straw-blonde hair tied back in a bun. She set the plate in front of me and gave the man in uniform a polite nod before heading away. I watched her go for a moment, then turned my attention on the food, if you could call it that. Sitting in the middle of the silver plate was a white, fist-sized block that looked more like soap than lunch.

There was a metal fork beside it on the plate.

They expected me to eat this?

I glanced around the table under my brows. The other seven kids were eating their weird soap. Their faces didn't show any signs of disgust, but rather seemed to relish in their chewing like starving orphan children.

Quickly, I retracted my last thought, realizing they may very well be alone now, without family or friends. That *I* may be alone now, for the second time in my life no doubt. I blinked hard, trying to force my thoughts away from those dark places.

"You can expect meals like this regularly," the uniformed man beside me said. "Everything we eat is grown within these facilities."

"What is it?" I asked, picking up the fork to poke at it. It reacted like canned cranberry sauce, firm yet somewhat gelatinous.

I'd always hated cranberry sauce.

"It's completely plant based," he informed. "The chemical that ultimately brought you here had unhinging effects on the animals but also enhanced plant growth, making farming much more efficient. We've been able to use this excessive growth to our advantage."

I didn't bother responding.

He crossed his hands behind his back, refusing to be disgruntled by my lack of enthusiasm. "Eat up," he said. "It may seem like a small portion, but it packs more than enough energy. It doesn't taste that bad either, I promise you." With that, he turned on his heel and trudged off to a group of people in uniform a few tables away.

CHAPTER 8

If those scientists had decided to give me a better sense of smell, I probably could have known from one whiff if something was wrong with it, but alas, I was short of one super sniffer. So instead, even though I doubted they'd try to harm their precious creations, I poked absently at the food while secretly watching to see if any of the others croaked.

The guy sitting next to me glanced over with a slanted line for a mouth. He had nice features, sharp and handsome. He looked down at his partially eaten food and set his fork aside, seeming to take my cue.

My eyes flicked over him with some interest. He had chocolatey brown hair with a little bit of curl to it, and neat eyebrows the same color as his hair. His skin, exposed all the way down to his waist, was a lighter shade of natural brown with a warm undertone, appearing Latino. Muted brown feathers like the ones on the tops of his wings lined his hairline and other parts of his body; across his shoulders, down his chest.

I instinctively shifted my eyes up and suddenly found them looking straight into his. His eyes, like the feathers, were unnatural. They were a light brown but had a silver tone to them that caused me to feel like I was looking into his soul.

We both looked away.

"What's your name?" he asked out of nowhere.

I glanced at him again. "Rory. Yours?"

"Adler."

Adler. Hmm. My mind immediately tried to bring back the list of kids from Carson's screen. With a dozen descriptions, however, he was a little hard to place. The only thing I really remembered was that he'd been mixed with some type of eagle.

Remembering this, my gaze shifted to his back, grazing his wings. The edges of his wide wings curled ever so gently around his shoulders, and the tips brushed the floor as mine did. While his marginal coverts were a muted brown, the bottom rows of larger feathers were black, with the very ends of each feather tipped in white. The first seven long, solid black primaries were the only ones without any white.

"Steppe Eagle," he spoke up.

I flicked my eyes away from his wings, realizing he'd caught me looking at them. "Hm?"

He nodded down at his wings, giving them a twitch.

"That's what I'm hybridized with, apparently. Steppe Eagle."

"Ah." I looked back at my own wings. Testingly, I brought my right wing a couple feet around my side, displaying it for the both of us. My feathers were pretty, speckled with flecks of gold. Even so, looking at them made me frown a bit. "I got handed Siberian Eagle Owl and Golden Eagle," I told him, feeling like someone comparing Pokémon cards. It was more than that though; it gave us a way to connect in all the horrible, messed up weirdness.

He raised his eyebrows in surprise. "Two?"

I nodded numbly, tucking my wing back in against my back. "Yeah." A small, empty grin tugged at the corners of my mouth as I looked at Adler. "We're both part eagle now."

He gave a small huff as a laugh, but his expression remained tense.

Now I was curious about everyone else at the table as well. I looked over each of them. With Adler's slender, well-toned body and good posture, it was easy to see the others past him.

Sitting to the right of Adler was a girl with blonde hair that gave off a golden sheen. She had a soft, round face with thin eyebrows, giving off an overall innocent, sexy vibe. Small, greenish feathers lined her hairline and caressed other parts of her body, matching the yellow-green color of her wing feathers. My eyes wandered over her wings, following them to the floor. Her folded wings were shorter, the tips hovering a good two feet above the cement.

Beside her was another girl around my height, dark brown wings fading to black hanging behind her. Hers weren't as short as the other girl's, but they didn't reach the floor either.

Her soft, squarish face sporting small eyebrows and half-moon-shaped eyes was gently framed with long, somewhat curvy, dark brown-black hair. With her chastened posture, she gave off a modest and lonely vibe. Her brown eyes saturated with an orangey-amber looked for hopeless answers in the table's shiny surface.

At the end of the table sat a small girl with little brown wings curled around her shoulders as if trying to hide. Her small, soft-looking plumage was cryptically colored to resemble bark or leaves. It was hard to make out much more with her curled up and sitting four people away.

Across from her, a youthful boy with almond-shaped eyes scooped up his last forkful of food from his plate. His pushed-up black hair had a thick white streak at the front, the feathers along his hairline also changing to white where they overlapped that section of hair. As he chewed, his deep yellow-amber eyes skipped around the cavernous room. It was hard to see his wings from my angle, only glimpsing a crescent of white, speckled with big black spots, curling around his right side. With my acute ears, I could hear his long primaries scraping against the floor.

He said something to the girl next to him, but I didn't really care what he was saying. The girl beside him didn't seem to care much either, looking held-together and sedate.

She had a strong Asian appearance, with long, shiny, mocha-colored hair, brown eyes, and gray-brown wings that were lightly striped and dotted. The hard top edge of the wing I could see had an interesting iridescent green highlight to it. It reminded me of the swallows that sometimes tried to nest in Jody's barn.

At this thought, I quickly moved on before I could get too caught up in what might have happened to my adoptive mom. My eyes skipped over to the last person, completing the uneven loop around the table. I tried to focus on his features to occupy my mind.

His features turned out to be a good distraction; chiseled and cunning. Muscles kept jumping out in his jaw as if he was grinding his teeth in anger. It was then that I realized none of the men here had any facial hair, but it was more of an absent thought. This young man was overall good looking, maybe a little older than the other couple of guys here, with medium-length, messy black hair with a bit more length on top, and eyes like Black Emperador Marble. Black-gray feathers ran along his hairline and other parts of his body like everyone else, with the ones traveling down the middle of his broad chest being white.

The densely striped undersides of his wings were unmistakable. He was definitely the Peregrine Hybrid.

Something nudged my right arm, making me jump and whip my head over. Adler nodded past the table, his eyes trained on a distance spot. I followed his gaze to the double doors. The left door cracked open, a man in a white lab coat who was not Carson holding it open. In the next moment, another person came hesitantly through, her round eyes (the left a chocolate brown, the right a startling blue) flicking nervously around.

"How many more are gonna show up?" Adler vexed, mostly to himself.

I did a quick count. Without looking over at him, I answered quietly, "Three more."

He seemed surprised I knew.

The short girl jumped when the scientist behind her urged her on. Her petite golden-brown and gray wings curled around her arms fearfully, prominently displaying the familiar black circles of a mourning dove. Choppy, semi-curly, brown hair fell just above her shoulders, long bangs pushed over to the left. The feathers around her hairline were a soft gray-brown, melting into her darker brown hair.

The same general-like man who'd led me over to the table led the new girl over, walking up to her from somewhere behind my left. He brought her to the table while explaining something, and she took a hesitant seat at the edge, away from everybody.

I looked her over where she sat on the far opposite side of the table, but quickly lost interest in her as I heard the double doors swing open again. This time two more people walked through, both boys around twenty years old. One had big, lanky black wings with a purple iridescent patch peeking over the first half of his left wing. They were dark and alluring, a stark contrast from his light skin and blond hair. The taller of the two had turned toward the scientist, talking to him about something. I got a nice view of his wings which were black as well, though his were long and angular with tan patches, like the color of one bird fighting to show through the more dominant black one.

As he turned back around to walk with the other guy, my eyes moved from his wings to the rest of his body. He had black, brown, and muted tan feathers along his hairline and down his chest. But that honey-brown hair, that face...

Why did it look familiar?

My eyes widened with realization and I hopped out of my seat, making the others around me startle. I ignored them and ran up to the boy, crushing him in my arms, making him produce an audible *'oof.'*

Frankly, I hadn't really cared for him before, but being the only somewhat familiar person in this place made my heart swell when I saw him.

He placed his arms hesitantly around me.

73

I let go of him. "I can't believe it's you," I said, feeling more emotional than I wanted to be. "I thought for sure that between the two of us you'd be a goner."

When he stared at me blankly, I thought for a tense moment that it actually wasn't him. How embarrassing.

"Rory?" he asked in wonder. In the next instant, a wide smile grew on his face, his fingers tightening into my shoulders. "Oh my gosh, you're alive!"

That's about as good as 'hello' was gonna get around here. I smiled as well, feeding off his increasingly energetic energy.

CHAPTER 9

Sitting at the table together, I couldn't stop staring at him. Will used to have a scrawny frame, but now he looked more filled out and lean rather than scrawny.

Also, I couldn't remember exactly what his eyes had looked like, but I was pretty sure they didn't used to be pale yellow.

"When did you wake up?" he asked. "Linda — the scientist lady that ran a bunch of tests on me — she said we were in stasis for the past ten months? Is that even possible?"

Why are you asking me *how it's possible?* I wanted to say. *Heck if I know!*

"I only woke up a few hours ago," I said. "And yeah, apparently ten months have passed. Oh, and we're in Iceland." *Just so you know*.

His face dropped. "What?" he asked meekly.

"I saw it myself, outside. This whole operation is

underground," I insisted.

"You've been above ground?" someone else asked. I looked over at Adler, who was peering at me skeptically.

I hesitated, wondering if I should even be telling them this. "Yeah, only for a moment." I shrugged. "Nothing really out there."

"But," Will complained anxiously, halting the rest of his sentence.

I watched him curiously. "But what?"

His eyes were searching the air in front of him, his straight eyebrows furrowing the skin between them. He mumbled worriedly to himself, but with my excellent hearing, I could still make out what he was saying. "Noah… How do I…? This can't be happening…"

"Your family?" I asked sadly.

He looked at me, a hint of surprise flashing across his pale yellow eyes. "Yeah," he said smally.

"Mm." I nodded absently. "Did, uh, Linda tell you why we're here? What the rest of the world is like?" I asked, trying to sound gentle. It didn't really work for me.

"Yeah," he said, frowning with uncertainty.

"Do you think it's true?" I inquired. If anyone could come up with a better reason we were in an underground base in Iceland, it would be Will, I was sure of it. He was the conspiracy expert, after all.

"Do I think it's true that some chemical from the bottom of the ocean has turned all the animals in the world into massive threats against humankind? That only five percent of the human population remains?"

Okay, so they told us the same information at least. I didn't answer, only waited for him to.

He swung his hands up in an exasperated motion, then turned and planted his elbows on the table. "I don't know," he said, rubbing his palms into his eyes.

I wanted to consolidate him, but I'd never really been good at that sort of thing. Didn't help it was basically the wounded helping the wounded.

I was saved from attempting an awkward pat on the shoulder when one of the double doors cracked open again. My head whipped over before the door was even halfway open.

Out walked another birdkid. The twelfth and final one. He appeared to be of strong Asian descent, with dark brown hair with lighter red-tinted streaks up front like a hawk's plumage, and red-brown eyes. But I mean, like, *red*-brown eyes.

Under a pair of sharp S-shaped eyebrows, his dangerous gaze swept over everyone who was looking at him, including me. Instantly, I knew he'd cook up trouble in some way or another. That was alright though; not like we didn't all have enough on our plates anyway.

I ignored him as he was walked up to the table like everyone else had been, only glancing at him again out of curiosity toward his wings. He himself was maybe an inch taller than me, so it was easy to see the several-foot difference of our wingspan where his wingtips hung above the floor. His feathers were a gray-blue tinted black, with faintly striped primaries. By my best guess, he was hybridized with some type of hawk, a perfect match for his challenging attitude.

He sat down in really the only space left, between the blond guy and the shy dove. The small girl became even more nervous beside this new guy, and I almost felt bad for her. Almost.

"That's everybody now, right?" Adler asked quietly from my side.

"Twelve, yeah," I said. "Should be."

The graying man in uniform didn't leave this time. He stood at the end of the table, standing very still as his alert, steely-blue eyes swept over us. Once everybody's attention naturally gravitated to him, he addressed us.

"If you were expecting a formal introduction or fancy presentation on your new life, too bad. All you get is me," he stated.

I heard someone further down the table curse under their breath.

The man waved away the kid's words. "Yeah, yeah." Then he stared at us seriously, taking all joy from the surrounding air. "I want you all to take a good look at the others around this table," he said slowly, carefully scanning each of us. "These are the people you will see every day from now on. You are all part of one unit, Unit 3. *This* is your family now." He paused, daring any of us to speak up or cry.

I spared a glance around the table, uncomfortably meeting the eyes of several others.

He eased up a little, even checking his short, square nails as he began clipping slowly back and forth at the end of the long table. My sharp vision focused on his nails annoyingly, and I frowned as I tried to blink the image away.

He spoke each of his next words thoughtfully, ending each sentence on a careful note. "Most of you have been made aware to some extent what's going on, and why you're here. It's simple, really: you're part of a small genetic population possessing what we call the Hybrid Gene. This special little gene is what gave our scientists the power to alter each of you, effectively hybridizing your genes with one or more species that are not your own."

He stopped checking his nails and laced his hands behind his back, continuing to pace slowly. "Whether you like it or not, you are humanity's best and only remaining hope," he said darkly. "The world has fallen into chaos and death, caused by a chemical that alters the brains and physique of nonhuman animals. I know you all had families, friends, that you want to get back to...but they're dead, along with the other ninety-five percent of the population," he said without remorse. "All that's left of them is you, and it's up to you to carry on the human legacy."

Okay, so no pressure then, I shrugged off internally.

Yeah, right. I was sure the others could hear my heart pounding irregularly through my chest.

"Now that you're all here and done with your initial testing, after you eat, we can move on to the next phase: training. Your primary job will be learning how to survive. After all, that's the whole reason for any of this." He glanced around at our plates. "So eat up, and do so quickly. We have much work to do."

He clapped his hands together in a single chalky bang, making three of us flinch. Guess I wasn't the only one with enhanced hearing.

The bossy man in black turned on his heel, walking a short distance to talk to a couple other guys who had been waiting on him. They were dressed in black as well, though they looked subordinate somehow. Call it a general feeling.

Well, I suppose it was time to eat that block of soap now. Nobody had died yet, so hopefully it would be fine.

I picked up the fork and cut into the bar. I brought the white chunk to my nose, giving it a sniff with my normal snoot. Smelled like peaches and old kale. It tasted like buttery apples. Overall, not bad.

As I ate, I wondered what kind of 'training' this new life would entail. Hopefully it wouldn't include bunkbeds, 'cause I'm not sure I could jam with that now that I had such good hearing.

CHAPTER 10

"First thing's first," our trainer announced, his voice carrying over the gray field to our messy row. "In order to train effectively, you need to master your own body. Today we will focus on using your wings."

Our group of a dozen kept looking around at our surroundings, not paying full attention to the trainer. The sloping plains, endless water, and gray sky were pretty empty and monotone, but they were still a beautiful sight. I doubt any of us had ever been to Iceland before. Mark that down as yet another new experience for our group in only the past few hours.

"Unit 3," he ordered, gathering our attention with a forceful tone. He was well-built like most of the men and women in uniform around here, but his light-brown hair, matching his chestnut-colored eyes, curled at the base of his nape and around his temples, a good two or three inches longer than most of the close-clipped hairstyles I'd seen. He was tall and appeared lightweight, having a lanky frame despite his rippling muscles, making me think he'd be a good specimen to add to the avian Hybrid collection. Five other guys in dark uniforms stood off to the side at the bunker entrance like statues while the trainer stood fifty meters out in the field with the rest of us.

We looked over at him with varying levels of difficulty. With all our eyes somewhat trained on him, he carried on, looking pleased under his attentive and serious attitude.

"Each of you will have a slightly unique way of taking off, landing, and how you fly once in the air. We can't fully predict your method, but have prepared a functional starting method by combining your human form and your hybridized bird species in simulators."

I glanced over at Will, who stood two meters to my left. He met my eyes and gave me a nervous grin. Neither of us let what the general-like man (who Will and I decided to call Bossy Bob) said about our friends and families get to us. We wouldn't believe him until we found proof.

"There is one general rule of flying, and that is flying typically requires flapping. Today, the hope is that you will get familiar with the feel of your wings and learn how to control them on even a rudimentary level." He scanned the dozen of us with a quick flash of his gaze. "Space out and practice expanding and moving your wings." He clapped his hands twice, signaling us to get to work.

The energy flowing around our group was mostly nervous and eager, filled with anticipation as we spaced out ten to twenty meters from each other. There was plenty of field to go around.

Jody used to have ducks on the farm. When they'd come to the age where they'd molt and grow in their full, pretty wings, I'd see them flap in place or run about on the ground, testing their strength and learning the motion of flying.

Right now I felt like one of those ducks.

It was windy outside, and under normal circumstances it likely would have felt cold in the past. That is, before being genetically altered.

I only really kept an eye on the others to make sure they wouldn't run into me (or vice versa). Right now I was more focused on my own body and wings. As of yet, I still felt that flying was my best bet at getting back to Virginia. Therefore, I took this flight training stuff very seriously.

But really, who doesn't want to fly?

I could feel certain muscles and tendons in my chest and back stretching pleasantly as I slowly unfurled my wings. Stretching them out wasn't so hard; I'd already done it in Carson's lab. It was weird using my arms and wings at the same time, but it was more like using your thumb and pointer finger together rather than trying to flex your pinky finger without flexing your ring finger. Know what I mean?

I could feel every feather, the way they overlapped, the wind pressing against them. It was…honestly, amazing.

Looking at my wings, I tried to move them in different ways. Curl, extend out behind me, turn, fold and open from different angles; anything and everything I could try. It was sort of like learning to write with your opposite hand, only somehow more natural. I felt I would get the hang of it with time.

But I didn't want to wait. The wind had picked up, luring my feathers and tossing my hair around behind my head. A spark scraped against the inside of my chest with a growing desire.

I took a quick look around me. Everyone else was occupied with themselves, some looking ecstatic, others horrified as they moved their wings. The trainer was distracted, helping the blonde-haired girl with the yellow-green wings.

My heart hammered excitedly. With a grin creeping up my mouth, I opened my wings again testingly, unfurling them like a soft curtain. The wind was blowing into me, my wings feeling like big sails. I curled them in most of the way, as I'd never seen a bird take off with its wings already open. I leaned over slightly into a bit of a crouch and tilted my mostly-folded wings to be more parallel with the ground. Time to see if my legs really were as strong as they'd said.

My legs tensed, looking like a cat not sure it wanted to pounce just yet. Throwing caution to the wind, I jumped as I simultaneously unfurled my wings, throwing their tips upward.

With legs like springs, I was able to jump four feet up and out from a standstill no problem. *Holy crap!* My eyes were wide with shock at my ability, and I almost forgot to flap down.

Momentarily filled with panic, I flapped down hard. My wings naturally came down in a more forward position, and I thought for sure that I'd go backward. Yet, somehow I gained lift. Panic turned into elation as my feet remained off the ground, my body moving forward through the air.

Up, out and down, repeat. My wings moved in a fluid motion, my huge, soft, hybrid owl feathers barely making a sound.

Through the pounding in my ears, I heard the commotion of the others as they shouted and pointed at me in surprise and astonishment. Grinning euphorically, I wondered what else I could do.

With the strong Icelandic winds buoying me up, I barely had to flap to stay aloft. I tilted my head to look down the lines of my wings, all the way to the very tips ten feet away in either direction. My long, sharp primaries resembled a Golden Eagle more than an Eagle Owl, curling gracefully against the wind. I gave them a flap, entranced by their golden sheen and cryptic patterns. So I could fly straight, but what about…

I faced forward, looking where I wanted to go. I gave my wings an extra flap, then shifted my body and tilted my wings at the same time. The effect was instant, carrying me upwards twenty feet in only a second.

"Woah," I breathed, leveling out a bit unsteadily. I stared with wide eyes at the rolling plain beneath me. I wanted to go higher, I knew I could.

I angled my wings again, still flying into the fierce wind. With barely any work, I rose an additional two-hundred meters. Feeling like this was a good enough height to practice flying, I testingly tilted my wings, letting the wind take me around to the left. The wind rocked me a bit, and I focused on trying to steady myself, feeling my heart beat harder in my chest with every teeter.

As the direction at which I flew with the wind changed, I had to alter my movements to stay steady. I practiced soaring in wide circles with seventy-foot diameters. When I'd circle back around into the wind, I'd sometimes have to give my wings a little flap to keep my pace. For sure I thought my hair would fly into my face, but I was ahead of it for the most part, even when the wind came from behind me.

Having gotten the general feel of it, I looked down. I'd say the others below looked small, but with my raptor vision, it was incredibly easy to make out their every detail. In fact, I could even hear them speaking and shouting below.

"I want to try!" Will said, staring up at me in wonderment. With a look of great excitement, he tried to mimic me.

My heart wanted to cheer for him, but all I could think was: *uh-oh.*

Will opened up his long black wings splotched with tan and bunched his legs. With a simultaneous flap, he jumped up. He made it *maybe* five feet off the ground with the help of his wings, though that may have been a generous estimate.

In the next instant, he fell back down, his wings whapping painfully against the ground. I winced just watching it. My wings tilted into the wind as I curved back around again, completing yet another lazy circle.

The trainer rushed over to Will, seeming both scared and happy, looking between me and Will as if not sure which was more important at the moment. Will got up and spat the grass out of his mouth.

"Your wings are different," the trainer hastily explained to Will. "Also, your legs aren't as strong. You're hybridized with two seabirds, so your wings are longer and thinner. You need to open your wings out while starting on the ground and flap them in small motions to gain lift."

Will extended his wings slowly, as if testing their strength. He examined them with a determined frown.

"More running, more flaps," the trainer reinforced.

"Got it?"

Will nodded. "Got it."

The trainer stepped back with light footsteps, giving Will an excited double thumbs-up. It seemed his serious attitude had all but vanished after seeing one of his students actually get off the ground. The others in our unit stopped to watch as well.

Will gave his wings a lanky flap and looked over each of them. "Okay," I saw him mouth silently to himself. He rolled his shoulders, making his wings jerk a few inches, and got into a bent stance, looking like someone about to run a race.

Suddenly, he started off, running down the small incline of the field. His outreaching wings worked, flapping in almost round motions.

I watched with great interest as he steadily made way off the ground. Five feet, seven, twelve. Soon he was flying low over the ground some thirty feet up.

CHAPTER 11

I thought for sure he'd lift easily up into the air as I had, but that's not exactly how it went down.

With his long, angular, incredibly slender wings, he seemed to have a bit of difficulty controlling them. I could see the panic etched into Will's face as he started flapping more erratically.

"Slow, deep wingbeats!" the instructor called from the top of the plain.

It seemed the trainer's words pierced some part of Will's panic, for his motions became more measured. I felt the wind pick up where I was, and I saw it slam into Will down below. It hit his wings like a breeze might hit a sail, snapping them taunt. Amidst the hit, his wings stopped flapping for a moment.

He gave them another single flap to steady himself, but then held his long wings out straight and rose fifteen feet, pressing into the wind.

He was doing it! He was actually getting higher! I stopped arcing and glided in place to get a good look.

Will tilted his wings, but instead of curving gently to the right, he nearly toppled over himself. I heard him gasp.

"It's okay! Go with the wind!" the trainer called.

His dark wings fell into sync with the breeze, making a full 180. With the aid of the wind, he rushed thirty feet over the others' heads, making them instinctively duck.

Will flapped in small motions. I bet if he were to make a snow angel facing forward, its quarter-moon wings would replicate Will's. Looking like a clumsy seabird, he rose higher into the air and circled back around.

Feeling happy, I lost altitude and curved around to meet him where he flew some three-hundred feet behind me.

"Hey!" I said, flapping closer to his right side. "We're doing it!"

He grinned at me. When he looked over, he lost his balance for a moment, his grin flashing into panic. I flapped out to the right before he could ram into me.

"My bad," he said, looking sheepish. Despite his momentary fumble, he looked extremely lighthearted and excited while flying for the first time.

I stayed a safe distance away from him still, and looked back down at the ground. The others had crowded around the trainer, who had his binoculars he'd pulled out of *god knows where* trained on me and Will, asking him how *they* were supposed to get up there. Everyone but the small girl that had been sitting at the end of the table, looking fearful of her own wings. Also, two boys, one of whom I recognized as Adler. The two boys had separated from the group and were walking down the field. I could hear their conversation as they speculated with each other.

"She's both eagle and owl, right? So I'm think'n that you're eagle, and I've got owl, so maybe just copy her and we could get off the ground too," the other boy reasoned. He was the one with the white streak in his hair. His coverts were white and splotched with black dots, the rest of his longer feathers fading into a darker color.

"Yeah, maybe," Adler agreed. "Let's try it."

The other boy nodded. He split off from Adler as if giving himself room to take off.

"Wait!" Adler said, jogging back over to him. The other boy looked at him in question. "The trainer said her legs are stronger. If ours aren't, we'll likely end up eating grass like that other guy."

"Sooo, jump around a bit first, is what you're saying?" the other clarified.

Adler gave a halfhearted shrug, a grin tugging at his mouth. "Yeah."

The other boy pressed his lips tightly together, thinking. Finally, he agreed. "Alright."

Movement in the corner of my vision snapped my attention back to my immediate surroundings. Will darted by me, then rose like the beginning of a roller coaster. Watching him, I felt I should practice some more new things. How about just simple up and down, side to side? I flapped a few times then practiced angling down and up, left and right, until I could do so smoothly. I also practiced allowing the wind to push me backward, taken along its stream by fanning my wings out, then flap forward again with extra gusto. My muscles had a euphoric sensation coursing through them. Not quite the burn you feel from exertion, but rather a tingling that seemed to give me even more energy.

And by the way, when I say 'muscles,' I don't just mean the ones powering my wings. I was using literally every muscle I had in order to direct my body and keep a good, least air resistant form. This included keeping my core firm and not letting my legs or arms fall.

Go ahead and try something for me. Lie down on the floor facedown and try to hold your legs up behind you, your arms down your body, and look straight ahead. Now hold for half an hour. Easy, right? Ha, well, it was for me now. That's genetic alteration for ya.

It was weird and scary and amazing being able to control my movements, flying so high up with nothing but the air touching me. Practicing, I came to the conclusion that flying could be mastered with the same techniques I used in Jeet Kune Do and Armed martial arts. Basically, I followed these principles: simplicity, directness, and freedom. I wouldn't follow or establish any specific pattern; I'd just flow with the wind.

I noticed those two boys below jumping into the air. About ten minutes had passed since I last listened to them planning, so they must have been through some trial and error since then. It seemed to pay off, though, for the guy with the white streak in his hair made it off the ground. He flapped into the wind then stopped flapping altogether, only tilting his wobbly wings to gain lift. Adler was up a moment later, looking like a clumsy raptor.

Oh geez, is that what I looked like at first? I hoped not. And if so, I'd definitely have to work on that. Yikes.

Now there were four of us out of the twelve up in the air, really practicing flying. I still couldn't believe it. I mean, *flying* kids?

I wanted to get out of dodge, though, so I banked north.

Wait — north? How did I know that? Not like I had a compass.

Surprised, I looked around and realized I knew which direction was which without trying. I could *feel* it, without thinking about the actual words. So...I had an internal compass now, too?

Cool.

So anyway, I banked north. I scanned the stretch of land below which ended abruptly, dropping off into a small, yellow beach.

Sitting like a beached whale in the sand was a little ship. Its dull red sides and white top with rust leaking through did not give it a particularly nice impression, but it really caught my eye being the only unnatural thing out here.

With my eyes trained on the ship, I pulled my wings in closer and felt the rush of losing altitude. I angled them more parallel with the ground after dropping a hundred or so meters, and began circling over the ship.

It was just…sitting there.

Okay, I mean, *obviously*. It's just…ninety-five percent of the population was supposed to be dead, right? This beached ship gave me a haunted feeling, laying abandoned here.

I shivered, not from the cold. Frowning slightly, I angled my wings and let the wind carry me up and away.

CHAPTER 12

The scenery was really quite stately, even in its bare state. Off to the north, the plains fell away into a few beaches while the western and southern edges ended abruptly at cliffs with impressive drops. The tallest was at least a four-hundred-meter drop, straight into the deep blue-gray ocean below.

Speaking of the ocean, it was *everywhere*. Besides the continuation of hilly plains off to the east, we were quite literally surrounded by water with not a smidge of land in sight. And let me tell you, I have good eyesight, and I couldn't see crap.

Feeling a hint of defeat, I coasted back to the base. It was going to be a really long flight back to Virginia... I mean, I could probably jump over the Denmark Strait to Greenland, then make my way into Canada, but that was still really far. Would I be able to make it? Plus, what would I eat? I had no idea if every food store in existence had long been raided of canned beans and spam or not. And how was I planning on dealing with all these supposedly super-evolved animals I had yet to actually see? The more I thought about it, the more I felt my plan was incredibly flawed.

My heart felt a little dim. When I folded my wings partially in and fell into a dive, however, my worries seemed to be ripped off me with the wind. My heart was beating fast as the ground quickly approached, my lips involuntarily curling into a grin.

Wait, I don't know how to land!! My grin vanished.

Fearing I would faceplant into the grass if I tried to flap all the way to the ground, I got as close as I could before swinging out of the dive and letting myself drop. I landed not as heavily as I thought I would, stumbling only slightly. It was only about an eight-foot drop, which, in hindsight might actually seem like a lot… Eh, I was alright, wasn't I?

I brushed myself off, even though there wasn't anything on me, and folded my wings in. They felt warm from exercise; another new, pleasant feel.

My first flight and I didn't die! My grin had returned, and I couldn't wipe it off. Flying was amazing!

The others on the ground came up to me, encircling me.

"What's it like?"

"How'd it feel?"

"How did you know how to do that?"

I wasn't really seeing any of them as I looked around at them, the exhilaration from flight leaving my mind both blank and on hyperdrive. "It's awesome," I said in total honesty, grinning at them. "A little scary, but totally worth it."

"How'd you know you could do it?" The girl who'd spoken looked at me with earnest eyes.

I shook my head a little, still in wonder. "It's part of me. Whatever those scientists did, it's natural on some level to me now." I actually looked at each of them this time. "Can't you feel it?"

"Ahhh!!" Will's panicked sound made me jump and spin around to my left. He came flapping down, going in all sorts of directions. His misery ended as he stumbled into the ground with half-cocked wings, catching himself right before doing another faceplant.

"I'm okay," he coughed.

I gave him a thumbs-up.

The trainer made his way through the crowd of dispersing birdkids and gave me a hard pat on the shoulder. "Nice job," he remarked. "First one up."

I looked after the trainer as he went over to congratulate Will as well as make sure he was alright. Will gave him a nod, and the trainer turned around and called out over the field.

"We have another twenty minutes outside," he announced.

Some of the group grumbled while others seemed

happy it was almost over.

"Why?" Will asked from behind him. "It's still so bright out."

The trainer threw a meaningful glance at the black watch on his left wrist. "It's almost six. Still need to get you back for dinner, then the CQ has to show you to your quarters."

"Ah," Will replied weakly.

The trainer walked off down the field a bit, then pulled out his binoculars. I followed their direction and spotted Adler some four-hundred meters away, and that other boy fifty feet in front of him. Now that their wings were fully spread, it was a lot easier to see their resemblance to other birds. Adler's Steppe Eagle mix was apparent in his brown, white, and black feathers as he soared in the sky. The other boy (whose name I still didn't know) looked more like an Osprey I'd often see by the lake near Jody's house. He had four very long, very dark primaries that curled in the wind, the undersides of his wings being a lighter striped color with white underlining feathers.

But he had said he was mixed with an owl? Judging by the soft contour of his secondary feathers and the white, dotted pattern on his coverts, I'd say maybe Snowy Owl. I didn't know of any other white owls, and Ospreys had solid black-brown coverts.

My eyes kept wandering to the trainer where he stood some twenty feet in front of me. I walked down to him while he was still looking up at the sky.

"Hey, let me ask you something," I said.

"Hm?" he asked, changing the focus on the binoculars with his right finger.

"How come my eyes didn't dry out or anything while flying?" When I'd ride my motorcycle, if my visor wasn't down, my squinted eyes would dry out in seconds. While flying, the wind didn't faze my ability to look around with wide eyes in the slightest.

"Ah. All bird Hybrids have an additional, transparent eyelid," he explained simply. "It's called a nictitating membrane."

I stared at him in dismay. That couldn't be true, could it?

A loud series of flapping off to the left drew my attention over. "Hey, someone else is getting off the ground," I pointed.

The trainer lowered his binoculars and quickly turned to where I was pointing. "Michael!" he said in surprise. "It's about time!"

The kid, Michael, was the guy who'd been sitting the most directly across from me at the table, when I'd first sat down. He had chiseled features that made him one of the most attractive men here, with messy black hair and determined, dark eyes. He flapped his dark gray-black wings, each triangular-shaped feather laced in a lighter gray, revealing the barred white underparts typical of a Peregrine Falcon each time he brought his wings up. His primary feathers were long and well-trimmed, complimenting his sharp features.

Michael had a look of concentration, determinedly flying higher off the ground with robust flaps of his wings. With only twenty minutes left to go, I guess he couldn't bear not to make it into the air as well.

While the trainer was distracted with Michael, I turned around and headed back up the slope to Will, who was realigning some twisted feathers.

"Hey," I said as I jogged up to him.

"Wassup?" he asked without looking over.

I glanced imperceptibly around as I slowed. The five men in uniform were still standing at the heavy doors. I pulled on Will's arm, bringing him further away from everyone else.

"What're you doing?" he asked, letting himself get led by me.

I only stopped once we were a good fifty meters from the doors and everyone else. "Look," I said, facing him. "While I was up there, I was thinking about how we're supposed to get back to Virginia."

His brows creased slightly. "Okay? What're you thinking?"

I chewed on my lower lip. "I think we're going to have to wait. We shouldn't leave until we have a better grasp of what's out there — what the world is like now." Will looked as if he was about to protest, but I carried on. "Even if we manage to fly all the way back," I pressed, "what then? How do we survive?" My eyes began searching the air around Will's head as I thought. "That's why they brought us here, right? To learn to survive? So maybe we stay here until we know we can, then go."

Will opened his mouth, but closed it when it seemed he didn't know what to say.

"It's been ten months, Will," I said softer. "If they've lived this long, then staying for a while longer shouldn't change much." It was a conclusion I'd found tough to come to, but it seemed like the best course of action.

We searched each other's eyes, trying to find answers there. I saw the rage bubbling up beneath his gaze of denial.

"You can do what you want," he finally spat. Looking aggrieved, he angrily trudged back up the hill.

I didn't chase after him. I only watched in understanding as he walked away. Sighing, I turned around to look out over the grassy plains. That beached ship should be directly in front of me in the far distance. Waiting was the smartest thing to do. We had no idea what was out there.

CHAPTER 13

Those out flying came back soon after. Will didn't look at me as we shuffled back through the thick doors behind the trainer.

"You were pretty good out there," a warm voice said next to me.

I pulled my eyes from Will to look at Adler, who was looking at me earnestly. "Oh, thanks," I said lamely.

Adler nodded toward Will where he walked half a staircase ahead of us. "You two knew each other before coming here?"

"Sort of."

"Ah, okay." I saw him frown slightly. "Hey, so, Iver and I were thinking the two of us and you could train together," he brought up.

"Iver?" I asked.

"Yeah, he got up into the air too," he explained. "We were thinking that since I've got eagle feathers, he has some owl, and you've got both, that it would be helpful to train together. Might learn quicker."

So that's what the boy's name was: Iver. It felt better to place a name to his face and feathers.

I didn't give him an immediate answer. Usually I was the kind of person who liked to go about things solo.

"Well, just think about it," Adler suggested, seeing me hesitate.

We emerged back into the cafeteria-like room and settled down at the same table as before. I unfortunately got squeezed between two other girls I didn't know, but when they saw my agitated hazel gaze flick over them, they gave me more space.

Will was wedged into a seat at the far right end of the table on the opposite side. His eyes passed over the group and paused on me, our gazes meeting. I saw him swallow and look away, feigning a nonchalant air.

He would get over it.

Metal plates and forks with more white blocks were passed down from the left end of the table by a couple of people in white, cook-like coats. I didn't bother holding out this time and ate quickly, wanting to move on.

Down the table to my left, I heard sniffles in the beginnings of a cry. I woofed down the last of my food. *Here we go.*

The sniffles inevitably picked up into a muffled sob. I glanced over. It was the dove girl, with long bangs hiding her sullen face.

BANG!

The boy across from the girl slammed his tight fist onto the metal table, making his plate clatter against its shiny surface. His red-brown eyes were staring just beyond his plate with a badly suppressed fire, his tense figure the definition of 'barely holding it together.'

"Shut *up*," he snarled quietly. The tendons along his forearm were prominent against the strain.

You can imagine this didn't go the way he wanted it to. The girl, now terrified, burst into tears.

"*Shut up*," he seethed, jumping to his feet. "You think we don't *all* feel like that? You're not helping!"

I glanced over my shoulder at the table where the trainer had gone to eat with other guys in uniform. They didn't make a move to stop what was happening, but they *did* stop to watch. One even laced his fingers as if preparing for a show.

Useless, I scolded.

"Hey, back off," the blond-haired guy spoke up from beside him. His deep blue and turquoise eyes were the opposite of the other guy's angry red ones, dousing his fire with his mere appearance.

"No! This is bullsh*t!" he yelled.

"Sit down, Ronin," Michael scolded disapprovingly, shaking his head.

Aggrieved red-brown eyes turned on Michael. He strode down the table to where he sat, which happened to be directly across from me.

"What did you say?" he mocked behind Michael's head.

I'd said this guy would cause trouble, didn't I?

Michael turned his head to the side, though he still wasn't looking right at Ronin. "I said sit down," he said evenly, looking very calm. I could see the muscles in his neck twitch, though, exposing the power simmering beneath his surface.

In the next instant, Ronin slammed into Michael, making the table shake and plates clatter. I jumped up from my seat as quickly as it had happened.

Michael turned and slammed a fist into Ronin, but the latter didn't stop. Those around the fight had backed off, not wanting to receive a stray hit.

The two boys ended up on the floor, rolling painfully over their wings which flared aggressively.

Oh geez. If they got themselves injured and couldn't fly, would it set us *all* back?

Worried that this would be the case, I jumped over the table in a swift motion, landing lightly before the two boys who had managed to get to their feet, still throwing punches.

My eyes followed their movements as if they were in slow motion. When Ronin pulled his arm back with the intent of throwing a swift hit, I moved in with lightning speed and grasped his arm in a firm hold, simultaneously taking advantage of Michael's proximity to sweep his feet out from beneath him. Using Ronin's backward momentum and the movement of my sweep to Michael's feet, I had timed it so that when I jerked his arm, Ronin's whole form was thrown off-balance and went swinging around. All of this happened within a second.

Michael crashed to the cement floor, looking startled, and Ronin stumbled to regain his balance.

"Cut it out," I snapped at them. My eyes shot dangerously between the two boys, my body tensed. My adrenaline had started pumping into my veins, and I can't say I didn't enjoy it. I'd been fighting for six years, remember?

Ronin jerked forward an inch, and my startling hazel gaze rounded on him, daring him to try. His eyes looked me quickly up and down, frowning. He seemed to be wondering if it would be okay to try to fight a girl.

"How did you —?" Michael asked in a voice of wonder, staring at me from the ground, his hands propping him up.

I looked between the two of them, not dropping my ferocity. "You think the two of you can stop acting like imbeciles long enough for us to at least finish dinner?" I rebuked.

"Sure," Michael agreed numbly.

After a moment, I stepped over and held a hand down to him. He looked at my hand for a few long seconds, then took it. We had both been genetically altered, and both of us were stronger than we used to be. It was far too easy to pull him to his feet. Michael brushed the back of his gray mesh pants off, looking tame.

I turned my full attention on Ronin. Raising my eyebrows at him, I asked simply, "Good?"

His lips twitched in a displeased fashion, but eventually he gave two slow half-nods.

"Great." I looked around, my eyes finding Bossy Bob a few tables away where he had been sitting by watching. "Can we maybe move on to the showers now?" I inquired loudly, tossing my hands up at him across the distance.

Both boys looked ruffled, in both a figurative and literal sense. Their feathers were worse than their bedraggled hair, sticking up all over the place in need of some serious TLC. Not to mention we'd all worked up a light sweat while practicing earlier.

Bossy Bob stood. "Sure," he responded coolly, his deep voice carrying over the distance without actually having to raise his volume. He gave me a pleased, avid nod, meeting my eyes. The corner of his mouth curved up approvingly.

CHAPTER 14

The others acted a little differently around me now. I couldn't quite place it. It wasn't fear... Respect? In any case, Will didn't seem to be giving me the cold shoulder anymore.

Bossy Bob handed us off to the CQ, a stocky woman with a no-nonsense attitude. I watched her short ponytail of black hair bounce with each step as she took us further into the facility. We went down several sets of stairs, but the thing was, there weren't doors at each flight like the topmost three levels.

With each step, I couldn't help but feel like we might be stepping deeper and deeper into our own expensive tomb.

"Here we are," the CQ announced, stepping down to flat ground and striding toward a set of double doors. She paused with one hand on the right door, turning her head around to peer up the stairs.

Once the footsteps pretty much ceased as everyone gathered, she pushed past the doors with both hands, sending them flying open.

I don't know what I was expecting when she opened the doors. A hallway? Another long cement room? All I know is that it definitely hadn't been *this*.

"Woah," someone murmured behind me.

Woah indeed, friend. Woah indeed.

I understood why there weren't doors at those other levels now. This massive space rose at least thirty meters up, an open combination of three levels. The ceiling was lined in large, flat panels that replicated the sky, though the walls were still smooth concrete. The floor started out as concrete as well, but only continued into wide paths around the outskirts of the room which was four times the size of a football field.

Disappearing into the distance were endless rows of crops. I didn't recognize most of them, and the ones I did recognize didn't look quite how I remembered. Some had small, pointy leaves, others were wide and shiny and as big as a person's face. Some were green, but some were purple or blue and decorated in interesting patterns. Plenty were dotted with fruits and berries, some the size of a thumbnail, others twice the size of my fist. People in simple tan uniforms walked up and down the rows of tall and short crops, tending to the plants.

"Stay on course," the CQ ordered as she purposefully and undistractedly turned on her heel and headed right, down a path which was ten feet across.

I forcefully pulled my attention from the cavernous, surreal space and followed the little bossy lady.

At the far southern end of the space, I noticed that the wall was lined with a strip of blue-tinted glass. The glass started around waist height, topped off about seven feet off the ground, and ran one-third the length of the southern wall. Positioned at the end of the walkway directly in front of us was an open doorway as wide as the path.

As we neared the far wall, I couldn't help but let my eyes wander over to a massive tree sprawled elegantly near the edge of the crop rows. This tree seemed to have its own plot of land, with a small pond and little stones placed in winding paths through its gnarled roots as big around as my body. I felt it deserved it though; its sparse canopy brushed the ceiling with a crown spread of fifty meters. Its base was easily ten feet in diameter — as wide as the path we were currently walking on.

We didn't stop to admire the tree though. Instead, we went straight through the open doorway at the end of the path, emerging into a long, wide hallway. It was lit with a soft blue light, giving the whole cement tube an open, underwater feel.

The CQ started down the hallway, but I paused to gaze around, feeling like I was in an aquarium.

The lady turned around to us and started walking backward. "What's the hold up?"

My eyes moved over to her as if she was an after-thought. I continued walking in a somewhat dazed state, and only then realized that everyone else had only moved forward once I had, staying behind me.

Walking with the long glass panes on my left, we passed a couple random doorways. Through one, I noticed a small room that looked a lot like a laundry room, though its units were silent at the moment. Another was closed, but I could hear someone talking on the other side. Some sort of office? Then we reached another open doorway, this one decoratively lined with little light blue tile pieces.

The CQ stopped at this doorway with her hands clasped behind her back. The rest of us came to a stop in front of her. I tried to peer inside.

"These are the bathrooms," the CQ said to the group, her loud voice making me flinch and look back to her with a displeased frown. "Inside, you will find twelve packs, each labeled with your names. Get your pack. There's a change of clothes inside, among other things. Afterward, you'll go to your rooms. They're not as-signed, and there are twelve total." She pointed down the hallway. "Those are the only other rooms down the hall-way. If you can't find them, then immediately proceed to G3 to get your eyes checked by a Labcoat."

I huffed in a small laugh. The CQ's eyes shifted to me, and the right corner of her mouth jerked up in a small show of appreciation.

"Well? Get going," she urged, scanning the group.

I didn't bother wasting any time and walked through the big doorway. *Ugh,* this was high school locker rooms all over again, except *fancy.*

CHAPTER 15

I managed to find my pack without much difficulty. There were a dozen of them, just as the CQ had said. Each one was a gray, thin cylinder half the size of a normal backpack, sporting a small, stitched-on white rectangle with our names.

Rummaging through it at the side while everyone else grabbed theirs, I found a second set of clothes, which I sat aside, a large, stainless steel water canister, a toothbrush, and a small metal tin about the size of my fist. Upon unscrewing it, I found it to be holding what smelled like toothpaste. The minty scent was more natural though. Probably more of their plant-based stuff.

Shoving everything back into my pack, I looked around. Set in two rows on either side of the room were twelve showers (excessive?), each with a light blue curtain pulled to the side. The showers themselves were larger than your typical shower as well, around five feet by eight feet. With these dimensions in mind, you can imagine how large the bathroom was.

Half a dozen sinks lined one wall near the front, and a long bench sat along the front wall opposite of the sinks. Above the bench were shelves holding stacks of fluffy towels. The bathroom curved around to a separate section holding toilet stalls, thoughtfully separating the showers from any unfortunate scents.

I grabbed a towel off the shelves and went to the first shower on the right. Checking it out, it seemed alright. At least the shower knob hadn't been genetically altered as well.

With a sigh, I hung my pack and towel up on a hook they'd conveniently installed on the outside of the stall.

I'd like to say it didn't take me until we were all getting naked to notice, but… Was it just me or were we all, like, *super* attractive? Maybe whatever in our blood that got us selected was more prevalent in highly attractive people? No, thinking of Will and how he used to be, I'd say that maybe wasn't quite the case. My physique hadn't really changed in stasis, so I didn't consider it before, but perhaps the bird adaptations weren't the only change forced upon us.

I shrugged internally as I got undressed and turned the water on. I tested the temperature with my hand under the two-foot-long shower head, except I couldn't really feel it. It could have been cold, but I guess the cold didn't affect me so much anymore.

I'm not sure why, but as I stood under the downpour, the droplets felt incredibly refreshing. I was like a flower experiencing a desert rain for the first time in a year, and for a long while I just stood there with my eyes closed.

◆ ◆ ◆

So, as it turned out, hair now structured as feathers? Yeah, it doesn't like water.

It was as if my body was repealing the water. Only with a thorough amount of scrubbing was I able to efficiently wash off. My wings were pretty much hopeless, every droplet sparking from my massive feathers like ice off a windshield.

Eventually I gave up and dried up whatever water had managed to stick to me. The second set of clothes was identical to the first set, and it was a lot easier to get on this time around now that I was 'experienced.'

Most of the others in the group were still showering when I left the bathrooms. Padding past the lightly decorated doorway and down the long, empty cement hall, the haunted blue appearance made me feel cold.

Peering through each bedroom doorway, they all seemed the same: around twenty feet wide and forty feet deep, with a ceiling reaching ten feet up. The back wall was strange; a moving image of sorts. I picked a random room, this one being the fourth room down from the bathrooms.

Unlike the bathrooms, the bedrooms had doors. *Thick* ones. Hopefully I wouldn't be able to hear as much going on outside my room with this, otherwise I doubted I'd ever find sleep.

I clicked the heavy door shut behind me and looked around with careful eyes. There was a light switch beside the door, but I didn't bother turning it on. The room was dim, filled with a melancholy silver-blue one might get from the moon's glow over a cold forest. Of course, that didn't stop me from seeing everything perfectly well.

Padding lightly forward, I let my fingers trail over a smooth white desk. A backless chair on wheels was tucked beneath it. Two gray, saddle-stitched notebooks lay in the center of the table. I flipped through the pages, all blank. Two ballpoint pens also sat nearby.

What's this? I wondered, spotting a peculiar device at the end of the table. It was half a foot long and triangular-shaped, so that a wide face stared up at me. I realized that this black face was actually a dead screen, its shiny surface giving it away.

My curious hands searched it, and I found a button. The screen lit up, a bright white light in an otherwise light-lacking room, making me squint my eyes against it slightly. It looked like...a playlist.

Music?

I don't know why its presence was so startling, but it was. I stared at it for a long minute before reaching a hand out and scrolling through the options. A decent song popped up amidst my scrolling, and I tapped on it. To my welcome surprise, it actually began playing.

"Huh."

As "Ordinary World" by Duran Duran began softly playing, I walked around the rest of the basic room. Besides the table, there was a long eight-foot mirror, a small metal sink, and a queen sized bed. I came to the very back of the room, with its unforgettable images.

My hands came up to the glass, resting only my fingertips upon its cool surface. I tapped on it. It must have been at least six inches thick, secured into the walls on all four sides. On the other side of the glass, dark gray waves clashed against the rocky cliff base some two-hundred meters below.

I was standing behind the face of the towering cliffs, overlooking an endless horizon. A horizon which I was supposed to fly across.

CHAPTER 16

I wasn't sure how long I stood in front of that glass for. My trance was only interrupted when a soft rapping sound came from behind me. With a startle, I realized it was my door.

"Uh, come in," I offered uneasily.

The door cracked open. My heart started beating quicker, but then Will's head appeared.

I let out a silent breath. "Hey, what's up?" I asked, relaxing a bit.

He stepped inside, looking around for a moment as if searching for something. Then his eyes found me and he sucked in a breath as if startled.

My brows creased slightly, confused why he was acting in such a way. "What?"

"Your eyes," he stated, looking stiff.

I looked around and raised my eyebrows in inquiry. "What about them?"

"They — they're…" He was failing miserably at explaining himself, but finally stuttered, "They're green, like a cat at night."

I stared at him blankly for a moment. "Oh," I realized. Recalling my brief genetics lesson from Carson earlier, I said with a small frown, "It must be a result of the tapetum layer in my eyes. I can see in the dark."

Will managed to click the door shut behind him. "Ah, makes sense," he said tensely.

I eyed him with a quick up and down flick of my apparently glowing gaze. With measured steps, I went to sit down at the edge of the bed, placed near the back wall. My wings trailed behind me across the sheets. "So what did you need?" I asked without looking at him.

"I…"

I snuck a glance at him. He seemed stuck, but upon my subtle gaze he came slowly over.

He looked at the music device to his left and ran two fingers gently across its ridge.

"I'm not sure, really," he finished quietly. A doubtful frown curved one corner of his mouth down.

I could guess.

"Come and sit," I said, giving the empty space next to me on the bed a single pat.

He obliged a bit reluctantly.

I waited for him to settle down, positioning his wings more comfortably behind himself over the bed like mine were. "I know it's hard," I began steadily. "This isn't fair to anyone, and it's not fair of me to ask you to wait to see the people you love."

Will shook his head, so slight it almost wasn't noticeable. "No, you're right though — the first time. And you're in the same boat as me and everyone else." He turned his head toward me, and after a moment I looked over as well. His pale yellow eyes which looked silver in the dim light danced between my glowing hazel ones. "It's not fair to you either."

"'Unfair' is nothing new to me," I said, giving him a sad shadow of a smile.

His brows creased a little, drawing his eyebrows over his honest eyes in a confounded manner. "How do you do it?" he asked.

"Do what?"

"Stay so strong." He jerked his chin out at me in a single, small nod. "What's your secret?"

I huffed in a light chuckle. "There's no secret," I insisted, my mood turning gentler. "Just takes practice."

"Mm." Will nodded absently. His damp honey-brown hair fell over his eyes as he turned toward the floor.

A couple minutes passed, with only the scuffing of Will's heel against the smooth floor to fill the silence as he kicked his foot distractedly. We both sat there think-ing…or trying *not* to think.

"We should get some sleep," I suggested finally.

"Yeah," he agreed with a sigh.

Neither of us made a move to get up right away. Feeling tired, after a few moments, I shuffled back and lay down on my stomach with a sigh. It felt so good to finally relax that my eyelids suddenly felt like lead.

I heard Will reposition himself. When I cracked my left eye open and slanted my gaze over, he was facing down the bed, sitting with his knees drawn up a foot from his chest. With his bare, lightly-toned chest covered only with some small feathers, and large, dark wings trailing behind him off the edge of the bed, he looked like a despondent painting of a lost angel.

He turned his head to the side and looked down at me, and it was too late to take my gaze from him. We seemed to hold a silent conversation between ourselves.

After a pause, Will tried to lie back, but elected to turn on his side after a bout of uncomfortable fighting with his wings. He settled so that he was facing me. His eyes flicked over me like a child.

When we both stilled, I could feel his breath on me; gentle and warm.

"Shove over a bit," I said, my voice muffled from being partially covered by the pillow.

"Why? Do I smell bad?" he inquired with a note of worry.

"Yeah, you smell bad," I joked with a one-eyed roll. *That's* why, nothing else.

He scooched back a bit. We didn't say anything more, only letting ourselves feel some sort of ease through each other's silent company. Lying there, it occurred to me that I'd made a friend in this crazy place. My second friend in ten years. I was on a roll.

CHAPTER 17

Warm water pressed on me from all sides, filling my vision with hazy blues. Little fishes darted around me as I swam up to the surface of the lake.

A deep breath of humid air filled my lungs once I breached the surface, my thick, dark brown hair fading to lighter strawberry ends fanning out around me like beautiful flower petals. I wiped the water from my eyes and swam in place, looking around. Spotting me from the shore, Jody waved to me with a smile. Her wavy black hair, which usually fell just below her shoulders, was tied back in a loose ponytail. Her skin was tanned from the sun, making the crinkles around her smiling brown eyes that much more apparent.

I lifted my hand from the water to wave back, but something in her countenance made my hand freeze. Her joyful expression was replaced by horror, her mouth forming a fearful 'O' shape. I felt my blood turn to ice.

A startled cry escaped my lips as something dragged me underwater. I was unable to use my limbs to paddle back to the surface, completely at this force's disposal. Paralyzed, I watched as the bubbles escaping my mouth floated up in the opposite direction. My surroundings got dimmer and dimmer, and the distance of the bubbles got farther and farther. I was sinking downward, away from the happy memory.

My vision was that of a normal person, and within seconds I was entirely enveloped in darkness. The water around me was cold, seeping into my bones. It was *painful*.

Somehow I realized my eyes were shut. In the next instant, they flew open and began darting around. I could use my limbs now and reached out through the water around me. My fingers hit invisible barriers, and no matter how hard I punched and kicked at them, they wouldn't break.

I couldn't hold my breath any longer. All of the air had already escaped my lungs.

My fists made dull sounds against the glass that resonated throughout the water. My heart was beating faster and faster, feeling like it might explode. My lungs burned.

I jolted upright, breathing hard. Massive gulps of air filled my enlarged lungs, yet I still felt gripped in a cold clutch. My heart was racing. I brought a hand up to my chest and squeezed my eyes shut for a moment, but closing them only brought everything back. Panting, I flung them open again and looked around myself.

I was in bed, sitting upright in a kneeling position since I had fallen asleep on my stomach. Smooth concrete walls surrounded me, forming a somewhat spacious and sleek room. To the right was a wall of glass, displaying void-like waves clashing outside under a dark sky. My eyes wandered to my left. Will was out cold, lying in the exact same position he'd fallen asleep in. His breathing was slow and even. Behind him, dark feathers trailed off the bed.

I moved my own extra set of limbs, not sure I really had wings, even reaching around to feel them. Yet, there they were. *Sigh. Still here.* I let a wide feather slide numbly from my fingers as I glanced around the room again. So…this was real, then. The true nightmare had only just begun.

Silently, I swung off the bed. Another look at Will said he was still oblivious. I padded gently across the smooth floor to the door, where I slipped out of the room. I didn't really know where I wanted to go. I just knew I had to go *somewhere*. Walking past the long, blue-tinted glass panes to my right, my eyes naturally went to the massive tree nearby, standing prominently in the dim cavern. My steps became a little quicker.

Entering the massive farming level, I couldn't help but pause and gaze around. It was way too big to be underground, practically forming its own horizon. After a brief pause, I continued on toward the tree. A small stone path wove around its thick roots, trailing off the concrete path. I stepped onto the first stone.

Would I get in trouble for this? I quickly dismissed the thought. Since when did I care, anyway?

My feet moved nimbly across the winding stones until I was led to the center of the tree. Its size was incomparable. I could hear my breathing change under its monumental presence. As if my hand had a mind of its own, I reached up and splayed my fingers over its rough bark. Amidst my wonder, the small sound of rustling leaves reached my sensitive ears, making my head whip over. On the other side of the closest row of hip-high crops, one of the farmers had noticed me. She dropped her eyes and continued examining a wide green and blue streaked leaf in front of her.

I didn't take my eyes off her, feeling wary. To me, she was like a deer in a forest unfamiliar to me; strange, and almost mythical. The farmer looked back up at me a second later.

"You like it?" she asked, her tame voice reaching me quite clearly in the stillness of the cavernous room.

"I've never seen one like it," I admitted after a moment.

She nodded in understanding, continuing to tend to her crops in an absent manner. "Just so you get a taste of what the world is like out there, that used to be a standard

Living Oak tree. *This* is what the chemical did to it," she said, raising a hand toward the massive tree. She gazed at it with a certain longing that made me uncomfortable. "Some plants are more severely affected, this tree being an example of such affections."

The tree beneath my fingers seemed all that more impressive — scary, even. "The chemical did this?" I asked, following the trunk up into its twisty canopy.

"Mhm." She nodded. "It's grown thirty meters tall — nearly one-hundred feet — in only ten months. Something that used to be only remotely attainable after a good seventy or so years. We believe it only stopped growing because it can sense the limit on space."

I was at a loss for words. Was this really the case? It was almost terrifying to think it grew so large so quickly.

Looking up through its branches, I had the urge to go up there and get a better view of the whole level. It might make the place less eerie to know what it all looked like.

Before, I'd look at such a large tree and be determined to climb it. Now, I had another idea in mind. Stepping back to give myself space, I searched for the perfect branch. High above me through a cavity in the canopy, a thick branch jutted out over all the rest. With my eye on my target, I bent my knees a little, getting into position. I could do this. I could —

I couldn't do this. I let out an exasperated breath as my legs straightened, and I walked myself in a tight circle. *Get it together, me.* Slapping myself mentally, I looked back up at the branch and bent my knees again. "Okay," I murmured under my breath.

Several long seconds passed. Then, I jumped up an easy five feet into the air. My wings spread open as my bare feet left the floor. They came down in hard, quick strokes, lifting me into the air.

I actually managed to fly up to the branch. Luckily the branch was thick, otherwise I just may have missed it and tumbled back down the other side.

"Woah," I breathed quietly, tightly grasping the rough sides. My legs were clenched around it, and I carefully pulled myself up so that I was straddling the branch. Excitedly, I looked up, expecting to see the entire level. A frown crept onto my mouth when I found my vision to be unfortunately blocked by a thick cluster of oak leaves.

Okay, no problem. I just have to... I held myself steady with my hands, then brought my legs up under me in a single, swift motion. Taking a few breaths, I deftly stood up, taking my hands from the branch.

Balancing had never been an issue for me. In fact, I had always been quite good at it. The only difference was that now my body was altered, and I had a pair of wings hanging from my back. Somehow these adaptations actually made it easier to hold my balance, however. I walked heel over toe down the thick branch until I was near its end, which flared out in half a dozen directions. *Now* I could see. Up here, I had a great view of the whole room. It truly was huge. I had no idea it was possible to build such a large room underground. Then again, I didn't think it was possible to give humans wings, so…

A weight settled in my gut. It was difficult to accept this as my new reality. My old life had been snatched from me, just like in my nightmare. It really was happening for a second time, wasn't it?

After staring out at the endless crops dotted sparsely with farmers for quite a while, I jumped back down from the tree. With wings like soft sails, I landed quietly, without nearly tumbling over this time. I went down the hallway and slipped back into my room, the only sound being the little *click* of the door as I closed it behind me.

I hadn't bothered using the covers supplied the first time, but now I crawled under them, needing to feel some sort of security in even the smallest way. My nightmare hadn't woken Will up, but now he stirred. I froze in my actions.

Will blinked his tired eyes open with a yawn. He blinked again and focused on me huddled under half a blanket.

"Hey," he said quietly, his rusty voice coming out as barely a whisper.

"Hi," I responded. Since he was already awake, I finished getting situated under the blanket and settled down with my head comfortably on the pillow.

Once I was settled, Will slurred sleepily, "Everything alright?"

"Hm? Yeah, fine."

He swallowed tiredly, letting his eyelids fall back shut. "Mm," he replied.

I was initially planning on going back to sleep, but I let my eyes travel over the relaxed plains of his features for a while. He was admittedly quite handsome, in a nerdy coffee barista sort of way. Not that it really mattered, what with the whole 'end-of-the-world' and everything. But still…

My gaze flicked to his closed eyes when his dark, straight eyebrows creased a little in the middle. I watched them slowly relax again, and he remained asleep.

I took a deep breath and let my eyelids close as well.

CHAPTER 18

I'd say the next seventeen days went by in a blur, but I could remember every minute of them. There was a different trainer for each area of study on level G1, and we got passed around between them every day.

The first week, we continued to focus mainly on flying, with intermediate lessons on survival tactics. Since I planned on going it alone, out in this big bad world, I paid attention to everything they taught us. Later, I'd go back and make notes in the saddle-stitched notebooks in my room.

The next week, they began introducing medicinal techniques in case of injury, including methods specific for our new bodies, aka *those with wings*. Covering our new biology got a little awkward when they brought up reproduction. Splitting our unit up so that there were an even number of men and women had not been without its intentions. The only bright side was that I'd only have a period once or twice a year now, near the beginning of spring. And since spring was already halfway over, I wouldn't have to worry about it for another year!

Besides all that good stuff, they also made a point to cover fauna and flora in Iceland.

"What about other places?" I had asked, needing to know about the rest of the world I would encounter.

"In due time," the trainer had dismissed.

It was irking to wait, but I had to do what I had to do. Not like I could explain why I needed to know *now*, not *'in due time.' "Yeah, so, I'm planning on escaping at some point in the near future. You good with that?"* Yeah, right.

Another three days of training passed without anything too new. At the end of the seventeenth day, I showered like usual. I was the last in and the last out, as I'd managed to find a place to practice my fighting moves on the fifth day and had stayed there late again tonight. Lately, I'd started integrating my wings into my techniques, adding a whole new wealth of possibilities. Who knew getting hit by a wing could hurt so much?

I turned the shower knob to the off position. I'd gotten better at bathing, too. And drying off. With a rapid flicking motion of my wings, almost every stray droplet of water came flinging off. Nature's air drier. The towel was really only more of an accessory at this point. I got dressed, brushed my teeth at one of the many sinks, then went back to my room to put my stuff away.

Afterward, I headed down to the end of the blue-tinted hallway and made a right into the farming level. Without a pause in my step, I headed straight toward the massive tree curling leisurely over the ground.

Eleven birdkids dotted the thick branches of the oak tree, gathered near the middle of a few select branches. I jumped into the air without a hitch and flew up to them, weaving nimbly through the tree and landing on an especially curvy branch beside June. She was the Tree Swallow-American Kestrel Hybrid, with straight, mocha-colored hair that used to be very long. Last week, she'd chopped it off above her shoulders, so now it looked more wind tossed and wild.

"— would definitely make more sense. All you'd have to do is roll your body as you bring your wings in, and it would be more effective," Samuel was arguing. He turned to me then with his deep blue and turquoise eyes. "Rory, what do you think?"

I flicked my eyebrows and settled down on the branch. I'd heard what they were talking about before I'd even exited the hallway. I'd already tried the move he was considering and had formed a slightly better method. "Well," I started, "have you ever tried it?"

"Well, no," he trailed.

"Then try it and prove it yourself," I offered simply.

He clenched his square jaw, sliding his teeth together in thought. "Huh, yeah. Okay," he agreed. He reached over and tagged Adler on the shoulder. "Think you could time me tomorrow?"

"Sure, I'll time you," Adler said. "That way I can prove you're wrong." He gave us a pearly white smile.

"I think it depends on your wing shape, too," June spoke up intelligently. "For us with sharper, shorter wings, we have to control our bodies to an even greater extent."

"Whiplash is a *thing*, people," Aubrey reinforced with a raise of her thin eyebrows. Her gray-blue eyes which were abnormally silver flicked over us seriously. She was hybridized with a Blue-faced Honeyeater, a bird with promise to be agile but no dive potential. She also had the strongest legs out of all of us, able to jump nearly eight feet into the air with an initial quick fwip of her yellow-green wings. Second to her leg strength were those mixed with an owl, then eagle and hawk.

"Only when you don't know what you're doing," Ronin remarked with a teasing back-and-forth motion of his head.

"Oh, she knows what she's doing," Will said. He flashed his pale yellow eyes at Aubrey, who gave him a sweet smile.

I mentally rolled my eyes. *Lovebirds.*

"Right, because *crashing* means you know what you're doing," June hassled.

Aubrey narrowed her silver eyes at June.

I heard the familiar fast-paced clip of the CQ's thick boots and looked across at the path some three-hundred feet away. I sighed internally. She was always ruining our fun.

"CQ is back," I stated.

The others turned to take a look.

"How do you always do that?" Samuel asked me.

"Do what? Know when she's coming?"

"Yeah. You always know before anyone else."

I tapped my right ear. "Good hearing."

"I can hear her too," Elena said in her small voice.

I eyed her. She was the Elf Owl Hybrid. Besides her and myself, the only other member in our group hybridized with an owl was Iver. "Yeah, owl Hybrids have better hearing," I explained. Personally, I could hear a mouse squeak on a quiet night half a mile away. My hearing was only getting better the more I focused on training my ears.

"Oh," she responded. The others took note as well.

As the CQ neared, she shouted up at us. "Get to your quarters, Unit 3! More training tomorrow!"

The group responded with a collective of sighs and groans. We flew down, some dropping directly below the tree, others (like me) gliding over to the entrance of our quarters.

I coasted down and gave my wide wings a few silent flaps to land. Tucking them neatly in behind me, I walked through the wide entrance and down the hall.

Several boys jostled each other as they ran down the hall past me. Not joining in their fun was Michael, who was typically more steadfast in nature. He slowed beside me.

"Hey, wanna try some tandem moves tomorrow?" he asked mildly.

I looked over at him. His jet-black hair fell handsomely over his forehead, try as he may to push the messy strands away. Sharp features gave him a quick-witted appearance, while his dark eyes flicked over me calmly. Michael and I could be said to have become the leaders of the group. 'A power pair,' the others liked to call us. I found their words amusing on some level, but the position they managed to put the two of us in was rather taxing sometimes.

"Sure, couldn't hurt. Feels like rain is coming, but you never really know with Iceland's weather," I joked, though there was truth to my words. Iceland's weather was worse than Florida's 'bright one minute, drizzling the next.'

Michael chuckled. "Very true. Guess we'll just have to see, won't we?"

His obsidian eyes shimmered with something more intense beneath their charming surfaces. My lips parted, but no words came, caught in his gaze. "Guess so," I managed to murmur.

We said our farewells once I reached my door, which was fourth down the hallway. I only paused to look after Michael for a brief moment. He stayed in Room 6, two more down from mine. There was just something about him… He made me feel comfortable yet questionable at the same time. Michael looked over his shoulder, and when he met my eyes, realizing I was stalling outside my room, he gave me a charismatic smile the others rarely got to see. Being put in a leadership role together, I think he just felt more comfortable to be genuine around me, versus with the others.

Hiding my rising grin, I turned back to my door and pushed it open with absent fingers. I shook my head slightly, trying to shake away my rising thoughts of him. Inside my room, I closed the door and went over to the smooth white table. Like usual, I grabbed one of my notebooks and splayed it open.

Click. The pen made a satisfying sound under my thumb, and I began neatly scribbling down notes from today's lessons under a section about toxic and nontoxic plants.

Since our lessons had primarily been about life in Iceland, I'd taken the liberty to talk to the farmers outside our quarters in my free time. They gave me insight on plant life around the world, not just the sparse vegetation in this frozen country. Apparently some foods that had always been safe for human consumption had turned poisonous. They'd figured this out in an unfortunate manner.

On the bright side, water pollution had drastically decreased in the past ten and a half months. We could probably drink from any old river nowadays and be fine.

'But what about the bacteria, and parasites? Didn't they evolve too?' you ask. Sure, but so did we. The bird genes gave us better immune systems capable of taking on these bacteria and other pathogens. Cool, right?

I didn't finish my notes until half an hour later, getting caught up in drawing detailed images of safe plants to eat and ones that could kill you on the spot. Some looked very similar to one another.

With a yawn, I clicked my pen and closed my notebook. I walked over to my bed and threw the messy covers to the side. Holding a pillow under my head, I curled up in a warm ball. My feathers lay gently over my exposed side like a big feathery blanket, the other wing half-cocked off the left side of the bed.

It took a while of watching the wind-driven waves caress the night sky to fall asleep. *Wait for me*, I said as I drifted off to sleep, sending my thoughts out across the ocean.

CHAPTER 19

The following morning began with flight training as usual. We came out here to practice no matter what the weather conditions were, building and testing our endurance.

This morning, the entire field was covered in a dense white fog. Even with my excellent eyesight, I was limited to only seeing as far as twenty feet in front of my face.

We split up the field and outward areas into four parts to avoid colliding with one another. "Adler, Clara, Iver," I said, "you guys take the south. Anna, Aubrey, Elena, you three go east. And June, Ronin — you two go with Will and Samuel to the west. Michael and I will take the northern section."

Nobody questioned my instructions. With a few nods around the group, we split into smaller groups and went our separate ways. Michael jogged beside me down the slope. I jumped into the air first without pausing, throwing my wingtips up and out. Michael was up in the air behind me a moment later and swerved around to my right side.

There wasn't much of a breeze today. With the blinding fog in all directions, it felt like the beginning of some eerie nightmare.

Our wingtips came down in time with each other, sticking close as we navigated through the fog. Down below, I could hear waves lap against a sandy shore.

"There's a beach eight-hundred meters below us," I informed.

"I can't hear anything." Michael frowned, knowing how it was I knew. He grunted. "We should be good to start practicing once we're far enough out over the water."

"Mm," I agreed. After another ten seconds of flying at an even pace, I asked, "So anything you wanted to practice in particular? Or just the standard double flying?"

Michael didn't seem to need to consider it, probably having thought about this already. "Let's try transitioning between formations and maybe some diving. I wanna test Samuel's technique."

I chuckled. "No need," I said. "There's a better way. I just didn't feel like popping Samuel's bubble, ya know?"

Michael raised his eyebrows in question. "Oh? Feel like teaching me?"

I turned my head to look at him under my right wing, which spanned a full ten feet out into the air. "Sure." I grinned lightly.

Tilting my wings, I split off from Michael into the fog. I heard him draw in a breath as I disappeared from view. He may not have known where I was, and I may not have been able to see him, but I could *hear* him. I curved around and dropped in on his right side.

He jumped, which really just meant he tensed and glared at me. "Trying to give me a heart attack?" he accused.

I smiled at him.

He rolled his eyes and curved his wings in, diving into a free fall like the beginning of a rollercoaster. I gave my wings one more forward-thrusting flap with a simultaneous twist of my body, spinning to make a ninety-degree turn straight down.

We lost altitude at a rapid rate, our wings held in close to our bodies. Michael's smoky form seemed suspended fifteen feet in front of me, slightly off to my left. Fog rushed by, making my view of him go in and out. Besides the quick rush of wind, there were no sounds.

I tucked my wings in closer and gained speed, floating over to Michael. Our eyes met, and it was just the two of us with no thoughts, falling through nothingness as we circled one another in a downward spiral.

The water was quickly approaching. I glanced down, then back up at him knowingly. He understood my look.

In sync, we broke out of the dive and rocketed parallel over the ocean. The fog let up in some spots, revealing the dark waters some fifty meters below. I weaved around like I myself was a wave, turning and folding my wings in a graceful and efficient manner. Michael joined in after watching me have fun for a few moments with an entertained smile on his roguishly handsome face, and suddenly we were flying around each other in the fog without running into one another, curving and ducking and weaving to our hearts' content.

This was fun, but it was also good practice. Learning to be in sync with each other wasn't something to be mistaken as easy. If you messed up by even a meter — which proved challenging when the wind was your guide — it could send you both tumbling.

The tips of my primaries grazed Michael's back as I curved over him. He turned to smile at me and came at me playfully.

I laughed and shifted twenty feet away with an easy shift of my body and tilt of my wings. Leveling out, I looked at him for another few moments, then curved away. Michael followed after me this time.

We practiced formations on the way back to the beach, shifting between side-by-side, hanging back to catch the other's slipstream, falling in line, and flying directly above and below each other. Doing this with Michael was easier than, say, doing this with one of the short-winged Hybrids. Everybody's wings were better and worse at different things.

The sound of the water changed, turning into the unmistakable sound of cresting waves, the type of waves that were mainly seen along the shoreline.

"Follow me," I said.

Michael turned his head to look up at me where I flew directly above him, my primaries just missing him on the downstrokes. I sped up and dove down in front of him, the creamy undersides of my wings flashing in front of him like a mirage. I could hear him following as I lost altitude.

The beach came into view as I expected, and I lost speed to glide smoothly down to it. My feet made small craters in the sand as I dropped down and tucked my wings in. I looked around while keeping an ear out for anything strange.

The scraping of large feathers sounded from behind me as Michael flapped down. I heard the soft impact of his feet on the sand, and the feather sounds ceased.

"What'd you want to come here for?" he asked, walking up to my side. He scanned the beach as well.

Surrounded by fog, it looked like we were on the surface of some other planet. It was kind of relaxing.

"I just wanted to see what it looked like in the fog," I said. "It's cool, isn't it?"

"Yeah, but…"

I waved him off. "But we're not supposed to land outside the fence, I know."

I continued to gaze around, feeling wholesome inside.

"It *is* pretty cool," Michael admitted after a while.

"Right?" I grinned at him. I walked away, closer to the water. After staring out at it for a long moment, I determined it was safe and sat down in the sand, my wings trailing behind me.

Michael came over and sighed comfortably as he sat down on my left, digging his toes into the sand.

We watched the waves together.

"Do you ever...?" His words trailed out.

I was caught up in the rhythmic lull of the waves. "Miss the taste of chocolate? Yes, yes I do," I answered.

He laughed. "Ha, no." His mood turned a bit lighter as he shook his head a little. "Sometimes I just wonder if they're still out there. My folks, I mean."

I pressed my lips tightly together.

He seemed to notice my expression and leaned forward to get a better look at me. "Are you alright?"

"Yeah, I'm fine," I deterred. I hesitated in my next words. "Do you ever think about finding them?" I finally asked. I peered at him out of the side of my eye.

"Yeah," he sighed, leaning back in the sand with his hands supporting him. He looked neither shocked nor outraged in the slightest. I don't know why I expected him to be.

"Why don't you then?" I inquired nonchalantly.

"Because," he frowned, "what if what I find is

worse?" He shifted in the sand. "Right now they probably think I'm dead, and right now I'm still able to have the hope they're alive. But, what if — what if they're —"

I watched him more apparently now. "Wouldn't you still rather know?" I asked gently.

He remained quiet for a while. Then he turned to me. "Would you?" he asked, honestly looking for an answer.

I looked back at him, into his eyes which appeared as obsidian among the white background. "Yes," I stated clearly.

CHAPTER 20

His cheek twitched, his eyes studying me. "What're you planning?" he concluded carefully.

I know it couldn't have been *that* obvious. *Michael, you are too good.* I looked away, turning my attention to the sand at my bare feet. My instinct was to play it off, but he'd seen my detailed notes. He'd seen how seriously I took all of this.

"Rory," he urged.

"Just a runaway hope," I said. Maybe he'd let it go at that.

When he didn't say anything, I slanted my gaze over to him. He was still studying me.

"What will it take for you to tell me?" he asked, his eyes squinted at me under dark lashes, the kind that was unfair for men to have, making women jealous.

The corner of my mouth flicked in a grin. "Beat me in a fight," I thought up teasingly.

"Oh, you think I'll lose, do you?" He raised his eyebrows roguishly while a smile tugged at his lips.

"For sure," I said.

His eyes flicked up and down my person and I tensed, sensing an incoming attack. He attempted to tackle me, knowing full well I could take it, and I sprung away to my feet, having seen it coming from a mile away.

He puckered his lips sourly as he looked after me. I tensed again. He jumped up and started after me. My face broke into a grin as he chased me around the beach, laughing to myself.

"Give up!" I called behind my shoulder.

"Never," he mumbled determinedly. Suddenly, I didn't hear his footsteps chasing after me anymore. Instead, I heard a whoosh of air.

I whipped around in just enough time to get an eyeful of feathers. I let out a breath as he tackled me into the sand.

He had me trapped with his wings wrapped around me, his body hovering above me while his left hand held my right wrist down, his right forearm planted in the soft sand beside my head. I could feel my own pulse quickening against his grasp. "Got you," he said, though his voice had lost its fire.

His eyes flicked over my face, and I froze, feeling caught by more than just his wings. I realized my left hand was still pressed against his chest, my fingertips tousling those small feathers there. His heat was seeping into my palm, and I could feel his strong, even heartbeat growing quicker beneath my touch.

My eyes moved up from my hand to his face, catching his gaze. Longing stirred deep beneath those dark eyes. How easy it would be to just…

He blinked hard and cleared his throat. Michael sat up, rolling off me and releasing his grip on my wrist which had never really been tight. His wings were taken aside with him, sliding out from around me like someone tearing away my sheet in the morning.

I sat up in the sand as well, feeling odd. My heart was still palpitating, but I schooled my expression into a casual one. Getting to my feet, I dusted the sand off of myself.

"Right, so," he started.

My eyes flicked over him as I shoved down my disappointment. "Do you want to keep practicing?" I asked, slapping the last grains of sand off my arms.

"Sure," he said, scratching his dark hair, "but I —"

I wasn't looking at him anymore. A strange sound I hadn't heard before snapped my attention off to a distant spot.

"What is it?" he asked, dropping his voice.

"Stay here," I whispered. I walked past him into the fog, down the beach.

A few minutes later, an old, rusted ship came into view, beached in the sand. It was an eerie scene amongst the fog, protruding from the dense white cloud like a sullen iceberg.

I'd seen this ship before, my first day out flying. It'd been as unsettling then as it was now. Up this close, it also appeared much larger. The weathered red hull was taller than I was, sitting crookedly in the sand.

While looking at the half of the ship that was visible in the fog, my ears pricked, and a moment later, a small figure emerged from the white background. A bird flapped down and landed clumsily on the railing, its white paint peeling, giving way to rust.

A puffin? I wondered, feeling startled. I wanted to be amazed — *the first living thing outside of the base I've seen!* — but a cold chill coursed through my body, making the feathered hairs along my skin rise in warning.

This little round bird was so cute, with his poofy white chest and shiny black back, but something about him sent warning shivers down my spine. It was his eyes, I realized. The beady little things were trained on me, no sheen to them in the hazy atmosphere.

I picked up on footsteps getting louder behind me. I heard Michael begin to say something, but I held my hand up at my side. He seemed to notice this subtle gesture and let his words die out. The puffin, too, tilted his head down at us. I could practically feel Michael's tenseness growing from where he stood out of view.

Okay, puffins, puffins... I racked my brain on what we'd learned about them last week. They liked to roam in flocks and had a natural tendency to copy one another. So where were his friends? I inconspicuously glanced around for more. My sensitive ears picked up on random, sparse flapping that came in and out, but I couldn't see anything through the dense fog.

"Maybe we should get out of here," Michael urged under his breath.

The puffin turned his eyes on Michael. He clicked his orange-tipped beak, and my eyes unconsciously zoomed in on it, revealing its finely serrated edges, sharp as razor blades. The sounds of small wings grew louder, and my vision clicked back to normal as two more appeared, landing on either side of him. I could hear Michael begin to back up very slowly.

"*No,*" I urged quietly, trying to glance over my shoulder without turning my head.

Too late.

The puffins honed in on him. They clicked their narrow beaks and opened their little wings, flapping up into the air one by one. As they rose, flapping came from all directions, not just from those few in front of us. In an instant, thirty more appeared beside their three friends, forming a tidal wave of black and white.

They converged, diving down at us. Only, they weren't looking at me; all of them were looking *past* me.

Oh god — Michael.

The birds made a bee-line for him. My breath hitched, and all I could think was: *protect him.*

My feet jumped into motion, spinning in the sand, and I raced toward Michael. Staring at the swarm of birds diving straight at him, he looked between frozen and ready to spring into the air. I made it to him only a moment before the birds did.

With my back to Michael, I threw out my wings, all twenty feet of them. The wave of birds broke around me with distressed cries, the whirring of their wings filling my ears. My threatening act warded off their attack, sending them to regroup above us.

Shocked as I was, I was not planning on sticking around to see if my threat worked a second time.

"Okay, *now* we go," I said, giving Michael a hard look.

He didn't need to be told twice. We ran ten feet down the beach, gaining speed, before jumping up and unfurling our wings. Being a Peregrine Hybrid, Michael was inevitably faster than me. I held my own, though, forced forward through raw fear. We booked it to the base, flying back through a plain of white.

The trainer saw us landing with haste and jogged over. "Hey! Why're you two back so soon?" he reprimanded.

"We were attacked," Michael said urgently. "By a bunch of birds."

"Puffins," I corrected. "*Lots* of them."

The trainer's face hardened. He pulled some blocky device from his jacket pocket and brought it to his mouth.

Turning away from us, he said in a steady voice, "Right. Sound the alarm. Birds seen due north."

Michael and I looked at each other, sharing similar expressions of foreboding.

Well, this can't be good.

CHAPTER 21

"How did you know that would work?" Michael asked me discreetly while the trainer was distracted.

"Uh…" *Should I tell him I DIDN'T?* I shrugged tensely. "Call it an instinct."

He eyed me skeptically, but in the end let it go. "Well, thanks."

I looked him over. "No problem."

The trainer turned back to us. "Alright, you two get back inside," he said, motioning toward the base door.

"Inside?" I repeated argumentatively, my brows creasing. "But the others are still out there."

"We're not going inside until everyone else is here," Michael reinforced.

The trainer looked between the two of us, his mouth drawn into a tight line.

I jumped as a blaring siren went off, filling the air. It was so loud that I held my hands over my ears. I wouldn't be surprised if I took my hands away and there was blood there, with how sensitive my ears were nowadays.

Words spread over the plains from seemingly no-where: "ANY AND ALL PERSONS ABOVE GROUND RETURN TO BASE IMMEDIATELY. ANY AND ALL PERS..." The message repeated five times before the siren was finally silenced.

Hesitantly, I let my hands drop from my ears. There was a ringing, but I thought I heard a clicking, too. Frowning, I screwed my pinkie fingers in my ears.

"You alright?" Michael's wavering voice filtered through my muffled ears.

"Yeah, I —" I turned in place, my eyes darting around the dense fog. "I thought I heard something else."

"I don't hear anything," he drawled. Though, he too glanced around alertly.

It was coming from the north. "There it is again," I said. Something suddenly occurred to me. "You don't think... The birds wouldn't go *toward* the sound of the sirens, would they?" I asked carefully.

The trainer regarded me uneasily. "Yes, they very well might," he said seriously.

You don't think you should have thought about that before setting the sirens off? I scolded.

We watched our surroundings even more alertly now.

I heard three pairs of hefty wings coming toward us

from the east, one much quieter than the other two. A minute later, three people appeared through the fog, flapping down haphazardly. Aubrey was running before she even touched the ground.

"What happened?" Aubrey asked us hastily as she ran over, sounding like she needed to catch her breath. She spun her head in every direction. "Where is everyone?"

Anna and Elena came over timidly, standing behind Aubrey.

The trainer held his hands up in a calming gesture. "We just need to get everyone back inside. Wild birds were spotted not too far from here."

Aubrey's face contorted like she'd eaten something sour. "*Birds?*" she asked accusingly. "You called us back for *birds?* I thought someone might be dying!"

"They very well could," the trainer said darkly.

This toned Aubrey's fire down a bit, and she gazed around more cautiously.

It was another couple of tense minutes before I heard several more sets of wings. Two sets landed in a similar manner, the other only flapping a few, more silent times before ceasing. I could tell that it was Adler, Clara, and Iver that had landed somewhere in the fog.

"Over here," I called down the slope.

I heard them talking anxiously among themselves, appearing ten seconds later.

"What's going on?" Adler asked. "We were kinda far

out when we heard the alarm."

"*Birds*," Aubrey stated, folding her arms over her chest.

The three who just came up glanced at me and Michael questioningly, looking for clearer answers where they couldn't get them from Aubrey.

"Several dozen puffins in the north, near the beach," I explained.

"*Not* as cute as you'd think," Michael muttered.

"You saw puffins?" Clara asked, sounding a little too happy about it.

"Trust me, you don't want to meet them," I said. "They tried to attack us."

Clara's face fell.

"How'd you get away then?" Iver asked.

The trainer also watched me, waiting to know how.

"Intimidation," I answered plainly. "I was the larger bird, and we both knew it. I guess if everything is more aggressive, they expect us to be too."

"Huh," the trainer said. My eyes shifted to him. He was nodding slowly, looking at me carefully. "Yes, that was a good move."

My head whipped over to the north as the clicking sound rang out over the barren plain again. "You guys should get inside," I said without looking at them. My eyes were trained on the foggy space to the north.

"Oh, *now* you want to go inside," the trainer huffed.

"No," I said. "*Them*."

Michael gave a curt nod to the group. "Rory and I will stay out here until the other four arrive. You guys wait inside."

"Sure thing," Aubrey said. I heard her start off toward the door and the others follow.

Adler and Clara hesitated, but then they, too, went with the others.

"Be careful," Adler called over to us as he left.

Some twenty seconds later, I heard the mechanisms in the door moving and the group walking inside.

"Why are the others taking so long?" Michael murmured to himself.

I was wondering the same thing. "They probably went further out. You know how those seabird boys are."

We waited, and waited. The trainer checked his watch. "Been five minutes," he stated. He looked out through the fog with subdued apprehension. "They should be back by now."

Yeah, thanks, Mr. Obvious. I took a step in the western direction. My fists clenched and unclenched at my sides.

"Rory..." Michael's voice held a warning.

"Stop trying to read my mind, will you?" I scolded.

"You shouldn't go out there," he urged anyway.

The trainer picked up on my thoughts now. "Uh, he's right, you know. If anything, you should go inside with the others."

"Really?" I sighed. "You're gonna try that one again,

'cause it worked so well the first time?" Uh-oh, my inside voice was becoming my outside voice. That's how you really knew when I was tense.

The trainer growled under his breath.

I still couldn't hear so much as a distant scrap of feathers. They weren't even close. "I'm going out there," I said and moved forward.

A sturdy grip planted itself on my upper right arm. I whipped around and glared at the hand's owner. Michael looked down at me from his whole two inch advantage. "I'm going with you," he said sternly.

My glowing hazel eyes flicked up and down his person. "Fine," I agreed tersely, taking my arm from his grasp. He let go and stared after me.

I turned back around and ran forward a few meters before unfurling my wings and launching into the air. A powerful and unfettered feeling coursed through me, just as it did every time I took to the sky. I heard Michael join me a second later.

Will was out there, possibly in trouble. I couldn't just leave him. Of course it *would be* his group. I'd have to beat him up for it later.

CHAPTER 22

I swerved slightly as my head looked this way and that, trying to pick up on anything useful. The first sound I picked up on was that of the waves rolling against the bottom of the cliffs far below.

I kept flying, further out over the ocean. Then, I heard it: that useful thing I was talking about. Amidst a storm of tiny wings, the strong beats of our group's massive feathers pounded in the air, accompanied by the panicked breathing of people.

"They're ahead of us," I informed Michael. "And they aren't alone."

I picked up speed, working my wings. Suddenly, the fog lightened up into a smoky cavern hovering a thousand feet above the churning water. A terrifying scene opened up before my eyes. At least three-hundred black and white birds were diving, biting, and clawing at three birdkids from our unit, chasing them in and out of the fog. I weaved down and to the right five feet when several puffins came barreling toward me. I looked over my shoulder with wide eyes as they flew by.

Further out in front of me, Ronin swept away ten birds with a billow of his wings, the fog swirling around him. He looked over his shoulder and brought his wings in, dropping fifteen feet before tossing them back out and flapping haphazardly away. He had managed to drop some birds that had tried to bite onto his wings, but they converged toward him like a living cloud.

I was about to dive down and help him, but then June whipped by like a torpedo, nearly running into me. Her wings flashed as she dodged the birds. Several of her iridescent feathers floated down through the fog behind her.

Someone else was fighting birds another hundred meters below. I titled my wings and angled down, losing altitude.

My wings snapped out gracefully when I got down to Samuel's level. "Why aren't you guys booking it outta here?" I yelled. "You're faster than them!"

"Down there!" Samuel shouted, pointing below. "Can't get him back up!"

What? I scanned the air below me, but all appeared clear. Then I heard him — his cries of pain.

I had no idea where Michael was or how the others fared back above, but I brought my wings in again and dove further down, only tossing them out to their full lengths once I was fifty feet from the ocean's surface. The fog was thicker down here, but still lighter than in the north, aided by a stronger breeze. I followed Will's voice and the enraged flapping of small birds, and spotted a hunk of metal bouncing on the surface of the water a moment later.

An old, red navigation buoy the height of a bedroom door swayed dangerously in the dark, sullen water. Clinging on for dear life, his feathers and skin covered in a sheen of cold water, was Will.

"Will!" I called.

His head turned stiffly to the side. My vision focused on him as my heart twisted, the panic in his eye becoming clear. He ducked down again as two puffins swooped at him, tearing off several feathers from his wings. Will hissed in pain but didn't let go.

My brain felt like it was on hyperdrive. What was I supposed to do? What to do??

I circled around. Several more puffins began their speedy descent toward Will, and I angled my own wings, diving sharply toward them.

WHACK!

Three small birds made large white flowers on the surface of the blue-black water as they were sent slinging away by a hard slap of my left wing. *Take that, devil birds!*

I felt victorious for approximately three seconds. That's how long it took for another thirty puffins to dive down at me in an attempt to avenge their friends.

Immediately, I began weaving to avoid the birds. They ripped several small feathers off from the top of my wings, producing a sharp stinging sensation. Their claws managed to score thin red lines along my arms as I brought them up to defend my face.

Anger welled up inside me toward the birds, and I spun like a torpedo, flicking out one wing while curving the other to produce such a movement. I felt the impact of at least ten birds against my halfway flared wing. Leveling back out, I didn't give them any opportunities and flapped straight up. Their little wings couldn't keep up, and soon I lost them in the wind and fog.

Coming up through the fog, I witnessed firsthand how the birds likely managed to take down Will. Ronin seemed to be holding out his own initially, but a wave of birds pouring down from his other side caught him off-guard. The puffins latched onto his wings twenty at a time, but only ONE wing, weighing him down unevenly. Unable to throw them off or keep his balance, Ronin fell through the air, dropping straight past me.

My breath all but disappeared. He fell in both slow motion and in the blink of an eye, and I found myself curving around. I had been flying straight up, and now I had twisted my body, diving straight back down.

Ronin fell faster than me, too fast for me to catch up to him in the two-hundred-meter window.

Just like the puffins had, Ronin fell into the water

with a cold splash, tossing up large white droplets around the impact. My wings faltered for a moment from the shock, but I caught myself and leveled out. Circling a hundred feet over the waves, I searched for any sign of Ronin. My eyes scanned the endless water, flicking back and forth anxiously.

It had to be a full twenty seconds later when I finally spotted his head emerge from the water. Breathing a deep sigh of relief, I glided down to him.

"Swim that way!" I said, pointing toward the buoy a hundred feet away.

His head turned to look at me, his expression riddled with shock. He followed my finger, and in the next instant, began swimming toward the buoy.

I protected him from any birds that still felt aggrieved toward him, and eventually he made it to Will. Ronin hoisted himself up onto the slippery metal, water trickling from his hair and wings in thick streams.

I circled around the buoy, then went and landed at the very top of it. I nearly slipped on the wet frame and crouched down to gain more balance.

"Can you fly?" I asked them. They couldn't stay here forever.

Will shook his head. "My wings are too heavy. I can't get a chance to shake them out."

As if on cue, a puffin swooped down to attack. I swung my right wing out at him, sending him twirling away into the waves. Doing so almost made me lose my balance, and I scrambled for a hold.

Breathing hard, I looked back at Will and said, "Well do it anyway. I'll cover you."

He nodded, his eyes wide.

Ronin was looking up at me through wet dark brown and red-streaked hair as well.

I jumped back into the air, throwing my wings out with nimble yet forceful flaps. The two boys worked to rid their wings of water while also trying not to fall as I circled the buoy, knocking aside puffins that dared to get too close. Luckily, Michael, June, and Samuel were taking on the bulk of the belligerent birds higher above. I tried to stay further in the fog to avoid bringing more attention down to us, only coming out to go after any stray puffins.

I was getting ready to urge the two boys to hurry it up when I heard their wings flapping. Gliding out of the fog bank, I watched Ronin get back into the air with quick flaps of his Cooper's Hawk wings.

"Come on, Will!" I said.

He shook his head, looking panicked. I knew he needed more space to take off, but we didn't exactly have that luxury at the moment.

"I can't!" he said.

I cursed under my breath. Okay, time for plan B. Or was this C? Who cared. I curved over to the buoy and flapped down beside Will, grasping onto the swaying metal frame to keep from slipping off.

"Okay, Will," I said. "I'm going to lift you up, and you're going to flap like you've never flapped before. Got it?"

"Uh… Got it," he said, looking nervous.

While the buoy swayed precariously, I stepped around so that I was standing behind Will. I could feel the heat blaring from him onto my chest.

"Reach higher up," I commanded.

Will looked like he wanted to ask questions, but did as he was told amidst the panic.

"Get ready to let go," I said. *"Don't hold on."* Before he could respond, I pushed off from the buoy. I grasped his forearms as I flapped upward, and his fingers which had turned white slipped from the metal.

I carried him up with me, though each stroke of my wide wings only brought me half as far up with Will's additional weight.

"Flap!" I urged.

Will opened his long wings. He started working them, and soon he was gaining his own lift.

"Letting go," I said, my voice strained from his weight, and I did just that.

He dropped a good fifteen feet, but then he didn't fall any further than that. With powerful beats of his long, angular wings, he started flying on his own. Elation broke over his face, then vanished. "Look out!" he called, pointing behind me.

Without looking over, I dropped down ten feet. Five

puffins went sailing over me.

"Ronin, Will, stick close," I said. "We're getting the others and flying the heck out of here."

CHAPTER 23

Ronin and Will had no qualms against my plan. They stuck with me in a tight triangle formation as I flapped higher up, each stroke of my wings lifting me an additional fifteen feet.

"Michael, we're gett'n outta here!" I shouted as I passed by him.

He let out a sound of exertion as he sent four puffins tumbling away with a lusty sweep of his wings. He gave me a deliberate nod and curved away.

June came into view, still being chased, and I called out to her as well. "Get back to the base! Everyone's up!"

She looked over, and her eyes widened even further. After looking past me at Will, she didn't hesitate to turn on a dime and go full-speed toward the base. Thirty or so black and white birds were left in her wake.

Michael came around with Samuel, and all of us booked it after June.

The puffins had nothing on our speed. We easily reached a hundred miles per hour without so much as a breeze, leaving the angry little birds far behind.

Or so I thought.

Staying close to the ground so that we could see the base, we passed over the ten-foot-tall barbed wire fence. Amidst the rush of adrenaline in my ears, I heard them before I saw them: more little flaps and weird clicking noises.

The fog had lessened enough to let us see fifty feet instead of just twenty, and as we soared over the plains, a hundred puffins circling the field came into view.

"So, that's a no on the 'can we get a break'?" I muttered to myself.

Unfortunately, I spotted June a moment later. Since she was the first to fly out toward the base, she was the first to arrive — *alone*. Yet again, she was faced with trying to fend off a group of puffins, which kept trying to pick at her feathers. If she fell now, there would be no water to cushion her.

"Follow me," I said diligently to those trailing behind me.

Ronin, Will, Samuel, and Michael flew with me back into the thicker fog. I could hear the puffins gathered in the field. Even without a visual on them, their clicks and cries were overwhelming.

The usual entrance was blocked. I circled us far out to the east, around the field to the other door, some hundred meters from the one under attack. We landed quietly for the most part.

Tucking our wings in, we went quickly toward the door. I waved a hand in front of one of the cameras, hoping they'd see us. The trainer was obviously no longer outside. The door creaked open and I stood by, keeping watch, while the others filed inside.

Michael, taking up the tail end, turned around once halfway inside. "Aren't you coming?" he asked, sounding a bit worried.

"No," I stated plainly. "Stay here at the door though. I'm gonna go get June."

He opened his mouth to say something, but I turned and jumped back into the air before he got the chance.

I'm going to level with you. Flying straight into a cloud of birds with razor-sharp beaks and claws, knowing that if I wasn't careful, I could plummet to my death? Not as easy to make yourself do as you might think. My heart was beating like crazy, my eyes darting around at every moving speck as if it was a laser that might kill me. I tried to focus my eyes on June. She looked like a mad Swallow, flapping speedily around.

"June!" I called.

I wasn't sure if she'd heard me. A breath escaped my lips as half a dozen puffins turned their beady little eyes on me. They broke away from the swarm and headed straight at me with steely determination.

Mistake! my brain cried. I swerved away, dropping

swiftly to the right. I leveled out like water spilling up to the edge of a tilted container, sloshing back to center.

This wasn't working.

Thinking quickly, I jerked my wings and angled off into the fog. Once the birds couldn't see me, I gained altitude, flapping with vigorous, forceful beats, my wings coming up above my head with each upstroke.

Deeming I was up high enough, I circled above the battle scene, trying to see through the patches of fog. My eyes locked onto June. I took a quick breath in and flapped forward a single time before bringing my wings in closer to my sides. I fell downward, straight at June.

"Incoming!" I called briskly.

June looked up when I was only ten meters from her. Right before I hit her, I spread my wings and grabbed her around the backside of her waist, snatching her away from the puffins. My wings tucked in again and we curved across the field. I practically threw her from my grasp when we reached the door, then landed down a moment after.

The birds cried out malignantly. I tried to pull the door shut. Suddenly, Michael was there beside me, helping to close it. Between the two of us, we managed to pull it closed just in time. I heard the *thump, thump, thump* of birds hitting the outside of the fortified door.

I breathed heavily, resting my hands on my thighs. "Are we all alive?" I asked through pants.

Someone chuckled, and then there were half a dozen

laughs. I looked over at them to see the whole unit there.

Michael patted me hard on the back, wearing a tense but relieved smile. "Yeah, we're all alive."

CHAPTER 24

We didn't get to hang around congratulating each other for long. The trainer was nowhere to be seen, but several other guys in uniform instructed us to head directly to G3 to get looked over.

I saw Carson again, and he did not look happy to see me. He did his tests mostly in silence, taking x-rays, inspecting my feathers, and all that. When he did finally speak, it was to angrily tell me how stupid I was.

I slanted my gaze over to him. I didn't need to say anything for him to know what I was thinking.

He rolled his eyes aggravatedly and focused on my x-ray with a deep frown. "I just don't want to see all my work go down the toilet is all," he grumbled.

I lowered my head, hiding my small smile. *How sweet*, I thought sarcastically. *He was worried about me.*

Once he was done examining me, he rolled around to me in his spinny chair. "The good news is you'll be fine.

Just give those few feathers about six weeks to completely grow back. Also, your healing rate is three times that of a normal human, so the cuts should be healed completely in a couple days."

"Alright."

He handed me a small tin half the size of my fist. "And take this. Apply it to your cuts." He shrugged one shoulder. "Just to be extra safe."

I took it from him and turned it in my hand with a small, irresolute frown. The cuts wouldn't be a problem, would they?

He motioned toward the door. "You know the way out," he said exasperatedly.

I left him to be annoyed and walked back out into the hallway. I saw Ronin walking through the double doors at the end of the hall, small cuts all over his body and gray-blue wings. He had a similar small tin in his right hand.

Feeling jumpy from the puffin attack, I tensed when a door swung out right when I walked by it. "Geez," I muttered, taking a breath.

"Oh, sorry," Will said, abashed.

I glanced at him and continued on.

He jogged to catch up to me. "Hey, uh…" His left hand messed up his now-dry hair as he searched for the words. "Thanks for what you did back there. I probably would've been a goner otherwise."

"Don't mention it," I said. I glared at him. "Ever."

His mouth formed a tight line.

We all gathered at the cafeteria level, G2. I slid into a seat beside Iver as Bossy Bob came over to us, looking between grim and impressed. One of the trainers, who served as our Icelandic teacher, was standing nearby.

Bob looked over all of us with a meaningful sweep of his gaze. "You all did good today," he said. "You've managed to do what many Icelandic natives could not: survive."

Shivers went down my body. It seemed I wasn't the only one affected by his words, for it looked like a cold gust had swept over our table.

While his words sunk in, he turned to the teacher-trainer. "How far are they through their native course?" he asked the trainer.

"We still need to cover the last two sections."

He nodded thoughtfully. "Have them finish that and then prepare them for the journey."

"Yes, sir."

"And make sure they've got their flying formations down," he added after a second of thought. "I want them working as a single unit before being dispatched."

"Dispatched?" Michael spoke up.

The military-like man turned his attention on Michael. "Yes, son. You've all earned yourselves a mission."

We looked around the table at each other, visibly quelling our slew of emotions.

"To where?" June asked. She still seemed shell-shocked from our recent experience. Long and short cuts were all over her fair, porcelain-like skin.

"A couple places," Bob said mysteriously. He circled a thick finger in the air above him. "Bring them food," he said loudly. "Then let them rest. Lots more to learn tomorrow."

And then, just like that, without allowing us to ask any more questions, he turned on his heel and clipped away.

◆ ◆ ◆

That afternoon, after a hot shower and a change of clothes, I sat in my room while everyone else was gathered at the Tree of Mahogany, as we liked to call the giant tree. It wasn't mahogany, of course. I'm honestly not sure how we even ended up calling it that, but it was kinda catchy.

I scribbled more carefully thought-out notes in one of my notebooks. This time around, I was trying to figure out the aggression seen in those puffins. The tin of medicine sat nearby on my other notebook, serving as both a paperweight and a reminder. Sure, DODG screwed with animals' brains, but it didn't just make them more aggressive — it also made them more intelligent.

So what actually drove the puffins' aggression? What type was it? Was it territorial? Protective? Just plain nasty?

I was deep in thought when a knock sounded at my door. On reflex, I flipped the book closed and slid it away from me, tossing the pen aside with it.

Taking on a nonchalant position, I said, "Come in."

The door opened softly. "Hey, is this an alright time?" Will asked.

After a pause, I asked, "What's up?"

He came in and closed the door, then walked up to me and sat lightly on the edge of the table. His eyes wandered across the white surface, and I saw them stop on my notebooks. He flicked a finger toward them. "Writing some more?" he asked.

I sighed. I reached out for the book I had been writing in and began tapping my fingers across its cover in a steady motion.

"You ever —?" I pursed my lips, trying to figure out how to phrase it. "I can't help but feel like the more we learn," I said carefully, "the less we know about anything anymore."

Tap. Tap. Tap.

My fingers made thoughtful sounds, filling the silence that followed.

Will nodded slowly. "Right… That's because everything's changed. We're relearning the world."

Looking at his face which had several sets of thin red lines scored across it, my heart ached for him. It really must have been terrifying to fall into the ocean like that. He was lucky there had been a navigation buoy out there.

I looked away from him, feeling distressed. What would have happened if we didn't have the base to fall back on?

"Do you really think we could survive on our own out there?" I asked, my voice subdued.

Dark waves lapped against the cliff base far below, filling my ears with a mocking invitation. Even though it was only the afternoon, the thick fog outside the panel of glass set into the wall produced an eerie light in the bedroom. It looked as if the fog had invaded my room as well.

Will shifted on the table a bit. "I hope so. It would kind of suck not to." He gave a feeble attempt at a laugh, coming out more like a weak gust of air.

I bit my lower lip, chewing as if I could take my unease out through it. My eyes found their way to Will again and I ceased my chewing. "What did you come here for initially?" I asked, feeling like I led him way off-topic.

"Oh." He scratched the back of his hair, suddenly becoming livelier. "You know, I was just wondering..." He glanced at me. "What if we got the others to come with us?"

My eyes steadily narrowed at him.

He hastily continued. "It just wouldn't feel right to leave them all here. I mean, at least not without a choice." He looked like he wanted to say more, but quieted down. I knew him well enough at this point to know that when he said 'the others,' he really meant *'Aubrey.'* "Right, well." His eyes shifted about uncomfortably, and he stood up. "Think about it."

Will left the room rather quickly. When he looked up as he entered the hallway, he startled. "Oh, hey," he said to someone I couldn't see. He glanced back through the half-open door, then left, going around something, or *someone*, awkwardly. I could just make out the edge of a chiseled jawline as this someone turned toward the awkward Will.

Even though I knew Will hadn't actually meant telling *everyone*, I had started to really think about it. My brain was distracted when Michael rolled around the corner into view, leaning coyly on the doorframe. His hands were clasped loosely over one another in front of him, his pointer finger tapping against the back of his other hand. My eyes flicked to them in a somewhat agitated manner. What did he want?

"Are you gonna just stand there or tell me something?" I asked a little harsher than I meant.

He tapped the backside of his hand a few more times, then pushed quickly off the doorframe and came inside with a couple even strides. "Tell you something," he said decidedly, closing the door behind him. I watched it click shut, a small, discreet frown forming on my face. His mouth parted as if about to continue zealously, but he hesitated, his dark eyebrows drawing together with sudden consideration.

I found myself easing backward under his strong gaze, and I tilted my head at him, watching him carefully.

Michael noticed the tin of medicine on the table near me, and I glanced at it as well, wondering what he was planning to do. He came closer, a meter away at best, and lightly swiped the tin off the notebook. He leaned against the edge of the table and unscrewed it. "You know," he said, his voice soothing, "it only actually works when you *use* it."

I hadn't bothered applying it to the cuts on my arms and face when I got back to my room — I'd gone straight into making notes. "I'm aware," I said tepidly, my voice falling far from haughty. I'd turned placid in Michael's presence, an effect that would have made me angry and guarded toward anyone else.

He dipped two fingers in and set the tin aside, stepping carefully forward and bringing his other hand up to steady my face. I wavered, and he paused amidst my hesitation. He met my eyes and suddenly I was caught by them, and he was able to reach the rest of the way, holding my face still with a gentle but firm cup of his fingers. I didn't mind this perspective, looking up at him from the chair, his tall form not feeling domineering in the slightest. I noticed his broad, well-toned chest, his defined arms, the dips and flex of his muscles, but I stayed focused on his eyes as his attentive gaze followed his fingers applying the salve.

It stung where the medicine met my cuts, but I didn't so much as flinch. His touch was ginger, and I felt myself yearning for more. I remained still, however, not wanting to risk ruining the moment and making him stop.

"There," he said quietly. He took his hands away from me and his warmth with them, turning back to the table to screw the lid back on the tin.

"What would I do without you," I said, giving him a teasing but thankful smile. He smiled down at the table and set the tin aside. His hand fell upon the glossy white surface of the table and his fingers tapped against it, his smile gradually waning. "What is it?" I asked him.

He faced me, looking serious, the tenderness he showed me stirring somewhere beneath the surface now. "I want in," he said.

"Want in...?" I led. What was this fellow getting at?

He swept his tongue between his lips. "I'm not an idiot," he said casually. "I've put the dots together. Our conversation on the beach... The meetings between you and Will..." He raised his eyebrows at me as if expecting me to finish his thought.

"Okay?" I asked, feigning ignorance. His visit was taking a drastic turn, one I did not care for. My defenses started rising back into place.

He shifted as if he wanted to get closer to me again, but he restrained himself with a small frown when he saw my adverse expression. His eyes became gentler as they flicked over the floor, under attractive lashes. "I've been thinking a lot about what you said — about knowing the truth — and I believe you're right. I want to come with you."

I only stared at him disapprovingly. He could be bluffing, couldn't he? "And where are you trying to go?" I asked.

His long, dark eyebrows drew in slightly. "I used to live in western Wyoming. I guess I just have to start there."

Ah. Brilliant plan. Very well thought-out. It was because of plans like this that Will and I were procrastinating on leaving for so long. The base was helping us learn a lot, sure, but all of our plans still sucked. Like, what would we do once we got across the ocean? Everyone probably wasn't still living in their same old house after the world went crazy, so how would we find them? Worst of all, what would we do if our mission turned out to be futile? Then we'd just be two birdkids flying around aimlessly, when we could have been living a relatively good life in a super-secure base in Iceland.

I didn't crush his hopes and instead asked, "You used to live in Wyoming?"

He seemed a little surprised by my interest. "Yeah, outside of Cody Yellowstone." He became a little more coy again. "I figure the distance doesn't matter so much, now that I can just fly there."

It was true; Yellowstone was a good distance from Iceland and central Virginia. However, it was also true that traffic was no longer an issue.

"Mm," I responded, still secretly miffed inside.

He looked me over earnestly. "So? What do you

say?"

Standing up, I whispered harshly, "I say there could be microphones in this room." I began shoving him out the door. "Now, go away."

He protested, but I got him out. I closed the door and leaned my back against it, letting my muscles relax again.

Sigh.

CHAPTER 25

The next couple days seemed to go by rather quickly. It wasn't long before I found myself packing in my room, getting ready for this mission I knew nothing about. For example, where we would be going; I had no idea.

There wasn't much for me to pack. I had my change of clothes, toothbrush and toothpaste, full water canister, and also included that little tin of salve Carson had given me for my cuts. I shoved my notebooks and pens into the pack and then glanced around the room.

Yep, all set.

I slung the cylindrical pack onto my back and clipped it. The pack, like the clothes, had to be made to accommodate our wings. The dark gray pack itself sat comfortably between my wings, only rubbing some scapular feathers near the middle. Two soft straps the width of two fingers shot from the top of it, coming over my shoulders and connecting in a sharp V-shape above my navel. Another two straps attached to the bottom of the pack came around my sides and clipped onto either side of the V-shaped end. It was a simple design, really, but it worked.

I exited my room, closing the door behind me, and joined the others who were gathering at the end of the hall. I got in line behind Anna, who looked a little nervous. Anna had been more of an introvert from the start, with delicate dove wings to match her quiet personality.

The CQ stood at the entrance of the hallway beside Bossy Bob, waiting for everyone to arrive. The rest of our unit filed in behind me, and not two minutes later, we were all ready to go. Except, they didn't lead us away yet.

A third person, this one a man with neatly trimmed salt and pepper hair, came out of the office room I'd never actually been inside of.

"Oh, good. You're all here," he said with a pleasant note. My eyes dropped to what he was carrying: a bunch of circular black bands. In the next instant, he began passing them out to each of us. As he walked down the line, he explained, "You're all flying further from the base than you have before."

I was handed one of these items as well. It looked like a bracelet, only thick and metallic, like a watch.

"If you get lost in the mountains or wherever else, we'll be able to find you a lot smoother this way," he carried on.

"So, these are tracking bracelets?" Will quizzed.

"Yes, these are tracking bracelets," he said with a certain level of zest. "Please, everyone put them on. Oh, and —" He pulled something out of one of his inside pockets, holding it up and giving it a little tilt from side to side. Passing his intelligent gaze down our line, he said, "Your unit will need one of these, too, in order to communicate with us if needed. I'll let you decide who takes it." With that note, he passed it off to the person at the front of the line, Samuel.

Samuel leaned out into the hallway some half a dozen people in front of me, and his eyes found mine. "Rory, catch," he said.

He tossed the palm-sized block underhanded. I reached out and grabbed it from the air. A quick looksie said it was like a normal handheld radio, except more compact.

"Well alright then," the man said. He pointed at it. "It's already set to the right channel. Do you know how to use one of those?"

"Of course," I responded briefly, examining it. I slipped the bracelet on to get it out of the way. There was a Velcro-like strap on the back of the radio, so I attached it securely to the bottom right strap of my pack.

"I guess you're set then," he said.

Bob cleared his throat. The tracker bracelet guy looked over at Bob with eyebrows raised in question. "Oh," he said, jumping back into the office. He emerged a moment later with a folded paper in his right hand.

"Here," he said, striding over and handing it to me.

I unfolded it into a foot-by-foot square of glossy paper. "A map?" I asked. My eyes scanned it. It was a general reference map of Iceland, with stylized relief, and red dots spaced at intervals along a single looping road. "Where're you trying to make us go?" I asked with a note of distrust.

"That road is what's known as Ring Road. Hits all the populated places in Iceland," Bob spoke up. Man, I still didn't know that guy's real name. "Your unit is tasked to examine every red dot you see on there. I don't care if you get there by walking, or flying — just get there. Go to *all of them*. You will circle back once visiting each red dot and come back to base."

"What do we do for food?" Michael asked from where he stood two people in front of me.

Bob wagged a finger at Michael. "Yes," he agreed, reaching down for something out of view. He returned to a standing position, holding a black canvas bag. "CQ, take them above ground, will you?" he asked almost politely.

She gave a terse nod. "Mm. Yes, sir."

"Everybody take two packets," Bob ordered as the CQ started off. "Each packet contains six rations. I'll let *you* decide if it'll last the whole way."

How helpful. Our line began moving, everybody reaching into the bag to grab a couple shiny silver packets as they passed. I grabbed two as well. It was just another test, really, and I got how it *was* actually helpful. Made us think for ourselves and for our own survival and all that.

"Need me to help you with those?" Clara asked, walking behind me.

"Hm?" I turned. She was gesturing to my pack. "Oh, sure." I gave her a small smile of gratitude, and she zipped the food into my pack for me.

We all helped each other out, and soon it was just me who was still carrying something in my hands. The feel of the glossy paper beneath my fingers did not put me at ease. It felt like a weight in my hand.

The CQ took us up the multitude of stairs, climbing our way to freedom, and we emerged into crisp, clean air. No puffins or birds thereof in sight.

I took a deep breath, taking it in. I would say the late afternoon sun was shining down brightly upon us, but the sky was covered in a light gray canvas. Something fell onto the bridge of my nose as I looked up. My nose twitched as a wetness developed, slipping down its contour.

Little specks started falling delicately from the sky. At first I thought it had begun lightly raining, but my eyes were able to focus on the individual specks. My breath hitched in wonder. Each little speck had the most beautiful designs, gorgeously etched into geometric flakes.

Crystals in the sky... Oh my, this was snow! I had no idea how truly beautiful snow was!

"Any more questions before you head off?" the CQ

asked.

My attention only vaguely returned to her. I was too entranced by the magnificent new outlook on the natural phenomenon floating around me.

"Yeah," Ronin spoke up arrogantly from the back of the group. "How about, why are we flying around the entire country?"

"Good question. You get to figure that out your-selves," she said. Her eyes glinted with something bor-derline humorous, but it was hidden beneath a dark, haunted pool. "Wouldn't want to spoil the surprise."

"Sure, sure," Ronin scoffed.

The CQ looked at me now. "Your only mission is to hit all of the locations on that map dictated by a red dot. That, and make it back without dying."

"Not dying would be preferable," I said.

She gave me a nod, then turned back to the rest of the group. "If that's all you have to ask, then head out," she said, jabbing a thumb over her shoulder at the field.

There were angry and curious murmurs around the group as we headed off, leaving the CQ behind.

"Stupidest mission ever," someone muttered behind me. Sounded like Elena, making me take a glance over my shoulder. Her clear yellow eyes flicked up at me, then hastily shifted away.

There was already a fine layer of snow covering the grassy plains. As we walked away from the base, I unfolded the map. *Okay, so we follow the road around this island? Sounds easy enough. What's the catch?*

"It's almost like they planned it!" Iver complained, shaking the powder from his hair.

"It's the first time it's snowed in the past three weeks," June concurred.

Michael nudged my arm, appearing beside me out of seemingly nowhere. "Hey. What's it look like?"

"Here." I handed the map over to Michael and looked out toward the mainland in the east. "The first dot is about a hundred mile straight shot that way," I said, pointing southeast. The base was located on the most western peninsula of the country, at the tip of a thick piece of land that looked like it wanted to separate from the mainland and form its own island. The dot I was referring to was placed far below, on the western edge of the oval-shaped country.

"So, bosses?" Will asked, slinging an arm around each of our shoulders. He turned his head between the two of us. "Where are we heading first?"

I had in mind to punch him in the face. Those thin red lines the puffins had scored through his skin were almost completely healed, leaving behind faint pink lines that were also quickly vanishing. Since this was the case, it would be alright to injure him now, right?

"Shove off," I said, reaching around to mess up his hair. Michael, too, had stopped to stare at him coolly.

Will only scrunched his face up and endured it, then let go with a sigh, as if I was no fun. Hearing the ruffled-haired Will ask, though, the rest of the group inevitably crowded around Michael and me in a loose crescent moon.

"We're going to fly southeast. Shouldn't take us more than an hour of flight time to reach the first dot," I went on for the group, turning to face them.

Michael nodded along at my words as he looked over the map seriously.

"We're really doing this?" Adler asked. "Flying around the country because they told us to?"

I opened my mouth to respond.

"They could have at least told us *why*," Aubrey said before I could speak. "Plus, why would they send us out only a couple days after dealing with those puffins? I thought the whole point of being here was so we *don't* die."

"We're doing it," I said resolutely, and before anyone else could interrupt. "Not for them — for us. This could be a good lesson."

"A *lesson?* A lesson for what?" Aubrey contended.

I looked around at them calmly and evenly. "For what else may be out there. For how the world is now, and how we'll survive in it."

CHAPTER 26

"Lucky for us," Samuel sighed, bringing something out from his pack, "I brought music." He gave us a tight-lipped smile, waving a black, triangular-shaped device in his right hand.

The corner of my mouth flicked in a faintly entertained smile.

Aubrey slanted her agitated gaze over to him. "Uh-huh," she said, looking unimpressed.

"Play us somethin' good," Iver said gaily.

Samuel tapped and scrolled his finger across the screen, then stuck it to one of his pack's straps as music began playing. Seeing some of us look at him in confusion, as those devices were never supposed to attach to anything, he hastily explained, "Oh, I modified it the other day. Just in case we'd need it." He smiled at us.

"Nicely done," I said, giving him a positive look. Then, I turned and started down the hill. "Time to go."

My wings unfurled as I jumped, revealing hundreds of tan-blonde feathers washed in a brilliant caramel butter, mottled with organized white and black flecks, my primaries and secondaries striped in dark gold, as I soared powerfully into the sky. My curled, silky hair whipped softly behind me as I pushed down with elegant, even strokes, rising easily. Wind rushed over my skin and the feathers along my hairline, shoulders, and chest, making pleasant shivers run down my body.

I curved around to wait for everyone to get into the air, circling high above. One by one, they ran or jumped forward and tossed themselves into the air, flying up to me where I waited patiently in the sky.

Once we were all together, we headed southeast in a loose formation, toward the first location. Samuel's device played "Wrapped Around Your Finger" by The Police against the gentle sound of the wind and snow as we flew.

The view was astounding, I will not lie. It was enough to distract me from the chill of the frigid wind. Flying above Iceland's jagged coast? Amazing. Empty, rolling white plains collided in a stark contrast against the dark ocean. Snow swirled around me, my wings cutting through it leisurely. We cut over an expanse of water to save time, inchoate gray waves churning below. Thirty minutes later, we were soaring over white plains again with beautifully carved mountains in the near distance.

Coming up to the mountains, we lost formation and I

floated upward on the soft breeze of a thermal updraft. Those of us with soaring-style wings circled higher and higher, while those with shorter wings had to flap harder and quicker to catch up.

I closed my eyes, relishing in the benign feel of the wind surrounding my person. When I eventually opened them, I was easily over two-thousand meters above the ground. I knew the ocean was off to my right, but the snowfall only allowed me to see the peaks of the mountains in front of me.

"Should be another twenty miles or so," I announced. "If we stick close to the ocean, we should find it no problem."

"Can't we just find that ring road thing and follow that?" Clara asked innocently, floating along the air currents thirty feet to my right. It was easy to hear each other amidst the wind. Small feathers protected our ear canals, allowing the wind to pass over smoothly, without all of that whistling.

I shook my head. "We're not using the road initially. The road actually avoids the mountains," I explained.

"Oh."

Adler tilted his wings and shifted smoothly over to me, a good twenty feet above my head. "What do you think it'll be like?" he asked. "It's some populated place, right? That's what the general said."

"Was," I corrected.

"What?"

"It *was* populated. And I don't know what it'll be like," I answered honestly. All I knew is that it probably wouldn't be good.

"I bet it'll be a ghost town!" Aubrey said. "Like in one of those zombie movies."

"I never did like those movies," Anna said sourly. A shiver of unpleasantness ran through her slim body to her wingtips, and she frowned.

Michael chuckled to himself. "You're in the wrong movie then, sis," he told Anna, his brows bowed up in the middle with pity.

Anna sighed.

We continued to fly mostly in silence for the next while, with only Samuel's music to fill our ears. A new scene unfolded eventually. The ocean cut into the land, producing a large waterway shimmering among the pristine landscape. Jutting into that waterway was a small peninsula, but not just any peninsula. My eyes had to zoom in to make sure I was seeing things correctly through the flurry, but there seemed to be a small town gathered on that piece of snow-covered land. Red and gray roofs peeked through the snow carpet.

I started losing altitude, diving down the first two-thousand meters, then leveling out to circle above with watchful eyes, peering down through the snow falling around me as if looking down through the eye of a storm. The others circled with me, and the half of us with raptor vision scanned the town below. Seeing things becoming more intense, Samuel shut down the music.

"I'm not seeing any movement," Michael stated, scanning the ground diligently.

"Anyone?" I asked.

There was a consensus among us that none of us saw anything. With this, we flew down to a narrow part of the peninsula, landing on an empty stretch of road. Of course, the only reason I knew it was a road was due to the parallel indents in the snow on both sides. The powder was a couple inches thick, and my bare feet, arched perfectly like those of a dancer, created delicate prints on its surface. I bet they were the first human footprints this town had seen in a long time.

"What now?" Anna asked a bit fearfully.

"I believe the next step is investigation," June spoke up quietly.

It felt like if we spoke too loudly, we'd awaken the dead. Our group of winged oddballs went carefully down the road, our heads turning at any conceivable sound or suspicious shadow.

Not four-hundred feet down the road, houses on either side, my eyes caught on yellowed spikes erupting from the snow. I walked closer despite the unease growing in my heart. I stifled a gasp. Hidden in the snow, those spikes suddenly resembled someone's broken ribcage.

I couldn't move. I only stared at it, feeling increasingly nauseous.

"Oh god," someone said, their voice muffled as if it was hidden behind a hand raised to their mouth.

"Is... Is that...?" Will asked meekly, his voice wavering.

I swallowed and clenched my teeth. Flexing my fingers to release the tension in my heart, I forced myself to turn and move on. "Keep moving, guys," I said.

It did not get better the further into town we got. There was more than one skeleton in the streets, most still wearing tattered, faded clothes. I saw half a corpse through a store window. Elena ran to the edge of the road and puked up what little food she had in her stomach.

"I think I'm gonna join her," Iver said queasily, sounding close to it.

It was no coincidence that the two owl Hybrids besides myself were the most affected by the sight. We had better vision than anyone, especially looking into the dim storefront. This person — man or woman, I couldn't tell — was not fully decomposed. That meant they had survived, for a good while anyway.

Through the gentle rush of snow, my sensitive ears picked up on something similar to the sounds our group's feet made on the smooth concrete hallway outside of my bedroom back at the base. I tensed and tried to peer through the shattered glass window in the direction of the sound. Michael seemed to pick up on my sudden change and urged the others to become still.

One bloody paw in front of the other, a dog-like

creature walked around from behind a counter at the back of the small, homey store. His thick brown and white fur made me sure this animal used to be someone's huge pet dog. You wouldn't catch me owning a dog like this one though. Repugnant white drool dripped from his black mouth. My eyes traveled to his yellowed teeth, each like thin knives.

He didn't seem to notice the dozen birdkids standing motionless in the snow some fifteen feet outside the shattered window. The 'dog' stepped up to the corpse lying near the wall. I couldn't watch, yet I couldn't look away, as his muzzle was bloodied with the body's innards.

At my side, I motioned discreetly with my right hand for the group to get outta here. *Slowly*, obviously. I heard their footsteps back up carefully in the snow, the faint crunch of the crystals beneath their feet.

It seemed the dog heard it too. He raised his head, chomping up a sloppy chunk of meat into his mouth. Eyes glazed over with the fog of death fell upon us, and his pointed ears swiveled forward.

Every feathered hair on my body pricked, those feathers along my scalp and down my front nearly hurting from it. "Go. Go now," I said, almost not getting the words out.

My feet started moving backward, but I forced them to stop. Acting like prey might make me appear like prey. The dog's ears followed the sounds of flapping wings as the group began taking off without hesitation. His eyes stayed on the few of us nearest to him: me, Michael, and Ronin. We seemed to be enough of a distraction for the rest to leave.

Seeing the others fly away, the dog bared his knife-like fangs dripping with blood, the skin atop his muzzle and forehead wrinkling into grotesque lines. A deep rumbling emanated from his throat as he lowered his head aggressively.

The three of us were caught in a standstill with this savage dog, but then he barked. It was a thunderous warning. He barked again, then turned on a dime and bounded forward.

Michael pushed Ronin aside and I leapt away just as the dog threw himself through the broken window. Red stains were left on the glass, but the animal didn't seem to care about his wounds. When I leapt, I managed to get my wings under me and flapped above the road. Michael and Ronin managed to get to their feet pretty quick under the imminent threat, and the two of them started into a run as the dog's hind legs scraped through the snow to stabilize himself.

I wanted to shout out to them, but did they really need me to tell them to run faster?

The dog ran with a ferocious gusto, growling hungrily. He was quickly closing the gap between them within only seconds. Ronin jumped into the air with quick flaps of his short but wide wings. Michael was right behind him, practically glued to Ronin's back.

Snapping jaws jumped up and grabbed the air only a meter from Michael's foot. I felt that my heart really did stop beating. I couldn't even let out a breath of relief when the dog fell back into the snow.

My wings worked in overtime, speeding up to Michael and Ronin. Michael met my eyes, and I was sure he could see the fear in mine just as clearly as I could see it in his.

We met up with the others circling higher above, and the dozen of us flew away without instruction. It took a while for the dog's chaotic howls to die out, only silenced with distance.

CHAPTER 27

When they'd sent us out on this permanently scarring mission, they'd done so in the late afternoon. After we'd finished our last few training sessions, I guess they didn't want to give us the rest of the day to laze around. Instead, they'd dumped us outside and told us to go follow this little death map. Now, after an hour of flight and at least thirty minutes of looking around town, evening was setting in.

None of us were really feeling up to jumping to the next town anytime soon, and since it would be getting dark within the next couple hours, we kind of used it as an excuse to find a place to sleep for the night instead. Okay, so not 'kind of.' That's exactly what we did.

"The mountains might be a bit safer," June offered, trying to sound unaffected by what we'd all witnessed just ten minutes prior.

"Not as easily spotted…yeah," Iver agreed uneasily.

Those closest to me gazed toward me for the ultimate approval.

Since the cold didn't really affect us too much anyway, I didn't object to it. "Alright. The mountains it is," I sighed.

We didn't backtrack, and instead flew directly into the Highlands, the inner region of the country that was widely considered impassible.

…Unless you're us.

It was surprisingly difficult to find a place that would shelter us from the snow, however. Everything was flat, even in the mountains. Sure, you had your weathered rocks which peeked out from the dirt and shrubs, but no *caves* or decent *ledges*. We flew over a twenty-foot-tall waterfall, and several wanted to stop there for the night, but I kept us moving. Fresh water was a magnet for living creatures.

Eventually, we ended up having to settle for a spot on the side of a random mountain, against a small drop in the steep. Some snow was being swept over it entirely, so it seemed decent enough. We flew down and landed on the shrubby, rock-filled slope and trudged through the snow to our little spot. Using our wings as plows, we swept the snow into low walls, creating a nice little area for ourselves.

Iver sighed as he sat down against the dirt wall, pulling his pack onto his lap. He took out one of those silver food packets and tore it open. I looked over my shoulder at him to make sure I was hearing things right, then turned back to the mountainside, scanning for any trouble.

"How can you eat right now?" Adler asked him, watching him take a bite out of a dry cookie.

"Good question," Iver said through his chewing, studying the food ration between his fingers. He popped the rest of it into his mouth.

Adler rolled his silver-brown eyes to the sky, then sat his head in his hands.

I turned away from the view and walked past them, lightly ruffling Adler's thick, dark chocolate hair as I did so. Snowflakes fell away from his curls at my touch, fluttering to the ground. It wasn't too cramped with how long the dirt wall was, and I comfortably sat down in a nice empty space between Clara and Michael.

Okay, so maybe 'comfortable' was an overstatement. I brought my wings around my sides and rested my head at the top of the short wall, getting snow in my curls. I closed my eyes, but images from that decimated town started a slideshow on the back of my eyelids. With a silent sigh, I stared out at the snowy landscape.

"Do we really have to go to *all* of those other locations?" Anna asked feebly.

"They're tracking our locations, remember?" Will sighed, sitting beside Anna further down the wall.

"Well...maybe we could just fly over them and not actually go down?" she tried.

There was a pause, in which Anna shuffled uncomfortably. "Hey, it'll be alright," Will comforted her.

"I'm not sure anything about this is alright," Aubrey said. "It's screwed up that they didn't tell us what they were sending us into beforehand, too."

The group got a little silent, none of us wanting to think about it too much. The weight of the dead had settled on all of us.

"Too bad we can't just get out of here," Ronin said, sounding vulnerable for the first time since I met him. "Out of Iceland, out of this life." He hit his head against the snow bank behind him, looking angry and helpless.

I turned my head to the side to see him better. I never knew the color red could look so blue. "Where did you come from?" I spoke up, more on the quiet side. "Before all this, I mean."

Ronin looked over at me, as if not sure I was talking to him. "I used to live in Indy. Eastside." He studied me. "Where'd you come from?"

I studied him as well. Wasn't Indianapolis one of the most violent cities in America? I guess that explained his personality to some degree.

"I doubt you'd know it," I said. "Let's just say west of Richmond, in Virginia."

"Virginia, huh?" An almost teasing smile played on his lips all of a sudden. "State of lovers..." He twitched his eyebrows up at me.

I groaned, turning to look back over the barren

mountainside instead of him. "Kill me now."

Ronin's chuckles died out, and Michael nudged me with his left wing. "Mm?" I looked over at him.

"There's another one," he whispered.

My brows creased slightly in confusion. *Another one? Oh.* "Michael," I started, a cautionary note to my voice.

"How many of you agree with Ronin?" Michael asked aloud, turning to look down the group. "If you could choose between staying here in Iceland, at the base, or flying somewhere else, which would you choose?"

Instead of speaking up rashly, I waited to hear their answers. I can't say I wasn't curious.

"It's terrible here," June said carefully, "but other places used to be much more heavily populated. It's probably worse elsewhere."

"Don't you want to try to find your family though?" Will questioned, trying to repress his passion on the subject.

June eyed him. "What makes you think they'd be the lucky ones?"

'The lucky ones.' Part of the five percent remaining? Some might argue the opposite case was luckier, especially after what we saw in that town. Decimated towns were probably all that awaited us.

"Wouldn't you still want to know?" he asked with an unsure frown.

"My father and mother lived in Nevada, near Mount

Charleston," June asserted. "Do you know how many mountain lions there are around that area? I saw one *walking down our street* once."

Will didn't keep pushing her.

"We have a lot of grizzly bears in our area," Samuel sighed. "*But* we also have a lot of guns, so... I bet my family made it. I'd say yeah — get out of Iceland and go find them. My sister especially."

"Can you imagine what they'd think of us now?" Iver exasperated. "With *wings?* I mean, my family is pretty cool, but Hybrid cool? Ehh."

"I wonder if the rest of the world even knows about their whole Hybrid project," Will said, giving his head a sad shake. "It's not like they gave *us* advanced warning or anything."

I didn't want to think about how it must have been for Jody and Vixen to have me suddenly disappear like that. Did the government at least inform them after the matter? Or did they rudely kidnap me and say that's that? Thinking back on it, a cold laugh escaped my lips. Virus. Yeah, sure. 'Side effects may include *growing wings.*'

"With a show of hands, how many of you would want to leave?" I asked advisedly.

I looked down both sides of the group. Slowly, hand after hand was raised. I raised mine as well, throwing aside a fraction of caution. That made it a total of ten hands in the air.

I knew why June had her reservations against it, but I

didn't expect Elena to want to stay. Well actually, I didn't expect this many people to want to leave in the first place. Dropping our hands back down, I leaned forward to look down the line. Elena was at the very end at the far right. "Elena," I said. "Why wouldn't you want to?"

She looked very small, sitting with her knees hugged to her chest, her brown wings wrapped gingerly around her arms. Elena looked up at me with her downturned eyes, with irises that were pure yellow. She looked away a moment later.

Samuel, sitting closest to her, tapped her leg with the back of his hand. "Come on," he urged gently. "Why wouldn't you?"

Elena shook her head, making her long, tawny brown hair sway. "We really shouldn't. It's not safe," she said quietly.

"Right," Samuel drew out. "But, that's the whole reason they hybridized us. To deal with the unsafe things." Elena didn't respond. Samuel waved her off. "Ah, it's just hypothetical anyhow. Don't worry too much about it."

Right… Hypothetical. I laughed inside, though it wasn't really funny.

"And if it wasn't hypothetical?" Michael trailed.

I shot him a glance. He looked at me with no signs of giving it up. One rotten egg and we could all be screwed. That's all it would take.

"What're you talking about?" Adler asked, sounding

curious amidst the tiredness.

"I'm talking about leaving," Michael stated. "All of us — or everyone who wants to — flying out of here. It seems like we were all taken from America, so we could travel together."

"*Leave* the base? Just up and ditch it, no questions asked?" Aubrey reinforced. She laughed. "Count me in. When are we leaving?"

"No, but seriously," Iver said. "You want to just leave? Is that even possible?" He was leaning forward now, looking very earnest as he watched us with deep yellow-amber, almond-shaped eyes. The patch of white hair at the front of his hairline matched the snow perfectly, making it look like a chunk was missing in some sort of matrix glitch.

I gave a one-shouldered shrug. "I haven't seen any chips or other implants in any of my x-rays. These bracelets must be the only things they're using," I said. And I *did* look thoroughly. Tracking implants were one of the first concerns Will and I had, spawned from Will's theorist brain.

"Why wouldn't they take more precautions?" June inquired. "After everything they've done to make us what we are?"

"So you do want to leave then?" Michael questioned her.

June's brows furrowed, and she sat back. "Well, no, I never said that," she argued. "I'm just saying."

"I guess they aren't expecting us to be brave enough to try to fly across the ocean," I offered, ever the optimist. I sighed and leaned back against the packed dirt wall. "Eh, who am I kidding? Who knows, honestly."

Anna was looking thoughtful and tapped her fingers against her knees. "You might be right," she said hesitantly. "I mean, no way would they put anything in place that would possibly hurt us, right?" She rolled her eyes. "Okay, besides sending us out here. But by their own hands, I doubt they would."

Some of my optimism was coming back to life. "It's not like they expect us to live at this base forever," I added. "We're only here to prepare to live in the rest of the world. At least, that's how they've made it sound."

"Maybe," Clara drew out, "we should trust in whatever process they have cooked up. Why not just stay and wait it out?"

Will huffed, seeming no longer able to hold back. "This isn't where we belong!" he said with intense conviction. "We shouldn't be holed up in some crazy underground base in freaking Iceland! I've been waiting long enough. I'm ready to go find my family."

Nobody really said anything after that. What else was there to say? We forced ourselves to eat something and settled down for the night.

I let my eyes fall closed again. This time, it wasn't the town I saw; it was Jody and Vixen. Will was right; we'd done enough waiting.

CHAPTER 28

Thankfully, nothing tried to sneak up and eat us over the course of the night. With varying levels of rest the next morning, we slung our packs back on and walked into the snow to take off. It was easy taking off from the sloping side of the mountain, and I tossed myself effortlessly into the air, rising steadily.

No matter what plans we each had cooking up in our minds, we seemed to have a general agreement that we would finish flying around the country. If we couldn't handle the distance or the sights here, flying home was only a pipe dream.

I circled around until everyone was up in the air, then the dozen of us started off toward the next town. I'd checked the map first thing in the morning while we all ate something, and I didn't need to check it again to know where we were going. It wasn't long before the next town came into view. In the east, the sun was breaking over the pristine landscape, filling the gray sky with deep yellows and reds. Despite the circumstances, it felt serene.

Before landing in the town, I didn't expect anything better than the first time around. However, I also hadn't expected it could be even worse.

An abandoned, chilly playground was filled with the remnants of children no older than ten. We saw a group of twenty-something rats feasting on the bones of a five-year-old and quickly moved on, though the odious *clip clip* of their teeth on the skull might never leave me. Some houses looked as if they'd been caught in a terrible fire, burned to a black crisp. Under a tree, in an area where the snow was less, a family picture lay half-buried under old soot. The skeleton hanging from that same tree was arguably more remorseful.

We didn't stick around for too long in any of the towns, but we DID go to all of them. All of them were empty; devoid of human life. The streets were owned by ghosts, the only things to touch their surfaces being the placid soft flakes from yesterday's flurry and the feet of those towns' murderers.

By the time I finally caught sight of the somewhat familiar fenced-in field miles ahead of us, to say we were deeply troubled would be an understatement. I know that, personally, I was greatly disturbed.

It was still light outside by the time we got back, though the light was quickly waning. There were two-dozen sets of footprints in the fresh snow, traveling all the way down the peninsula and through a locked gate, into the field. They must have been busy doing *something* while we were gone.

Feeling strange, we landed in the field and walked up to the doors, where several armed guards were waiting. They let us in without hesitation, like, 'hey, back from the store already?'

Bossy Bob was waiting inside the moment we entered. He scanned us with his ever-watchful eyes. "Now you know," he said. "It's mandatory for all units to go through this experience. I hope you've managed to take something away from it."

We glanced around at each other, sharing similar looks. It was evident that we were all thinking along the same lines: Can we just smack this guy?

Maybe if I wasn't feeling so disordered from our recent experience, I would have put more thought into what he meant by *"all units."* I found out soon enough though. Our group went down the endless stairs to go shower, sleep, stare at the walls, whatever, when at the doorway to the farming level, I caught sight of strangers hanging out under our tree across the distance.

"Who are *they*?" Adler irked, halting in his steps beside me.

"I'd like to know the same thing," I murmured. I stopped to stare at them, still feeling too numb to fully care.

We kept walking, but the closer we got to these

strangers, the more confused I was. Were my eyes lying to me? Ah, I knew it! The horrific scenes at those towns were finally getting to me.

"What the hell...?" Ronin muttered.

Okay, so it wasn't a fluke that I was seeing things.

Heads below the tree turned to watch as we walked by. Ears pricked to listen. Yes, *ears pricked. Literally.* All of these people, over twenty in total, had furry ears at the sides of their heads where their human ears should have been. They ranged in color and size, and even shape if I wanted to look that close, but they were there nonetheless.

"Suddenly I don't feel so weird having wings," Will said. I could only agree.

It was then that I noticed that furry ears weren't the only strange part about these people. They all had *tails* as well. Half of them also had nails that looked too sharp to be human, and all of them had peculiar eyes that made it uncomfortable to look at them for too long.

"Let's just deal with one thing at a time," I said. Some of my group were giving these strangers hard looks, but reluctantly abided by my words. "Come on, guys," I sighed. "I dunno about you, but I could use a shower."

"Yeah, fine," Ronin said. "I'm still gonna go give them a word after."

I started opening my mouth, then realized I didn't really care enough and let it fall shut.

Flying around Iceland didn't take as long as I thought it would, which was good. Now we'd have extra rations to last us during our flight to America.

We all left our bracelets outside of the office, in a basket purposefully labeled "UNIT 3 MISSION ITEMS," and I placed the map and radio with them. We took showers, changed into clean clothes, and brushed our teeth extra well. Showers: one thing I would miss about this place. Our dirty clothes got tossed into wash machines, our packs got tossed into our rooms, and we headed upstairs for dinner.

When we exited our quarters, those other Hybrids were no longer under the tree. For a relieving moment I thought maybe they had been part of my imagination, but nope. When we got up to the cafeteria, there they were, chatting and jostling.

The cafeteria felt much livelier now, making the cavernous space make more practical sense. Even so, there was still so much space left. It made me wonder if there weren't more Hybrids in waiting. The thought somehow made me feel nauseous.

Our unit took our seats at our usual table, which, unlike the tree, had not been taken over. I had to look over my shoulder to see any of them properly, so I mainly just listened. The food came, and I eavesdropped on their conversations while I ate.

So here's what I learned... They'd all been on the same mission as us. They'd just left a lot earlier, right before we woke up, and had gotten back a lot later. It made sense though. I mean, comparing my group, which typically flew at a steady pace of a hundred miles per hour, to theirs, which likely traveled around three or four miles per hour, maybe five at a jog… It made sense, no? I was just having a hard time imagining how they dealt with the altered animals they'd come across, like that crazy dog.

When they talked, I tended to hear animal-like variations to their voices. Pretty sure a normal human's laugh didn't also sound a bit like a snarl, for example. I could hear some of their tails scrapping softly against the ground, while others didn't touch it at all. Since they were also separated into two tables, I had the suspicion that this was really two units and not just one giant unit.

Would the weirdness ever end???

"Hey, birdkids," someone called from behind me.

"What do *they* want?" Will grumbled under his breath. He was looking past me at their table with a dissatisfied expression.

I didn't want to at first, but I turned to the side to look at the Hybrid that'd spoken up, with a no-nonsense glare.

The half-cocked grin on his face faded when he met my eyes. Sometimes I still scared *myself* in the mirror, so I can only imagine how this guy felt under my cold, glowing gaze.

The guy next to him, with unruly dark hair and tall,

dark ears, shoved his shoulder. "How come we haven't seen you before? How long ago did you wake up?" this handsome stranger asked. His piercing yellow eyes were trained on me.

I didn't really care to answer him, but said, "About a month ago."

Michael also turned to look at them, his elbow grazing mine on the edge of the table. "How about you guys? When'd you wake up?" he asked.

The wolf-like man shifted his eyes to Michael. "We were in the tanks for seven and a half months."

Over two months less than we were? I shared a glance with Michael.

"That long, huh?" Michael asked absently.

CHAPTER 29

Only seven and a half months. It kind of made sense… They had a lot less that needed to grow, I guess.

Honestly, I was still a little caught up on the fact that there were more units living in the base. I felt stupid for not realizing it sooner: *Unit 3*, emphasis on the THREE. I don't know why, but I suppose I just assumed we were part of some greater list of birdkids in bases everywhere. It hadn't occurred to me that maybe they'd numbered the units *in this specific base.*

I was also definitely not expecting there to be people hybridized with species besides avian types.

"What're you hybridized with?" I asked, examining the people sitting at their table and those behind them.

"Me? Wolf," the dark-haired lad laughed with an arrogant huff. "Our unit? Canines." He jerked his chin at the table behind him. "They're the felines."

A girl sitting next to him, with almost white hair and

white ears to match, flicked her appealing beigey-yellow eyes over us. "And you're obviously hybridized with birds," she said, her voice light and airy.

"Gee, what gave it away?" I asked with dull sarcasm.

The girl laughed lightly, exposing pointed canines. When the boy beside her looked at her, his eyes crinkled faintly at the corners.

"So what's it like?" the canine Hybrid, who I'd first turned around to glare at, spoke up. He had dark red-chocolate hair, with even darker ears turned toward us curiously.

"What's what like?" I asked.

He rolled his eyes. "Flying, of course."

I actually considered it, though it felt odd sharing my experiences as a Hybrid with another Hybrid. Just another kid experimented on against his will. "Freeing, and powerful. There's nothing like it," I answered, feeling nostalgic for the feel of the breeze in my feathers already.

"Mmm," he murmured, as if reminiscing. "Awesome. Definitely better than tails, ha. Incredible balance, sure, but still not as cool."

I laughed unsurely before turning back around to finish my food. This was way too weird, even for me. I was sure I'd wake up from this dream at any moment. When we finally got up and headed back downstairs, I was relieved. But when the other two units were close to follow, I once again was made uneasy.

The number of footsteps echoing in the stairway tripled, making my head feel cluttered. I practically burst through the doorway to the farming level and tossed my wings out the moment my feet touched the concrete pathway.

"Hey, where ya going?" Will called after me.

I had to get my head cleared. No way could this be my new reality. A world where the human species was on the road to extinction and Hybrids existed, not just avian-types, but *all* types.

I gravitated to the towering tree. I don't know why. I guess us avian-types just really liked trees.

With skillful tilts of my wings and a watchful eye, I navigated through the huge, twisty branches. Soft, for-ward flaps allowed me to land carefully upon a top-notch perch only fifteen feet from the ceiling. I balanced easily as I began walking steadily up and down the branch, thinking.

The soft scrapping of large feathers got closer. Will landed within the tree canopy, his wings stirring up a breeze. I pulled a curl from my cheek as Will tucked his wings in neatly behind him.

He stepped toward me and reached a hand up to a smaller branch above him. Will stood there in an easy-going manner, watching me pace thoughtfully.

My eyes flicked over him, then I turned and walked the other way again. Since when was he so calm? When I first met him, his bouncing foot seemed to be running on never-dying batteries.

"What're you doing?" he asked.

"I'm thinking," I stated. I reached the middle of the tree and turned, walking lightly back toward Will.

The ruckus caused by the three separate groups made me look through the cracks in the wide, oblong tree leaves at them. Units 1 and 2 were headed through the field of crops, along a narrow dirt path. The rest of Unit 3, my glorious winged group, started taking off to the air, undoubtedly to join us in the tree. The canine and feline Hybrids turned to watch as the birdkids flapped and soared over the crops.

It was a spectacular sight, truly, to see them flying so gracefully and powerfully. The first week, we'd all looked like gigantic, clumsy raptors, but now there was a certain natural grace about each and every one of us. Somehow, it looked *right*. When I was flying, it also felt right. The thought of waking up from stasis to be hybridized with something other than a bird made me shudder.

Will only took his eyes off me when our group started landing in the tree near us. Samuel and Aubrey landed on our branch, causing it to sway ever so slightly beneath my feet.

While the top of the tree was being filled with birdkids and the sound of their wings, I looked over the field at the other two units. They went up to neighboring doorways similar to the entrance of our quarters, but the walls beside them didn't have any fancy glass panels. I never saw the farmers using those entrances, now that I thought about it. It never occurred to me until now that they were additional quarters.

"Mahogany Meeting?" Adler offered.

I turned my attention back to those of us in the tree. A Mahogany Meeting was just a cute name we came up with for a serious group meeting. "Which part of today's events did you wanna talk about?" I asked sardonically, sitting down on the branch with my legs hanging over one side, my wings over the other.

"How about all of it," Ronin huffed. "Can we maybe start with the part where there are other Hybrids? Or maybe jump straight into how we're gonna *bail* from this place."

Michael, crouched agilely on a branch across from me, with his arms resting over his knees in a comfortable manner, tossed the fingers of his right hand in a dismissive gesture. "Let's not start with the other Hybrids," he said, sounding tired of it all. "There's another day to mull over how messed up all this is."

"Escape plan it is then," Iver said, somehow able to pull off a joyful countenance.

Will came over and nudged my leg with his toes. "I know you have a plan already," he said. "What is it?"

I looked over our group. There was a restless, apprehensive air among us.

"We leave tomorrow, during our morning flight," I said, keeping my voice low. "They shouldn't expect anything is amiss if we're already out flying over the water."

There were nods of approval around the group.

"So soon?" June asked, her eyes wide.

"You can still come with us, you know," I induced after a moment. She busied herself with picking off bark pieces beside her left leg. "You have tonight to think about it," I said. "Let me know your final decision tomorrow morning."

June nodded without looking at me.

"You too, Elena," I added, shifting my eyes to the girl sitting behind everyone else.

Elena didn't respond. I'd have to keep my eye on her... Something about her just wasn't sitting right with me. Call it paranoid intuition.

We stayed in the tree a while longer, discussing various matters. Forty minutes later, we had a loose plan in place for tomorrow and the days thereafter. We'd fly across the Denmark Strait to Greenland, where we'd take a breather, then jump over the Davis Strait to Canada. Each strait was about as wide as Iceland was from coast to coast, so it was doable. Once in America, we'd hit the closest homes and move outward from there. Hopefully there'd be some clues as to where to go from that point on.

Finally, we went to our quarters, splitting off for the night.

The night proved to be a restless one. I couldn't stop

tossing and turning, which was made a struggle in itself by the sail-like wings folded against my back.

When I finally drifted off to sleep, it wasn't long before the soft padding of feet outside my door woke me up. I'd always been a light sleeper, but it was ridiculous now.

My eyes opened, alertness washing over me, and I rolled to face the door. A shadow passed through the dim blue light peeking under my door, reflecting in my glowing irises. The padding continued down the hallway, toward the exit. Wariness spread through me, making the speckled gold and brown feathers along my hairline prick. I got up and quietly went to my door. My hand paused an inch from the handle as I listened. I couldn't hear anyone in the hallway anymore.

I cracked my door open as slowly as I could and peered through. Still nothing. I slipped out of my room, easing the door shut behind me, and trailed after them with footsteps lighter than that of a mouse. I crouched low at the wide, open doorway and peered around the side. Always go low when looking around any wall or doorway; never look from the level they'd expect someone to peer around an edge from.

The person who'd left must have flown to the stairwell, for I only caught a glimpse of their feathers disappearing through a closing door some two-hundred feet away. Brown with a heavy pattern. That's all I got. It was enough though.

My curled fist made a dull sound as I hit it upon the wall beside me. I cursed under my breath. No way could this be good.

CHAPTER 30

I didn't get any sleep after sneaking out. There wasn't a clock in my room, but the change in lighting outside the glass wall told me only an hour had passed since then. I swung out of bed, took a moment to brush my teeth at the small metal sink, then shoved everything into my pack and headed out of my room.

I went down the row of rooms and rapped my knuckles against each door. "Up and at 'em!" I called.

Groggy voices, ruffled sheets, and shuffling feet sounded from inside the rooms. I did the same to those three rooms before mine as well, then waited patiently for everyone to show up despite my growing unease.

One by one, tired birdkids emerged from their rooms, their packs slung over one shoulder or dragging against the ground in their hand. Bringing our packs outside with us was not uncommon. We usually just brought them for the water, however, but no one should think anything strange of it.

"Morning already?" Will asked as he shuffled down the hall to me, rubbing the sleep out of his eyes. Seemed no one got a good sleep last night.

"Unfortunately, yes," I said. Eyeing his bedraggled hair and the messy feathers along his chest, I couldn't take it anymore and reached out to fix at least one problem for him.

He yawned and didn't stop me.

"You're a mess," I said. "Did you pack everything you need?"

"Uh-huh."

"Alright."

No matter how I tried to fix his soft, feathered hair, one curled tendril refused to listen. I gave up and looked past him at the gathering birdkids, most of which wandered into the bathrooms. A couple more trickled out from their rooms. If my count was correct, there was still one of us missing. Of course, I never heard anyone come back in the past hour of no sleep. And by 'anyone,' I mean — who else — Elena.

We've gotta move, I thought anxiously. I had no idea where she went, and now that she remained unseen, it only made my misgivings that much more prominent.

Our flight trainer appeared at the entrance right as the last person was coming out of the bathrooms. "Oh, you're all up already," he said as he halted in the entryway, sounding somewhat surprised. "Good." He peered down the hall as if checking that we really were all awake, then turned and said, "Let's get going then!"

A poor check on his part. Unless...he knew something?

With the group looking overall more awake now, however slight, and everyone's packs situated between their wings, we followed the trainer up the endless stairs. At the top floor, we paused outside the gates to freedom, and I watched as the trainer placed his rough hand on the foot-long panel beside the right door. My enlarged heart was beating hard in my chest. *Just open.*

The panel beeped and turned blue. A suspenseful moment later, the heavy doors cracked open with a hiss. Ignoring the guards, the trainer stepped aside and we piled out. The trainer gave a nod to one of the guards, and he leaned toward the panel and placed his hand upon it. Just as the stout doors began to recede, I heard heavy boots racing up the stairs, Bossy Bob's ever familiar voice calling out for the guards to not let us out.

Iver and I glanced at each other in the same moment. We'd both heard it.

"Up up up!" I shouted, urging the group forward with my open wings.

"Wha'?" Ronin indignantly shoved my wing away, but his fingers did nothing against my thick feathers.

"Up now!" Iver concurred, sprinting forward. He tossed himself into the air a second later, bringing his white and black wings down hard over several peoples' heads.

The group was spurred into motion, all remaining sleep leaving their expressions.

"Don't let them leave!" I heard Bob yelling, some two flights of stairs down.

Too late.

We flapped into the air, knowing this was now our only chance. Amidst the rush of adrenaline, I distinctly noticed June in the flock of fleeing birdkids. Seemed she made a decision after all.

The flight trainer seemed startled, turning between his students flying away and the heavy doors which were being reopened. I guess he hadn't known anything after all, by the alarmed expression on his face.

As we flew over the field, passing over the barbed wire fence, I heard Bob burst through onto the grass. I looked back to see him staring after us, enraged and somewhat worried. To my surprise, he ordered the guards to fire tranqs.

Just as the guards were loading their guns and taking position on the field, I saw none other than Elena run out onto the grass behind Bob. The regret and fear etched into her face was my last glimpse of the base before turning forward and flying away with all my might.

The click and snap of loaded guns hit my ears like a pin dropping in a still room. They couldn't fire from *that* far away, right…?

A trigger was squeezed, and seconds later, a pointed

object whizzed by some twenty feet to my left. My eyes expanded.

"They're shooting at us!" I yelled.

I didn't need to see the panic or determination in my group's eyes — I could hear the change in their already brisk breathing. Two more triggers were pulled, and I heard the darts travel through the air. I rushed down and threw my right wing down at the ground, causing me to curve in the air. At that very same instant, a shiny dart hit my durable feathers and ricocheted.

Will looked over his shoulder at me as I curved back around, his mouth agape with the realization he'd been *this close.*

My steady gaze conveyed to him that it was alright, and to keep moving. He looked forward and kept going, and I reached around the creamy buttermilk underside of my wing to feel my lower back, near my right side. There was a stinging sensation in a very localized point, but there was nothing there.

Another dart flew by below us, narrowly missing Anna. Then another, and another. How were they able to aim so relatively well??

My flaps became lethargic, my movements unbalanced. Normally it was very easy to breathe, more so than for a normal person, but now it felt as if my lungs had evaporated, my breaths coming out as shallow pants.

"You guys?" I called, my voice sounding distant and weak in my ears.

Soon I couldn't even feel my wings, and I fought my hazing vision, coming in and out of focus. I shook my head to clear the cotton, but my eyelids had started to droop.

Despite the lax wave flowing over me, my heart felt incredibly tight in my chest, panic racing through my mind. The only thing to quell the panic was a curtain of darkness, falling over me, diminishing any conceivable thought I may have.

Goodnight, world.

CHAPTER 31

Within the darkness, I could feel the time pass. Light would filter in through my cracked eyelids, looking like shiny, translucent rays past my dark lashes.

Someone was above me. I could *feel* them. When I caught a hazy glimpse of the world, it was all blue. But above me, there was a strong warmth. And wrapped around me, over the limp edges of my wings and around my chest, was that same staunch warmth.

I faded away again, and it felt like hours upon hours had passed by the time my eyes fluttered open again, my eyelids feeling like chainmail.

The landscape was unfamiliar, and even the air felt different. My senses started coming back to me, and I noticed the sun was closing in on the horizon already, illuminating the lower sky a fiery red. Nearly a whole day had passed?

"Where are we?" I slurred. I tried to sit up, making

me groan. Ugh, it felt like I'd been back in stasis. Rough grass dug into my palms, helping me to sober up.

A firm hand steadied me, coming around to my back over my soft scapular feathers. Michael was there beside me, helping me up. Had he been there all along?

"Somewhere in southwestern Greenland," Michael said with a small shrug, as if our location was the least of his concerns. A smile tugged at his mouth, his eyes lighting up with relief. "Here." He lifted a water canister up to my mouth.

I took it in one hand and sipped on it, but I couldn't drink much and handed it back soon after. My eyes kept shifting to Michael. He wouldn't stop looking at me like that — like if he took his eyes off me for one moment, I'd evaporate into dust.

I ran my hands down my face, trying to clear the grogginess. It was coming back to me now. "They tranqed me, didn't they?" I sighed. I passed my tired eyes over most of the group, who were gathering around me. "You guys carried me?"

"Well, Michael did," Iver said sheepishly. "I'm glad you're awake. You really gave us a scare, ya know."

I was both embarrassed and deeply touched. My eyes fell on Michael, his striking features washed in blue by the nautical twilight. "You carried me the whole way here?" I asked curiously, feeling my cheeks involuntarily heat up.

With his hand not supporting me, he reached up and

gingerly swept a curl away from my face, making my breath catch quietly. "Of course. I'd never leave you," he said. His voice was calm and deep, and it sent shivers down my spine.

Help me now, I thought, feeling the need to gulp.

"He was the only one fast enough to reach you, at the base," Clara informed earnestly, tugging on a lock of her long hair distressingly.

I didn't know what to say to that. So, basically…if there wasn't a good-hearted Peregrine Hybrid within our group, I could have ended up as a birdkid pancake? My body felt tense all of a sudden.

"How do you feel? You've been out for a while," Will said. I turned my attention gratefully toward him, glad for a distraction.

"Alright, I think," I replied. Will looked rather coy, keeping his distance. That was enough about me though. I got to my feet, my wings sliding against the ground as they came up with me.

A dizzy spell washed over me, and I stumbled. Michael caught me with strong, sure arms, his brows drawn in as if his fears had come true. I took a deep breath, clearing the fog from my head.

"I'm good," I said, releasing my tight grip on Michael's forearm. I felt embarrassed for a second time.

"You sure?" he worried, looking over me, uncon-vinced.

"Yeah." I stepped forward by myself, up to a small

ledge jutting out from the sloping, grassy hillside.

The scene before me, lain out to the southeast, was even more beautiful than anything I'd seen in Iceland; beautiful enough to take any bad feelings from my chest. I drew in a breath at the turquoise waters sparkling under a velvet blue sky littered with only the brightest stars, at the mountains dipping and spiking powerfully behind them. A massive lake, extending outward on both sides by miles, sat nestled at the bottom of a burgundy and light green grassy plain, framed in the distance by a mighty mountain range. I'd never seen anything quite so literally breathtaking.

"Rory," Will started, "I'm sorry. I'm so sorry."

I tore my gaze from the peaceful scene to look at Will. "What? What for?" I asked, feeling a little startled.

Will shuffled uncomfortably, and the others threw sorrowful glances at him. He stepped toward me, and in only a few wide strides was standing before me. I had to tilt my head up now to look him in the eyes, which took on an unusual lavender tint in the twilight. He grasped my right hand in his like a pleading man, worry and guilt etched into his features. I'd never seen him like this before and could only watch him without words.

"If it wasn't for me, you wouldn't have gotten hit. You were only in its path because you were protecting me," he divulged. "You — you almost died! If —"

"Hey," I soothed, taking my hand out of Will's grasp to plant both of my hands on his shoulders. "I didn't though, okay? I'm alright." I pursed my lips, feeling bad for him. "I'd still do it again in an instant. Don't feel sorry."

He lowered his gaze and nodded smally after a while. "Yeah," he responded quietly.

I patted his right shoulder, over the small black and tan feathers there. Letting my hands fall away, I took in the rest of the group.

"Is everything else alright?" I asked them. "Obviously, Elena..." I let my words fall short, a sour feeling surfacing.

"She betrayed us, plain and simple," Ronin spat. "She couldn't handle leaving, so she tried to ruin it for all of us."

Samuel opened his mouth, looking to object on some level.

"What," Ronin spurred, "you're gonna say she was scared? We were all faced with a choice, and she made hers."

"She's just..." Samuel made an attempt anyway. He didn't finish his sentence, however. A doubtful frown cast the corners of his mouth downward.

"Tame it down, Ronin," I sighed, feeling too tired to deal with him. "It's not Samuel's fault."

Ronin crossed his arms over his well-toned, light bronze chest. His wide, hawk-like wings twitched irritably behind him.

Getting to serious matters, I rubbed my aching

temples and asked, "Do you know if we were followed? Any drones or whatever else they might cook up?" Never knew with these crazy scientist types.

"Haven't seen or heard anything," Michael said, looking all 'down-to-business.' "We checked our packs, too, just in case someone managed to slip in any trackers or something. Everything's clear."

"That's good," I said, thinking. "We shouldn't stay here too long." I looked west, along the side of the long, sloping hill we were on. Smaller mountains blocked my view, but I knew the Davis Strait should be in the distance somewhere in front of me, if they followed the correct course while I was, eh, out for the count. "Any troubles staying on course?" I asked no one in particular.

"No, we'll be heading to Canada next," Michael said pleasantly.

I glanced at him. I wondered how much my incapacitation slowed them down, but I wasn't planning on asking. "Okay. How long have you all been resting here then?"

Michael didn't seem to have an answer, which was odd. "Less than an hour," June answered for him.

Michael's brows furrowed slightly, and he looked down the hill. I saw a muscle in his jaw twitch. I couldn't tell if he was upset at himself for something, or if it was some form of worry seeping through.

Trying not to think too much into Michael at the moment, I did some quick math. Flying across the

Denmark Strait should have taken four to five hours. If we were near the lake-filled eastern side of Greenland, that was easily another five or so hours of flying time. Seeing as how close the sun was to the horizon, however, having to carry me indeed slowed them down by an hour or two. I cursed myself for getting hit, but there wasn't much I could do about it now.

The Davis Strait would take an additional four to five hours. There's no way we'd make it to Canada before nighttime really set in, and only three of us had night vision. Well, *two* of us now...

"Alright, well, night shouldn't stick around for too long so far north, but it sounds like you guys deserve a break," I said. "I'll keep watch while you all rest, and wake you up when it's light again."

This sounded like a decent and fair plan to everyone, and after a bout of approval, they found places to rest some thirty feet up the sloping hill, near a cluster of lichen-covered boulders. It was only then that I realized all of our packs were also up there, including mine. I'd totally forgotten about it. Will looked after me hesitantly. I gave him a reassuring nod, and only then did he reluctantly go off to rest with the others.

I brought my hands up to my upper arms in a manner reassuring to myself, feeling odd, but also satisfied. We were really doing it — we *had* been doing it. Michael slanted his obsidian eyes over to me, looking at me under thoughtfully handsome brows, his head still tilted slightly toward the ground behind him where the others were settling down.

My eyes flicked away from him, and I turned around to face the lake, walking gently to the edge of the short outcrop. Behind me, footsteps approached through the rough grass. Michael came up to my right side in silence, standing only half a foot away, our wings nearly grazing each other. Soft blue light illuminated the two of us standing there side by side.

"Thank you, by the way," I spoke softly.

Michael didn't respond immediately. He looked over at me with shadowed eyes. "Just try not to get shot again, okay?" he asked a bit coolly.

A comment like that normally would have made me chuckle, but Michael's tone made me pause instead. He looked back out over the lake with a reserved expression, and I was left to examine his chiseled side view, which looked softer in the twilight.

I wouldn't misplace his frustration. I knew he wasn't actually mad at me, but rather, it spawned from a place of fear.

"Yeah, I'll try not to," I practically whispered, still watching him. After another long moment, I sighed and turned to look forward as well, rubbing my arms, feeling chilly even though it shouldn't have been possible.

My eyes were skipping absently across the twinkling lake, when suddenly, a firm hand found its way to my left cheek. I was pulled around, and for a moment our gazes met, searching each other's eyes, his much more forth-right, and then he leaned in, his mouth pressing to mine with all the warmth in the world. When I didn't resist, his other hand came up to cradle my head as well, his finger-tips seeping into my curly hair.

At first I was startled, but then I began to melt into his warmth, his unsuppressed passion. I hadn't realized how much I wanted this; not fully. I brought my own hands up his firm chest, skimming his small, soft feath-ers. My fingers found their way into the base of his wild black hair, and I pulled him closer.

I felt him heat up from my total abandonment of inhibition. We tilted our heads the other way and kissed each other more deeply, sending an oddly peaceful sense washing through me. His hands traveled intimately down my sides and around to my back between my wings, pressing me to him, making me fold into him like delicate silk.

Oh geez. This is happening. This was... It was amazing. We were in total sync, our kisses a dance with no routine, falling into a hungry passion beneath the twilight.

My mind went blank kissing him in the middle of an empty landscape. By the time our actions turned gentler, I was only thinking of him. His wings had curled around us both, my wingtips curving around his legs. Breathing more heavily, his lips touched mine — not a kiss, just a brush of lips against each other, but it was enough; it was more than enough. I wanted him, his heat, his passion, and leaned forward to capture him once more. But of course, I heard jibbing coming from the boulders higher up the low-incline hill.

I broke apart from him, our wings gradually sliding away from one another, and cast a fruitless glance at the birdkids watching us from a distance. Michael looked over as well, letting his hands drop down to my waist, his fingers gentle but firm against my bare skin.

He laughed quietly, coming out more as a light huff, the corners of his lips, reddened from our kisses, curled into a smile. "Seems we have an audience," he murmured teasingly.

"Seems so." I brought my right hand up to his sharp, smooth jawline and turned his head back to me. I pulled him back in and kissed him again.

CHAPTER 32

Michael stayed out on the ledge with me while the others slept. We sat on the exposed stone side by side, our legs hanging off its edge comfortably. I swung my feet absently, keeping watch over the landscape.

Michael yawned beside me.

I glanced at him quickly, not wanting to take my eyes off my surroundings for too long. "You should sleep. If anyone should rest, it should be you," I said. Flying all day was tiring in itself, but carrying someone else the whole way with you?

"Well… Okay," he obliged after a moment of hesitation. He lay back on the slab of stone, leaving his calves dangling off the side of the ledge. "Wake me if anything happens," he said, folding his arms under his head.

I snuck another glance at him. With his arms like that, it attractively displayed his muscles, and I was immediately brought back to our intimate actions.

Chewing my lower lip to quell my desires, I forced myself to continue scanning the hills and mountains.

◆ ◆ ◆

Have you ever performed a stakeout? No? Well, I don't know about other people, but this felt an awful lot like a stakeout, and I figured I liked it.

I have no problem being still for hours, in both body and mind. In fact, I was rather enjoying it. It was extremely peaceful out here, with only the sounds of the gentle breeze coursing through the scraggly grasses and the light snoring of my group, and for the first time in a month (wait, technically eleven months?), I got to see the stars, totally unobstructed.

The world was in a permanent state of twilight. Astronomical twilight for the past several hours, but twilight nonetheless. The sky was a canvas of deep gray-blues and violets, splashed with diamonds. Unfortunately, my excellent raptor vision still did not allow me to see Messiers in great detail as a telescope might. They were still very cool-looking, though, scattered among the densely packed stars as random bursts of color.

What's it like looking at the stars with night vision, you ask? The same as with normal vision, really, but a lot brighter; maybe three times brighter. The plains and mountains were also brightly illuminated in my eyes, though I could only see so deep into the lake waters. A light breeze created ripples in the lake, and so much light was being reflected off its surface that it looked solid.

Very beautiful though.

While admiring the glowing lake, something off in the left corner of my vision made me turn my head, my mind snapping to attention. When I didn't see anything, I thought maybe I'd imagined it, but then a little furry head popped up above the scraggly grasses.

I sat very still, watching the creature as he traveled over the hills some five-hundred meters to my left. I saw his every detail very clearly across the distance. You didn't need to be an animal expert to know that this was an Arctic fox, decked out in his springtime grey-brown and beige coat.

Rounded white ears swiveled about, and brown eyes were on a constant move, zipping around. He jogged briskly through the burgundy grasses, up and down slopes neighboring the lake. More importantly, he was jogging *this way*. It had only been a matter of time when his ears stopped swiveling, fixed in my general direction. I saw him train his eyes off to a spot behind me, and my breathing paled.

He picked up the pace, galloping through the grass directly toward those sleeping among the boulders higher up the hill.

Okay, you're asking for it, I growled internally, jumping up stealthily. He showed no intention of stopping. I tossed myself from the ledge and unfurled my wings. I gave them a few minimal flaps, floating down the hillside, then curved left.

The fox saw my furtive form gliding soundlessly straight at him one second too late. I angled sharply and dove down upon him with killing intent. With precision only possible through hours of training, I brought the hard edge of my right wing down upon his neck in a hard, swift motion, effectively silencing the creature with a cold *snap*. Straightening, I let out a slow breath and frowned at the limp animal.

Droll dripped from his open mouth full of sharp teeth. We'd learned about Arctic foxes at the base. They'd evolved to be venomous. One bite from this little critter, and anyone in the group could have been in serious trouble.

I flicked my wing feathers, shaking them out to release any built-up tension. Without a second glance, I turned and jumped back into the air, landing just as silently as I'd left on the stony ledge. I eased back down, resuming my watchful position.

◆ ◆ ◆

When daylight finally returned, casting a pink glow over the landscape, everyone was none the wiser of what could have become of them.

I'd been sitting here near motionless for so long that a light dew had collected on my delicate, feather-like hairs. I stood up with a groan and stretched, bringing my arms above my head, my wings following them up as if attached to strings. Letting my arms fall back down, my wings leveled out, but I left them fully spread open above

the ground. The first rays of daylight warmed the undersides of my feathers pleasantly on this chilly hill, and I let
my eyes fall shut as I soaked it up.

"You're beautiful." A deep, silky voice, husky from
sleep, reached my ears, making me smile.

I opened my eyes and turned to look at Michael,
where he'd propped himself up on the stone, his amorous
gaze flicking up from its lustful wandering, meeting my
eyes. Folding my warmed wings back in, I asked, "Sleep
well?"

"Surprising well," he said. He sat up and ran a hand
through his dark, messy hair. Tendrils fell back across his
forehead despite his efforts, though it looked very attractive. "Did all go silently through the night?"

The corner of my mouth flicked higher up. "You
stayed asleep, didn't you?"

"Hmm. Fair enough."

"I'm gonna go wake the others up," I said. I lightly
ruffled his already-messy, jet-black hair as I walked past
him into the grass, making him grunt as his futile efforts
were affectionately sabotaged. I trudged up the hill to a
cluster of boulders, the tallest boulder coming up to my
hip. I began lovingly nudging awake the group members
closest to me with my toes. "Up and at 'em. Day again."
Some of them needed a shake to wake up.

"Wha'?" Adler mumbled sleepily, raising his head to
look around in confusion. His silvery eyes focused on
me, and he set his head back down with a sigh.

"Five more minutes," Samuel slurred, his arms hugging the pack beneath his head of blond hair.

I walked through the birdkids, picking up my pack as I went, and whapped Samuel with a wing.

"Ah!" He startled, jolting upright. He looked around in alarm, then his eyes fell upon me, and his face twisted up sourly. At least he looked awake now.

"Get up," I said, then flapped up to a nearby, lichen-covered boulder.

"How long were we asleep for?" Aubrey yawned. When she sat up, her golden-blonde hair stuck up in random places.

I stifled a chuckle and shrugged. "Six, seven, eight hours?" You tend to lose track of time when being still for so long.

"Mm." She nodded along.

"We'll leave in fifteen," I said. With that, I jumped into the air again and glided down past the ledge to the lake with my pack.

Using the fresh, turquoise water, I washed my face and filled my water canister to the brim. I purposely took a very small sip of water, knowing I wouldn't get the chance to go to the bathroom for a while. I went ahead and stuffed a portion of food into my mouth before brushing my teeth, then walked back up the hill.

Everyone was awake and getting ready. After eating a portion from their own packs, they, too, went down to the lake to brush their teeth and fill their canisters. It wasn't long before everyone had done whatever they needed to and we were all ready to leave.

The last few clipped their packs, and we went up the hill together. It didn't take long for the sun to appear completely over the horizon, warming a clear sky. A good day for flying.

We took to the air, knowing our feet wouldn't touch ground again for hours. Reaching a decent altitude, we flew at a steady pace of around a hundred miles per hour. A stray, strong oceanic wind occasionally added an additional fifty miles per hour to our speed. None of us talked for the first good while, and soon we were flying out over the ocean, only intermediate flapping to fill our ears.

Michael flew beside me, some thirty meters above the others. His wingtips sometimes touched mine on the downstrokes, and electricity jolted up my wing each time.

I had no regrets about what happened the other night. Well, except for maybe one, but I'm not sure it counted. Will was acting strangely around me now, avoiding my gaze and such. I watched him coasting below with squinted eyes, as if staring at him long enough would give me all the answers to the riddle that was Will.

Aubrey flapped over to him while I was watching him. He wasn't so awkward with her, and she got him into a conversation pretty quick. You save a guy, *twice*, and still get less from him than Aubrey.

Okay, so I'm not dumb. I know there was a decent

possibility that I was growing to be more than a friend in Will's eyes. But this was not a reverse harem situation, people. I would be taking only *one* man. Granted, he'd never outright said or tried anything that went past friendship, but there was a certain look in his eyes every now and then... Nothing in particular would spark it; I'd just catch him with an enamored discretion about himself before he'd look away and continue on as normal as if it had only been my imagination.

I hit a warm gust of air and coasted leisurely, taking my gaze off Will and relaxing into the breeze. Hickory curls streamed behind me as the air buoyed my wings, carrying me effortlessly.

"There's really nothing better," Michael said, reading my mind. I looked past my left wing at him, my long, golden wingtips curling gracefully against the wind, to see him smiling at me.

"There really isn't," I agreed with a grin.

If there was ever a perk to being stolen from your family and being genetically altered without your consent, it was being able to fly. Whether or not it made up for it was another question I refused to consider.

I won't get into the long journey across the ocean. It was mostly a lot of soaring, watching the endless waves, and avoiding the rare seabird. We were lucky to not run into any bad weather, only the occasional zealous wind pressing us in the wrong direction.

The sun was making its way high into the sky by the

time land finally came into view miles away. Our group shared excited and nervous looks, and the lot of us poured on the speed.

A rugged, mountainous landscape rose up immediately from the ocean. We coasted along the broken shore, thoroughly inspecting it before descending upon the base of a snow-capped mountain range, beside a wide waterway cutting into the land. The ground here wasn't flat, but rather was a slope of grass transitioning into sand and worn, light-colored pebbles.

I left my wings slightly agape to allow the heat from exercise to dissipate as I looked around from the ground. A last few flapped down around me, landing along the sandy shore.

"We actually did it," June said in wonder, stepping tentatively through the sand with long, slim legs, gazing around at nothing in particular.

I nodded absently, feeling amazed myself. "Yeah. We flew to North America," I agreed. A grin spread across my face, a giddy feeling rising through me. *We actually made it!*

"Now what? We just fly south?" Clara asked. She laughed to herself. "Heh. South for spring? Makes no sense."

I chuckled at Clara's thoughts. "Don't question it," I teased.

"I guess we'll have to decide which states to hit first now," Michael said. "Since we're already on the east coast, I figure we should continue straight down before spreading west." He was speaking of cardinal plans, but he distractedly nudged a small, worn stone from its seated position near the top of the sandy embankment, watching it roll down toward the water, leaving a grooved line in its wake.

Ah, yes, the mission. I got my head in the game and considered it, watching the stone roll to the water's edge, stopping short of getting a nice soak by mere inches. Continuing east... That meant Virginia would be one of the first on the list. Why did I feel so nervous??

"So, just to be clear," Ronin said, "we *aren't* splitting up. Like, one group stays east while another goes west, then meet up later or something?"

"It's safer to stick together," June dismissed.

Ronin tightened his lips.

"I guess we've gotta know who lives along the east coast then," I spurred. "Will and I are in Virginia, so that'll kill two birds with one stone." I arched an eyebrow at myself when I realized what I'd just said, and coughed.

"I'd probably be first on the list," Anna said. "I'm from Portland, Maine."

Adler raised a hand at the elbow. "I used to live in New Jersey, near the middle of the state. Should be easy to find."

I looked around at them. "Anyone else on the coast?" When all I got was a few 'nope's and head shakes 'no,' I said, "Alright, so first is Anna, then Adler, then Will and I. Who's next?"

States were listed, plans were made. This was not going to be a short journey, but we didn't fly across the ocean for nothing.

CHAPTER 33

After a short rest, we got back in the air and skipped over a fifty-mile-wide waterway to the edge of the next peninsula, then continued following the coast south. Then we flew over *another* hundred miles of water before finally reaching a solid landmass. *To Maine we go!*

Let me tell you, that oak tree back at the base was not the only gigantic tree around. It was startling to see such towering forests as we got further south. Some plants seemed to have completely overtaken towns, only the rare and lonely roof peeking through as a sole reminder of what used to inhabit the land.

We eventually made it to Maine, outlined by a run-down port of entry border, mostly overtaken by dense vines and trees sprouting from the wide highways. The sun was threatening to close on the day as we flew down the state, but Anna didn't want to stop for the night yet. The whole group of us were sizzling with energy, and we forged onward, coasting beneath a blanket of clouds, those of us with raptor vision helping Anna to spot town names on rusting highway signs.

I heard Anna's breathing quicken and looked over at her. "There it is!" she pointed. "Right down there!"

I looked over the group, then rested my eyes on Michael. "You guys hang back. I'll go down with Anna," I said.

Michael gave me a nod and circled around, telling the others to stay in the air with him while Anna and I went down. Anna didn't waste a moment. She tucked her head in and brought her wings in closer, losing altitude the best a person with dove wings could. I sped after her, giving my wings a few good flaps and throwing myself downward, angling my own wings in closer. I gained on her rapidly and had to pull up a bit.

Anna flew straight down to the quiet city. She flapped her wings out fifty meters from the ground and shot around buildings. Anna's relatively little wings allowed her to make quick directional changes, but I held my own as I followed swiftly and silently after her, floating around buildings and lampposts.

She landed in an empty street and strode purposefully up to a five-story apartment building, her semi-curly, dark brown hair bouncing behind her. I coasted down to the street and tucked my wings in as she went by a wrecked car, sitting on its side on the sidewalk. I spun in a slow 360, scanning for danger, before walking up to the front of the building.

Anna was glaring at the doorknob. I could actually hear her heart beating in her chest as she fruitlessly punched in a code in a panel beside the door for a second time. It was dead. She tried to turn the knob, and when it still didn't open, she slammed her fist on the dull gray door.

She cursed desperately under her breath, turning from the door with her hands on her hips.

I stepped back and looked around, my observant gaze traveling up the side of the red and white brick building. My excellent eyes spotted the locks on the bay windows, all in the *locked* position. Couldn't get in that way. No balconies to slip in through either.

I sighed. "Step back," I told her, waving her away.

"Huh?" She looked after me with confusion, and I waved her away again. Anna stepped back unsurely.

Standing in front of the door, I took in a deep breath through my nose.

CRACK!

I slammed the bottom of my foot squarely against the door beside the handle, sending it swinging back against the inside wall. Little pieces of wooden door frame, where the bolt had been, went flying, clattering onto the cheaply tiled floor.

Anna sucked in a breath, then quickly rushed inside as if I wasn't there and her door hadn't just been kicked in.

I shrugged, keeping my shoulders loose, and walked in after her. She disappeared up a staircase as soon as I walked through the doorway, and I took a moment to peer around. Seemed quiet enough, though I was pretty sure I heard a scraping and squeaking in one of the rooms ahead of me. Wrinkling my nose in distrust, I went up the wooden stairs after Anna.

I heard her down the hallway shooting off from the third-story stairwell. Cautiously, I padded down the hall and hesitantly entered a room several doors down.

"Anna?" I called softly. I peered around the room. Drawers lay misshapen and items were scattered over the hardwood floor. Toy trucks and games lay forgotten near a window, the sight making my heart sink.

Walking further into the apartment, I spotted Anna in what looked to be the kitchen, raided as it was.

She plucked a dusty note from beneath a magnet on the fridge. Anna held it in both quivering hands, her delicate brows creased as her dual-colored eyes scanned whatever was written on it.

I went around to her side. Written on the square of creased paper, was a note telling someone named John that they were headed to a safe house. An address was scribbled beneath it.

Anna turned to me suddenly. "We have to go here," she impelled.

I opened my mouth to reasonably object, but hesitated. Looking past her, out of a small window set into the wall over the sink, I saw the light quickly waning. Anna didn't have night vision.

"It's not far from here," she insisted. She held up the note and urgently waved it around a bit. "I know where this is."

I eyed the paper skeptically. After a sad glance at Anna's desperate expression, I agreed. "Alright," I sighed.

Her eyes lit up, and she practically ran from the kitchen into the hallway. I tossed my eyes toward the ceiling, asking for help, then jogged after her.

We emerged back out onto the street, and the sun was no longer visible. Its only remnants were those bright orange patches on the gray-blue clouds slinking by above.

"Let's head back to the others first," I said. When she looked at me as if about to object, I explained. "It's getting dark. They should know what's going on. It'll only take a moment."

Anna let her mouth fall shut and came with me reluctantly. We flew out from the buildings and back up to those of our group still wheeling a thousand meters up. Michael dropped down a few hundred meters to meet us.

He looked at me questioningly, shooting a glance at Anna. *What did you find?* his eyes asked.

"I'm taking Anna to another place," I informed. "An address from a note. We shouldn't be too long, but you guys should find a place to rest for the night."

Michael seemed to mull it over, looking unhappy about the idea.

"There're some small islands nearby," Anna interjected helpfully, pointing southeast. "Just that way."

"Alright," Michael finally said, a bit gruffly. "Don't be too long."

I gave him a half-nod and a small smile of assurance. The corner of his mouth turned up in response, his eyes softening toward me, before curving away with steady wings. I watched him go, taking a brief moment to admire his grace and strength, fond of the way the last bit of amber light highlighted his feathers copper, then curved in the opposite direction with Anna close to my side.

"Lead the way," I encouraged, tossing my hands forward.

Anna cast me a thankful glance, then sped up, taking us back toward the city.

I had no idea where she was taking us. Five minutes later, we were landing outside a short, gray concrete building with heavy double doors busted in. The faint light from the setting sun cast an ominous, dark orange glow upon the building. I still wasn't convinced Anna knew where we were going, but after a hesitant moment, her feet moved forward, and she walked through the doors.

A rotten stench wafted from inside, and I fought the nausea rising up. *Nevermind. Right place*, I thought stiffly.

As much as I DID NOT want to, I followed Anna inside. Anna dusted off a stocky flashlight she'd picked up from the floor, and to my surprise, the light flicked on when she clicked the button. My eyes had already adjusted to the lower lighting, and I had to hold my hand up to guard against the sudden onslaught of brightness.

My eyes readjusted as we walked down a long, musty corridor. The corridor opened up into a massive underground room, concrete support columns lined at intervals. Ragged bunk beds sat in messy rows. But among the beds and scattered in piles among the floor, were people, all dead. Hundreds of them.

I paused in the entryway, feeling sick. Anna stumbled on ahead of me through the corpses, her hands shaking. Some were reduced to bones, others retaining some mostly disintegrated form or another.

Near the back of the room, Anna fell to her knees, the flashlight clattering to the ground. It rolled in a crescent along the floor, coming to a gritty stop with its light illuminating the legs of three corpses. Anna cried out in anguish, and tears gushed from her eyes, her face an image of horrible sorrow.

I came quietly over to her and rubbed the top of her back between her wings, trying to sooth her. With her face crumpled, she reached out to the smallest corpse, but her shaking fingers couldn't bear to touch it. I gazed sadly at the couple and little boy sitting together, their faces hardly recognizable.

CHAPTER 34

It was hard to pull Anna from that horrible room, from her family, but I couldn't stand to let her stay there.

The scuttling of small claws within the vents finally allowed me to lead her away, my arms wrapped around her shaking shoulders. I kept glancing back at the vents, the noises getting louder.

"Come on," I said softly. "Let's go."

Anna continued to sob quietly as I took her back through the corridor. We emerged onto the open road, and already, the air felt much more refreshing.

I tried not to look too relieved for Anna's sake. Turning toward her, I placed a hand on her shoulder and asked, "Do you think you can fly back now? We really shouldn't stay here."

She blinked the tears away, her long, dark lashes sticking together from the wetness. Anna nodded, glancing between me and the ground. Her face was blotchy and snot was running down her nose, yet she still had a certain endearing nature about her. It was hard not to have your heart ache for her.

"Alright. Let's go find the others," I said, pressing my lips into a tight line.

She sniffled and swiped at her nose, and I looked at her for a long moment before taking a few strides and jumping up, tossing my wings out. Anna stumbled forward a few steps and jumped up maybe two feet as her wings came down in quick strokes. She joined me in the air, and the two of us curved away, toward the water.

There were multiple islands, and I had no idea which one Michael had decided to take the others too. As we flew over the water, it turned out I didn't need to know.

Michael flapped up to us and led us to the others. They had found a giant tree to rest in, this one rising fifty feet above the surrounding trees, all also exceptionally tall. I didn't ask why they chose a tree. In fact, I was glad they had. Sleeping in a house, or any man-made building for that matter, just seemed...*wrong*, somehow.

Everyone noticed Anna's sorrowful state the moment we landed in the tree. No one really seemed to know what to say or do, except Samuel. He got up and jumped down to our branch, which was as thick around as two people. Anna found her way into his arms, and he comforted her in a way only he could.

Seeing Anna in good hands, I felt more at ease. I turned my head up on instinct to find Michael looking down at me, crouched artistically halfway down the length of a thick branch. He jerked his chin to the side, motioning for me to come over.

With a final glance at Samuel and Anna, I turned and flapped up to the branch some twenty feet above me, near Michael. It was easy to balance upon, and I walked along its curvy length to the middle of the tree. I eased down with my back against the trunk, sitting for the first time all day, my wings trailing down either side of the branch. One knee was left bent in front of me, while my right leg hung off the side comfortably.

Michael watched me heedfully for a moment, then came over and sat down in front of me, dropping one athletic leg over each side of the smooth branch. His eyes searched mine. "What did you see down there?" he asked, keeping his voice quiet.

I shook my head, my eyes traveling away. The awful images were still plastered in my mind. "I just hope it won't be like this for everyone," I said, a note of sad bitterness in my voice. "There was a safe house," I said. "No survivors, out of hundreds."

Michael let out a long breath. "Geez. Anna..." He shook his head dolefully and gazed pityingly down at her. Her sobs still sounded from a lower spot in the canopy. "This wasn't a mistake, right?" he asked out of nowhere.

I stared at him. "You wanna ask that *after* flying across the ocean?" I quizzed.

The corner of his mouth flicked up. "No," he huffed

humorously.

I rested my head back against the smooth tree bark. My right foot swung absently as I thought. "Let's just try to get some sleep," I said. "I can take first watch."

"That's alright, I've got it," he said mildly, swinging his legs over to the same side of the branch. He placed a comforting hand on my shin, his thumb gliding across my skin in ginger motions.

My breathing became shallow as I watched him. It felt as if my only source of warmth was coming from that hand. It was a simple action, but it sent electricity running up and down my leg, making me dig my toes discreetly into the bark.

Get it together, me! I scolded myself desperately. *You just saw hundreds of dead people!* But it didn't seem to matter. I still wanted him there.

I swallowed and casually said, "Just wake me up when you get tired."

"Mm," he agreed in so little words.

I folded my arms loosely over my chest and let my eyes close. It was the best I could do to clear my mind enough to allow me to slip into sleep, where the nightmares soon found me.

◆ ◆ ◆

"Hey. Hey, wake up." Someone called out to me softly.

My mind was pulled from the darkness of my subconscious, blinking the morning light from my eyes.

"Wha'?" I mumbled. I looked around. "Damn*t, you

let me sleep through the whole night?" I leaned forward and rubbed my eyes.

My face was brought away from my own hands, and my eyes were left to look straight into Michael's. I was suddenly caught in his gaze, as I often was. I never realized it before, but with the way the sun cast its first rays, there was a light spark crackling through his obsidian irises, so deep it was like a ravine breaching his soul.

A gentle but firm thumb brushed over the plain of my cheek, and I realized I had been crying in my sleep. Michael's gaze was soft as his eyes grazed me. "You were having a bad dream," he murmured, his dark eyebrows creasing delicately in the middle.

I covered his hand with my own, pulling it gently away. "Yeah, I have a lot of those," I mumbled distractedly, feeling somewhat embarrassed to know he'd seen me crying. I pulled my eyes from him and looked around again. It seemed everyone else was still alive, so that was good. "Did everything go alright?"

When Michael didn't respond, I turned back to him. His lips curled up in one corner. "You stayed asleep, didn't you?"

I rolled my eyes, a teasing grin flashing across my own face. "Well played."

Michael laughed lightly.

Anyone still asleep got woken up by the two of us. We didn't shout out for them to get up, but rather, we had to go to each one and nudge them awake. Best to attract as little attention as possible to our group in the tree.

Today, we were heading to New Jersey. Anna's depressed, shell-shocked state put most of them in an uncertain mood, but Adler was holding his own. Seeming to press aside any dissuasion, Adler got ready quicker than anyone else, anxiously waiting to go.

"Hold your horses," I joked. "Can a girl go to the bathroom first before flying to another state?"

Adler paced impatiently on a thick branch hovering thirty feet off the ground. He waved a distracted hand in the air. "Yeah, yeah, just make it quick."

I laughed to myself as I jumped down the tree into a thin layer of fog that had gathered over the ground, my wings stirring up the fallen cloud.

Another ten minutes later, we were all ready to go. We rose into the air, daybreak casting a hopeful glow over us. My mesmerizingly patterned wings looked especially golden in this lighting, light sparking off my feathers as I curved along a chilly breeze.

New Jersey wasn't *that* far away from Maine, but it did still take us a few hours before descending down to an inconspicuous suburban neighborhood, half of which was overtaken by vegetation, like a contagion. We circled above the neighborhood some five-hundred meters up at first, scouting for danger.

A pack of wild dogs jogged through the streets, following a herd of several dozen beefed-up deer, and we soared higher up while waiting for them to clear out.

Fifteen minutes later, when they were a comfortable enough distance away, Adler circled downward.

The brightly lit day gave the illusion of safety, but we knew better. Half of our group continued wheeling in the sky above as Adler and the rest of us went down together. I looked around with alert eyes and ears as we landed in a street being overrun with plants, thick leaves curling around fences and telephone wires. Adler folded his wings in and shook his hands out. I could hear him trying to psych himself up under his breath.

Adler jumped up the stairs to the front porch while I, Clara, Iver, and Anna waited in the street outside the house. Anna still looked dejected, rightfully so, kicking at a crack in the asphalt with her arms crossed. Anna's terrible experience hadn't left any of us too hopeful, instilling a realistic fear in our hearts, and Adler's hand was shaking slightly as he reached nervously for the door handle.

A familiar rotten stench permeated the air in this neighborhood. Watching Adler turn a handle that was apparently unlocked, I only hoped he wouldn't take whatever he was about to find too hard.

We waited outside for a good twenty minutes. The only reason I didn't go in after such a long time was because I would have heard if he was in danger. Instead, I was forced to listen to his muffled sobs, my good hearing feeling more like a curse.

He eventually came out of the house, not meeting

any of our eyes. A beaded blue necklace was clutched in his right hand. His silvery eyes looked like shimmering pools, reddened at the edges.

"So," he said, his voice sounding dead, "I found them. I can't say for sure, but I'm pretty sure it was our pet dogs that did it." He nodded, his face twisting up contemptuously. He lowered his head to the street, poorly hiding the tears that slipped from his cheeks.

We gathered around Adler supportively, hugging him and patting him. He rested his forehead on Clara's shoulder as several more muffled sobs came.

"Shh," she cooed, running her right hand down his muted brown wing feathers. She folded her lower lip, biting it as her own face creased sympathetically, Adler's pain visibly etched into her countenance and in the way she gripped him tightly to her.

This was really not looking up for us. A terrible feeling was taking hold in my gut. Virginia was next. *I* was next.

CHAPTER 35

No one needed to be told the outcome when we flew back up to the others in the sky. If they hadn't seen the episode on the street, then they saw the answer in Adler's torn expression.

I met Will's eyes, a wealth of excitement and fore-boding swirling within his pale yellow irises. We were next. Will looked more eager than me by a long shot, even after seeing the outcome for Anna and Adler. Me, well, I was just trying my best not to let the dread show too prominently on my face.

Even though I almost didn't want to, I ran through our next course of action in my head.

Finding Anna's and Adler's houses hadn't been so difficult. They were both very close to, if not right on, the coast. Finding my little town outside of Richmond shouldn't be too hard either. We'd just continue to follow the coast, down Maryland, then shoot southwest toward

Richmond. If we found Richmond, I'd be able to follow the interstate to our town. Easy-peasy.

◆ ◆ ◆

After an hour and a half of flying, my dread turned into something slightly different. Something in me was telling me to turn around and fly the other way, but I forged on despite the nagging intuition. I could feel it; a fore-warning in the air.

Another half an hour later, we were fighting the winds as I followed the highway, west. Will, being hybridized with two seabirds, did not have as good raptor vision as I did. Therefore, even though we had to find Will's house too, I alone had to navigate our way there.

That was alright though. I didn't really mind that part so much. It was Will's backseat driving that I had a problem with. A couple times, I had to lean over and whap him with one of my wings to get him to shut it.

The closer we got to our destination, the gloomier the sky got. Our group had to dip down in altitude to soar under the gathering clouds. The sun, sitting high in the sky like a glowing overseer, disappeared behind a thick, gray blanket.

"Are we getting close?" Michael asked, raising his voice against the growing winds. "We might need to take shelter soon."

I glanced up at the impending storm, hovering and churning above us. The cloud coverage spanned for miles.

"Yeah, we're almost there," I called back.

Should be right around… There.

I spotted Jody's farm some ten miles away. That dinky little house was unmistakable, even from this new aerial perspective. As we circled down upon it five minutes later, it shocked me to see no horses on the farm. Immediately after, I felt silly for feeling shocked about that. Obviously, why would the horses still be there? It was just… Different.

I dove down the last few hundred meters, coming to a graceful swoop for a stop. My bare feet tousled the tall, wet grass, the blades left shiny by the light rain.

When the others flapped down behind me in the field, I was already striding toward the front door. The door turned out to be locked. Without a second thought, I jogged around the side of the familiar house to what used to be a semi-decent flower patch, now filled with unruly stalks shooting out in every direction, tall grasses threatening to choke the lanky flowers out.

"*Yes,*" I whispered, pulling up a dirt-covered key between my fingers. I ran back around the side of the house, along the long, flaking, white siding panels, to the front door. Small water droplets skipped off my feathers as I stood in front of the door, my shaking hands making it difficult to get the key in.

I finally got it and threw the door open. The house wasn't very big, and it didn't take long for me to check every inch. No Jody, and not a single clue. I hadn't exerted myself, yet I was panting. *Where is she??*

The front door flung open again as I jumped down to the grass, which reached up to my knees. Ten birdkids stood off to the side, turning their heads around alertly, but looking awkward standing in the empty, rainy field.

I turned in place, scanning for, well, I'm not sure. Evidence of life — *anything.* Desperation welled up inside my chest as I looked around. All I was doing was scanning an empty field, for goodness sake!

Then I saw it. I saw that thing, the one that changes your life forever.

I don't remember making my feet move, but I found myself treading numbly across the field. The wet grass hugged my shins as I went forward.

My legs, which absently carried me, suddenly gave way once I reached the edge of the field, under a line of dark trees. My knees crashed into the damp ground, my hands falling limp in my lap.

Beside a line of old family headstones, a new one stuck out from the ground. It didn't really *look* new though. Its aging white surface was rough, with words that looked like they'd been chiseled out by hand.

"Jody…" My words were too quiet to even be considered a whisper. I couldn't be sure they'd actually escaped my lips.

My right hand came up to trace the letters etched into the stone face, feeling rough under my fingertips: JODY BAKER. And directly beneath that, my eyes struggling to focus on it: PASSED OCT. 3RD, THE LAST YEAR.

Whoever did Jody the respect of providing a final resting place must not have known her well enough to include anything else. The mere thought of a stranger taking such niceties was enough by itself to make tears well up in my eyes.

She'd lived another five months after I was taken. So, it turned out that leaving earlier from Iceland really wouldn't have done anything…

Before I knew it, a stream of tears was pooling along my jawline, falling in a string of delicate pearls from my chin, wetting the ground alongside the raindrops. I barely noticed that the rain was picking up, coming down harder and thicker, its pounding upon the field and surrounding forest serving to hide my mourning sounds.

My heart felt crushed in a way all too familiar to me.

I didn't hear Michael come up behind me. A sure hand was placed upon my right shoulder, but I could barely muster the strength to turn my head. Raindroplets ran down my skin like water off a duck's back, and I was no longer able to tell them apart from my tears.

"Rory? You should come inside," he offered peaceably. When I didn't turn him away, he started helping me up. "Come on," he urged gently, supporting me with a wing around my back.

I walked numbly back to the house with him. My tears had already left me, my heart too empty to cry anymore.

Some part of my brain registered that our group needed to get out of the rain. I tilted my head up to look at the clouds, and heavy droplets exploded like tiny white flowers off my skin.

Turning back to the group, I blinked the rain from my eyes. I tried to rid the weakness from my voice and, after clearing my throat, gestured lamely to the house. "You guys can stay in here while the storm passes," I said.

"You sure?" Adler asked hesitantly. His thick, wavy hair was weighed down by the pounding rainwater, but he continued to stand in the field outside the house.

"Yeah, I'm sure," I said, beginning to walk toward the front door myself.

I didn't look back at them as I went inside, and a minute later, they began awkwardly filing into the small house behind me. I glanced at them. It was weird having them here, allowing them to glimpse into my life.

Thunder rumbled outside, stirring the lot of us into varying levels of anxiety. Storms shouldn't have been an unusual occurrence for any of us, but I suppose it hit differently when you're all a bunch of highly-tuned Hybrids living in a post-apocalyptic world. Who knew.

The rain came down harder. It sounded like the roof itself might come crashing down at any moment from the drumming impacts. Storms used to give me a sense of comfort, listening to the rain and watching the droplets streak down the windows. Now it rang through my ears like a war drum, stifling my senses.

I went to the kitchen and checked the fridge and cupboards, needing to distract myself. Not so much as a single measly can left. We were running out of the food rations we'd brought with us from Iceland.

With a loud, aggravated exhale, I set my hands on the counter with my head bowed. Too much was wrong right now.

My ears pricked. I didn't need to see him to know who it was.

"Stop hovering," I ordered. "I'm *fine*."

"Yes, I'm aware," Michael said, trying to sound serious.

I turned my head to the side to glare at him tiredly. He was leaning in the kitchen doorway, his arms crossed over his chest in a relaxed manner. His eyes were skimming the kitchen counter, then flicked up to mine.

I sighed and let my head fall forward again. This sucked, royally. I shook my head and took in a deep breath to steady my thoughts, lest I break down. It was only a little after noon. This rain didn't seem willing to let up anytime soon, and we still needed to check up on Will's place. I also wanted to fly by Vixen's old house, where she stayed when she wasn't in college.

My fingers started tapping on the counter, coxing my brain into coming up with something helpful. *Ah, I know.*

Pushing off from the counter, I strode purposefully out of the kitchen, past Michael. He looked at me questioningly as I went, and turned to watch me as I trifled through a stack of old papers and books near the corner of the living room, beside the kitchen.

"Rory, what are you…?" Michael's words trailed out, a faint note of humor teasing his semi-worried voice.

It had to be here somewhere. I'd been with Jody when she'd bought them. She'd insisted that you couldn't rely on technology, and had proceeded to make extra sure I knew how to read them once bringing them home.

"Ah-ha," I said, startling a few birdkids hanging out nearby. I lifted a thick, folded sheet of glossy paper from the pile.

I selectively grabbed a few pens from the kitchen, reaching distractedly around Michael to do so. Bringing the pens and paper, I went to the dining room table and splayed out what I'd grabbed. I took care to smooth out the creases at the corners of the paper as it lay unfolded on the wooden table.

Some of the group had started to gather around me out of curiosity, looking over my shoulders.

"A map?" Ronin asked.

"Yeah," I said, my eyes running amok over its detailed surface. "I'm gonna map out our next steps. Finding places along the east coast was easy enough, but I'm sure it won't be quite as easy when we fly further inland."

"You sure you don't wanna…?" Clara's voice fell out.

"*No,* pretty sure I don't," I responded stiffly. The edge of my right hand swept across the glossy paper as I went from state to state, finding and marking the locations each person in our group had given.

I could feel the group pass glances around at each other behind me, wondering if I was alright or going crazy. They knew me well enough by now to know not to push me, however, and decidedly went along with it.

Samuel pointed over my shoulder, pressing his finger to the paper. "I'm right there," he said, pointing to a spot in northwestern Montana.

He lifted his arm away, and I circled a small town where the tip of his nail had been. I nodded absently, connecting each location with a dotted line in the most reasonable and fastest order. *This is the least fun game of 'connect-the-dots' ever.* I tilted my head and raised my eyebrows vaguely at my moving pen. *Or...is it the most fun?* I pondered to myself. 'Connect-the-dots' with high stakes and hours of flying! What could go wrong!?

This would give us a good (or better?) directional idea. I don't know, I mainly just wanted something to distract myself while also being productive and not mopey. While we all had internal compasses, we did not have exact locations written on the inside of our skulls.

"After we're done in Virginia, we'll fly west-northwest for..." I measured the distance with my fingers, comparing it to the key. "Six-hundred miles and some change. If we're flying for any more than six hours, then we know we passed it."

"So, we're going to Missouri after Indiana?" Aubrey asked. I detected a note of nervousness in her voice. Aubrey was the stop in Missouri.

"Yes. It's quickest to stay south and hit this line," I said, my finger traveling along the path, "then shoot north from Nevada to Wyoming. And then Samuel is right above that."

"Looks good," Michael determined.

With no more need to write, I snuck a furtive glance at him. My eyes traveled discreetly from his hand planted on the table beside me, up his well-toned arm, to his handsome facial features. His brows were creased with rumination, his dark eyes flicking across the paper, studying it.

He turned his head to look at me. "We should come up with a spot to regroup if anything ever happens."

I let my eyes fall away. "Mm. How about, if we get separated from the group, we agree to meet up at the next dot. That way it'll be somewhat close no matter where we are at the time," I suggested.

"That would work," Michael agreed. He turned back to look around at the rest of the group. "Does that sound good to everyone? You'll have to memorize each other's locations."

Shrugs and nods were passed around. Some 'should work's and 'yeah, alright's echoed behind me.

CHAPTER 36

After creating a course of action, I didn't know what else to do. I knew that if I simply sat still, I would surely burst into tears again.

Leaving the map splayed on the table, I edged around the cluster of birdkids in the small house, and they gathered closer around the map in my absence. Glancing over my shoulder one last time, I paused for a moment at the base of the stairs before padding up to my old room.

Upstairs, a draft crept across the wooden floor. I thought it would bring some sort of comfort to be back in my old room, but really, it only felt odd. It was as if…this was only the memory of who I used to be. I hadn't realized it as it was happening, but I'd changed in more ways than one over this past month of consciousness.

I walked slowly across the floor, my eyes following my hands as they swept gingerly over the edges of blank canvases and unfinished paintings, leaving a thin layer of dust on the pads of my fingertips. With zero water, all of the plants in my room had died, reduced to shriveled brown husks. Louise still sat in one corner of the room, and a faint shadow of a smirk flicked upon my lips.

I no longer needed something to distract me. Instinctively, almost naturally, a pad of paper found its way into my hand, a pencil in the other.

The simple metal bed squeaked as I dropped onto it, my unmade blankets still tossed aside to one corner in an untidy heap. A couple old pillows shoved behind my back provided a nice backrest, while my wingtips grazed the dusty floorboards, hanging over the low metal headboard.

Who can say for sure how long I sat there, my head drawn in attentively toward the paper, my fingers expertly navigating the pencil across the page. I certainly could not tell you. It could have been twenty minutes or three hours when the familiar creak of the old boards made me snap my attention over to the opposite side of the room. I continued to look toward the open doorway, and a moment later, Ronin leaned his head in, his hawk-like plumage for hair falling over one eye.

"Ronin," I stated, somewhat surprised. "Everything alright?"

He huffed in an uneasy laugh, which was uncharacteristic of him. "Shouldn't I be asking *you* that?"

The corner of my mouth curved up, but the faint smile faded just as quickly as it'd come. "I don't believe so," I said simply, resting my pencil at the edge of the paper, leaning back into the flat pillows. Ronin had never come to me like this before. Since he was, something must have really been bothering him.

His eyes shifted momentarily to Louise, and he took a second glance. He pointed, raising his arm at the elbow. Turning his gaze toward me suspectedly, his head tilting in bemusement, he accused, "Is *that* how you beat me that first day?"

"Call it a hobby," I joked, though it was nothing like that.

"How long have you been doing it, then?" he inquired, stepping up to Louise to take a better look.

"Since I was fourteen," I said, watching him size up the wooden structure.

"Huh. Long time." I was tempted to ask him what he came up here for, when he finally turned and said, "I wanted to ask… Do we *really* need to go to Indy first? Because really, I could wait if someone else couldn't."

I pursed my lips and squinted my eyes, my gaze wandering off to the side with suspicious thoughts. My face relaxed to its usual state in an instant, and I slapped my hand lightly down against the pad of paper in my lap. "Right, well," I started. Without turning my head, I slanted my gaze over to him. My mouth parted, but I hesitated. After a moment, I said, "It's okay to be afraid, if that's what you are."

His countenance twisted. "What? No, of course not."

His features relaxed, and he shuffled his feet against the wooden floorboards. "I'm just saying. I — It —" He huffed with annoyance. "Can a guy just try to do something nice for once?"

I chuckled lightly. "If it's you, no."

He rolled his eyes and turned to leave in a gruff, disappointed manner.

"Hey," I called. "Wait."

He stopped in the doorway and turned back toward me, a frown casting a doubtful appearance to him. "What?" he asked, rather than retorted. The anger had nearly all but gone from him, revealing a fragile anxiety he kept hidden.

"You don't have to," I said gently. "You don't have to go to Indy if you don't want to. None of us will make you."

His eyes fell to the floor somewhere below me. His mouth puckered off to one side, looking as if he was chewing the inside of his lip. After a while, he admitted quietly, "It was just my grandmother there with me. I already know she didn't make it out of all this."

I nodded slowly in understanding. "If you really feel that way, then we won't go."

Ronin sighed, and I was unsure whether he felt relieved or weighed down. He slapped his hand upon the doorframe, his knuckles turning a shade lighter from his tight grasp. He leaned forward, holding himself up with that hand as he swung, attempting to delay thought.

"Let's skip it," he decided with a lingering frown, pulling himself back up.

"Alright. We'll skip it."

He gave a terse nod, suddenly looking uncomfortable. He turned to leave, and a thought occurred to me. "Oh, Ronin?"

He backed up into the room once more, looking like he'd rather be anywhere else, but too lost in his own thoughts to substantially portray such feelings. "Yeah?"

"There are extra blankets and pillows in the closet near the front door. I don't think this storm is going to stop anytime soon."

He began to open his mouth, but the words stalled on his tongue, as if reconsidering what to say. "Alright." His wings twitched behind him peevishly, and he left the room.

I pursed my lips, staring after an empty doorway. Once his footsteps no longer lingered on the steps leading downstairs, I turned back to my artwork. It was only a herd of horses, but each was crafted thoughtfully, careful lines bringing the image to life. The pencil tip, which had dulled greatly from use, glided over the paper again.

My carefully sketched lines became blotched by a teardrop, and I tried to wipe it away before it warped the paper. But more came, and I threw the pad down on the floor to my left, feeling overwhelmed and angry all of a sudden. Pressing my palms to my tightly shut eyes, I tried to take deep breaths and stop crying.

After a few minutes, I lifted my left hand away, sliding my damp palm up into my thick eyebrow, and looked down through a watery lens at the sketch on the floor. The herd of horses galloping across the page only brought Jody front and center in my mind. They were her joy and passion in life.

Running from the dark places creeping through my mind, I turned away from the drawing and looked out of the window instead, dropping my hands from my face. The tears running down my cheeks seemed to race with those droplets streaming down the window.

Another shaky breath in, another breath out, despite the firm clench of desolation on my lungs.

The breathing helped for only a moment, then had a reverse effect. It cleared the tension in my heart enough to let all of the sadness back in, at full force.

I felt small, curled up on my old bed, in my room which had been abandoned for months. My heart, which had never fully healed the first time, after the death of my parents, felt as if it'd been cracked open.

◆ ◆ ◆

The only sounds were those of the heavy rain and wind lashing outside, the range of conversation taking place downstairs, and the steady beat of my own heart and breathing.

I lay there in bed on my side after some time had passed, unable to bring myself to face the window which cried tears in its own respect when I was unable to. My wings lay limply behind me, like silk sheets with no warmth.

The wooden stairs creaked under the soft padding of someone's bare feet. I was aware enough now to register it, but I didn't bother to move, not even when Michael appeared, leaning his head in with a gentle knock on the wooden doorframe. I only looked at him, then let my gaze fall idly away.

Stepping into the room, he paused for a moment but then decided to come slowly over. My eyes flicked to him again when he knelt down beside my bed. I watched as he gingerly picked up the sketch pad from the floor.

"Did you do this?" he wondered, appearing fascinated. His eyes lifted to mine.

I nodded against the pillow under my cheek.

He looked back down at it, his brows creasing ever so slightly. "It's…beautiful. Powerful," he said. He sighed and rocked back onto the floor so that he was sitting, with the pad in his hands. Michael looked at it for another while, then set it aside with a careful touch, as if handling a king's crown. "Rory…"

He didn't seem to know how to phrase whatever he wanted to say. "Don't," I whispered. I knew I would be alright eventually. I just needed time. That's all I needed.

Michael chewed his lower lip, appearing somewhat anxious. After a moment, he turned to me in sincerity and asked, "Do you want me to leave you be?"

I wasn't looking at him anymore though. I wasn't

really looking at anything.

When I didn't respond for a while, he got up to leave, as disappointed about it as he may have seemed. "Alright," he breathed. "Goodnight." He looked over at me from the open door and gave me a small, fleeting smile, then reluctantly ducked through the doorway.

I heard the creak of the first step, and it jolted me. I pushed myself into an upright position, feeling achy from the effort. "Wait," I spoke out suddenly, my voice sounding a little hoarse from the crying.

The footsteps paused. Michael then stepped back into the room, stopping in the doorway. He didn't have any reservation in his eyes, but he did delay.

"Stay," I said, though it sounded more like a question. I felt lame for asking, and felt my cheeks heat up from some form of embarrassment.

Without asking any questions, Michael walked back to me. He shifted onto my bed and pulled me close to him, hugging me as if it was him that was in need of relief. My heart involuntarily sped up a bit, and after a second of hesitation, I allowed myself to relax in his comforting arms, laying on his firm chest, nuzzling my face into the soft feathers covering his broad muscles. His warmth was greater than mine, and I fell into it sleepily.

Soft, wide wings wrapped tightly around me protectively, while he stroked my curly hair with careful fingers. He didn't say anything. He only had to hold me close to him. With him there, the bad thoughts and feelings still floated nearby, but they became tamed by his warmth, making it easy to relax. I wasn't even sure when it happened, but not long after, I slipped away into sleep.

CHAPTER 37

I blinked slowly awake the next morning, feeling well-rested physically, but drained emotionally. A warmth surrounded me, and I wanted to stay there forever. But of course, as the light filtered into my eyes, the events from yesterday came rushing back.

I blinked, staring at gorgeous, large feathers.

Had that all really happened? It was hard to believe any of it, and I lay there motionless for quite some time, soaking it in. Jody was dead.

Something from my subconscious was nagging me, and I realized what it was: I'd had a strange dream last night about Vixen. *Vixen!*

I jolted upright in bed, startling Michael as his feathers, which had stayed wrapped around me all night, slipped down my sides. My head whipped toward the window beside the bed as a spry energy surged through me. A dull light lit the world, covering the fields outside with a mist only seen at dawn.

"It's stopped raining," I remarked.

Michael, looking confused in a manner characteristic of someone who'd just been woken up at the break of dawn, looked over at the window with squinted eyes. "Okay?"

I jumped out of bed, my bare feet touching the floor that was chilly in comparison to the warmth I'd just left. "I have to go somewhere," I said hurriedly, keeping my voice on the quiet end. "It's not far from here. I'll be back soon."

"What? Where're you going?"

I leaned down to him and planted a sweet kiss on his lips, which he accepted without question. Pulling away, I looked at his face which was so handsome even when like this — tired and confused — and brushed some dark hair from his temple.

My eyes shifted back and forth between his. "I'm going to go see about my friend."

His befumbled expression grew some clarity. "Won't you —?" His words ended abruptly as I raised an eyebrow at him in a daring arch. Michael knew better than to ask if I needed a chaperone, but I wouldn't put it past him to try to come anyway. He stopped himself with a bit of difficulty. "Be careful," he said instead, him being so tired probably what tipped the scale, otherwise he surely would have kept pressing me.

Accepting a victory as it came, I gave him a smile,

which, for the first time in a while, was genuine. I still had hope.

Michael reached up into the back of my hair and pulled my head back down, taking me in another kiss. I could feel his deep passion, and when he let his fingers slip away, letting me go, I felt momentarily dazed.

Pulling myself away from him, I sucked in a breath and mustered the strength to leave the room. But once in the open doorway, I halted. That door...that creaky front door...

Simply by listening, I could tell that everyone else downstairs was still asleep. I pursed my lips and spun back around, striding straight up to the largest window. The latch to lock it was long broken. I heaved the old window up, then slammed my arm up into it to get it to jump up the last six inches.

"Good enough," I shrugged to myself. "If the others wake up before I get back, tell them I went out but that I'm not dead."

Michael propped himself up on his elbows to watch in confused humor as I hoisted myself up and out of the window, onto the roof. "Sure," he replied distractedly.

Once out, I turned around and poked my head back through. "Bye for now," I said to him. He gave me a strange look and lifted his right hand in a sort-of wave. Feeling funny inside, I pulled the window back down, lest the stray rabid squirrel wander by.

I went carefully down the roof a few steps, the gray

shingles still cool, not having had the chance to warm up under the sun, then pushed off near the edge, throwing myself out and away from the house. Jumping straight off the roof into nothing would surely have landed me in the hospital, but my wings unfurled, collecting the air like huge, feathery sails. My long wingtips, striped with gold, grazed the tall grass as I brought them down in adept, elegant strokes, their pale blades getting tossed around in my wake.

The sun was still in its early phase, barely peeking over the treetops. I flew in the direction I knew Vixen's house to be, using the roads as guides. It wasn't soon after that I managed to find her house: a squat, two-story thing that was fancier than Jody's house but still considered low-rent.

After circling above for a couple minutes, I determined it was safe enough to land. I dropped down agilely onto the street outside her house riddled with potholes and tucked my wings in. It was eerily quiet, even with my good hearing. In this neighborhood of suburban, two-story houses, there wasn't the faintest sound of human life.

Setting my eyes on the familiar house in front of me, I found myself hesitating for reasons which spawned from unease, trepidation, and just plain strangeness. Scrunching my nose in determination, I forced myself forward.

The front door was unlocked. In fact, it was cracked

open. I stopped outside the door and listened for anything suspicious for a while, but when I didn't hear anything, I gingerly pushed it open further. Inside, the tiled entryway was wet from last night's rain. My feet made light pattering sounds as I went inside, looking around. It felt wrong being in the house like this, uninvited. Especially since Vixen's dad had always been a stickler for the rules of pleasantries.

Shoving aside the strange feeling that I was doing something wrong, I searched the house for clues. No one was inside, dead or alive. Even after twenty minutes of inspecting each room, I found nothing helpful. In fact, her room even looked untouched. So did her parents' rooms. Was this normal?

Out of curiosity, I went back outside and checked a few neighboring houses. All of them had the hasty attestation of people packing up to leave. Drawers were not only open, but selectively emptied. In one house, I found my way into a study. A safe, in a cubby atop a dusty desk, hung open. I eased the safe's door around with two fingers and a curious frown, my keen eyes inspecting it. There wasn't so much as a single scratch on the outside, suggesting it was not opened by force. A looter must not have done this, but rather the people who used to live here.

Something was off. I walked out into the street feeling nonplussed. I glanced back at Vixen's house, staring at it pensively as if it would give me verbal answers. I could stare at it as long as I wanted, but alas, houses could not speak, even in this new, crazy world. With a troubled frown, I jumped into the air and flew off.

I made one last stop at Vixen's dorm at the college which now looked like an abandoned wizard's courtyard, tall stone buildings emerging from an otherwise barren landscape. This desolate cluster of castle-like buildings could have looked grand, and even mysteriously eerie, if not for the surplus of red plastic cups strewn about, unable to decompose. Again, none of Vixen's belongings had been touched. I didn't know what to make of it. It made no sense to me.

Feeling troubled, with no real clues to go off of, I had no choice but to fly back to my old house. It was raining lightly when I landed outside the door, tiny droplets skipping off my large feathers like diamonds. I could hear the others chatting and speculating within.

I went straight inside, tossing the door open without any qualms toward the others. Ten pairs of eyes fell on me as the door clanked shut behind me.

"Where the heck did *you* come from?" Samuel interrogated with a joking note. "Also, I didn't know your last name was Baker." He grinned, an old, unopened envelope between his fingers.

"It's not," I said, casting my gaze briefly upon him and over the envelope. "It's Sorren."

Samuel, appearing confused, squinted down at the paper. He looked as if he was going to ask more about it, but Will spoke up before he got the chance.

"Where did you go?" Will asked, his brows drawn in with something that resembled anger.

"Out," I responded obscurely, as I strode past them into the small dining room. "It's raining outside, but it's pretty light right now. Should be fine enough to leave."

As I gathered the map up, Will didn't give up. "Out?" he retorted. "Michael told us as much already, but that doesn't answer the question."

Michael made a 'hmph' sound from somewhere else in the room behind me.

That's it, I thought crossly, reaching a tipping point with Will's impudence. I shoved the map into my pack, which I'd dropped into a dining chair last night. My stomach was starting to hurt, but seeing as how I only had seven rations left, I tucked it away, untouched. Leaving my zipped-up pack in the chair, I spun around and strode up to Will, then promptly grabbed his arm as I passed and dragged him toward the front door.

"Hey!" he protested.

Ignoring his minimal struggle, I tossed the door open and brought him out with me. The door clanked shut again as I led him into the grass. A good twenty feet from the house, I turned on him suddenly, making him startle. "What do you think you're doing?" I scolded him.

His face twisted, looking insulted. "What d'you mean?"

I pointed at him accusingly, squinting my hazel eyes.

"You've been acting strangely ever since Greenland."

He turned his head left and right, as if looking for someone to back him up. Unfortunately for him, his only backup was an empty field. He stared into my eyes with some form of angry determination. "I have not," he stated indignantly.

"You have," I contested.

"Well…" His lips kept working into different forms, as if about to say something but stopping himself.

I only continued to stare him down coolly, unamused.

He hardened his expression and looked me up and down accusingly. "Maybe if you weren't so chummy with Michael —"

I held a hand up, stopping him, and huffed incredulously. "Really? You're gonna talk to me about Michael? What about you and Aubrey? How's it any different?"

He pressed his lips tightly together, looking like a man considering a bad idea. I saw it in his eyes but didn't react in time. Will suddenly stepped toward me, closing the gap between us with surprising speed, and took me in a firm kiss. His hands held my head as he kissed me like I was a craving he could no longer resist.

Caught off-guard, my hands came up to his chest, a warmth briefly infecting my palms in the sparse rain, and shoved him away. I stared at him furiously, but he only looked hurt and still a little angry himself.

"*Damn*t, Will.* What'd you go doing that for?" I

scolded, glaring at him. I swiped the side of my hand across my mouth, as if that could somehow undo what just happened.

Will scrunched his face, looking somewhere between pain and wanting to punch *himself*. "I know," he seethed. "I'm sorry, I'm sorry." He dragged his hands down the sides of his neck, leaving flustered red marks in their wake.

I raised my eyebrows and splayed my hands out in a universal *'then what the hell??'* gesture. If he had tried this a few weeks ago, I may have — *just may have* — reciprocated, due to what I could only pretend to assume would have been an influence of his nerdy coffee barista charm. But now? I mean, could his timing have been any WORSE?

He dropped his hands and used them to gesture to me indeterminately. "You know what? No, I'm not sorry," he said, force coming back into his voice.

I grinded my teeth together, resisting the urge to punch him or just sideswipe him with a swift leg. The worst part was that his words left a strangely warm mark on me, but I quickly doused the small, auspicious flame. I wanted to be so mad at him — I was — but at the same time I just couldn't.

With a composure coming across as all too calm, I stepped very carefully up to Will. I heard his breathing hitch and become shallower with cautious yearning. His eyes flicked up and down my face, holding a certain reservation.

Looking directly into his eyes, in a lowered voice capable of bringing shivers even to myself, I said, "Do that again, and Michael won't be the only one you'll have to deal with."

I saw a hint of fear flash across his eyes at the mention of Michael, but he quickly covered it up with a hardened gaze.

I gazed at him a moment longer to reinforce my position, yet I found my eyes unconsciously flicking over his lips before I walked around him to the door. Even though it frustrated me, I had to admit he wasn't a bad kisser.

Ugh, so annoying. I ought to have just punched him.

CHAPTER 38

The moment I entered the house, a strange atmosphere made me pause. I swept my suspicious gaze over the birdkids in the living room. They tried to act nonchalant, but my eyes flicked to the curtain which was still floating back into place.

"We should get going," I said calmly, walking studiously to the dining room to grab my pack. I slung it over my shoulders and clipped it, then looked back toward everyone.

They averted their gazes and got ready to leave. I didn't look at Michael as I waited, despite my great desire to snatch a glance at him. I knew he must've seen what had happened.

Will walked in and paused before the door even fully closed. Half a dozen heads glanced at him knowingly. Aubrey refused to look at him, unavoidably hurt and potentially angry at him, as any girl would feel in her position. Back at the base, her and Will had started to hang out as more than friends, even if it wasn't anything definite. Ronin gave Will a hard pat on the shoulder as he headed out of the door Will stood beside, and Will pressed his lips tightly together, suppressing his agitation.

More birdkids filed out after Ronin. Will walked further into the room, looking after those leaving. "Does this mean I'm next?"

Michael leaned back against the edge of the table with a sigh, his arms crossed sturdily over his chest. "If you mean next for a beating, then yes," he said with a deceptively easygoing tone.

Will looked tired. "Look, Michael," he began to dissuade.

Michael held up a hand with a concurrent minimal, downward tilt of his head, stopping him. "No, that's alright. I get it." Michael got up and put his pack on over his shoulders. He walked toward the door, planting a firm grasp on Will's shoulder as he passed. "Just don't let me catch you doing it again," he advised warningly.

Will tensed uncomfortably, even after Michael let him go. Michael looked over his shoulder at me before going through the door, meeting my eyes pointedly.

Sigh. Though, even with this new, uncomfortable air, a small part of my heart couldn't help but enjoy Michael's protective nature about me.

Not wanting to be alone with Will in the room, I headed out after Michael. Everyone was gathered outside, portraying various levels of eagerness and nervousness. Once Will joined us outside, looking annoyed and slightly perturbed, we were able to head off. The group began jumping into the air one and two at a time, sending the long blades of grass around them into a state of panic with the strong gusts their wings produced.

I cast my gaze toward Jody's headstone one last time in a silent goodbye, then turned and ran forward a few steps before throwing my own wings out, lifting myself into the air. Quiet, steady strokes lifted me easily, surpassing those who'd jumped up before me.

Only Will knew the way to his house. Initially, the plan was for me to help him spot the signs while we all soared a healthy distance from the ground, but this morning's events changed things. He was the last one up. Once he finally flapped up to us, he didn't hesitate to tilt his long wings and lead the way. The rest of us banked southeast after him.

I didn't think Will lived that far away, but after a solid fifteen minutes of flying some four-hundred meters above Will, I was beginning to have my doubts. As usual, I looked toward Michael to get his nonverbal opinion on it, but then I stiffened, nearly forgetting what had happened, too caught up in the pleasure of flying and in the mission.

Michael was flying off to my right not too far away. He seemed to sense my gaze, turning to look at me. His eyes took me in without the faintest hint of anger or blame, and I felt my palpitating heart finally get put to ease.

He tilted his primary feathers and shifted smoothly over to me, close enough that his sharp wingtips grazed mine. He gave me a faint, reassuring smile, and turned back to watch the world below us. I let my eyes fall back to the landscape as well, a small smile teasing the corners of my lips.

A minute later, he spoke up, turning back to me in a kindly peculiar manner. "So, Sorren, huh?"

The name was familiar, making me react to it immediately and glance over at him. "Yeah," I said with a shrug. I don't know why, but it felt odd to be talking about myself, about my pre-apocalypse life, in any way. But since it was Michael, I went ahead and admitted, "I kept my biological parents' name. I only moved in with Jody when I was fourteen, after they, uh…died."

"I didn't know," he said, sounding regretful.

"How could you have?" I brushed off. I chewed my lower lip discreetly, not really wanting to talk about it anymore. "What about you? I don't think I've ever heard your last name." Or *anyone's* in our unit for that matter. Guess there had just always been more pressing matters at hand.

"Knight," he said. "Like the knights of the Round Table."

I found a grin spreading across my face. "Michael Knight." I nodded, feeling unexpectedly pleased. "It's kind of charming. I like it."

Michael laughed lightly, and I felt warmer inside as I flew, feeling closer to him yet, in a way I hadn't expected to.

It wasn't for another ten minutes that Will began losing altitude. We were already flying relatively low over the ground since Will didn't have the best raptor vision, and now we went even lower, following after him to some degree.

I don't know what I was expecting Will's house to look like, but it surely wasn't this. It was practically a mini mansion! Will didn't seem phased about it in the slightest, though I guess he wouldn't.

Will swooped down with long, slender wings. In this light, the lighter tan patches looked like gold nuggets amidst his shiny black feathers. I wanted to stop him, tell him to let us scout it out for a minute first, but by the time I opened my mouth, he was already too far away. I felt tense as I watched him come to a running landing, on a paved driveway that took up one-third of the front yard. He hastily folded his wings in behind him and strode purposefully up to the front door.

Like several of the large ground-level windows, the front door was busted in. Will strode inside without having to so much as turn a door handle.

I wheeled in the sky a third of a mile above the house, waiting, and watching for danger. About ten minutes passed, and I spotted a curious group of creatures leap out of a nearby, overgrown yard into the paved street. They bounded along in a series of smooth arcs.

What the...? I focused my astute eyes on them. I didn't recognize them at first due to their burly sizes and excessively long teeth. Low and behold, they could only have been the world's new squirrels.

I could hear their chittering and grunting from my position high in the sky. They seemed to be communicating with each other. One stopped and chattered at the others, causing all eight of them to stop as well. They looked toward the same direction: Will's house.

The feathers along my chest pricked, and those along my hairline raised in alarm. I wasn't the only one who saw them; Adler and Michael pointed them out as well.

"Are those — *squirrels?*" Adler asked in disbelief.

"They look more like rabbits to me," Michael huffed, clearly alarmed. Well, not clearly. It was just that I knew him well enough to know such things.

It was true, though, that these burly, grey-brown squirrels were much larger than they should have been. Honing my eyesight even further, I also noticed that their bushy tails were riddled with hidden spines, like a thinner version of those on a porcupine.

"There's something else, down there!" Adler pointed somewhere off below us, further down the street. My eyes followed his finger, and I caught sight of yet another potential problem.

A cat-like creature the size of, well, definitely larger

than a house cat, pounced from a broken, two-story window, following after another waiting at the bottom. Once they were both down, the two felines looked to each other in taciturn understanding for a brief second, then trudged agilely down the house's driveway. Pronounced muscles moved like thick ropes beneath their thin layer of black and brown fur, their skinny tails flicking with every other step.

It seemed as if they were hunting the squirrels, probably having spotted them from their window perch.

Okay, time to go do somethin' dangerous.

Hardening myself mentally, I shot a forceful glance between Michael and Adler.

Michael's expression dropped immediately. "I know that look," he said, a warning edge to his voice.

"Wait, are you gonna —?" Adler couldn't finish his words, perhaps out of sheer disbelief.

"Yep. I'm gonna," I stated resolutely. "Don't let the others get too close. I'll call if I'm dying." And with that, I folded my wings and angled my body, dropping straight down. The two boys' protests were lost in the wind as I fell away from them.

I didn't want to be spotted by the squirrels, if you could even call them that anymore, so before getting too close to the ground, I shot closer to a bank of tall pine trees. With a sharp tilt of my primaries, I swooped around the backside of their canopy, circling around (hopefully) undetected toward Will's house.

My exceptional hearing picked up Will's scuffling on the second story, in the southwestern-most room. Lucky for me, breaking windows seemed to be a hobby around here, and I angled straight down toward a giant, busted-in window at the far corner of the house. It was one out of a set of three side-by-side panels, the other two sealed in by intact glass.

I shot my wings out right before reaching the side of the house to slow my speed, then tucked my wings in at the last moment, shooting through the open window into the house. I nearly smashed into a wall that seemed to have jumped out from nowhere, and had to quickly tuck-and-roll. My wings, encasing my body and over my head, provided a decent level of padding as I tumbled across the floor, somehow missing the plethora of ornately carved wooden furniture. In the next instant, I jumped to my feet and spun around, ignoring the pain in my left shoulder.

"Will!" I exclaimed. Will was staring at me in horror, taken by complete surprise. Something fell out of his hand and clattered to the floor; a book of some sort. I pointed to it while catching my breath. "Do you need that?"

CHAPTER 39

His fingers spread open, his palms splayed toward me as he stared at me with wide, belligerent eyes. "Rory!? Did you just —? How —? *What the hell!?*"

My head spun toward the hallway when a crash sounded downstairs. It sounded like glass, or maybe a very expensive vase, breaking against the floor. Alas, the squirrels must have arrived.

In the next instant, a low *meowl* sounded from the backyard. *Dang, those cats were fast to arrive.* They wouldn't see us through the massive, one-third broken window taking up almost half of the room's back wall, would they? *Sarcasm.*

I strode toward Will, taking him quickly away from the window. I pressed myself up close to the wall separating the room from the hallway, forcing Will against it as well.

"What's going on?" Will asked beside me, panic

rising in his voice. He kept looking between me and the gaping window I'd shot through. "You've got that whole 'something is tryna kill us' vibe going on."

"If it's so obvious, *why are you asking?*" My voice had dropped to a near whisper. "You really have *got* to stop making this a habit," I said, keeping my voice low as I peered around the corner. I couldn't see anything down the stairs, which sat right outside the half-opened door. However, I heard the scrapes of tiny, sharp claws and the gentle flick of their tail quills against a stone floor. I took my head from the edge and pressed myself back against the wall. The cool paint seemed to seep into my skin, and I knew it must have been my imagination. Probably the 'I have more money than you' wallpaper getting to me. "I mean, really," I continued. "How many times am I going to have to save you?"

"I don't know," Will confessed with a shrug. "Maybe three, four, five more times?"

"I'm being serious!" I whisper-yelled. "This can't keep happening!"

Will's voice had dropped down as well. "What, and I'm not? You think I like being the one at the center of all these near-death experiences?"

I rolled my head toward him, wearing an exasperated expression. "*Well, apparently.*"

His nose crinkled, his lips pressed into a tight, agitated line. His narrowed eyes stared me down, though he couldn't argue with me. Then he looked around as if searching for something. He nodded toward the window I'd come through. "Why don't we just fly back out through there?" he bargained.

"Because," I said, hating myself for saying it, "there are *cats* out there." They were obviously capable of jumping to great lengths, and I didn't know what effect a bite or scratch from one of them might entail. However, Will's idea wasn't horrible.

"Cats?" Will questioned with a puzzled look.

I craned my neck, trying to glimpse the backyard without being noticed. I didn't see the cats. I didn't hear anything either, though I'm not sure I could have heard much past the pounding of my heart in my ears anyway.

The scratching downstairs seemed to move into a different room, as if they were wandering throughout the entire lower level of the house. Outside, all was quiet. Maybe it would be alright now to slip away…

I peered forward again.

"AH!" Will and I jumped back simultaneously, nearly crashing into one another. Will let out a manly shout, while I yelped and slammed back into the wall behind me in horror-struck surprise.

A dark feline bounded through the broken window at us, like a demon coming to collect his souls. I had only one thought snap through my mind: *We're gonna die!*

This was not an overreaction, I assure you. If you saw what I saw — an image of death conveyed through a hissing cat the size of a medium goat, dark fur bristling, eyes like translucent pearls and teeth like needles — you would probably have the same thought.

A wooden end table went flying through the air. Will chucked the furniture at the cat, and it crashed against the animal, sending it sprawling into the floor.

I was too terrified to rejoice. My body reacted before my brain did, and I practically flew through the doorway, sending the door crashing outward.

"Come on!" I breathed, hurtling into the wide hallway. My scattered thoughts snapped a plan together. I'd seen them from outside — the wide windows lain into the opposite side of the house. I glanced back to see Will stumbling out after me, and he followed me as I ran into the room across the hall.

A collection of angry chirping came from down the stairs. Of course the squirrels wanted to join the party! Why not!?

I burst into the far room, Will right behind me.

"Now what?" he wheezed.

My darting eyes trained themselves on a single window. "Now we bust outta here!" I yelled. Leaving no room for hesitation, I sprinted forward. Bringing my wings forward and jumping up at the last moment, I tucked my head in as the hard edges of my sturdy wings slammed into the glass.

CRASH!

Glass shattered, sending jagged daggers through the air. A weightless feeling engulfed me, and I knew I was outside, about to plummet. I snapped out my wings, grasping the air. The ground came all too close to calling itself my pillow, but my wings worked powerfully, sending the overgrown grasses below into a whirlwind.

"*Woah*," I breathed, bringing my wings down hard. I shot up a good twenty feet, just as the second cat launched itself up at me from the tall grasses.

Coordinated cat attack! my brain screamed, only slightly impressed. It would have been more impressive if they *weren't trying to KILL me.*

I looked over my shoulder. Will was not as brave as me and had not sprung through the window with no regrets. He was standing precariously in the windowsill, looking as if he was talking himself into jumping.

I angled my wings, my right wingtips pointed almost directly straight down at the ground, curving around in a sharp arc. I heard it just as Will's head spun to look over his shoulder into the room behind him: a throaty growl. It was inevitably pissed.

"*Jump!*" I shouted, fear for Will rising in my chest.

Will turned forward. In the next moment, he jumped out from the side of the house, his wings expanding on reflex. His flaps were quick with panic, and he came closer to the ground than I had. Lucky for him, that second cat had chased after me and wasn't a direct problem for him.

His wide eyes spotted me banking over the street, and he flapped directly toward me. I kept an eye on the house as we flew higher and further away, quickly rising above the house and the threats within. A dark form lingered in the windowsill Will had jumped from, baring its pointed fangs up at us in a rueful hiss.

My heart pounded in my chest, making me feel like I needed to catch my breath, though my enlarged lungs would agree otherwise. "Please tell me you at least found something helpful," I implored, turning to look at him in an almost pleading manner.

Will was visibly shaking. He didn't respond, only continuing to flap higher and higher beside me. After a long moment, he shook his head reluctantly, and I stifled a sigh.

CHAPTER 40

"You're bleeding," Michael stated, staring intently at the middles of my wings.

I looked down their lengths. Indeed, it seemed the glass had cut me. Thin lines of blood were seeping across my feathers where they'd impacted the window.

"It's fine," I dismissed. "It doesn't hurt." In fact, if Michael hadn't said anything, I probably wouldn't even have noticed.

Michael pursed his lips, looking like he wanted to argue with me. "I saw you bust through that window. You should make sure the lacerations didn't cause any tendon or nerve damage," he said.

I paused, peering over at him. The teacher-trainers back at the base hadn't gone over such specifics. "You sound like a doctor, you know that?"

"Probably because I was halfway through med school before all this happened," Michael disclosed, sounding as if he'd rather not be telling me.

My eyebrows arched faintly in surprise. *Convenient? I think so.* Meeting him in the middle, I said, "I'll deal with it next time we land. Clean it out and whatnot." Looking around at the landscape below us, riddled with disgruntled neighborhoods and towns, I really didn't want to go back down yet. "Let's just get out of civilization first."

"Mm. Fine," he grunted. He rolled his shoulders as if easing some tension. "A mountain range should be coming up soon enough. We can stop there."

That was right; we'd be passing over the Blue Ridge Mountains. I'd always loved those mountains. I'd drive up there to go hiking multiple times a year. Never *flew* over them though. Should be interesting.

As we soared onward, several miles above the ground, I kept inconspicuously glancing at Will. He was flying off to the side of the group, at a slightly lower altitude. Will never told me what he'd found in the house, which I gathered must have been nothing. A good sign or bad sign, who could say for sure?

I didn't want to push him, still feeling the devastating effects from my own search. Such inquiries could be dangerous to the mind and heart. Even so, finding Jody's headstone had put me to some ease, as depressing as that ease may have been. At least I had a definite answer. On *one* person, at least. I still had no idea what had become of Vixen, and it was driving me crazy.

Already feeling agitated, I angrily grunted at the sun, trying to block its intolerable rays with my hand. Flying east put us in the position to fly directly into the rising run. Apparently the others could tolerate the sun better as Hybrids than they could as humans, but my tolerance had actually gone in the opposite direction.

"That's it," I stated, frustrated. Several of those closest to me glanced over.

"You good?" Ronin goaded.

"*No*, I'm being *blinded*." Covering my eyes from the sun, I searched the ground miles below us. *How convenient. A town.*

Spotting a gas station was no problem. The mere sight of it brought back bad memories, especially after what I'd just gone through with Jody, but action had to be taken.

"I'm going down real quick," I informed.

"Are you? Take a look at those injuries while you're at it," Michael said.

I shot him a glance. "Okay."

Facing forward, I set my eyes back on my target and brought my wings in closer, tilting my body downward. I began losing altitude, feeling the rush in my feathers and deep in my bones. Roller coasters had nothing on me.

The town, like every other town we'd come across, was empty. It was worse than a ghost town — you had to be on constant alert, lest something *eat* you.

I floated down to the gas station after taking a brief

moment to scout it out. Tucking my wings in silently, I edged closer to the storefront. Old posters lay rotting against the glass, sporting ads about lotteries and ciga-rettes. *My, my, what humans used to consider important.* It was enough to make me audibly sigh as I walked through the broken-in front door.

I scanned the small store, and my eyes fell upon a rack of glasses further down the frosty front window. It seemed *sunglasses* weren't at the top of peoples' ran-sacking lists. Lucky me. I padded down to the rack, and my fingers traveled across the neatly arranged rows. Well, 'neatly' may have been an overstatement. It was mostly alright, at best, what with the apocalypse and everything. I tried a few on, checking myself in the small mirror provided at the top of the rack.

I was there for the sunglasses, but my eyes couldn't help but wander over myself. How different I looked… I still couldn't believe it at times. As I glimpsed myself in the mirror, those small gold and dark brown speckled feathers merging into my hair rose forward in a hint of surprise. When I tilted my head toward the light coming in from outside, I also noticed a gold sheen reflect off the edges of my dark, kindly arched, attractively thick eye-brows. People used to comment on my eyebrows a lot — how much they wished they had them. I wonder if they'd still say that.

I laughed inside and put aside my thoughts, trying on another pair, these sporting a thin, gold metal rim, holding two smoky, stone-blue lenses. They were aviator glasses. This alone impelled me, never one to hinder a good use of irony. I gazed outside with them to test their effectiveness.

Feeling pleased with them, I left them on while searching for another pair. Once I found a decent pair, I folded them up. I was about to stride back out of the store and fly away when I remembered I was injured and had told Michael I'd check on it.

Bringing my left wing around in front of me, I picked at where the blood was seeping from. It had coagulated by now and was dried over my feathers. I brought my right wing around. Same thing. I plucked a tiny glass shard from between my feathers and flicked it away. Seemed alright, but could probably do with a cleansing-out. Looking around the store again, I found that, unlike sunglasses, fresh water had been high in demand.

That was alright. I'd just wait until we reached the mountains to use the cooling water from one of their many streams to wash my wounds out. With this in mind, I left the store and jumped back into the air.

The others wheeling leisurely above started forward again as I neared, flying in a loose formation. I angled my wings and let the wind carry me upward, then flapped out into place. I went over to Iver, where he flew near the far left side of the group, and handed him the second pair I'd grabbed.

"Here," I offered.

"Oh, thanks," he said, pleasantly surprised. He took them from me gratefully and unfolded them, shoving them onto his face. I raised my eyebrows. Not bad.

I coasted back toward the front of the group. Michael was gliding off to my right, and gave his wings a few extra flaps to catch up to my position, Samuel coasting leisurely off to my left.

Iver turned to June, flying nearby him at the back. "How do I look?" he asked her.

"Mmmm. Have you ever seen the movie *Top Gun*?" June led on.

"Yeah?"

"Better now?" Michael asked, covering up the rest of June's response.

"Definitely." The world was tolerable to look at now.

"Heh. You look like you should be some model on the front page of a sunglasses ad," Samuel said. He peered at me with semi-squinted, deep blue and turquoise eyes. "You sure you never actually modeled before?" He huffed gratifyingly. "'Cause, you definitely could have."

I turned my head toward him, my face a mask beneath my new, dark glasses, my lax mouth portraying nothing. His humorous smile, laced with earnestly, faltered, and he gave a last, weak laugh.

"Pretty sure," I said.

"Mm." He nodded and busied himself with looking back over the landscape, pretending to scan it in a diligent manner.

I looked back to what lay in front of me as well. The small upward curve of the corners of my lips remained unseen.

Not two minutes later, as we neared the edge of the pocket of desolate remnants of civilization, the beginnings of a mountain range folding the land, I picked up on a strange glint from far below. I probably wouldn't even have been able to see it if not for my new sunglasses.

Out of nowhere, a shiny bullet whizzed by some hundred meters to my left. My eyes widened. *Can we not just go* one day *without something trying to kill us?* I exasperated. I mean, really.

There were a few gasps, and a startled yelp, by whom, I will not say.

"Evasive maneuvers!" Iver cried.

Luckily, their aim was pretty terrible. Two more shots were fired, but neither came remotely close. It was easy to swerve away, and Michael and I led the pack into the foothills of the mountains.

As we soared away, Michael and I looked over at each other at the same moment. His brows were drawn in seriously, conveying startling realization, and I looked back at him knowingly. Only humans could shoot guns. At least... No, I'm pretty sure only humans could.

That meant there were survivors here.

CHAPTER 41

We dove down through an opening in the canopy, on the opposite side of the rising mountain. Not all of the trees here were as large as the ones in some forests, so we landed on the leaf-strewn ground instead of in their branches.

"What the heck was that?" Aubrey asked immediately upon landing. She strode up to our gathering group and glared around at us as if it were our faults.

I took my sunglasses off and tucked them into my top. "Well, it would seem there are others," I said, my tone rather calm. After nearly getting mauled by a rabid cat the size of the family goat, I guess the effect of this attack on our lives was lost on me to some degree. Not like it was the first time we'd been shot at, either.

"We should go check it out," Adler urged.

June nodded. "If there are humans down there, we should see what they're like."

"I agree," Michael said. "This is the first time we've come across anyone outside of the base."

I held up a hand midway. "Just hold on a moment," I said, dousing their enthusiasm. "They just *shot* at us. We can't simply go up to them." I huffed in an unamused laugh, and my eyes traveled to Michael. We shared a nonverbal agreement, assuring me that I wasn't crazy for having common sense. Then, I saw Will's mouth open out of the side of my eye. I can't say for sure, but before he even spoke, I'm almost positive I could read his mind.

"Then we go incognito," Will declared carefully.

I gritted my teeth. *Yep, there it is.* I'm not entirely sure why, but I didn't actually want to go say 'hi' to these random people, even if they *were* the first living souls we'd come across. Even before the apocalypse, I'd always been happy to live my own life, without the interference of other people. Purposely going to meet a group of post-apocalyptic survivors was my nightmare. However, I did like a good investigation, also being one of great, undeniable curiosity.

"How? We have *wings*," Clara stated unhelpfully. "We don't even know if they're aware Hybrids exist." Anna, standing next to Clara, nodded along supportively.

"Right. So let's not let them see us," I drawled obviously.

"Spy mode?" Michael clarified.

"Spy mode," I said.

"Sweet. I'm in," Will said, inviting himself.

"Hey, no, we shouldn't all go down there," June interjected, raising her hand, her palm facing parallel to the forest floor. "We'll be too easily spotted."

June was right. "A couple of us with long-distance vision will go down to check it out first," I said. "Do some surveillance."

June looked as if about to disagree on reflex, but hesitated. She gave a one-shouldered shrug. "Yeah, I guess that seems okay."

"No way! I'm going down there too," Will argued.

My gaze slanted over to him. "You wish to jump back into danger then, do you?"

He looked troubled, a frown tugging at his mouth. His pale yellow eyes were a shade duller, ever since leaving his house. "They're pretty close to where my family lived." He tossed a hand at me. "Yours too," he encouraged. "What if they managed to gather here?"

Honestly, the thought hadn't occurred to me. The thought of Vixen living in some form of survivor camp just didn't compute. But who knew. Months upon months of death and other turmoil could change a person, undoubtedly.

Will was getting in my mind. I had to stop him. "I'll go down with Michael to scope it out. I have the best senses and fighting skills out of all of us, and Michael is capable of holding his own. The rest of you stay hidden in these woods, maybe move further up the ridge. After we get back, we can tell you what we've found and go from there," I said.

Will abruptly shut his mouth. I could see how hard it was for him not to argue with me.

"Okay. You guys be careful," Samuel said.

"No promises," I said with slim humor, shooting Samuel a glance with sparkling eyes. I tapped Michael on his left bicep with my knuckles and started off down the mountainside. "Come on. We'll have to hike there. Too risky flying over."

"Alright," Michael complied. He turned back to the group, walking backward for a few steps. "Set up camp or something, might be a while. But no fires — don't need a signal to draw in any attention."

Michael got a few responses from the group, a few variations of 'okay.' He turned back around, and the two of us trekked over the last hundred feet of the sloping ridge and down the other side of the mountain together.

Some time later, maybe twenty minutes had passed, voices, footsteps, and other faint human sounds were getting louder in my sensitive ears. There had to be at least thirty — forty — people further down the mountain.

We couldn't get too close. I tapped Michael on the back of the hand and jerked my head to the side, toward a clearing in the trees. He gave a minimal nod and followed me to the outcrop.

Staying low, we snuck over the boulders, shimmying up to the edge of the outcrop, where it abruptly fell away in a fifty-foot sheer drop. What appeared to be a camp, built over an old campground site, was nestled in a mini valley about a mile in front of us. There were fewer trees there, but it still had a decent amount of cover. The curious part was that I didn't think the bullet came from this mini valley, making me believe there must be scouts around the base of the mountain.

◆ ◆ ◆

I plucked a blackberry from a twiggy bush surviving at the edge of the outcrop and offered it to Michael, laying on his stomach to my left. "Berry?" I said, already chewing one myself.

Michael flicked his eyes over it skeptically. "You sure that's a blackberry? It's the size of a golf ball."

He wasn't wrong. It also tasted a lot juicer than I remembered blackberries being, and more sweet than tart. "Yep. It's one of the safe plants to eat." I held it out to him again. "Try."

He pressed his lips together, then took the berry from my fingers. Throwing caution to the wind, he popped the whole thing into his mouth. I watched him chew, waiting for a reaction. His eyes squinted, one more than the other.

Suddenly his expression lightened, and he turned to me with eyebrows raised. "Mm," he said through a full, closed mouth, giving me a thumbs-up. He held his hand out toward the plant and flapped his fingers in a 'gimme' gesture. A grin tugged my mouth to the side, and I plucked another for him.

We'd been up here watching the camp for about half an hour and going, learning as much as we could from a safe distance. As far as I could tell, post-apocalyptic humans were just as boring as pre-apocalyptic humans. They seemed decent enough though. Mostly just cleaning weapons, only three of which were guns, cooking something that looked like mystery meat stew, and going about other daily activities. There were a couple kids, playing with a ball, running around the adults. The oldest person there looked to be around forty, with chestnut brown hair streaked with silver. He acted a lot like what I'd expect a survivor enclave leader to act like, people coming to him and being directed in various directions.

A fence meshed together with metal scraps and wooden logs lined the perimeter of the camp, rising straight up a solid twenty feet. With only a few sparse white clouds in sight, the sun shone down through the trees and reflected off those metal bits like diamonds embedded in the wall. The whole camp was maybe the size of two football fields smashed together. It seemed they'd taken over a campground or something, a dozen wooden cabins arranged in three neat rows near the back southern side of the camp.

The people living there didn't look the cleanest, nor the most nourished, with thin frames, partially tangled hair, and worn clothes. Hard to hold them to any standards though. Besides the kids, I counted thirteen women and twenty-eight men. Wait — make that twenty-nine men. Another came up to the fence and was let in, a limp animal most closely resembling a rabbit slung over one shoulder.

But who was that other man behind him?

A second person, this one decked in what could only best be described as a dark blue cloak, trekked up to the garage-sized gates which had been reclosed. I willed my eyes to zoom further in, inspecting this person who was dressed differently from everyone else. Bare feet poked out from the long hems of the cloak. He lowered his hood, and my brows furrowed.

I reached over and lightly slapped Michael's forearm with the back of my hand. "Hey, check it out. Does he look...?" My words faded out before I fully finished the question.

Yes, he did look familiar.

"That's it. I'm gonna kill him," Michael said seriously, pushing his hands up under him as if about to get up.

I grabbed his arm, holding him in place. "No, wait."

I watched in dismay, digging my nails into the stone beneath me, as one of the two men guarding the gates from higher posts on either side turned and shouted for someone. The man I'd pegged as the enclave leader strode through the camp to the gates and conversed with one of the guards from the ground. I could hear their conversation clearly from my mile vantage point.

"Human?" he asked.

"Yes, sir. Seems unarmed, and alone," the guard said.

The leader gave a curt nod and waved his hand outward. "Let him in."

The two guards shared a glance, then opened the gate, cranking levers on either side. The boy in the cloak, with honey-brown hair, stepped back with some alarm as the gates opened.

Three men with guns stood off behind the leader. Their guns were pointed downward for the time being, but I didn't doubt they'd readily use them.

"State your name, son," the leader spoke up, facing the newcomer who stood thirty feet away.

"Will," he said. He held himself strongly, but his pale yellow eyes glancing around gave away his nervousness.

My cheek twitched.

The leader said something else to him, Will fed him a lie, and he was invited in. Will stepped hesitantly through the gates and jumped a little as they cranked shut once more, with him standing *inside* the camp.

That sneaky rascal. He truly did have a death wish.

CHAPTER 42

"He's going to get himself killed," Michael said. His muscles were tensed beneath my grip.

"Just wait," I said quietly, my eyes trained on Will as he continued talking to the camp's leader. I wanted to watch and see what happened before diving down there. Just because Will was reckless didn't mean *I* had to be. Besides, maybe Will would get out on his own.

What I didn't understand is how the others in our unit could have let him go. Surely, they wouldn't have. He must've snuck away unaided.

"It's always curious what people tend to adorn themselves with," the leader remarked, his eyes flicking over Will's hairline.

"Oh. These?" Will reached up to the feathers on his head. "I guess I got bored." He dropped his hand and shrugged.

The leader narrowed his eyes, and for a moment I

thought Will had been caught. Then the leader slapped Will's upper arm with a rugged grin. "Ha, don't we all." He turned and gestured for Will to follow. "Come, I'll get you something to eat. Rations are low here, but I'm sure we can spare something."

Will perked up. "What, like, a home-cooked meal?"

The leader laughed, his voice a bit rusty, as if he didn't laugh often. "Sure, like that."

Will followed after him eagerly, though he still glanced over his shoulders with an alertness that had been drilled into him.

I watched as the two of them walked further into the camp, their forms passing beneath trees, the three armed men following some fifteen feet behind them. They came to a campfire surrounded by carved-out logs and took a seat, thankfully where I could see them through a hole in the canopy.

"What's your name?" Will asked.

"John," the man said, scooping out a ladleful of mystery soup into a plastic bowl. "Here." He plopped a metal spoon in it and handed the bowl to Will, who took it gratefully.

Will picked up the spoon and examined the soup curiously. "What's in it?" he asked.

"Better not to ask," John said, giving Will a wink.

Will laughed nervously. "Heh…" He brought a spoonful to his mouth and chewed. His nose crinkled discreetly, and I saw him forcefully swallow what was in his mouth. Will coughed. "So, John," he started. "There's actually a reason I came here."

"Oh?" John peered at him skeptically.

Will nodded. "I heard of your camp and thought I'd take a look. I'm wondering…"

The two kids, a boy around ten and the other, a girl no older than six, came around the fire, still kicking their ball around.

"Lucas, Samantha," John raised his voice. "Don't play so close to the fire."

"Sorry!" Lucas called, kicking the ball away. "Oops!" Lucas covered his mouth with both hands, having kicked the ball right into Will's back.

Will set the bowl aside (a bit joyfully I might add), and reached around, taking the ball in his hands. He held it out to the kid. "It's alright," he said with a smile.

The kid, Lucas, stepped up carefully to Will. He reached out slowly, and Will set the ball in his small, worn hands.

"Thanks," Lucas said, sounding young and innocent. The boy couldn't seem to stop staring at Will. I couldn't say which aspect of Will was particularly intriguing to the boy, for there were many strange things about Will. The boy's eyes traveled over his cloak, for lack of a better word. His fearfully curious gaze came to rest at the bottom of the fabric, and I saw it as well. "What's that?" the boy pointed, bending down to pull the cloak's hem away.

"It's nothing," Will discouraged. "Don't you know not to go touching other people's clothes like this?" He reached down to stop the boy, but he'd already flipped the fabric away.

"They're feathers?" Lucas questioned, backing up a step in surprise.

"Decoration," Will explained hastily. Only Will would find his situation thwarted by a ten year old.

John's countenance became cold, examining Will oddly, and he rose to his feet. "Remove your cloak," he ordered in a low, careful voice.

Will turned to the man, and Lucas backed away with the young girl. "You want me to take my clothes off?" he said accusingly.

John didn't stand down. A frown cast a doubtful appearance to him. "Do it," he said.

"What're they saying down there?" Michael asked me. He could see it, sure, but Hybrids mixed with diurnal birds had the hearing equivalent around that of a normal human. Only those mixed with nocturnal birds, such as an owl, had enhanced hearing.

I had let Michael's arm go and was preparing to jump into action myself. "Will's about to be discovered. Time to interfere," I said adamantly, a cold river of fear slithering down my spine, battling with the determination rising within me.

"Got it," Michael said, pushing himself up as well.

Michael was always so willing to follow me into

battle. I knew he'd have my back no matter what.

With Michael one step behind me, I pushed off the stone and ran forward a few steps before tossing myself into open air. For a moment I entered a freefall, gravity doing what gravity does best. With a grace parallel to that of the majestic Golden Eagle, I unfurled my wings and caught the wind, swooping out of the freefall.

Every time I took to the air, with my body and wings which were powerful and capable, a sense of immense strength and fulfillment rushed through me. I felt completely free.

I tore down the mountainside, treetops swaying in my wake. Michael was the fastest out of our entire group, but he remained by my side. The two of us dove straight down to the small valley, where Will was putting up a struggle.

Michael and I were a pair that didn't need to communicate through words. First thing upon swooping down upon the camp, I rammed into two of the armed men with my outstretched wings. They went sprawling, knocked unconscious, their guns sliding away into the dirt. Michael took down the third in a flash of feathers, and we shared a battle-ready glance before simultaneously turning to face Will and John.

Will stared at the both of us with wide eyes. His cloak floated the last foot to the ground, leaving his bare, lightly feathered chest and large feathery wings fully exposed.

John spun around, looking between the three of us with a great amount of fear in his expression. His eyes caught on the three unconscious men, and he stared at us with new conviction.

"What are you?" he stammered, a note of anger reaching his voice.

I tilted my head a notch. "You don't know?" I asked. I shared another glance with Michael. The humans didn't know about the government's Hybrid project, then?

His eyes widened. "You're what we shot at earlier," he realized. "What are you?" he asked again, this time more forcefully.

I was about to respond, but hesitated. This felt like one of those special moments where a nickname was endowed forever.

"We're the Hybrids," Will responded, shedding his fear. Welp, there went my opportunity.

"Hybrids?" John mouthed to himself, appearing stuck in disbelief.

"You really don't know?" Michael questioned skeptically, taking a curious step closer to the man.

People had started to gather, some holding wooden spears threateningly. Nobody seemed to know what to do, all of them keeping a healthy distance of at least twenty feet. I kept an eye on the guns in case anyone tried to rush for them.

"What do you want with our camp?" a brave man asked, stepping out of the circle of gathering people. He must have been around thirty, with startling blue eyes that shined through his unkempt brown hair.

"Nothing," I said, a small frown forming on my lips. "Only to retrieve this one." I flicked two fingers at Will, and anger suddenly started to well back up toward the honey-haired boy.

The people around us looked...scared. I felt sad for them. This was how people lived now?

"Where did you come from?" that same man asked. "Are you...even human?" I turned my head toward him, but he was, for the most part, looking strangely at Will.

"This was done to us against our will," Will said, a sad note to his voice. "I only want to find my family."

Michael cleared his throat, signaling for Will to stop talking.

"Against your will?" the man asked. "Who did this? How?" John seemed to be waiting for an answer as well.

I shot Will a warning look. Will tore his eyes from mine, ignoring both me and Michael. "Some government organization," Will carried on. "They knew what was going to happen to the world and altered our genes to help us better survive."

"The virus," John thought up, the pieces visibly connecting in his mind. "Wait. You mean to tell me, *that's* what they were doing? They *knew?*" He looked startled, enraged, and helpless.

"Yes," Will said. "But we escaped."

"Will? Shut up," I said coolly, my voice carrying to

him dangerously.

John's eyes flicked to me, but he seemed unable to look me in my dramatic hazel eyes for long. The brave man looked to Will, however, seemingly drawn to him from the start.

"Your name's Will? You wouldn't happen to be Noah's brother, would you?" the man spoke up reluctantly, eyeing Will with pensive blue eyes. He hadn't been around to hear Will's name earlier, only gathering because of the ruckus.

Will stared at him as the feathers along his hairline steadily rose forward, disbelief filling his expression and making his wings twitch eagerly behind his back. "You know my brother?"

The man scratched his stubbled chin, then flicked a dirt-encrusted finger at Will. "You look near identical. Well, except for the feathers," he gestured.

My mouth nearly dropped open — *nearly*. Will's family was actually here??

CHAPTER 43

"My brother is *here?*" Will breathed, barely able to get the words out. He looked around as if he would spot him in the crowd.

"He left, maybe a month and a half ago," the man informed solemnly. "Thought his chances would fare better with that larger group we've heard rumors about." He waved off his own comment disinterestedly, as if upset at Will's brother.

I didn't know Will's brother or what he looked like, but I knew Vixen. She was unmistakable, and I didn't see her among the people here. I felt my heart squeeze.

"What? Why —?" Will began to ask.

"Where is this group?" Michael asked, his voice steady but forceful.

The man took a second look at Michael, and I saw his dusty boots shift back a few inches. I couldn't blame him. If I wasn't a Hybrid myself, and if I didn't know him in the way I did, Michael might appear rather threatening. With his large, intimidating wings, forthright posture, and steely, dark gaze, he looked like an avenging angel.

"I —" The man clamped his mouth shut. "I won't say," he said resolutely.

"And why not?" I spurned. A desperate hope made me wonder if Vixen could be with this other group.

He glanced a bit anxiously between the three of us winged people.

"You expect us to trust such information to you?" John huffed. He tossed a hand at us, his expression bordering on disgust. "Look at yourselves."

Well that's just insulting. I narrowed my eyes at John, making his anger hitch as his glare skipped over me.

"Can you at least tell me if any of my other family made it? Was it only my brother?" Will asked, his voice cracking at his last words.

The man who'd stepped from the circle frowned at Will, his eyes studying the winged boy dubiously. He seemed to be considering whether or not to tell him, but ultimately said, "He was the only one."

Will blinked. I could practically see the hope crashing down within him.

"What about a girl named Vixen?" I spoke up quickly, unable to stop myself.

"No. Now leave," the brave man said aloud. "We

don't want you here."

Feeling heartache, I looked around at the forty-so people gathered around us. They wore fearful and disdainful expressions. Hardening myself against their hateful glares, I turned to John, the enclave's leader. "Tell us where this other camp is, and we'll leave. You'll never have to see us again," I promised slavishly, my tone a commanding one.

He still could barely look me in the eyes, submissive fear passing across his expression each time he dared. Angry lines were etched into his face as he stared toward the fire. I could see the mental battle going on within his head.

"Just tell them!" someone whisper-yelled from the surrounding group.

"Tell them so they'll leave!" someone else agreed anxiously.

"*Alright,*" John snapped, making those surrounding us whisper to each other anxiously.

"If you give us false information," I added warningly, "then we *will* return."

John hesitated. Obviously, that was what he'd been planning to do.

"Montana," a woman spoke up. John shot her a cold glance. His anger told me she wasn't lying. "Near Canyon Mountain." She swallowed back her fear as my eyes landed on her.

"Thanks," I said, though I still wore a frown.

Montana… That was the last stop on our list of locations. That would work out perfectly!

I sighed. "Let's leave these nice people alone now, shall we?"

"Mm," Michael agreed gruffly. He picked up their guns. The men laying on the floor groaned as he walked around them.

Michael gave me a nod, and I turned to Will. "Will? Unless you're planning on joining their group…?"

Will could sense the malicious edge to my voice. "Nope, I think I'll be going," he coughed, appearing a little coy.

"Hey, are you taking our guns?" someone contested angrily.

Michael cast his eyes briefly over the man who'd spoken. "No, we're just making sure you don't shoot at us with them," he responded in an uninterested tone. "You'll find them outside the southern wall of your camp."

The man huffed agitatedly.

"Let's get out of here," I mumbled, feeling agitated myself.

There were audible gasps of fear, wonder, and dare I say awe, as we spread our wings and rose into the air, our powerful wing strokes kicking up a tornado of leaves, disheveling peoples' clothes and hair. We weaved around trees like pros, flying out of the camp. Michael dropped the guns on the other side of the wall like he'd said he would, and the three of us flew out from the forest and across the sloping mountainside.

We flew around the mountain in silence. I leaned over and whapped Will with one of my wings.

"Ow!" he exclaimed, bringing his hand up to rub the back of his head. He glared at me indignantly.

"Do something like that again, and next time I'm leaving you to get shot," I scolded.

Michael didn't dare laugh, though I could tell he wanted to.

Another period of silence passed as I tried to let my anger slip away.

"You wouldn't let me get shot," Will muttered.

Whap!

"Ow! Hey, fine!"

"That's more like it," I grumbled, while a smile played on Michael's lips.

We circled around, staying close to the treetops the whole time, and angled down through the trees. The three of us landed on the leaf-strewn ground, tossing up shriveled brown leaves and twigs. Michael and I came to graceful stops, while Will ran a few paces before being able to bring his long, slender wings in.

The group of birdkids got up, looking curious and eager, and came over to Michael and me.

"What did you find?"

"Are they like we'd thought? How many of them are there?"

Questions were thrown at us. I waved them down as Will trudged up through the leaves behind us. He passed us and walked behind the group to a fallen tree.

Michael began telling them what'd happened. I eyed Will as he slumped down onto the rotting tree trunk, looking lost in his own thoughts. I sighed at the sight of Will and turned back to the rest of the group, joining in on the story.

Once everyone was caught up, I suggested we move further into the mountain range and stay there for a while. No way could we stay on this mountainside; we were too close to the survivor camp. We could camp out near a waterfall or something and leave in the morning. I figured we could all use a healthy break to mull things over and just relax.

We packed up and flew northeast, further along the range of the Blue Ridge Mountains. Some of the outcrops we passed over looked familiar, which was no coincidence. I'd been to these mountains before, hiked every single one of their trails.

"Down here," I called. I tucked my wings closer to my body and began descending toward a mighty scar in the mountainside.

The mixed hardwood forest split open to reveal a stony ravine, tall walls on either side, a large spill of water from a massive waterfall up ahead gushing through it.

I curved my wings, flying over the ravine. My eyes scanned the surrounding ledges, and I swooped down to a rocky overlook jutting out from the forest, nearly a hundred meters above the base of the ravine.

"It's beautiful here!" Anna said admiringly. She made a tight circle over the ravine and flapped onto the outcrop near me.

"Did you see over there, too?" I asked, pointing down across the cliff.

Stepping closer to where I was, her eyes expanded, drawing in a gasp. "Oh my gosh! That's the biggest waterfall I've ever seen!" She shook my shoulder closest to her imploringly, staring out at the waterfall. "How did I not see that coming down?"

I chuckled lightly, glad to see that she was able to enjoy things, as she'd been mostly quiet after Maine. Anna went closer to the edge of the cliff while several others landed. I peered around the mostly flat, rocky outcrop and into the trees behind it. Seemed decent enough here. I didn't like staying near water sources, but I'm not sure it mattered while so high up from the actual water. Plus, the cliff made for an easy escape route.

I unclipped my pack and tossed it aside, beneath a cluster of trees. Athletic wing strokes tossed my hair around, large feathers flapping down around me. It didn't faze me in the slightest.

Ignoring the wings around me, I stepped up to the very edge, looking over. For a moment it felt daunting, like it used to before getting wings. My heart beat harder with warning, even though my brain knew there was no danger.

I remembered standing on this very same ledge, about two years ago. Back then, I yearned to leap from this cliff and fly. But back then, it was only a yearning, nothing possible.

I got a funny feeling in the depths of my stomach, spreading outward to my toes, fingers, wingtips, and I turned around and walked away from the ledge. Ten paces later, I took in a deep breath, and a smile crept up my mouth as excitement grew in my chest. I spun on my heel and RAN off the side of the cliff, earning multiple head turns, and jumped outward at the very edge.

"YAHOOO!" My enlivened shout echoed off the walls of the ravine below. My hair streamed behind me as the wind slapped against me. Sixty meters down, I snapped out my wings and glided upward, feeling the wind and exhilaration in every fiber of my being. It was a dream come to life.

Excited shouts and whoops sounded from above as multiple others jumped down the side of the cliff. We dove and glided to our hearts' content, immersed in the greatness of whom and what we were.

At the base of the waterfall, thousands of tons of water pounding against smoothed boulders, I curved sharply up with seconds to spare. My primaries grazed the falling river as I flapped upward with everything I had, hundreds of fine droplets being thrown from the curtain of water as I rushed alongside it. I wasn't sure which was pounding harder: the water, or my enraptured heart.

The water gave way to nothingness, and I allowed myself to fall backward, turning over in the air. For a moment there was nothing, simply peace, then I held my wings in and dove straight down.

Racing the waterfall with absolutely nothing holding me back, I felt truly alive. I'm not sure there was any better feeling than this.

CHAPTER 44

After a good-hearted flight, I retrieved my pack and tossed myself leisurely off the edge of the cliff. I followed the ravine, dropping down with each mini waterfall and swerving around trees as if it were a dance I knew the moves to.

A few minutes later, I came across a nice pool of mountain water, collecting at the base of a two-foot-tall waterfall. It spanned ten feet in diameter and was no more than five feet deep, filled to the brim with crystal clear liquid.

I sat my pack aside on a dry rock and dipped my toe in. I'm sure it was cold. Every other time I'd been up here as a normal human, the water had been freezing, even in summer. However, it felt perfectly fine to me now.

With one last glance around, I stripped down and tossed my clothes on top of my pack, long overdue for a bath.

The water engulfed me, and I sunk into it with relish. After a few minutes of just relaxing, I rubbed my body clean and ducked my head below the surface to wet my hair and face. I took time to look over my wings and make sure each feather was clean. I also washed out my wounds from earlier, where the glass had cut me. It really wasn't that deep, as I was sure Michael would be glad to know. I managed to scrub the blood off as well. Then I sunk back into the water, its touch just too relaxing.

For a while I simply lay there in the water with only my nose above the surface, the warbled sound of liquid in my ears. My eyes were closed, and I let my mind fall silent. It was nice to be alone.

Through the water, the wind habitually rustled the trees' many leaves high above, so I didn't startle when I heard an additional rustle.

"Beat me to it, did you?" someone said from behind me.

I turned and stood on the spot, forgetting I wasn't clothed. "Ronin! Where the hell did you come from?" Ronin's eyes widened a sliver and grazed my body. I looked down and realized I was still naked.

"Wow, I can see why Michael and Will fancy you," he said.

I abruptly covered my front with a wide wing and stared at him with a hardened gaze. "Do you mind?" I scolded.

He lifted his red-brown eyes away with a smile. "Not

at all." Rarely had I seen his smile, and it did not please me to see it now.

I emerged from the pool of water and walked over to the pack I'd thrown over a rock, ringing out my hair as I approached. I looked over my shoulder at him to make sure he was still turned the other way before skimming the water from my skin with my hands. For good measure, I rapidly beat my wings to remove any more water and dry myself off before pulling on a clean set of clothes.

Once dressed, I shoved my dirty clothes in my pack to be washed by hand later. I slung my pack back on and faced Ronin. "Okay, you're good now," I said, gathering my rapidly drying hair behind me. Ronin, who had waited patiently, turned around. "Don't go spewing your mouth, yeah?" I cautioned him.

"Sure," he said, a no-good glint to his eyes. "Can't say I'll forget though."

I arched an eyebrow at him. "Well we wouldn't want that, now would we?" I walked past him and leapt onto a fallen tree.

"The rest of the unit is still at the waterfall," he said as I walked up the trunk. "Not sure where Will went though. Thought he would've been with you."

I watched a ray of sunlight passing through a semi-translucent, iridescent leaf, sending out an array of purples and violets onto the forest floor. "Wanted some alone time, did you?"

Ronin remained silent. I felt the fallen tree wobble an inch and knew Ronin had jumped up behind me. Then he jumped over to a neighboring stack of rocks with half a stroke of his gray-blue wings, his darker, chocolate primaries barred with thick black stripes. He wasn't as talkative as usual, but I was fine with that.

I looked around the mountain forest placidly, feeling calm in a way only a forest could make me. It was very peaceful. Golden rays of late afternoon light filtered through the canopy like a warm glow. The treetops whispered in the wind, but there was no breeze down here, making the forest floor a very quiet place. The only immediate sound besides the rustling leaves was the trickle of water behind me.

I could imagine a chipmunk, one from before the chemical was released from the bottom of the ocean, hopping along through the undergrowth. There were plenty of fallen nuts around here, and I could imagine it stuffing its cheeks with them. Thinking of this, I suddenly found myself getting hungry.

"Hey, Ronin," I said. He looked over at me through dark hair streaked with lighter strands. He too looked calm out here in the forest, with no one other than each other around. "Wanna help me with something?"

"Like what?" he asked.

♦ ♦ ♦

We returned to the cliff high above the ravine over half an hour later, seven fish strung together on a vine over

Ronin's shoulder. Each one was nearly the length of my forearm, and their glistening brown and pink bodies were covered with neat black dots. Their camouflage proved useless against Ronin's and my excellent vision.

Ronin plopped the string of fish down upon the stone with a cold *slap*.

"Eww," Aubrey complained, who was, unfortunately for her, sitting closest to the fish.

"Did you guys catch all these yourselves?" Samuel asked, looking over them with an impressed light to his eyes.

"Yep. All stinking seven of them," Ronin said, prodding one with the tip of his toe.

"Someone get a fire up and running, would ya?" I said. I chucked my pack off to the side before picking up the string of fish and taking them down to the ravine, where I prepared them with a sharp rock.

While preparing them, I couldn't help but feel a knife would make life a lot easier. I made a mental note: sunglasses, check; knife, find soon.

When I was finished and brought them back to the ledge, a fire was burning brightly. Everyone looked both relaxed and lively at the same time. I walked into the forest and selected several sticks to serve my cooking purposes, then set the rest of it up and had the fish cooking over the fire in no time.

June chucked a small stone off the side of the ledge. "Are we staying here all night then?" she asked.

I glanced up at her. The fish was almost done. "It's nice to rest," I said, feeling relaxed against the warmth emanating from the fire. My face felt tingly under its heat, but I kind of liked it, spurring memories of those times I'd gone camping with Jody, and my birth parents before her.

"Plus," Iver added, "look around. It's beautiful here. We may as well come back to live here."

"Ehh, I don't know about that," Clara said. "Trees and rocks are alright, but beds are still a lot comfier."

"Well, sure, but if you could bring them up here?" Iver encouraged. "Theoretically."

Clara tilted her head in thought but didn't respond.

"Okay," I said, taking Clara's mind off the decision, "food is done." Those closest to me got their portion of half a skewed fish first.

"This isn't so bad," Iver decided happily, taking a sizable chunk out of the meat.

"Yeah, it's actually...good," Adler admitted. "And I was apprenticing under a chef — most popular in our city — so I'd know."

"Did you?" I asked, my eyebrows rising in pleasant surprise. "You're cooking next, then, Mr. Chef."

"Nice one," Michael chuckled, shooting Adler a teasing look.

"Walked myself right into that one, didn't I?" Adler grinned shamelessly at the stone ground, then took another bite.

"Thanks, you guys," Clara said with a sigh. "It's been a while since I've had something other than plant-based biscuits."

There was agreement around the group, and I found myself grinning.

"What kind is it?" Anna asked, studying it.

Ronin looked to me and shrugged his shoulders.

"Wild Brook trout by my best guess," I said. "They like mountain streams."

Anna took a tentative bite out of it and chewed slowly. It must not have been that bad, for she took another bite, then another, and another.

I munched on my own fish and looked around thoughtfully. "Do any of you know where Will went?" I asked, realizing he wasn't eating fish with us.

"No, we thought you knew," June said.

The group seemed to tense, as if feeding off my hidden anxiety.

"Maybe he went on a food run of his own without realizing he didn't need to?" Iver offered.

"...No," I said, my voice quiet with doubt. I set the skewed fish down against one of the stones lining the fire and got up, brushing my pants off even though they weren't dirty. "I'm gonna go look for him. You guys stay here and finish eating."

The group looked after me as I walked to the edge of the cliff, Michael watching me especially so, though he kept quiet. I looked around, hoping to maybe spot him from here.

Nothing.

I jumped from the cliff in a partial dive, unfurling my wings. The wind buoyed me up, each easy stroke bringing me fifteen feet higher. I soared away, along the mountain.

It wasn't ten minutes later that I found him, sitting alone at the top of a mountain where the rock was exposed. I angled down and landed a little ways from him, then walked over the impressive boulders. Will undoubtedly saw me before I'd landed, but he didn't make any action to recognize it.

I sat down on the hard stone beside him, my wings trailing across its surface behind me. I looked around, carefully admiring the view. The tips of the mountains were all that could be seen. Everything below was covered in a blanket of low clouds, giving me the impression of sitting up on Mount Olympus. It was nice up here; peaceful and still.

A crow coasted out of the low clouds, flying over the mountainside a mile below. A forlorn figure, its dark outline contrasting greatly against the white background. It gave a lonely cry, one that reached out for miles but found no reply.

"It's strange, isn't it? How we've barely seen any birds?" I wondered aloud. My voice was on the quiet side, barely reaching the treetops surrounding the outcrop.

Will huffed. "I seem to remember very clearly a swarm of puffins."

Between watching the bird, I took a glance at Will. "Yeah. I don't mean those though. I mean since we got to the states." I gestured absently to the crow coasting in and out of the fog. "Don't you find it strange?"

"Well, maybe a little," he admitted.

I considered it, watching the lonely bird. "I suppose humans weren't the only species to experience a decline," I murmured.

CHAPTER 45

I stayed with Will at the top of that mountain for a while. Eventually, though, I figured the others might be getting worried and turned my head toward Will. My eyes looked him up and down. "Ready to head back?" I asked.

He shrugged a shoulder almost imperceptibly.

"I made fish," I said as bribery.

Will turned his head partially toward me, his narrowed eyes glancing over me. "You? Cooking? No way am I going back now," he said and turned forward again.

I continued to stare at him. Finally, a grin cracked his mouth and he glanced at me. The two of us laughed, making me feel like I'd gotten my friend back. It felt like an accomplishment to get him to laugh, and my heart felt lighter.

"Come on," I said through a smile, getting to my feet. I tapped his arm as I rose. "Let's head back."

After a brief moment of reluctance, Will sighed and

got up. His smile had faded, reducing his countenance to a sad one. He turned to leave, and I stopped him with a hand lain over his bicep. "Hey," I said, inspecting him. "Are you alright?"

Will exhaled as if it took great effort. He didn't try to pull away from me, only glancing smally at my hand, making me suddenly conscious of it. His eyes traveled over the rocks, a small frown on his lips. "No," he admitted.

I remained quiet, only letting my hand drop back to my side.

Will kicked at a small protruding nub in the stone, his gaze downward, watching it absently. "I should be happy," he said. He raised his eyebrows slightly. "My brother is alive," he nodded, his head like a bobble toy. Will raised his head, and I found my eyes meeting his. "So why aren't I?"

I didn't want to give him a half-baked answer, so I considered it. "Just because you've found something good," I spoke carefully, "doesn't mean all the bad goes away."

Will searched my eyes, looking back and forth between them as if trying to find a deeper meaning behind my honest and patient gaze. He took in a breath and looked out over the sloping mountainside. "I suppose you're right," he murmured, almost as if to himself.

I watched him quietly, not wanting to push him when he was fragile like this.

"Can I ask you something?" he inquired.

"Sure, what is it?"

"Who's Vixen?" Now it was his turn to watch *me*.

"My best friend. She's the only other person I had besides Jody," I confessed after a moment, then bit the inside of my lower lip to prevent myself from saying anything else. If I got into it, I'd get sad, and if I got sad, it might ruin the work put into making Will feel better.

He sighed as if sharing in my grief, then flicked his eyes back over me. "Alright, let's go," he said, when I said nothing more. "Guess I'll try some of your fish."

A grin tugged at my lips again. "I'm sure you'll love it," I said.

Will huffed in a small laugh.

I jumped into the air first, then circled around to wait for him. Will leapt across the uneven rock surface, running ten paces forward with his wings extended before lifting into the air. Banking softly, I met him over the mountain ridge, and the two of us traveled back to the cliff together.

"Ah, you're alive," Iver said upon our return, looking relaxed, with his bare feet hanging over the side of the cliff.

"Yea," Will said lamely.

Besides Iver, the others didn't pay much heed. Half sat around the fire, the other half at the edge of the cliff, their feet dangling over the side. I could tell they felt relieved, even if they didn't make any fuss about it.

Michael, sitting by the fire, studied the two of us, then let his eyes travel away with a certain soreness. I saw Aubrey, sitting at the cliff's edge, take a glance at Will, her expression tightening.

I picked up the uneaten half of my fish and grabbed another for Will. "Here," I said, handing him the skewed fish.

"Thanks," he said tamely, taking the fish from me.

Seeing Michael look somewhat troubled, try as he may to conceal it, I walked around the fire and sat down beside him on his left, our sides bumping together. I rested my right wing across his, and he turned his head to give me an easy smile, nudging my shoulder affectionately with his. I felt him relax beside me, his worry dissipating. Turning toward the fire, I took a bite out of my fish, feeling good. There was no need for the fire anymore, but something about that intoxicating warmth and those flickering flames that were like the sun to my eyes was engrossing.

My eyes wandered over the charred wood while Will took a seat on the opposite side of the fire, looking somewhat out of place with his estranged disposition. I found it curious how the darkest shadows were those closest to the flames, hidden within the deep cracks of the burning wood. So engrossed in the peculiar nature of the fire, I didn't hear my name being called. It must have been the second or third 'Rory' when I finally lifted my eyes from the fire. "Hm?"

"We were asking how much further it is until the next stop," Adler told me. He watched me curiously across the fire.

"Oh." I did some quick calculations in my head, the map displayed on the inside of my mind. "Maybe six, six and a half hours?" I offered. "Less if we fly higher." Ronin still had no intentions on going to Indiana, so we were skipping ahead to Missouri.

"I wonder why we're so spread out," Michael said, poking at the fire with a charred stick.

"What d'you mean?" I asked him.

"Like, why not collect us from the same general area? Why so spread out?" he explained passively.

Hmm. I didn't have a good answer for that. While I thought, I watched the stick Michael was jabbing the fire with, sending sparks floating upward where it aggravated the burning embers. I knew there were other Hybrids, scattered around the world at different bases. I'd learned that early on. Why take people from a bunch of different states from across the country, however, I did not know.

"They must've had their own reasons," June supplied. "They're by no means stupid."

"They are *crazy* though," Ronin remarked.

"Crazy, sure," June agreed. "But not stupid. Who knows their reasoning behind it. Guess we'd have to ask them."

If June didn't have an answer for the minds of those scientists, I thought, it was likely none of us would. She'd told us a while back about her interest in chemistry, having majored in it before the apocalypse. When she'd told us, I'd nearly laughed. A smart girl studying chemistry gets turned into an experiment? Ha, there was never a shortage of irony around here.

At June's last words, we fell into a strange, uncomfortable silence. I felt like a mind reader again, knowing that everyone was internally shuddering at the idea of going back for *any* reason.

From the silence, Samuel asked in an ordinary voice, "What do you think Elena is doing?" I glanced up to see him frowning slightly at the fire.

"Probably backstabbing someone else," Ronin laughed coldly.

Samuel's frown deepened.

I picked up a small twig between my fingers and chucked it gently at Samuel where he sat at my three-o'clock. It bounced lightly off his chest, yet he still startled.

"Hey, try not to worry too much about it," I said. "She's where she chose to be."

Samuel ran a hand over his dark chest feathers and met my eyes momentarily. "Yeah," he said quietly.

My eyes flicked over him. "You have a good heart, Samuel," I said with a small frown, looking back toward the fire. I picked up another twig and chucked it into the flames. "There's nothing you can do about Elena though."

Samuel lifted his gaze to me; I could feel it. "Thanks," he said after a while, his tone sincere but somewhat small.

While there was still light, we bathed, washed our clothes and lay them out to dry, refilled our water canisters, took the time to smooth out our feathers, and just hung out. Nothing tried to attack us way up in these mountains. It was a refreshing change.

When the sun finally closed on the horizon, we got to experience a magnificent painting, as brief as it was, then lay down for the night, spread out over the rocky outcrop of the cliff. A smoky scent from the put-out fire wafted through the air, stirring familiar, pleasurable feelings. I could still hear the crackle and hiss of the charred wood as the last of the embers slowly died.

I lay down perpendicular to Michael, the back of my head resting on his lower back while he lay facedown, using his folded arms as pillows. The stone dipped just perfectly to accommodate my wing structure, making it not all that uncomfortable to lie on my back despite the fact I was indeed laying on hard stone. By the change in breathing around me, I could tell the others were drifting off to sleep. I, however, was not tired in the slightest and stared up with wide, alert eyes, taking in the night sky dotted with stars. The world was still plenty bright to me. Iver, somewhere off to my side, had a wing strewn over his head to block out the light I was delightedly letting in. I could tell he was still awake as well. Him, and Anna, whose tears slipped quietly onto the stone.

Michael's warm, feathered wing, which was tossed across me like a blanket, twitched. I turned my head to look along his back to his head full of attractively messy black hair, and saw his brow furrow into his arm.

Having bad dreams had become a common occurrence for all of us. Even still, my heart felt concerned watching him. I reached over, beneath his wing, and ran my fingers across his back in gentle, soothing motions.

"It's okay," I whispered. His wing twitched one more time, but then his brow lessened and his feathers slackened over me. I felt his body relax beneath me at my soft touch. With a small sigh, I turned back toward the stars.

CHAPTER 46

The next morning, we each ate another one of our precious rations left over from the base and packed up to leave. I was feeling well-rested despite my lack of sleep.

It was hard to leave the mountains. While the others got the last of their things together, I stood at the edge of the cliff, looking over an enrapturing scene. Unlike at Jody's house, I had only good memories from this place. Leaving made me feel like I was leaving home.

I'll be back, I promised myself.

"Ready?" Clara asked from somewhere behind me. I didn't know who she was talking to; maybe everyone.

Anna responded with, "Yep." I knew she had a rough night, but she seemed in better spirits this morning. Must have been the refreshing mountain air working its magic.

I didn't need to see when they were all ready to leave; I could hear it — the impatient shuffling of feet on stone. I pulled my sunglasses out and slipped them onto my nose.

"Alright, let's head out," I said without turning back. I was already at the very edge of the cliff, so I merely looked down and stepped off, dropping into nothing. Twenty feet down, I tossed my wings out and caught the air, then soared along a good part of the ravine's length before angling out and away.

I heard the unfurling of feathered sails behind me, and soon, ten pairs of wings were flapping around me.

When a horse is galloping across a wide, open field beside a whole herd of other powerful beasts, I bet he feels a whole lot like I did flying with a bunch of other powerful winged people. We were together, we were strong, and we were free. It felt amazing to be flying with such a group.

Today, we would be heading to southeastern Missouri. Aubrey's anxiety was poorly concealed, try as she may to shove it down. I heard Will give her some support, to which she made a brief, rude comment and flapped away from him. Seemed all was not right in paradise. Will had only himself to blame, but I still felt bad for him.

We caught up to some vigorous winds miles above the ground, and we soared along their lengths, easily adding an additional fifty miles per hour to our speed and greatly improving our time. Those with shorter wings that weren't meant for soaring had to flap a lot more, but it was manageable. It felt like barely any time had passed at all when Adler spoke up, announcing the name of Aubrey's town. Aubrey didn't have raptor vision, but Adler did.

I heard Aubrey suck in a breath. "So close?" The sound of the wind against her wings changed, and in the next instant, she shot by beneath us, diving downward.

"Down we go," Michael announced lazily. He brought his wings in close and began falling like a torpedo, quickly and easily gaining speed.

A giddy feeling rising inside me, I angled down into a dive as well. The first drop in altitude made my stomach feel full of butterflies. We were easily over five miles above the ground, and I was able to reach a much faster diving speed from this height. Back at the base, the flight trainer had clocked our speeds on trial runs. I knew that as I approached the ground, I was doing so at over five-hundred miles per hour, my nose specially designed with internal features that kept the wind from hindering my breathing. At this speed, I shouldn't have been able to see straight, let alone my hair look good.

Closest behind me, though still a large difference between us, was Adler, and Clara and Ronin behind him. Most of us easily passed Aubrey and had to level out and wait a few hundred meters above the decimated town while she caught up.

Although Aubrey was likely about to be very disappointed and have her heart crushed, I couldn't help but look over at Michael with a wide grin, avid for the exhilaration of diving.

He shot back a grin of his own, his dark hair even more windblown than usual.

When Aubrey caught up, we hastily looked away from each other to hide our joy.

Aubrey flapped out of her dive and peered around. She made a frustrated sound. "I still can't see anything. I have to get closer," she said. She dropped even further, but I held back the others with a gesture of my hand, looking back over my shoulder at them. Flying too close could be dangerous.

They held their positions while we watched Aubrey fly a mere fifty meters from the ground, swerving around and over tree tops and buildings. I was on high alert, should anything jump out and attack Aubrey, or, god forbid, were we to get shot at again.

She took a sharp left and continued southwest for another minute, then circled over a towny neighborhood for a moment before dropping down to a wide black street.

I assessed our surroundings and determined the top of a nearby four-story brick building should be alright to land on. It had a flat cement top with a protruding metal doorway near one corner, and it provided a decent view of the surrounding streets and buildings.

Signaling to the others with a twist of my hand, I pointed down to the building and swooped away. I coasted silently down to the rooftop and tucked my wings in, then stepped to the side so the others would have plenty of room to land. Clara and June came down next and moved aside as well, then Adler, Ronin, Iver, and so on. Michael landed last, balancing on the edge of the short concrete wall lining the roof with his wings flared elegantly behind him.

This was a strange neighborhood, in my opinion. I looked around from this new rooftop perspective while Michael jumped lightly down from the short wall and came over to me, his right hand sliding absently around my waist as he scoped out our surroundings as well. With a thick black road lined in variously sized red brick buildings chock-full of large glass windows, it looked like one of those towns you'd see in a winter romance movie. Except, it was the beginning of summer, and you couldn't watch movies anymore. Even if you could, there was no one left to film.

With so many alert eyes on the roof, we were well protected. Michael's hand slipped away as I walked over to the western edge of the building overlooking the street, and watched as Aubrey, who was a few blocks away, climbed through a second-story window of a red-brown townhouse. *Well, that's one way.* Me, personally, I preferred diving straight through them.

Although I couldn't see Aubrey, only her shadow passing across the inside of a dusty window every now and then, I could hear her. Seemed she'd found some answers, though not the ones she'd hoped for. None of us had any problem waiting, especially those of us who'd already had the privilege to be disappointed. Heartbreak from a tragedy such as losing your family didn't disappear overnight, but the first step to accepting it and moving on was actually facing it.

I'm not entirely sure how long we waited around on the roof for. Maybe thirty minutes? Forty? It didn't really matter. The sun was bright and warm, occasionally filtering in through a thin sheet of white clouds high above. I had my wings gently splayed against the sun, soaking up its warmth as I leaned forward against the concrete wall, my hands clasped lazily in front of me while my eyes wandered.

Good weather, no rabid animals, no guns, no —

My sensitive ears pricked, and I tensed, looking around astutely.

"What is it?" Michael asked quietly, having been leaning against the wall beside me. He looked over at me, then back out over the street apprehensively.

"Not…sure…" I got the words out distractedly, listening intently. I turned around, looking east. It was coming from that direction. I pushed off from the wall and strode up to the eastern edge of the building, overlooking a back section of town, some trees growing up from abandoned alleys. "Iver?"

"Yeah, I hear it too," he said anxiously, coming to stand next to me.

It was an abnormal sound, a shuffled scraping, like

rubber scuffing against asphalt. It was unlike any pawstep I'd ever heard. If anything, it was human, a rhythmic bipedal shuffling.

"Another human?" I questioned, my breath hitching.

"No way," Iver said, his deep yellow-amber eyes widening. "You don't actually think...?"

"What should we do?" Clara asked, her wings twitching in a panicked manner.

"Someone's gotta get Aubrey, for starters," I said, my eyes trained on a distant spot. It was impossible to see the source of the noise from down here; I'd need to get into the air, but then *I* might get spotted.

"I'll get her," Will said determinedly.

I nodded absently before I could properly think through Will's decision. The sound of wings came from behind me, kicking up wind, then disappeared down to the street below.

"How far is it?" Michael asked, not a hint of fear in his voice.

"Maybe a mile away, but it's walking toward us," I said.

"Mmm, I'm not saying it's not cool to see another living person, but, uh, maybe we should decline the invitation and get out of here?" Samuel offered.

You're probably right, I thought. But the prospect of simply leaving without even a glimpse would surely tear me up inside later. In a world where the streets lay dormant and the only sounds were that of the breeze and nature, add in the creak of old buildings and the flapping of tattered fabric clinging to skeletons in the wind, the shuffling of a single life was like finding a diamond among a field of coal.

Regardless, we waited for Will to come back with Aubrey.

"Where is he?" June reproached, turning on her heel to make another lap at the edge of the roof. "What's taking so long?"

I was generally calm and patient, but Will *was* taking a while. The footsteps were getting closer, having closed in by a third of a mile already.

I walked up to the western edge of the roof and looked down the street. Hearing the tense conversation — neigh, argument — inside the townhouse, I was regretting letting *Will* of all people go. He was the last person who should have fetched her!

Amidst my mental scolding, I said, "Someone else needs to go get them." I shouldn't go down there either, not unless I wanted it to take even longer.

Ronin sighed and jumped up easily onto the concrete wall, with great agility. "If I'm not back in five, send someone else in to save me," he said, then jumped right down off the side of the four-story building. The flutter of his sail-like wings traveled to my ears, and in the next instant, he was striding down the street, looking around apprehensively. He picked up into a jog.

I went back to the opposite side of the roof, trying to

peer out at the source of the noise. There were too many buildings in the way between me and the shuffling still some two-thirds a mile away.

"As soon as they come out of that building, book it to the sky," I ordered.

"Will do," Samuel agreed.

"Are we absolutely sure we shouldn't check it out?" June asked. A thousand more questions lay behind that one, none of which had to be asked aloud; they were already in each of our minds. What if we knew them? What if they could tell us something we didn't know? What if they needed help?

I hesitated, not wanting to divulge into my plans to do just that: check it out. They'd know soon enough though. "I'm gonna go see what, or who, it is once everyone is in the air and safe," I said.

"Alone?" June speculated.

I glanced at her. "I can be pretty stealthy when I want to be. It'll be safer that way."

June pursed her lips, looking in the mood to argue but knowing it was pointless.

"Like hell you are," Michael said.

I found my eyes narrowing as I turned around. Michael was steadfast, his gaze full of caring conviction. "Yes, I am," I said, a warning edge to my tone that meant 'don't cross me.' "I can be in and out before they even realize I'm there." *I've got those ninja owl genes, remember?* "Your wings are too loud."

Michael and I stared at each other, locked in a non-verbal battle. The other birdkids standing around us suddenly became uncomfortable, watching their two leaders.

"Fine," he said eventually, through gritted teeth.

I eased off, lifting my indomitable hazel gaze mercifully off him. Just as that was resolved, I heard a door opening and three sets of feet padding out onto the asphalt. I went to the edge and leaned forward expectantly. Indeed, an angry Will and Aubrey were walking behind a determined-looked Ronin.

"They're out. To the sky we go," I announced. "Make sure to head west," I reminded them. "I'll catch up to you."

They didn't have to be told a second time. One by one, they leapt over the edge of the roof and snapped their wings out, flying upward. They made sure not to fly too high, however, for fear of being spotted too easily by whatever was approaching.

In less than a minute, everyone was flying west over the town. Will had run down the wide street and lifted into the air, joining Aubrey and Ronin as they chased after the others. Michael was the last one on the roof, and he gave me one last, hard look before jumping over the edge of the roof after them.

Then it was just me, looking between those flying away and the footsteps approaching from the opposite direction. I took several wide steps forward and jumped into the air, unfurling my wings. I dipped slightly over the street, then curved around to sneak up on the approaching creature from the side.

The shuffled walking got nearer, echoing down an empty street, and I angled toward a three-story building squatting beside the road. I landed as stealthily as possible, which, for someone who had always been agile and was now hybridized with an owl, was pretty darn stealthy.

Staying low, I tucked my wings back and crept up to the far corner edge of the building. Cautiously, and very slowly, I peered over the brick edge. A shadow appeared on the ground, stretching out over the asphalt. In the next instant, a figure became visible, shuffling haphazardly down the street.

I held my breath, watching them. This person — he was human, but in all the ways humanity shined through, there was only a coldness to him. His torn jeans and gray shirt, loose against his thin frame, were stained in red, forming a sickening abstract painting. Black boots scraped against the ground, and I could see they were near their end, the soles rubbed almost completely off. Clean lines, pooling beneath his sky-blue eyes, ran down his dirt-covered face. Messy brown hair fell overgrown around his worn countenance, framing his face savagely.

Heartache toward this beat, worn man at first glance would have been anyone's natural response, but I could not feel such a thing when looking at him; those ragged nails crusted with blood, those incredibly light blue eyes which darted around hungrily, without a soul behind them.

Something was seriously wrong with this person.

CHAPTER 47

They'd said that it wasn't supposed to happen, that it wasn't possible. But looking at this man who had no humanity, blood stains at the corners of his dried lips, I knew it to be the case.

People weren't supposed to be able to be affected by the chemical. Yet, here he was, shuffling down the street right in front of me. I could see it in his eyes and in the way he moved — he was more aggressive, ready to tear apart anything placed in front of him. Whether or not his intelligence had become enhanced, however, was still up for debate. Though if he was still alive after all this time, wandering alone nonetheless, it must also be the case.

I shuddered. I had to get out of here.

Something further down the street crashed, muffled within a building several blocks down, like a pot falling to the floor. My head spun toward it, then back to the humanoid. His posture was scarily alert, his too-bright eyes focused on the source of the sound.

The man went faster down the street, his footsteps becoming quieter. It was like a switch had been turned on inside of him, turning him from a listless shell of a person into a stealthy predator.

I tried to focus on what had caused the noise, for a brief moment thinking maybe someone from my unit had followed me back here. But no, they wouldn't be so careless (except maybe Will, I scoffed internally), and what reason would they have to be *inside* the building?

Staying put, I watched as the affected man went up to the building the noise had come from. He used my move, the one where you crouch lower before peering around a bend. Then, in a flash, he darted into the building. Screams rang out, one a woman, another a child.

The feathers along my body pricked to full attention, feeling doused in a frigid bath. *Oh [insert your choice of curse word here].* That could not have been good.

I wrestled with myself for a moment, if I'm being honest, torn between keeping myself safe and alive and possibly keeping whoever was down *there* alive. I jumped over the side of the building a second later, throwing my wings out, and glided quickly to the building the man had entered, coming to a running landing on the hard asphalt.

Just as I rounded toward the flung-open door, two people came crashing out in a panic. I jumped back almost ten feet as a terrified woman and a young boy stumbled out onto the road. They were normal humans, and afraid.

Springing into action, I rushed toward the door again as the affected, hungry man strode out. Using my own momentum, I swung my folded wing around, my feathers barely touching the pavement as I pivoted. Aiming up and under his rib cage, I landed a deadly blow to his kidneys, sending him flying back through the air, crashing inward through the doorway.

"*Mom!*" a young boy cried, his voice muffled by his own fear.

I spun to look at them, and my heart clenched. I hadn't seen it before, but the woman, inevitably the boy's mother, had a bloody gash the width of my hand drawn across her left side. Her clothes, covered in dirt, were now stained with a deep crimson. The child, no older than seven, grasped at his mother desperately as she lay on the ground gasping.

An angry grunt made me spin back toward the door, staring into sky-blue eyes that wanted me dead. He clawed his way up the doorframe, one hand over his kidney where I'd hit him. The muscles in his neck were tight with pain, but he forged on, the ligaments under his thin skin tensing.

Another surge of adrenaline coursed through me, and I waited until he came at me, opening himself up to vulnerability, to strike out at the base of his throat with my fist. He choked, unable to draw in a single breath, but still stumbled toward me, and in the next instant, I bent forward and threw him over my shoulder, sending him slamming into the asphalt.

Before he could get back up, I dealt a final blow. Bringing my right wing around at full force, I slammed the hard edge of it into his temple, rendering him — finally — unconscious.

I huffed, staring down at the man whose fate I'd sealed, my eyes flicking over him for any sign of movement. His bony chest rose and fell with some difficulty, shuddering, then fell one last time.

The crying of a young boy brought my attention away from the dead man to a despairing scene in the middle of the street. I jogged a few paces over to them, standing hesitantly behind the boy, his shoulders shaking.

"Here, let me help," I urged, kneeling down next to him.

He looked over at me through red, watery eyes, tears streaming down his cheeks. "Who are you?" he asked through sobs. He pulled up his mother's hand into his, turning back toward her. "She's all I have left. Save her, please."

I didn't respond to him, not wanting to give him any promises. Pulling her torn shirt up to her rib cage, the exposed gash on her side did not look good. I looked around for something to use, but all there was were the clothes on our backs. My eyes landed on the boy's jacket.

"Quick, take off your jacket," I said. He looked at me as if I was crazy, still crying. "Quickly!" I urged.

My voice spurred him into action, and he tried to pull his jacket off. I helped him get it off the rest of the way and balled it up, pressing it to the woman's wound.

"What're you doing?" the boy asked dazedly.

"Applying direct pressure to the wound in order to try to stop the bleeding," I responded, trying to keep my cool. I'd just killed someone. Someone else was dying in front of me.

A feeble hand came up and grasped my wrist, making me suck in a breath. Her fingers were cold, the warmth in her palm also quickly waning.

"Please, take care of my son," she said, her words a series of gasps. Dark blue eyes pleaded with me, staring up at me with a dying wish. Her dirty blonde hair was swirled around her head like a halo.

My heart stammered in my chest. "I —" Now suddenly *I* was the choked-up one.

"Please," she said, her energy fading. "My son…"

I didn't know what to say — what to do. "Conserve your energy," I pressed, unable to look the woman in the eyes any longer. I continued to hold down the blood-dyed jacket to her wound, but it was just too deep. I wasn't making any difference. *No no no.* While the woman pleaded with me, I pleaded with the universe. *Don't let this happen!*

The boy broke down into another volley of sobs, his

head of dark blond hair hanging over his mother.

"I love you, Emery," she said weakly.

"Mom. Mom, don't go," the boy, Emery, said, holding back his sobs long enough to utter the words.

His young voice should not have been filled with so much pain. It wasn't right. None of this was right.

CHAPTER 48

I watched as the woman took her last breath. Her head fell back onto the pavement, her dark blue eyes staring up at nothing.

Emery broke down again, hugging his mother. "No… Mom."

I let go of the jacket, letting my hands slip away as I rocked back onto my heels. I didn't know what to do. I didn't even know this boy, and he didn't know me. The rest of my unit was currently flying west, gradually putting more and more distance between us.

I turned my head, looking in the direction they'd left. Glancing at the boy, I knew what I had to do.

"Emery?" I asked testingly. I reached hesitantly out to touch his shoulder, which was still shaking. He turned, and I drew my hand back before I'd even touched him.

"I don't want to leave her. I don't care what she told you to do," he said angrily. His dark blue eyes, just like his mother's, glared at me. "I don't need anyone to take care of me."

I frowned as he turned back toward his mother. Looking west again, I tried to figure out what to do. Obviously, I couldn't *leave* him here... He'd be a sitting duck! But I couldn't just take him away from his mother, either.

"Emery," I tried again. "There's nothing left to do. Your mother... You should come with me."

His sobs had turned to sniffles, probably from the shock. He shot me an angry glance, though the effect was lost by the sadness drowning him. "I'm seven, not handicapped," he snapped, a deep frown etched into his face. He swiped a wrist under his congested, dripping nose. "Not like I haven't seen one of my parents die before."

I pursed my lips, unsure how to respond to that. "I know you're not handicapped," I said. This seemed to be the right thing to say. His anger toward me lessened, and he swiped at his nose again.

"I can't leave her here," he said.

For a seven year old, I thought, he was handling this pretty well. I hadn't been around while the chemical was unleashed upon the world, but he had. Some became stronger — were forced to — I suppose.

"Do you want to...bury her?" I asked. I didn't know what his family's religion had been, but I was trying.

Emery looked at the asphalt beside his mother. He nodded.

"Alright. We'll do that," I sighed.

I waited for Emery, then eventually stooped down and picked up the woman in my arms. It wasn't all that difficult to carry her, what with my enhanced strength. It was just that the weight of the dead was more than literal.

Emery walked beside me as we went down the street. I'd flown over the town, obviously, and knew there was a nice park further down the street and to the right.

He blinked at me, his tennis shoes scuffing across the asphalt. "You have wings?" he asked, as if it was a casual question.

"Uh." I glanced over my shoulder. "Yeah, last time I checked."

A minute later, he asked, "Can you fly?"

I looked over at him. He seemed too numb to look back up at me. "Yeah."

He didn't say anything more, which I felt was odd, even in this scenario. When we got to the park, it turned out to be even nicer on the ground than from the air. The plants had overtaken the block, creating a mythical, forest-y feel.

I laid her down near a bed of blue and white flowers, then went to look for something to dig with while Emery stayed at her side. A garden house nearby luckily had some shovels in store.

Emery stood up when I neared, and I handed him a shovel. He took it in his small hands. It was sad to see, but I knew it served him better to help. We got to work, and it wasn't too much longer when we had, more or less, a rectangle dug out from the ground. I picked up the woman again and laid her down gently in the grave we'd dug. Then I stepped aside, allowing Emery to say good-bye to his mother.

Once he was done, I clamped a supportive hand on his shoulder, and he looked up at me for a moment, his eyes watery.

No words needed to be said from me. No words *could* be said. He tossed the first handful of dirt into the grave, and I filled in the rest.

I wasn't sure how long the others in my unit had been waiting for me at this point, but it was more so at the back of my mind at the moment. Even so, we really should have been going.

"Is there anything else you want to do?" I asked, peering sideways at him.

He shook his head 'no.'

"We should get going then," I said, jabbing the shovel into the ground next to me, producing a muffled *snick* as it slid into the dirt. "My friends are waiting for me."

Emery spun around to me. "There are more like you?" he asked. His countenance was still sad, but his eyes sparked with some interest.

Holding onto this spark, I said, "There are. I'm sure you'll find they're alright."

"But… How will we reach them?"

The corner of my mouth curved in a small, semi-mischievous grin. "How do you feel about flying?" I questioned.

◆ ◆ ◆

"Don't look down," I said, gripping his arms, which were wrapped around my shoulders. He had to lie on top of my pack, which actually served better for me, providing my wings with enough space to move freely.

His breathing was rapid and panicked. "I'm going to fall!" he cried.

"No, you're not," I stated plainly. "Just don't go moving around a whole bunch."

We flew at a low altitude, less than a mile above the ground. Not because I was afraid I'd drop him, in which case a higher altitude would give me a better chance at catching him in time, but because I didn't want him to get too cold. Just because I had a great tolerance to it didn't mean I'd forgotten normal people didn't. Not to mention I'd ruined his jacket…

Oh geez, was I crazy for this? Taking in some random kid? The simple answer: yes, yes I was.

It was no surprise to find that the others had waited for me, a few miles out of town, but I felt relieved nonetheless. Along the straight shot to our next location, heading west-southwest, I found them circling a couple miles above me. They dove down to meet me, and I was immediately greeted with strange, surprised looks.

"We were getting worried!" Will exclaimed as he flapped down, almost sounding angry. Then he halted midair, dropping ten feet as his wings stalled. He caught himself and stared at me in confusion.

"Rory...?" Michael led.

"I know," I said, flying in place. "Some stuff happened. I'll explain, but the short story is that the kid is with us now."

I felt Emery shift behind me, looking over my shoulder at Michael and the others. A gasp escaped him.

Michael's eyes shifted to my shoulder, looking at the kid. "Mahogany Meeting!" Michael called, his voice deep and demanding. He shot me one last glance, then dove toward the ground.

I crinkled my nose, knowing I was gonna get it. I didn't lose speed rapidly like Michael; I lost altitude in gradual wheeling arcs. Couldn't very well go saving the boy only to give him a heart attack, now could I?

Down on the ground, surrounded by forest, Emery waited off by a large tree, kicking its trunk absently, while I had a meeting with my group.

I told them everything that'd happened while they stared me down, taking a glance over my shoulder at Emery as I told the story. "I couldn't leave him," I finished, my voice nearly cracking from the pity I felt for the child.

The group shared looks with each other.

"We should take him back to the survivor camp in

Virginia," June said. "It's the closest place we know."

I shook my head. "We promised them we'd never come back, not unless their information proved to be false."

"Then, we'll drop him off near the camp and have him go there alone," June offered. "That way they don't need to know we were involved."

I opened my mouth to refuse, but the words were lost to me. I felt troubled and looked over at Emery again. He had his back against the trunk he'd been kicking, his skinny arms crossed over his tank top.

He looked toward us, knowing and angry. "I know you just want to get rid of me," he spoke up. "So just get on with it."

I pressed my lips into a tight line. "Nobody's trying to get rid of you, Emery," I told him. "We're just trying to figure out what's best for you." I gestured around the group. "In case you haven't noticed, we're not the most *practical* group for you to join."

"I don't care that you have wings. It doesn't bother me," he said. He folded his arms tighter over his chest, resolutely looking away.

I sighed.

"Hm. Strange kid," Adler murmured, peering toward Emery with a certain level of interest.

"Fine, we'll take him with us to the survivor enclave in Montana," Michael determined. "It should be safer for him there than in Virginia anyway." Michael gazed at the boy, and for once I couldn't completely tell what he was thinking.

"Won't that slow us down by a lot?" Samuel argued reasonably.

"It will," Michael agreed. "But unless you want to take the kid back to Virginia yourself...?"

Samuel sighed. "No, that's alright. He'll just feel like we're dumping him, and he doesn't need that right now."

"Poor kid," Aubrey said sadly, looking after him with a frown.

"He was lucky you were there when you were," Will said. "Otherwise he would have shared the same fate as his mother."

Ronin took in a breath, as if rounding on a thought. "You really killed a man?" he questioned me, looking at me with skeptical, squinted eyes.

I cleared my throat and looked down, nudging a twig with my toe. I'm still not sure how I felt about that ordeal, but more than that, I worried whether I'd have to do it again at some point in the unpredictable and foreboding future. But maybe — if that's how it would be from now on — it would get easier with each time. *Oh god, this is my life.*

"Way to be subtle," Will berated Ronin.

"I'm just asking," Ronin defended himself. He elbowed Will.

Will frowned at him and elbowed him back. In no time, the two boys were scuffling with each other.

"Cut it out!" I scolded them, punching each of them on the bicep.

"Ow," Will frowned, rubbing his arm. 'What did I do wrong?' his upset gaze seemed to say.

"Yes, I did, alright? I did what had to be done. Now, can we just get back in the air? We've got a lot of ground to cover and only half a day left to do it." I stared them both down, then looked briefly over the rest of the group.

"Yea," Samuel said submissively. His reply was followed up with a bunch of similar replies.

"Remind me not to mess with you," Ronin ragged under his breath.

I puckered my lips, staring at him dourly. He twitched his eyebrows in a regretful 'oh well' gesture.

"Alright then," I said to the whole group. "Emery?" I called over my shoulder. "Hop on. You're coming with us on a road trip."

"A road trip?" he remarked from the base of the tree.

"Whatever you want to call it," I said. "Now come on."

Yep, that's me: 'Ms. Motherly Instinct.' Ha. No. This was going to be a long trip.

CHAPTER 49

Carrying the boy, we had to stop a lot more often. A dark side of me was glad it was the kid who'd survived instead of the adult; no way could I carry his parent over this distance.

The day, while it had started out decent enough, was now speeding by. The sky had taken on a darker shade by the time we made it to western Oklahoma. We passed a couple tornadoes, tall funnels reaching for the sky but unwilling to part with their beloved ground. My body tilted to the side, and I curved leisurely around a funnel, keeping clear of it by a good hundred meters or so.

I can't explain it, but not even the tornadoes bothered me. Maybe it was the perspective; looking down at them was much less stressful than being at ground level with destruction raging around you. It felt natural to be curving around them, soaring through the air. Emery, on the other hand, was still getting used to this amazing perspective. Sometimes I'd glance over my shoulder out of the corner of my eye, behind my sunglasses. I'd caught him in a state of pure awe. I almost worried he might let go of my shoulders and try his own hand at flight.

We landed in a rural part of western Wyoming, following Iver. Emery slid off my back, his shoes producing a puff of dry, red dirt, as I took my sunglasses off and gazed around. We'd landed a little ways down Iver's property, which was basically a giant, empty expanse of dried grass and dirt. Still, not bad.

The grass, which only grew midway up my calves, crunched underfoot, baked under the sun's relentless summer heat. It seemed even these plants, with all their enhancements, still had limitations.

A crack of thunder made me look to the north. Overwhelming a salmon-colored sky was a dark mass approaching in the far distance. Lightning struck, a white and purple volt, illuminating the landscape tenfold for a brief moment.

Emery jumped, and I huffed in a light laugh, peering at him out of the corner of my eye. He didn't notice. I tapped his shoulder with the back of my fingers, making him jump a second time. "It's alright," I said, a teasing note to my voice. Us birdkids may get a little antsy around storms, sure, but we still knew we'd be fine.

He swallowed. "I know," he said in an almost convincing tone, but the waver in his voice gave him away.

We waited for Iver, but he came back to inform us

that his family was nowhere to be found. He had a second location in mind though. Squinting at the approaching storm, he said, "Feel free to bunk in the house tonight. That storm is going to hit us."

Emery glanced at me nervously. I really felt the need to tease him, but I held back. It made no sense, how he could be so strong in some areas, yet scared of a storm.

"You'll be fine," I told the boy.

There was a grin I was trying hard to hide on my face, but it flickered away in surprise when Emery reached up and grabbed my hand. I looked down at him, unsure how to feel about the young boy.

I put my feelings about him aside and led him up to the house, thanking Iver as I passed him. "Oh, and Iver?" I said, turning sideways as I walked. "Take someone with you, just in case." Didn't need him getting lost in a raging storm.

"Alright," he said, unopposed to the idea. Iver was too kindhearted. I sometimes worried about him, but hey, he was alive, wasn't he?

We walked up to the house, toward the wide front porch, while Adler flew off with Iver. Outside, the wood-paneled house looked old and weatherworn. Inside, it was actually pretty nice; a rustic, open-concept house you'd expect a couple of old, satisfied people to be living in. The dining room, capable of seating a dozen people, was openly connected to the living room, furnished with a full-blown stone fireplace. Partially separated from the dining room was a large kitchen with granite countertops and silver appliances hanging from a cook's rack above an island counter. A hallway shot off from the living room, but I didn't want to explore the house too much.

After peering around for a moment, I pulled a white lace curtain aside, looking out of a north-facing window at the storm.

"I'm gonna go look for some food before the storm hits," I said, letting the curtain fall and heading toward the front door, about to duck out of the house.

"I'll come with you," Michael said.

I opened my mouth.

He held up a hand to stop me. "Neh, I'm coming with you."

I closed my mouth. With a shrug, I went out of the door, leaving it open for Michael, who was three paces behind me. Secretly, as his footsteps neared the door after me, my heart involuntarily sped up a bit.

"Bring back somethin' good!" Ronin called from within the house, before the door fully closed. I rolled my eyes even though he couldn't see it.

As we went across the porch, stepping down into dry, itchy grass, Michael said thoughtfully, "I seem to remember Iver talking about peaches and apples. We could probably find some left over from an orchard or something."

"That was my line of thinking," I said. "Peaches. But probably not apples, 'cause you know, they'll kill you and whatnot."

Michael inclined his eyebrows. "Really?"

"Unfortunately."

It took us about twenty minutes, but we did eventually find what somewhat resembled an orchard. The trees may have been overgrown, but their roots were unable to magically shift the entire tree, so they remained in unnatural rows.

Upon landing, I strode up to the nearest tree, its branches weighted down with fuzzy red and yellow fruits, each the size of my hand. I plucked one and sniffed it, pervading my senses with an incredibly sweet scent. I took a bite, causing lukewarm juice to run down my chin.

"Good?" Michael asked, smiling alluringly.

"Mhm," I said through a full mouth, relishing in the sweet taste. I swiped the juice away with my free thumb and swallowed, already missing the taste. "It's amazing. You have to try it."

"Oh yeah?" Michael came over to me, moving in a relaxed manner, and I paused to watch him. He came very close, bringing two fingers under my chin as his eyes traveled over me temptingly.

My gaze, immediately softening by his touch, flicked over his features, between his cracked obsidian eyes taking me in and those soft lips, barely parted.

He lifted my mouth to his and kissed me sweeter than the peach, his lips lingering on mine. Then he pulled back a bit, running his tongue over his lower lip, and let me go. "Mm. You're right," he said, his voice like silk in my ears. "It is amazing."

I felt like his kiss had taken my breath, and I wanted it back. I closed the small distance between us, wrapping my arms gently over the back of his neck, one hand still holding the peach. Kissing Michael felt good every time, and I found myself unable to stop, the two of us alone in an abandoned, overgrown orchard at dusk.

◆ ◆ ◆

"What took you so long?" Ronin asked upon our return. The door clanked shut behind us, blown inward from the winds picking up outside.

I walked up to the dining table where Ronin sat, unclipping my pack and pulling it over my head as I went. I unzipped it and poured out half its contents, the other half being my personal items. A slew of huge peaches tumbled out onto the wooden tabletop.

"This did," I said.

Michael slid in beside me, his side grazing mine as he came up to the table's edge. I felt his touch very acutely, and I tried to hide my rising grin. He dumped out his half-a-bag full of peaches as well, making a total of two-dozen.

"Fair enough," Ronin said, in a manner suggestive of retracting his previous question. He reached out and grabbed one of the massive peaches, his red-brown eyes taking it in as if it was gold.

"Food? What kind?" Clara asked, coming into the dining room.

At the mention of food, the others were quick to jostle into the dining room, swarming around the table. Aubrey, the last to come over, slumped down depressingly into the chair that happened to be closest, still defeated from her findings in Missouri. She halfheartedly picked up a peach that had rolled nearest the edge she sat in front of, without the faintest hint of actually wanting to try it written anywhere on her frowning face.

"Oh, wow! These are huge," Anna said. "Are they even safe to eat?"

Michael and I shared a look. "If not, we should've been dead by now," I said.

"Which means, yes, they're safe to eat," Michael clarified with a small smile.

I plucked one off the tabletop and turned my head, searching for Emery. He stood off to the side, technically in the living room. "Here," I called out to him.

Seeming to know I was talking to him without having to say his name, he looked up as I tossed the peach underhanded. Emery caught it with both hands, then turned it over, examining it.

"Thanks," he said, his voice quiet.

To cover up the sounds of our relished chewing, Samuel found a battery-powered CD player, set it atop the table — right in the middle — and hit the play button without checking the disc. We all became still as the music began playing.

"Taylor Swift, huh?" I shook my head, unable to stop my humored grin from spreading. Iver's family certainly had their quirks.

"You didn't bother to check the disc?" Michael asked, looking amused.

"What're you guys talking about? This song is *great*," Will said. "All I need now is a piano and I'd be rockin' a one-man show." He started humming along to the tune, and his fingers moved across an imaginary horizontal plane in the air, pretending to play the piano. But, peculiarly, his hands moved in a way that made me suspicious he actually did know how to play.

We looked around at each other, grins growing on our faces. Not even Aubrey could go without the smallest of grins. As if connected through music, we all burst into song at the start of the next well-known line.

I abruptly shut my mouth, my eyes widening while my brows drew down. "Uhh, uh-uh. That isn't my voice," I said, shaking my head slowly.

Clara coughed, as if fretting her own voice as well. All of us died out, actually, rubbing our throats and staring at each other in shock, and maybe in some form of horror.

Will didn't seem to mind, as if oblivious to his own vocal chords. His voice carried over us like honey, extremely pleasant to the ears. The song line finished and he finally looked around at all of us.

"What?" he asked, noticing our strange countenances.

Anna pointed meekly at him, then looked around the table. "You didn't hear yourself?" she asked Will, looking back toward him with some hint of disbelief.

Will only looked at her in confusion.

"We sound like freaking *angels*," Ronin said. Even he sounded startled, though he looked happy, excited even.

And that, through the power of Taylor Swift, is how we found out we were all amazing singers now. And when I say amazing, I mean it. We should ditch this whole Hybrid operation and start up a band or something.

CHAPTER 50

Over an hour had passed, and Iver and Adler were still not back. The storm raged overhead in the night, knocking itself forcibly against the sides of the house. For the others, their only source of light was a couple yellow flickers from two candles' wicks. Granted, the hefty white candles were nearly the size of dinner plates, the wicks the width of shoe laces, so I'm sure they could see just fine.

I lay on my side on the hard floor of the spacious living room. There were a few brown leather sectionals forming a U in front of the fireplace, but Anna and Clara took up two spots, the third reserved for Emery when he wanted to go to sleep. My left arm propped my head up, my slim artist's fingers disappearing into my thick, curly hair. I stared absently out of the window behind Michael preening his feathers, watching the rain lash against the glass.

"How did you guys get like…this?" Emery asked out of seemingly nowhere, gesturing to the lot of us.

Michael gave a humorless laugh, looking over the feathers of his left wing strewn across his lap. "You don't want to know," he said. "Trust me."

Emery opened his mouth, but hesitated. He decided upon asking, "Can anyone be like you?"

Michael flicked his wing out of his lap, his long feathers scraping against the floor as they set into place behind his back. "No."

"Ah," Emery said, sounding deflated.

Will came over from the neighboring dining room, looking rather jubilant. "Don't worry, kid," Will said, sitting down near a decorated throw pillow tossed onto the wooden floor. "It's not all it's cracked up to be. Take it from me." He lay back on the floor with a sigh, shoving the pillow under his head, then stretched his arms and wings out.

Will, could you take up any more space? I pushed his long wing away with my right foot, folding it toward him.

"Oh, I'm sorry, am I taking up too much floor?" Will asked with false apology, raising his head to look at me.

"Yes," I stated. "Now shove over." Using both feet, I pushed him away, but only made his left wing flap over his front.

Will huffed, pretending to be indignant. "Rude," he said, though a grin played on his lips.

"You all are lucky," Emery said.

"Huh? *Agh.*" I looked over at the young boy but grunted in the next instant, receiving a pillow to the side of the face. I picked it up and narrowed my eyes at Will, who was guiltily missing a pillow. "Thanks for the extra pillow," I said, smiling.

"Hey, wait! No!" Will lunged forward.

I brought the pillow around and smacked his head with it. "Take that!" I said.

"Ah!" Will squinted his eyes against the pillow and reached out to grab it from me. I let him take it back, though I chuckled at his expense. I was glad things between Will and I weren't as weird anymore. It was nice being friends with him again.

Through my chuckles, I turned back to Emery. "What do you mean we're lucky?" I asked him.

"You all have a family," he said.

Except all of our families are dead. I suddenly found my smile fading. "Well, that's not exactly the case," I started hesitantly, not wanting to get into our depressing mission with this seven-year-old boy.

"You're one big family," he insisted. "You have each other." Emery sank further back into the wooden support beam behind him. "And I — I have no one," he murmured, as if to himself, staring at the wooden floorboards off to the side.

"That's not true," I said. "You have us." He raised his eyes, and I tried to give him a smile, but he averted his gaze.

"For now," he said. Emery got to his feet and disappeared down the hallway.

My growing frown faced his backside.

"He'll come around," Will said, repositioning the pillow under his head. "These things take time."

I figured Will was right, for once. I found myself thinking over what Emery had said, too. In a sense, our unit was becoming a family of sorts. I'd never thought of it that way before. Every one of us had experienced a great loss, even more than the shared ordeal of being genetically altered, but here we were, having a relatively good time while a storm raged overhead. We were stronger together, for sure. Without each other to prod and joke around with, I doubt we'd still be going. After all, what would be the purpose of flying alone, not just physically, but psychologically?

Seeing me mull over things, Michael came over to me and sat cross-legged on the floor. I didn't mind it at all when he began playing with my hair. "Just because you saved him doesn't mean he'll be grateful," Michael said reasonably, his voice more on the gentle side. "Take Will for example."

"Hey!" Will shot back indignantly.

"My point is," Michael carried on, "don't expect too much from him. And don't feel like he's your sole responsibility, either."

"I don't know how to help him," I divulged, feeling

bad. "I never had any younger siblings or anything like that."

Michael twisted a curl around his pinkie finger. "Neither did I," he admitted. "I have a sister, but she's my age."

I acutely picked up on his usage of present tense. In a weird way, Michael's hope gave *me* hope. I was already starting to feel better, but a part of me was still weighed down. The boy... He would forgive us eventually, right? We *would* have to leave him at some point in the near future.

I sighed and nestled my head more comfortably on the small, embroidered pillow. "I'm sure it'll be fine," I said, more so to convince myself.

"It will," Michael said. "You'll see."

CHAPTER 51

It continued to storm throughout the night, frequently waking me up. Each time a bolt of lightning struck, I'd be jolted awake, by both the brilliant flash of light and the defending crack of power.

Iver and Adler didn't return until the morning, when the storm had finally moved on. I was lying half-awake when I heard their wings and footsteps before the door even opened, and I jumped up, looking toward the entrance. Michael was startled awake by me, which seemed to be becoming a habit, and followed my gaze attentively. Their shadows passed over and then the door swung open.

"You're back," I said, finding myself relieved.

A quick glance over Iver, who poorly concealed his disappointment, told me his luck had been foiled. Not for the first time, I wondered: were we ridiculous for putting ourselves through all this? Was it really that important to know? The short answer: yes, to both.

Michael sat up, looking tired. "What took you guys so long?" he asked, running his fingers through the side of his hair.

The others, still sprawled out around the living room, started waking up.

"Oh good, you're finally back," Clara said, her voice slurring with the remains of sleep.

Adler gave her a faint smile, as if the motion took effort. "We camped out for the night while the storm was passing," he explained.

"I figured," I said, standing up and brushing the sleep off of myself. The hardwood floor was very uncomfortable, and it felt good to get up off it. Both boys had dark rings under their eyes, though Iver's were considerably worse. "Do you want some breakfast? Michael and I brought back peaches last night."

"Sure," Adler said.

I was already walking toward the table, the aches gradually clearing from my body. We'd only eaten half of them last night, so there was still one left for each of us.

I tossed two over to Adler, and he held one out to Iver, but Iver turned it down spiritlessly. I picked up a third and bit into it with satisfaction. *Mmm. Yep, still as good as the first time.* If this was the kind of food we'd be forced to eat from now on, I was alright with that. Indeed, I could live with it happily.

The sleepy birdkids managed to gradually get up and

eat something. We massaged the kinks out of our backs, brushed our teeth with well water, and got to use Iver's apocalypse-proof septic tank instead of the great outdoors. Eventually, once our little mission around the country was over, I felt a place like this wouldn't be so bad to live in.

While my unit got ready, I sought out Emery. Turned out that he fell asleep in a bedroom down the hall, a small human ball in the middle of a king-sized, wood-crafted bed. I just hoped it didn't used to be Iver's parents' room or something.

I shook his shoulder to wake him up. "Hey, gotta get up, kiddo. Breakfast is waiting," I said.

When all he did was jerk his body in a sort of sporadic twitch, I leaned over and realized he was stuck in a deep sleep, having a terrible nightmare by the looks of it.

"Emery," I said with more force, shaking his shoulder again.

He gasped awake, his dark blue eyes flinging open. He sat up quickly, looking around with wide eyes as if expecting to be attacked.

"Hey, it's okay," I soothed, sitting on the edge of the bed beside him and rubbing his back. For a brief moment, and for the first time I consciously realized, I was somewhat startled when my hand didn't meet wings. His back was bare! I wasn't sure when a normal human back became weird to me, but a small part of me felt it was odd now.

He shook his head, his face beginning to crumple. "It's not," he gulped. "It really happened."

The young boy turned and, to my surprise, buried himself in my arms. I patted his back gently while he cried, unsure what to do.

Michael appeared around the doorway, looking concerned. "Everything alright? I heard —" His words abruptly ended when he caught sight of Emery in my embrace, his small shoulders shaking. Michael pursed his lips. He gave me an imperceptible nod and left from the doorway, leaving with barely a flutter, as if he had been a ghost.

I turned back to Emery, who had his arms gripped tightly around my midsection. It was quite some time before his sobs quieted down, and he let me go, his face all red and puffy.

"We've got a long flight ahead of us," I said, rubbing his arm. "Let's get some food in you before we go, okay?"

He sniffled and swiped a wrist under his nose, then nodded innocently, looking dejected. I got him out of the bed, and he shuffled down the hall beside me, partially hiding behind my right wing.

It was a good thing I managed to get the boy to eat something, because we didn't get another meal the rest of the day. Flying from Oklahoma to Arizona, not to mention with a seven-year-old on my back? Yeah, not the *shortest* flight. The only upside was that Clara, our next stop, lived near the Grand Canyon National Park. Needless to say, I wanted very badly to check that out.

The sun was threatening to set by the time we neared Clara's place, maybe another hour before dusk would hit us. We were flying over an arid landscape, monolithic red and white striated rocks rising from the ground before us.

"Eh, maybe let's find a place to sleep for now and worry about me later," Clara said, trying to sound nonchalant. She moved with a certain anxiety, however, visible in the tenseness of her body and the quickened flaps of her dark brown and white, hawk-like wings.

"You sure?" I asked, looking sideways at her where she flew sixty feet to my left.

Her soft, squarish face was creased around her mouth and between her small eyebrows, her worried gaze searching the ground below. "Yeah," she said, glancing up at me momentarily. When she looked over, the color of her irises seemed to shift in the waning sunlight, at one moment appearing light brown, in the next a fiery amber as she faced the sun.

She was scared, I could tell that much. "Alright. How about the canyon?" I proposed, finding my opportunity and going for it.

Clara seemed to consider it. "It's not too far from here. Good cover... I'll lead us there," she decided. She flapped forward with measured strokes of her long wings, her somewhat curvy, dark brown hair streaming behind her as she flew ahead of us with purpose.

I tried to hide my excitement as we changed course by a few degrees, banking my wings ever so slightly, the setting sun catching my feathers in a flash of gold.

It didn't take very long for the canyon to come into view. If you were walking there from the ground, you may not even realize how close you were to it, but flying three miles above the ground, it opened up like a mighty scar across the landscape. My enlivened eyes widened as my grin did, taking in everything fervently, picking up on every little detail and silhouette in a way only an artist could.

"Well, here it is," Clara said monotonically, widening her arms out at the grand sight. Clara may not have been as excited about it, whether due to the situation she was procrastinating on or because she used to live so close to it, but I couldn't wait to get closer.

"Check it out," I said, nudging Emery with my right shoulder.

I felt him lift his head, which I knew he hid because of the constant rush of wind. His only saving grace was the windbreaker I'd picked out for him on our way over the very top portion of Texas, the black, polyester fabric now snapping in the wind. "Mm? Woahhhh." I didn't look over my shoulder at him, too engrossed with the scenery to take my eyes off it for even a second, but I could imagine his mouth dropping open in astonishment. "What is this place?"

"This is the Grand Canyon!" I said.

"Grand Canyon?" he repeated breathily. "I've never been before."

"You guys? I'm going down," I called out to the group. In a lower voice, I said, "Emery, hold on tight."

"Wha'?"

He'd been flying casually for long enough. He should be okay with a little drop, no? Excitement growing, I angled downward about forty-five degrees and held my wings closer to my body, directing myself in a streamlined manner.

I heard Emery's breath catch against the wind passing speedily over my ears, his grip tightening. Flying a little under three-hundred miles per hour, I had to hold his forearms tightly to prevent him from being ripped from my back.

The canyon speedily got bigger, unfolding itself to me. Around ground-level, I came out of the dive and followed the carved-out scar, a geological feat that took over six-million years to develop into what it was today. The dusty stone dropped drastically in a steep cliff, then sloped downward toward a river trickling by in the very center, a full mile down.

Amazing! Beautiful! Astounding!

I couldn't get enough. My wings were itching to go crazy swooping along the stone, but I couldn't so long as there was a child hanging on for dear life on my back. Not wanting to waste a moment, I began searching for a good place for our group to spend the night, where we could all be safe for at least a little while.

As I flew through the canyon, skimming its horizon as if it was filled to the brim with imaginary liquid, Adler's big Steppe Eagle wings flapped in from my left. He swooped down to me. "Hey! This is pretty awesome," he said, smiling at me. "Are you looking for a place to rest for the night?" I opened my mouth to respond, and before I could, he replied, "I'll help you. Are you think'n more along the lines of a cave or nice piece of rock?"

"I'll know when I see it," I said, not having any clue what it was exactly I was looking for.

"How about over there?" Michael proposed, appearing on my right as he leveled out of a dive.

I looked to where he was pointing and shrugged easily. "Sure, looks decent enough." It was basically an island, fifty feet across in a squashed circular shape, with two mile-deep gorges on either side. At least no one would be able to sneak up on us from there.

The three (technically four) of us swooped over to the island and landed upon its red, dry, relatively flat surface. Emery hopped off my back before I fully landed, my wings still fanned out behind me.

He ran up to one side, looking straight down with his hands on his thighs. "Cooool. We're so high up!" He spun around to me, looking excited, a nice change from the depressed kid from this morning. It was probably the high-speed dive that pulled him out of his depression for the time being. "We're gonna *sleep* here?"

I smiled. "Yeah, why not?"

"Nice." He was grinning as he ran to another edge, checking everything out.

"Just don't fall off," I called over at him.

Michael steadfastly scanned our scenic surroundings. "There's a water source, we're separated from everything else... It's perfect," he decided.

"We're running dangerously low on rations though," I said. "They'll do fine for tonight, but we really should figure out a more long-term plan."

"Hey — you find the food, I'll cook it," Adler said, shooting finger guns at us with a pearly white grin.

I laughed, but then I started thinking, making me quiet down.

"What's running through your mind?" Michael asked me.

I tilted my head, feeling funny inside. "We're basically gigantic birds of prey, are we not?" I led on.

"I suppose, in a sense," Michael said with a half-shrug.

"Then, I'd think we should be good at hunting. With some practice, at least."

Adler snapped his fingers. "We could build spears and take 'em out from above!"

Michael placed his hands on his hips as his studious eyes considered the two of us. "That's not a bad idea," he said.

"What would be *really* cool is using bows and

arrows. I went through a whole archery phase for like three years in high school," I said. I sighed pleasantly. "Yeah, got yelled at a *lot* for that one." Lots of missed shots, nearly hitting Jody once. Ha, good times.

"Did you now?" Michael questioned curiously. "You're just full of surprises, aren't you?"

I laughed lightly. "Maybe. I can throw a decent spear, too, so that shouldn't be a problem. The real issue is crafting one straight enough."

"When the heck did you get a chance to throw *spears*, too?" Adler asked, befuddled. "Michael's right, you're crazy, haha."

CHAPTER 52

Michael scrunched his nose and ran an uneasy hand through his hair, and I narrowed my eyes at him. "Am I?" My voice carried a warning, but I wasn't actually upset. I mean, he wasn't exactly wrong.

"Ehhh," Michael said, emphasized with his pointer finger and thumb in an 'itty-bit' gesture.

"Oh, okay, coming from the cook and the doctor who both got turned into *birds*," I exasperated, unable to stop a grin from forming on my face.

"Don't shoot the messenger!" Adler said, raising both hands defensively as he chuckled.

Our laughter was drowned out as a flurry of wings started landing down around us, tossing my hair around. Emery tried not to get blown off the side of the rock.

"Took you guys long enough!" Adler joked. "What'd you do, go on a joyride?"

Clara came over, folding her wings in, and punched

him semi-lightly on the bicep. "Shut up," she said, though the corner of her mouth was curved up happily.

Samuel swung his pack off the moment he landed. "Man, I'm hungry," he said, digging around in his pack. He pulled out a silver packet and took a dried disc-like portion out.

"We were just talking about food," Adler brought up. When the others glanced at him questioningly, he said, "Yeah. We're thinking of using spears and arrows and stuff to try to hunt. Instead of just nonstop fruit and what-not."

"That's not a terrible idea," Samuel said slowly, sounding a lot like Michael.

"And Rory can teach us," Adler added.

"Oh?" Will asked, his curiosity piqued.

I shot Adler a 'thanks for nothing' glare. "I know *some* stuff. I'm by no means an expert, but I should be able to get us started."

"That sounds cool," Will said lightheartedly. "I'll give it a try." He gave me a smile, and for some reason I felt slightly nervous. I gave him a small smile in thanks for the support.

For now, though, with the day closing fast, we all ate a dried vegetable cookie that had been cooked up by scientists, each of us losing another one of our precious rations. Even though I only had a few left, I broke one in half and gave some to Emery. He was only half my size and was burning a lot less calories on a daily basis.

I shoved my portion in my mouth, eager to check out the canyon freely. After a hearty swig of water from my canister, I rolled my shoulders and ran toward the edge of the island in wide, spirited strides. Pushing off extra hard at the very last inch of rock, I began my freefall into nothing. Only once dropping a good fifty feet did I snap my wings out, catching the air easily, gliding forward.

It didn't take long for others to jump into the air to check it out with me, with only a handful of minutes left until sunset. Emery was amazed, watching with jealous awe from the top of the canyon while I and some others flew around with grace and skill.

The canyon was a magnificent sight, its striated surfaces washed in vibrant purples and golds, the thin river below looking like a window to another world. I couldn't get enough of it.

Soon the sun finally fell behind the horizon, and everyone but me headed back to the stone island. I continued to coast leisurely a mere forty feet above the top of the canyon, barely flapping as I rode against some soothing winds. To my surprise, the South Rim and the North rim were actually only ten miles apart, a distance which took me minutes to cross while it would have taken someone driving, forced to loop around the canyon, five hours. I could've stayed like that forever, flying over a sight so spectacular, but eventually, I circled around and flew back to the others.

By the time I got back, Emery had already fallen

asleep, using someone's pack as a pillow. The group was absorbed in conversation, keeping their voices on the low side while the boy slept. They barely seemed to notice when I landed, ever silent, and walked up to them.

Dusk had faded, revealing the night sky. The stars here were unbelievably bright, totally and completely unobstructed. Even those without night vision could see each other just fine as they spoke about our travels and what to do next.

They were arranged in a giant circle, and I sat down in the only available spot, between Will and Ronin.

Will looked over at me as I settled down to his right. "Have fun?" he asked, speaking in a lowered voice as he leaned in toward me.

"It was really nice, yeah," I said, giving him a small smile. It was nice to get some time by myself every now and then.

"I'd go with you, but I'd probably crash into a rock wall or something," he chuckled.

"It's not *that* dark," I goaded.

"Well, then, maybe I will." His tone had turned unusually light, his personable gaze flicking softly over me, making me suddenly very conscious of him.

"What about that affected guy?" Aubrey was saying, sitting past Ronin on my right. "We've gotta live in a world with *them* now, too. Should we tell someone about it? No one at the base ever told us about them, so maybe they have no idea it's possible."

I cleared my throat discreetly, unsure of Will's intentions and of what to say to him. Flying with him didn't sound unpleasant to me, but...you know? "Tell who? The Labcoats back at base?" I nullified, turning to Aubrey and relieving myself from responding to Will. The affected man was a serious topic! A real concern, ya know?

"Well..."

"No way!" Ronin declared. "They tried to shoot us down with tranqs!"

At Ronin's outburst, I glanced at Emery, laying some fifteen feet off behind me. The others noticed and some glanced over as well, making even Ronin's countenance drop dramatically in volume.

Turning forward, I delved into thought. "Maybe it's the opposite of our case for some people," I said, squinting absently at a small crack in the rock, near the middle of our circle.

"What're you talking about?" Ronin shot down. "That doesn't even make sense. The opposite of us are just normal people."

"Hear me out," I insisted. It was making more and more sense inside my head. "We have some allele that allowed us to be hybridized, right? So maybe they have an allele that allowed them to be infected. Or, they're simply lacking whatever it is that prevented the chemical from affecting everyone else. Just because it's rare doesn't mean it doesn't exist." I naturally looked between June and Michael, the chem major and the med student, for assurance.

June and Michael glanced at each other across three people, sitting at my ten-o'clock. "Well, it's not *impossible*," June said slowly.

"Certainly not a *desirable* possibility," Michael added. "The allele... At least in our case, it isn't hereditary. They'd probably have no way of knowing how many people were affected by DODG."

"Alright, but how badly do we *really* wanna know more about these affected people?" Samuel pressed. "Bad enough to fly all the way back to Iceland?" He teetered his hand while scrunching his face. "Ehhh, I say no."

Ronin flipped a pointer finger toward Samuel and raised his eyebrows. "I concur."

I shook my head, my brows drawing in. "We don't need to fly back — we *shouldn't*. If we end up determining we should tell some scientists about the crazy people — though I don't think we should, because we just *escaped* from a base — there are other bases to go to; ones that *haven't* tried to shoot us down yet."

"Sure, but how do you suppose we find them?" Aubrey asked, her tone coming off a little angrier toward me.

Ignoring Aubrey's frustrations, I wanted to give her and everyone else a straightforward, totally helpful answer. But honestly, how was I supposed to know?

"They're going to be located in places that used to be sparsely populated and have fewer species," I came up with, thinking back on something Carson had said a while back. Using what I knew about animals and the world in general, I said, "My guess is they're either on mostly uninhabited islands, or located further north where it's too cold for most things to survive."

"Like Iceland. Ah," Clara realized. "Not bad."

"Wait wait wait," Will spurned, halting the discussion. "Are we actually considering doing this? Don't we have enough on our plates as it is?"

Amidst everything, I couldn't help but look over at Emery. His mother had died at the hands of a monster, a man turned soulless against his will. If either Emery or the man, before he became affected, had weight in our group's decision, what would they say?

I had disappeared into my own thoughts and hadn't heard what the others had been saying. Something about 'we just have to live with it now' and 'but I don't want to die.'

I turned back to my group, feeling that this life was undeserved. "Look, you guys," I interjected a bit forcefully, making their arguments die down and cease. "We've only seen *one case* of DODG affecting a human so far. Maybe there aren't any others, maybe there are. I think," I said more carefully, "that we should learn more ourselves before jumping into the fire right after escaping from the frying pan." I looked around at them with quiet expectation, waiting to hear their thoughts.

They all looked around at each other as they soaked

in my suggestion, communicating nonverbally. I could see what each of them wanted simply by the look in their eyes. Some were tempted to seek out the scientists and quell this issue before we really got into it, while most of them would rather be anywhere *but* another base.

"Mahogany Meeting vote says…?" Adler led on.

"Raise your hand if you agree with Rory, that we wait," Michael spoke up, sounding authoritative as his dark gaze swept calmly over the group.

Two, five, seven hands were raised. Michael looked across the flat, open rock between us, our eyes locking on one another. He raised his hand, and I raised mine. Then we all looked between June and Aubrey, neither of whom had their hands raised.

Aubrey let out an exasperated sigh. "Alright, fine," she huffed, and raised her hand.

June pursed her lips, and with a forfeiting shrug of her shoulder, raised her hand up as well.

CHAPTER 53

Everyone had gone to sleep. Everyone except me, as usual.

Even though the night had brought a twenty-degree temperature drop, it was still very warm. Warm, but not humid in the slightest. I was sitting on a ledge furthest away from the sleeping group, my left leg hanging off the side while my hands were wrapped around my right leg, pulling it to my chest, leaning into it comfortably. I hooked my left heel against an angled face of rock and absently tapped it gently against the side.

It was peaceful out here, almost enough to make me forget everything that we were facing. The world was quiet, the landscape dreamy. It almost didn't feel real.

Below, near the thin river flowing a mile down, I spotted movement. My eyes honed in on it, focusing on a tuft of yellowed grass. A tiny striped lizard, covered in spines, poked his head out of the blades, watching for danger. I stayed very still. The lizard seemed to determine the coast was clear and scuttled forward, running down the last few meters of rocky substrate to the edge of the river.

I picked up on footsteps and the soft rustle of feathers coming up from behind me but kept my eyes on the yellow and brown creature. Soft as the steps may have been, each one echoed tenfold through the quiet canyon, and the lizard darted back into the brush. Disappointed, I looked to my left to see who had spooked the lizard. Will walked over without making eye contact or any move for conversation. He sat down a meter away from me at the ledge with his legs dangling off the side, his hands pressed into the rock behind him, his feet crossed at the ankles.

Why is he awake?

I gazed at him with interest. A gentle breeze flowing up through the canyon ran its soft fingers through his shaded brown hair. A stray curl of my own hair tickled my cheek, but I left it. Will closed his eyes and angled his chin up to embrace the breeze, looking peaceful. His face and chest glowed a soft silver under the moon's light.

My eyes ran from the ends of his primary feathers, up the slope of his right wing, to the lean muscles atop his shoulders. I moved along the outline of his face, noticing his sharp nose, clean jawline, the way short tips of his hair curved gently around his ear, the soft glow upon his lips...

It didn't seem to matter to me that I was looking at him, admiring him. I just felt peaceful.

Will took a deep, calming breath and gently opened his eyes. Still he did not look over at me, but rather looked out over the canyon. "It's so peaceful," he said softly.

I didn't respond. I went back to watching the canyon as well, not thinking about anything in particular. Then my head turned slightly at a rustle somewhere off on the other side of the canyon to my left. Will tilted his head to the right. My gaze shifted to him to find his eyes resting on me.

Neither of us looked away.

"Wanna go night flying?" he asked with the gentlest of smiles.

The corner of my mouth curved up. "With you?" I asked.

"Sure, why not?" He got up slowly and lowered a hand to me. "I promise I won't bite."

My eyes flicked to his open hand then back up to him. I took his hand in the next moment and got to my feet.

"Where are you going?" a young voice questioned. I spun around to see Emery standing before me, frowning at me.

"What're you doing up?" I asked, wondering if he had another bad dream.

"Same as you," he said plainly. Emery swept a hand

out behind him, toward the feathered group sleeping on the dusty stone.

I tilted my head in question, my brows creasing ever so slightly. "What —" My voice cut off and my eyes widened. I realized they weren't asleep — they were dead, their feathers stained with blood. I sucked in a breath, horror washing through me. "Emery..." I could barely speak.

"Now we're *both* traitors," he said, continuing to talk in his simple voice, barely a sliver of emotion in it. He slowly shrugged his small shoulders with a simultaneous tilt of his head to one side. "I thought I might be alone, but you're a traitor too, in a way."

I was speechless. I stared at Emery, and his dark blue eyes shifted to Will, a dark knowledge swirling behind his gaze. I turned to Will, following Emery's gaze, but Will wasn't looking at either of us — he was staring down at his chest, his hands clamped over a spot near his heart. His breathing was ragged, watching blood seep through his fingers.

Will! My heart clenched.

I rounded on Emery, ready to take that little kid out.

Before I even fully spun around, something slammed into my stomach with such force that I was sent flying backward. My arms reached out, but there was nothing. I fell, right off the end of the ledge. Emery's impassive expression was the last thing I saw.

I bolted upright, feeling as if I couldn't breathe. Hard stone was beneath me; I wasn't falling. Immediately, I looked around, panicked I'd find everyone dead.

Around me, ten birdkids were sprawled out across the rock surface beneath the soft glow of the desert stars, their chests undulating with the rhythm of calm, steady breathing. Will, too, was among them, some ten feet away from me. I forced myself to calm down, steadying my own breathing while I listened intently to their gentle snoring.

They're still alive. I clenched my eyes shut, drilling it into my head that they were alright, and that it had only been a dream. Then I thought of Emery, and my eyes flung open once more, searching for him. He was lying in the exact same spot he'd fallen asleep, looking small and peaceful. Not at all like a killer.

What kind of mind jacking dream was *that?* I slumped forward and ran my hands down my tired face, then looked around again, this time able to feel more at ease.

Michael was asleep beside me, laying half on his side, half on his stomach. I suddenly remembered I'd fallen asleep next to him, feeling comfortable despite the hard, uneven ground. A frown tugged at the corners of my lips, recalling what I'd been doing in my dream, before a little boy had murdered my new family.

Traitor. That's what Emery had called me in my dream. But, I hadn't even done anything! Not in real life, anyway.

The stars were still showing, but I knew there was no way I'd be going back to sleep. Even though I knew Emery was just a boy, I now felt wary toward him. It was probably a stupid feeling to have toward a seven-year-old, but that dream really messed me up.

I stayed up, just sitting beside a sleeping Michael with my wings wrapped around my sides, warming my legs, while I looked out over the canyon. Eventually the sky lightened, hiding the stars behind a pink and yellow haze. As the sun broke over the red desert landscape, filtering in through gaps in the long, monolithic rock formations, my group began waking up.

"Arg. Is it morning already?" Iver asked, sitting up and rubbing the sleep out of his light-sensitive eyes. He reached over and nudged Anna awake. "Hey, Anna. Morning." Anna grumbled something in her sleep and turned away from him.

Others started getting up as well.

Clara looked groggy when she first opened her eyes, but then they widened and she jolted upright. "Crap," she muttered.

I looked at them from the side of my eye. These people were superficially placed together, sure, but staying together was a choice we all individually made. Now they were getting up in the early morning, rising with the sun, to go support one of our members.

Will sat up and groggily reached into his pack,

pulling out his water canister. He took a long minute to unscrew it and poured some water over his face. Lowering the canister, he shook his head, sending water droplets flinging, and blinked himself wide awake. "Don't even know what day it is anymore," he muttered to himself, taking a swig from the canister.

Michael stirred, and I pulled my eyes from Will. Though my gaze instantly softened when it landed on Michael, I still felt strange from my dream. Will dousing himself in water didn't help either.

"Hey," he said sleepily, blinking awake. His eyes took me in under half-closed lids.

"Morning," I said, watching him.

He pushed himself up off the ground into a sitting position, one leg bent in while the other lay across the rock surface. He let out a long breath and tried to clear the sleep from his head. Then his gaze concentrated on me and his eyes flicked over me strangely. "How long have you been awake?" he asked.

"Uh, not long," I lied.

"Mm." He peered at me a moment longer, then let it go.

They started getting up and stretching, fanning out their wings and yawning. Samuel went ahead and woke Emery, who looked around as if he couldn't remember where he was. I watched the boy skeptically as we all ate something.

We did whatever we needed to do, and less than

twenty minutes later, we were all clipping our packs and getting ready to leave the canyon.

Samuel came up from my right side and tapped my arm, making me jump slightly. "Woah, sorry," he said. I rolled my shoulders to ease my tension, looking back over the group. "I was just gonna say that I can carry Emery for a while. I'm sure it's tough carrying him all this way, so I thought we could split it up."

"What? No way!" A little kid's voice rang out somewhere to my left, making both me and Samuel turn to look. Emery came closer to us, looking borderline panicked. "I — I don't want to!"

"Don't want to what?" I asked calmly, though an imperceptible frown began pulling at one corner of my mouth.

"I only want to fly with you," he said — practically pouted. His eyes looked between us with a hint of fear, and I immediately understood.

"You can trust Samuel," I assured him. "He's a strong flier."

Emery hugged his arms to his chest, looking like he wanted to argue but too scared to know what to say.

"I think Rory could use a little break, don't you?" Samuel asked the boy, sounding kind. He looked at Emery expectantly and raised his eyebrows for reassurance.

Emery kicked at the dusty rock, frowning at the ground. His eyes moved back and forth as if he was thinking about it. "I guess," he decided, sounding small.

I tried not to breathe a sigh of relief for the kid's benefit, but I did give Samuel a small, grateful smile. He gave me a warm nod, though he looked somewhat deterred by Emery's fear of him.

As we started tossing ourselves into the open air one after another, I took another glance at Emery, who Samuel was carrying on his back. They looked like two brothers, with their similar hair color and blue-ranged eyes. Emery was visibly trying to quell his worries, and I thought to myself that to be afraid of this boy was silly. It was just a dream, after all.

With my feelings about my dream resolved, I ran forward and jumped into the air, ready for whatever would come next.

CHAPTER 54

As it turned out, just because one person felt secure about the events to come didn't mean everyone did. Clara? I definitely felt bad for her. She may have put up a stout appearance, but after finding her family — her mom and two sisters, all shot by her divorced dad, who then hung himself off the side of the stairs — her outer appearance came crumbling down.

Samuel didn't let Emery get close to Clara's house, but you could see the fearful understanding in his young eyes.

June was next on the list, and I could tell she wasn't surprised by Clara's outcome. However, her expression was still very tense when she came out of the tan, two-story house last with Clara. I saw her try hard to hold back tears of her own, but I knew she'd built up a hope inside, however small it may have been. After seeing Clara's family, I think whatever hopes she had about her own family were crushed into dust. June had been the realest one from the start, but she was still only human. Well...almost.

As we regrouped on the dirt-covered road outside, June came over to me and pulled me aside. I was a bit skeptical but followed her a healthy twenty feet down the road. She came to a stop and turned toward me, but her eyes refused to look at me.

"What is it?" I asked.

June tapped her bare foot a few times against the red dirt that'd blown across the asphalt. She took in a sharp breath and said, "I want to skip Nevada."

I felt a little surprised, but my countenance remained neutral. After seeing so many devastating outcomes, I was wondering when it'd take its full effect on those still on the list. At some point, the human psyche would choose to save itself, shying from, and even defending against, a discovery that could very well crack the fibers that held it together.

I watched her jaw clenching and unclenching as she stared concretely at the dirt. The only thing I could do was make sure she wouldn't regret it. It wasn't my place to *decide* to go to Nevada or not. "We're so close. Are you sure?" I asked.

She nodded. "I never wanted to in the first place. The closer we get, the more I know I don't want to."

"Well...alright, if that's really how you feel." I sighed internally and looked over at the rest of our unit still standing in the road, baking under the sun, taking sips from their water canisters. Only Michael and Samuel were left. "Let's go tell the others."

June nodded tersely but didn't say anything else.

The two of us walked back to the others, and I told them the change of plans, that we would be heading to Wyoming now. Michael became very still, and I knew it was finally hitting him.

I edged closer to Michael as the group talked amongst themselves and asked quietly, "You still want to do this, right?"

Michael looked grim, but determined. "Yes. I want to know," he said. He took in a semi-shaky breath. "It just feels a lot more real," he admitted. He blinked, hard. "There's no avoiding it now."

Michael was strong, I'd give him that. He'd gotten to see a lot of horrible outcomes, yet he was still brave enough to face his own. I gave him a tight smile and squeezed his hand. He returned the gesture with a pressure of his own, his palm extremely warm in this desert heat.

We let each other go, and Michael said aloud, "Let's get moving then. It's too hot here anyway."

A smile flicked across my mouth, and we started jumping into the air without hesitation. In this arid landscape, strong ground-level heating by the brilliant sun created warm updrafts that allowed us to easily climb tens of thousands of feet.

Once we were up, flying north at a steady pace, I tilted my wings and glided over to June. "Hey," I called out to her, flying a wing or two's distance above her sleek form. She was moving smoothly with the help of her brown, iridescent wings a little bit lighter than her mocha-colored hair, striped and dotted like a kestrel. June turned her head to the side to look up at me. "Last chance. You sure about skipping Nevada?"

She kept her head turned to the side, but her eyes fell away from me. "Yeah, I'm sure. To Wyoming we go."

I gave her a single nod. "Alright. Just had to check."

"Thanks," she said, flashing a sad smile, her brown eyes appearing especially exhausted. June turned forward, and I tilted my wings again, allowing myself to be carried away by the wind.

◆ ◆ ◆

"Hey, check this one out!" Adler said, and I could hear the familiar draw of a bow's tight string. "I feel like I'm in the Olympics."

"Yeah, it's nice," I responded through a doorway I'd had to kick in, not actually able to see what Adler was talking about from the back room I was trifling through. "Don't dry fire though. It can be dangerous."

I heard a laugh. "I think we're well past dangerous," Ronin remarked.

We'd been flying for only a few hours, but Emery needed a potty break and Samuel didn't mind setting him down. Since we had been flying over an interesting little town, a few of us had decided to go down to the local sporting goods store while we were at it, and now I was studiously looking over a selection of knives in the back room while Adler, Ronin, and Will combed through their bow options. Everyone else was wheeling leisurely in the sky a mile above the store, not wanting to lose their momentum.

"Well aren't you a beauty," I murmured, holding up a fixed-blade, six-inch, stainless steel combat knife with a bit of a straight clip point shape, the color being that of pure ebony. The handle, slim and extremely well-fit to my hand, was crafted of gray Micarta made to resemble wood.

Deciding I'd found the love of my life, I stowed the knife in a matching, dark gray nylon sheath, shoved a few extra hunting knives for the group in my pack, and walked out of the small back room into the main store area. Immediately upon walking through the doorway, I heard a large crash. I rolled my eyes and headed over to the boys.

"Having fun destroying stuff?" I asked them, eyeing the fishing supplies still rolling about on the carpeted floor some thirty feet down the back aisle.

"I, uh, meant to do that," Adler said, pursing his lips with a bow lowered in his left hand.

"Yeah, and I meant to do this," Will said, smacking Adler on the backside of the head with the feathered end of an arrow.

Adler jerked away from the impact and rubbed the back of his head with a frown. "Touché."

I tried not to grin too obviously, not wanting to support their boyish recklessness, and turned my attention on the bow and arrow selection. I had to break into a back room to find knives, but it seemed not many people thought to flush out the bow and arrow stock. "Did you guys find some you like?" I asked, running my fingers over a row of carbon fiber recurve bows.

"I mean, sure, but we don't really know what we're looking for," Will said.

"Mm. Well, these should work," I offered. I pulled a few out of their racks and pushed them into the boys' hands. Then I scanned the arrows and selected a few. "Try these," I said, holding them out to the three dumbfounded boys.

"Like right now?" Adler asked as he took the arrow from me. A grin spread over his face. "Sure, I could knock down some more supplies."

"You see that fake fish hanging from the ceiling down there?" I pointed down the aisle. "Aim for that."

"Way down there?" Will queried.

"Yep," I said with a fun pop of my lips at the end.

Will squinted down the aisle and pulled his lower lip in, gnawing on it momentarily. "Yeah, okay." He stepped in front of me and tried to situate the arrow on the riser.

Seeing him doing it wrong, I stepped quietly over and patiently positioned his hands correctly, notching the arrow on a little indented platform called the shelf.

"Like this?" he asked, pulling his arm back.

"More like…" I corrected his arms and the way his fingers lay around the string while Adler and Ronin took note from the side.

As I lifted his elbow higher, staring down the line at which he would fire as if I myself was the one drawing the bow, I caught Will watching me from the side of his eye.

Disrupting my concentration, I became conscious of my hands on his skin, over his lean muscles, and lifted them briskly away. I stepped back and gestured down the aisle. "Fire," I said brusquely, wishing my voice didn't waver slightly, and cleared my throat to cover it up.

Will took his questionable gaze off me and looked forward, becoming focused. He pulled back and breathed slowly, then after a long moment, he released his fingers, letting the arrow fly. A few *clangs* rang out an aisle over, and Will scrunched his nose disappointedly. Ronin chuckled behind us.

"So, some advice," I said, folding my arms loosely over my chest to prevent my amusement from becoming too prevalent, "don't do *that*."

"Yeahhhh, I'll try not to," Will said, still looking after his missing arrow.

"Okay, my turn," Adler said, shoving his way past Will and me. I leaned back to avoid his large feathered wings. He held his hand out to me and I gave him an arrow, then he carefully set the arrow like I'd shown Will.

I watched him with scrutinous eyes, flicking over his form and technique. I had to admit, this was kind of fun. "Keep your arm higher up," I pointed out. "And…" I kicked his left foot forward a bit, getting his stance right. "There you go."

"Okay, okay," Adler breathed, his expression one of eager determination.

He pulled his arm back, and, while looking down his line of sight, aligning it with the Styrofoam fish, released the arrow. It went sailing right under the fish, only a couple feet from it.

I turned to him with my eyebrows raised. "Heyyy, not bad," I applauded.

Adler let his arms rest and turned to me with a smile. "I think I'm getting the hang of it," he said.

We had Ronin try, but he was nearly as bad as Will. Still, they weren't lost causes, so we packed up half a dozen carbon fiber recurve bows and a ton of sturdy, lightweight arrows. For whatever reason, sporting goods shops didn't seem to carry spears, so that one was out for now. I also realized I'd need a belt of some sort for my knife, and settled on a simple drop leg sheath, a type of gray nylon belt also attached to two bands that strapped around my right thigh. It was comfortable and didn't restrict my movement at all, plus it made it so that my new knife wouldn't get ripped away in the wind while I was flying.

Samuel greeted us out front with Emery, and his eyes widened at all the supplies we were lugging over our shoulders, plus a small spool of fishing line in my pack.

"So I guess shopping went well?" Samuel asked.

"Couldn't find spears, but they had plenty of bows," I said, feeling pleased nonetheless.

"Cooool," Emery said, going around Ronin's back to touch the new weapons. "You guys are gonna use these? Like for real?"

"Yeah," I said, giving Emery an easygoing smile. "Wanna learn?"

He spun toward me excitedly. "You'd teach me?"

"Of course. You can train just like everyone else." I tilted my head, my thoughts wandering. "Well, except for the shooting while flying part."

"Awesome! I'd love that," Emery said. "When can we start?"

Large shadows the size of small planes passed over the town, and I shielded my eyes against the sun as I looked up at six familiar forms, appearing graceful and almost dangerous as they circled a mile above. I pulled my stone-blue aviator sunglasses out of my top and slipped them onto my nose. "On our next break," I said. And with that, I ran forward a few strides and leapt powerfully into the air, tossing my wingtips up and out, bringing them down in lusty, smooth strokes.

CHAPTER 55

The scenery was really quite beautiful. We flew over endless miles of gray mountains and thick, winding rivers. When we finally took another break, this time as a whole group, we landed down in a high-elevation, gorgeous grassy area surrounded by mountains on three sides like mighty seventy-foot walls. A handful of cerulean water pools were scattered across the ground, and red-gray rocks dotted the landscape, probably having tumbled down from the mountainsides at one point.

What a perfect place to practice archery.

We dumped our packs in a pile and got set up. Since there weren't any trees around, our group began taking turns firing at a cluster of low, small-leaved bushes. I walked up and down the line of five birdkids and one Emery, helping them out. A couple were getting the hang of it, including Adler and June.

Ronin, Clara, Michael, and Anna were awaiting their

turns, watching those practicing.

"You know, I can't hit it once. I bet you don't even know what you're telling me," Aubrey said, becoming flustered out of nowhere.

"Adler and June are getting it," I said, padding down to where Aubrey was at the far right end of the line. "Just give it time and you'll get it too. A big part of archery is patience."

Aubrey crossed her arms, holding the bow in one hand. "Then prove it."

I arched an eyebrow at her.

She shoved the bow at me, holding it out. "I haven't seen you shoot once. I'm not convinced you actually know what you're doing."

Will had always been the most punch-able person, but Aubrey was getting up there in the list for me. I snatched the bow from her and plucked an arrow off the soft, short grass as she turned to judge. The others got one another's attention and all stopped their practice to watch me.

It was natural, holding the bow. Without even think-ing about it, my feet got into an optimal stance, I notched the arrow, and drew the string back.

For someone with raptor vision and enhanced strength, archery was a whole new game. I released my fingers, and the arrow shot forward with great precision. I picked up another and walked steadily down the line, the others moving away as I went forward. Another shot, then another, and another. I went down the whole line, then let the bow relax at my hip once half a dozen arrows were consecutively fired.

Iver nudged Aubrey on the arm, making her scowl at him. "I think she's proved her credentials," he smirked.

Anywhere their arrows had landed on their last attempts — some barely missing the bush fifteen meters away, others seventy meters down the slope — I had placed an arrow less than an inch from it.

Reeeeahh! Reeeeeahhh!

My head swiveled toward the sudden, sharp cry as the lot of us tensed, and a moment later, a red-tailed hawk came soaring into view over the western mountainside.

I heard someone get up from the ground behind us and turned to see Michael getting up with a sigh. He held his hand out. "Let me give it a try," he said. His easy-going nature toward it made me curious, and I handed the bow to him.

Michael swiped an arrow of the ground near the front of the line and, to my surprise, got into a perfect stance and held the bow and arrow with a form seen in professionals. He followed the hawk through the air for a few long moments, then released the arrow.

The hawk let out a screech as the arrow imbedded itself in his stomach, and the bird tumbled downward.

I looked from the fallen bird toward Michael, a pleasantly surprised, impressed smile on my face. He handed the bow back to me with an appealing smile of his own, and I felt he could not get any sexier.

"You guys are awesome!" Emery praised, his eyes wide with astonishment. "I'll go get the bird. Don't shoot yet!" He set his bow down in the short grass and ran down the field to go fetch the hawk and arrow.

While Emery did that, I returned my attention upon Michael, bumping his shoulder with mine as we walked back toward an exposed section of knee-high boulders. "Where'd you learn how to do that?" I asked, unable to stop smiling.

Michael laughed lightly, as if about to tell me something embarrassing, and my bright hazel eyes flicked over him with interest. "While most new college students spend their free time at parties, I got super into archery." He scratched the back of his head full of jet-black hair, then tossed that same hand in a semi-shrug. "Probably because my dad was really into it before and I wanted to try it, but I ended up really enjoying the sport."

"That's actually really cool," I said. My smile grew softer. "I like learning new things about you. You're like — like one of those ghost-paintings." Michael gave me a very strange look, and I hastily tried to explain, "You know, like a pentimento. No?"

Michael shook his head slightly, barely hiding the smile on his face. "No," he chuckled.

"It's where there's a painting under a painting. Nobody knows about it unless they really look," I said, but my interest in explaining faded as he brought his right hand up, his fingers cupping my chin.

"You're very strange, Rory Sorren," he mused. His dark eyes, cracked with light, seemed to embrace me. "I'd be lying if I said I didn't love it."

My heart took a pause, momentarily confusing the word 'it' with 'you.' "Anytime," I said lightly, giving him a teasing smile.

I heard Emery returning already, his shoes clomping across the ground. I leaned forward into the kiss Michael was already planning to give me before turning toward the young boy, a dead hawk in his right hand, an arrow protruding from the bird's underbelly. Emery ran directly up to me and held the bird out by the legs, his tan and brown wings limp at his sides.

We made a small fire and cooked the bird. It wasn't enough to supply any of us with a whole meal, but we each tried a small portion of the meat. The overall consensus was that it tasted closest to dark turkey meat, but more pungent. Still, this small meal proved that the idea of using bows and arrows wasn't a bad one. In fact, it could very well prove to be a life saver.

After our snack and a bit more practice, we packed up and got back into the air, continuing north toward Michael's hometown. We didn't stop again, eventually reaching Michael's one-story rancher house in the mid-evening. With a pure blue sky, a peaceful landscape with mountains rising in the far distance, and a stream running along the base of the property, this house looked like something out of a dream.

I flew down with Michael while the rest of the group circled above, keeping a watch for any danger.

We'd been logging major hours every day nonstop in order to find out anything, anything at all, about our families, yet never had I seen Michael so hesitant once those hours were put to fruition. He paused in front of the door for quite some while, his hand halfway to the silver knob.

I looked between his face and that space between his hand and the knob, wondering if I should say something. Then I heard something from inside the house, a sort of muffled scrape and a breathy huff. Michael went to close the distance, but just as soon as he reached forward, I pulled his hand back.

"Rory —?"

"*Shh*," I urged, taking a step back from the door. My eyes searched the outer brick wall as if I could see straight through it. "Something's inside," I whispered.

Michael became tense, but he didn't step back with me. Instead, I saw something bordering on hope cross his expression, and I instantly knew what he was thinking.

"I don't think it's them," I said. I reached out and pulled on his forearm again, starting off around the side of the house. "Come on, let's go around."

Michael looked between me and the front door, but ended up following me around the side of the house. We ducked down at the side of a wide window, and the two of us peered through the glass at the very edge. I could feel the heat radiating from Michael's bare chest as he leaned over me. So close, I could also quite literally hear the anxious beating of his heart.

The interior of the house looked decent enough, albeit looking like a whirlwind had blown through the house, furniture overturned and papers strewn everywhere.

"What happened here?" I wondered quietly. I noticed the dark splatters staining the light-colored carpet, and my mind immediately jumped to 'someone got attacked here.'

I knew Michael had seen the stains too, his hand clasped around the window frame turning white at the knuckles, his body trembling slightly. "I have to go in there," he said, his voice steady and determined despite his shaken outer appearance.

"That's a —" Michael disappeared before I could finish my sentence, continuing stealthily down the wall. "...really bad idea," I finished, speaking to no one. I pursed my lips as I watched his wings trail around the corner of the house.

I was considering going after him but paused when I heard the faint creak of a door being opened from the outside. Not too long after, I saw Michael through the window, creeping carefully through the inside of the dim house. I felt my heart speeding up in my chest, my muscles tightening, ready to spring into action at a moment's notice.

Besides Michael, I didn't hear anything else inside. I wasn't so hopefully naive to think that I'd imagined that earlier noise, though, and kept my guard up.

Michael went through another doorway, out of my range of sight. I heard him stifle a gasp and his breathing become increasingly shallow. Further down the house, I heard a delicate shuffle of fur against furniture. My eyes widened, and I wanted to shout aloud for Michael to *get the heck out!*

In the next instant, the front door came crashing outward, slamming into the brick wall beside it. Michael somersaulted down the stairs and practically threw himself across the overgrown front yard. "*Run!*" he yelled over his shoulder at me, already spreading his wings.

My tensed muscles went into action, my legs not wasting a second to sprint away from the house and jolt me into the air as my wings unfurled. I was fifty feet above the house in only two seconds and didn't stop there, rising an additional fifteen feet with every wing stroke.

Michael was breathing rather heavily beside me and kept looking back at the house.

"What'd you find in there?" I quizzed, wondering what sort of creature would be living in his house. It certainly couldn't have been good to elicit him *throwing himself* through the front door.

He shook his head, looking startled and depressed. I didn't press him as we flew up to the others.

Michael didn't wait for the rest of the group once at their elevation and flapped forward with conviction, with me right behind him, trying to catch up. Everyone else eased out of their overlapping, seventy-foot-diameter circles and followed after us, looking around at each other anxiously, questions written all over their faces.

I worked my wings, willing myself to be faster. I may have been fast, but I was still only in second place as far as speed went in our unit, Michael taking up first place.

"Michael!" Ronin called from somewhere behind us. "Would you slow down?"

Michael didn't look back at Ronin, but I did see him lessen his flaps, falling back only a little. Still, it was enough for me to catch up.

I glided up next to him on his right and simply stayed by his side, flapping intermediately to stay aloft. I looked over at him, a frown tugging at my heart as I watched him smear a tear away with the back of his left hand.

Bitterly peering back at the house which was gradually getting further and further away, I wished I could take away all his pain. A massive white and tan dog most closely resembling a Great Pyrenees stood in the doorway, his front legs spread strong and wide as if claiming his territory.

The scraping of large feathers got louder, and Ronin appeared on Michael's left, looking partially worried past the initial miffed appearance. "What happened down there? Why'd you leave so quick, huh?"

"Don't worry about it, Ronin," Michael said, coming across as fed-up and irritable.

Ronin looked to me across Michael's back, and I pursed my lips, unable to give him an accurate answer, not that I would have if I could.

Michael must have seen Ronin trying to find answers through me, for he huffed and said, "They're all dead, alright? Same as Adler, the d*mn dog did it." He swiped away another tear, trying to harden his expression.

Ronin seemed taken aback, glancing at the house, and stared at Michael as if he was crazy. "You're just gonna leave him? You don't want to kill him or something? He murdered your family!" he proclaimed.

Michael quieted down in mind and body — I saw the way he became more relaxed, only his frown deepening. He looked after the house, getting smaller and smaller, his expression clouding over. "It wasn't his fault," he said after a while. "Won't change anything, either."

Ronin looked exasperated, but I understood where Michael was coming from to some degree. I had a chance to help put my parents' killer in jail — and I did — but that's not what had made me feel better. Only time did that, and learning to move on. Ronin fell back with the others, but I continued to fly next to Michael, keeping him silent company as we traveled further north.

CHAPTER 56

Nobody bothered Michael. I think they felt it was fine enough to let me handle it, if anyone. Our next stop — Samuel's place — was only half the distance it was from Clara's to Michael's. It was getting dark, though, so I suggested to Michael that we search for a place to land for the night. He agreed in so few words, appearing sad, if anything.

I wanted very badly to comfort him, but our unit also felt it was my place to lead them, so I set aside my feelings for him and diligently scanned the ground, the map in the back of my mind as I searched.

If state borders still counted for anything anymore, I'd tell you we were likely crossing over the Wyoming-Montana line at the moment. We were so close to completing our mission around the country and finding the survivor enclave. I didn't want to get my hopes up too much, but if I managed to find Vixen at the camp, there'd be no complaints from me.

The trees here were large, like the oak tree back at base. Countless pine trees, tall and relatively thin, with bright green needles, were nestled in the valleys of sharp, towering mountain ranges.

For a group of birdkids, sleeping in trees was definitely a safer option than sleeping on the ground. I led us a short ways down the sloping side of an imposing gray mountain to a cluster of pine trees that overlooked the rest of the forest. We landed in branches a good seventy meters above the ground, but instead of settling down for the night, we started grouping together between three trees to have a Mahogany Meeting that I called for.

Emery was looking more than anxious as he held on tightly to a rough branch as big around as he was. "Can I just go down there?" he asked, his voice shaky. Too scared to let go of the branch, his eyes flicked toward the ground instead.

"Sure, if you don't mind being eaten by wild animals," I said, leaping over to another branch two meters away. He looked as if he was actually considering it, so I said, "It'll be fine. I can take you to a lower branch that's thicker if you really want."

Emery nodded fervently, so I went ahead and leapt over to his branch, causing it to sway slightly and make his eyes widen with terror. I tried not to smile as I knelt next to him. He wrapped his arms around me, and I held onto him as I stepped off the branch, floating down to another a good twenty feet below, my wings acting like soft sails.

"Further down," he said urgently.

"Okay, okay." I dropped down another fifteen feet, but wasn't going to let him rest any lower than that. "You can let go now," I said, standing on a branch twice as thick as the one he'd previously been on.

He looked around hesitantly before carefully setting his feet down on the bark.

"Better?" I asked.

He nodded smally, though he still looked worried. I helped him get closer to the middle of the tree, and he eased down with his back against the bark, his knees brought in toward his chest. I was about to fly back up to the rest of my unit waiting to start the meeting, but then Emery asked, "Are we almost at the other camp?"

I paused and looked down at him, but he was picking at a lip in the bark beside his sneaker. Something in his voice told me he'd rather be far away from the camp. "Yeah... Is that alright?"

Emery glanced at me. "It was always the plan, I guess," he said, frowning.

"Hey," I said, crouching down to be eye-level with him. "It's not like you'll never see me again. After this, who knows what'll happen?"

His eyes flicked over me again, this time lingering curiously. "You're not going to leave me then?" he questioned.

How is this seven-year-old making me feel so bad?
"Not forever, no."

He pursed his lips and went back to picking at the bark. "Promise?" he asked.

I didn't take promises lightly. They weren't something I just *threw* around. But looking at the boy, his hopes bordering on what I uttered next, I said, "Promise."

He was still frowning slightly, but he did seem to relax, if only a bit. I gave his hand a reassuring squeeze, then stood and flew back up to the canopy where the rest of my unit was waiting, landing on a branch near June and Michael.

"Hey," I said to the group, smoothing out a few of my feathers.

"So what's going on? Why're we having a meeting?" Samuel asked.

My eyes flicked to Samuel, sitting in a branch ten feet away in a neighboring tree. "Because of you," I said plainly. Samuel's brows began to draw together in question. "We were told the camp is near Canyon Mountain. Canyon Mountain is less than an hour north of here, and we'll be flying over it to get to your house. The meeting is to ask you: do you want to continue on to your place further north, or dive into the enclave camp first?"

Samuel opened his mouth but couldn't seem to respond.

"It's up to you," I said. Looking around at the group, I added, "I'm sure I speak for everyone when I say we'll gladly pass the camp to check on your family first. God knows you've waited long enough." I glanced around at everyone again. "Agreed?"

A variation of 'yeah' and 'agreed' sounded around the group. Samuel looked around at all of us, seeming touched.

"Thanks, guys," Samuel said, sounding like a large load had been taken off his shoulders. "But...I know it's hard to ignore the camp when it's so close. And then there's Emery..."

"Emery will be fine," I dismissed with an easy shrug. "Don't base your decision off of him. Honestly, I don't think he'd mind sticking with us a bit longer; in fact, he'd probably prefer it."

"Well..." Samuel looked around at us. "Okay, then. I guess we're going to check on my house first." He was smiling, and we were smiling, and it was clear to all of us that we cared more about each other than anything else at this point, something I'm not sure any of us thought would happen when we first met in that underground cafeteria that first day.

I heard a fidgeting rustle a meter behind me, a swish of pine needles, and automatically I knew it was Michael. When I turned around, however, all I saw was his dark form coasting down the mountainside. It was just a guess, but Samuel looking so happy about getting to see his house again probably brought up too many emotions for Michael.

There was barely any light left, dusk reaching its breaking point, so I naturally didn't feel comfortable watching Michael flying off through the valley.

"I'll be back," I told the group. With a simple look around, they could tell I was going after Michael, who was nowhere to be seen in the cluster of branches.

I got a few nods from the others, and I turned and tossed myself off the branch after Michael, slipping from the confines of the canopy. Michael was too fast, these mountains too vast, and I'd already lost sight of him. I didn't have to flap to go speedily down the mountain, only hold my wings out steadily. Once I reached the valley, I slowed down and soared a mere fifty miles per hour over the dense forest, thinking he may have landed somewhere to be alone, since I didn't see him in the air.

I kept my senses pricked, listening for anything that could clue me in. A minute later, I heard a light rustle, and my heart sparked. *Michael!* I thought.

I brought my wings in closer as I flipped around and angled through a small break in the canopy of bushy needles, emerging into a whole new dusky world hidden by the treetops. I swerved around towering tree trunks, their bark so thick it looked like armor made from chunks of stone. Not many plants grew on the forest floor, covered in brown needles, with only the occasional boulder popping up.

I tried to follow where I thought the sound had come from, but that only led me to an empty clearing. Gray-blue light filtered in through the canopy, creating a dim circle of illumination thirty feet in diameter. My gaze traveled to a small creek gurgling down a thin stretch of weatherworn rocks, the water sparkling like molten silver in my nocturnal eyes.

The water seemed to lure me, and I stepped over and crouched beside it, dipping my fingers into the refreshing liquid. This was definitely a peaceful place for Michael to be, but where was he? I took my hand away and looked up, scanning the canopy.

Another rustle sounded somewhere behind me, and I spun around, thinking it was him. What actually stood before me at the edge of the clearing, though, made my breath hitch and my chest contract with fear.

Standing ten feet tall on his hind legs, each clawed paw larger than my head, a mighty roar rang out from the beast's elongated mouth, a guttural and deathly sound. I found myself facing a giant, ivory grizzly bear, his fur streaked with swirls of gold, no white in his eyes. It looked like something only the Greek gods could come up with, sent to destroy me personally. I could see it in those pitch-black eyes — he wanted me dead, and only me.

CHAPTER 57

He roared again and let his front fall, his paws slamming into the ground with such force that I could feel the vibration travel up the soles of my feet. I'd like to say I dashed away to freedom in a moment's notice, but the truth of the matter was that I was paralyzed with sheer terror.

The bear charged forward, faster than I ever thought a bear could move, and I stumbled back into the creek with light breaths. I slipped on the wet rocks and fell back onto the opposite bank, the impact of the ground jarring my bones and making me gasp. The massive animal came at me, his mouth wide enough to swallow me down to my shoulders.

Some sense returned to me, staring into his mouth, and I scrambled to my feet and ran, but only made it a few strides before a sharp pain coursed up the back of my right leg, pulling me down by my calf. I flipped over to defend myself, freeing my leg from his grasp, but the bear's claws came back down and ripped my pants and flesh, sinking into my left thigh. Each claw was nearly as long as my hand, the dim light, filtering in through the opening in the canopy above, glinting off each one like malicious blades.

I didn't scream like people did in cheesy horror movies, but I did put up a fight, the sounds of trashing water and the bear's ragged breath sounding out through the otherwise quiet forest. There was an initial searing pain, but it numbed just as quickly as it happened. There was only the shock and adrenaline. Raw instinct took over. The bear twisted his colossal head and snarled. With teeth exposed, his four fangs each as long as my pinkie finger, he brought his head down, his mouth opening toward my face as if in slow motion.

The realization that I could die wasn't something new to me. I'd seen my parents die. That doesn't leave you with a happy-go-lucky mindset. But even despite this, I lived. Every day, even up 'till now. My heart beat once, and in that time, I cried out in exertion as I brought my right wing around in a flash, slamming the hard edge of it into the bear's massive face. The force of the impact was so great that it redirected his snout into the dirt and needles beside my head. Its enraged breath huffed in my ear, and I snapped into action, my mind both on hyperdrive and totally, utterly blank, my right hand reaching for my uninjured thigh.

I let out an enraged sound as I plunged the six-inch-long blade into the side of the bear's throat, his neck as wide around as the branch Emery was likely still sitting on further up the mountainside. I brought my other hand up and twisted the blade into his flesh, blood dripping down my arms.

The bear screamed, if bears could even do that, a horrible feral sound escaping his mouth. He yanked his head back, twisting his body over to get away. I felt a pull in my leg, then heard a loud *snap*, and the pressure was released. The bear stumbled out of the clearing, blood staining his pure white fur, his breaths coming out as jagged wheezes.

I didn't dare to drop my knife, watching with wide eyes as he struggled to breathe. I sat up and crawled backward out of the creek, my body drenched, blood clouding the creek water.

The bear lay down forty feet away, past the tree line, and didn't move. I could still hear his breathing, see his chest undulating with difficulty, though he didn't get up. I held my own breath, waiting for him to take his last.

Finally, when his breaths became so faint I could barely hear them, I allowed myself to relax a little, if that was even possible. "I'm not dead," I told myself, hardly able to believe it. My thoughts got in order the best they could, and I looked over myself, assessing injuries.

My leg — it did not look good. There was so much blood that I couldn't tell what the injury itself looked like. I dropped the knife on the bank and scooted back into the creek. With a ginger touch, I cupped water into my shaking hands and poured it over my wounds. For a few seconds, five deep lacerations, each at least eight inches long, could be seen to be scored through my skin, before the blood would pool back and hide it again.

"Ah, crap," I muttered. My body was still sizzling with adrenaline, and I desperately tried to remember what I was supposed to do. *Lacerations. Lacerations are different from cuts. DON'T apply a tourniquet. DO apply pressure.* "Right..." I reached down and tore off the bottom of my pants midway up my thigh, exposing the bloody injury entirely to the air. My leg was still numb, and I took advantage of that, balling up the fabric and pressing it tightly to my wounds. There were more on the back of my other leg, but not as deep as these.

Something seemed to scrape against the inside of my tissue when I pressed down, making me draw in a hiss of air and take the cloth away. "What the...?"

Just barely sticking out of my leg was a jagged white material as big around as a nickel. I sucked in a large breath, gripped the end of it tightly, and yanked it out in the next moment. This time I did cry out, my vision blackening slightly. I shook my head to clear the haze and dropped the claw tip onto the bank beside my knife, resting at around three inches long. It had been embedded in my bone, probably breaking off from the rest of the bear's claw when he had twisted to get away from me.

Shooting a fruitless glance at the bloodied claw, I

pressed the pants material back onto my thigh. The only thing reassuring me, as I watched my own blood continuously stain the water around me, was knowing that I was supposed to heal faster than before. *I'll be fine. I'll be fine. I'll be — Who am I kidding? I'm going to freaking die out here!*

As I failed to reassure myself, I thought I heard another rustle come from the surrounding forest. I tensed, going on high alert, ready to see how well I could use my leg if another bear popped out of those d*mm woods.

Pulling the knife back into my right hand, while my left hand continued to hold the cloth down, I looked around at the base of the trees, each wide enough to hide an entire car behind them. I sat very still, listening and waiting.

Extremely wary, my head spun toward the smallest movement off to my right. I honed my eyes in the growing darkness as a figure emerged from behind a wide tree trunk, a soft face faintly illuminated at the edge of the clearing.

My breath hitched, and my brows knit together in disbelief. I blinked, not sure I was seeing things right.

"Vixen?" I stammered.

And

      all

            the

                  while,

                          we RISE.

AUTHOR BIO

Shaye F. Widlacki spent years creating whimsical and poetic stories before finally deciding to share a bit of her imagination with the world, in hopes of adding a bit of piquancy to the minds of all you lovely people out there. She has always had a great love for animals, leading to a major in Biology, giving a realistic feel to a fictional sci-fi series. When she's not out having spur-of-the-moment adventures or watching Psych with her majestic dust-collector of a cat, she's making an adamant attempt to further her writer's tendonitis and creating super-annoying cliff-hangers.

Made in the USA
Middletown, DE
28 August 2022

72478113R00276